She is staring into her own face, a shimmering curtain of light between herself and herself. She reaches up a hand to touch her mirror image's face and then . . .

    . . . freefall

She hits wood. She looks up, feeling splinters in her fingers, the roll and swell of the deck beneath her feet, seeing the white of billowing sails above her head and the bright blue sky beyond. She hears a cry of alarm, but cannot tell where it came from; smells smoke, pungent and acrid. She takes another breath and her lungs fill with it. She coughs violently, each spasm causing her broken bones to scrape together, agonisingly. She rolls with the pitch of the deck. She tries to turn her head to see, and as she does so a terrible pain shoots through her neck but before she can pass out there is a tremendous explosion, flames engulfing her, she screams but can make no sound, and then . . .

    . . .freefall

Her thoughts are disjointed, fractured. Betrayal. Destruction. Failed rescue. Her own face, and that of another, framed in black. A name. A picture of a man she does not know. A weapon. Vengeance. The supercilious smile of a grey man in a grey suit. Thirst. Hunger. Jolt awake. Flash of red. And always pain. Total pain, engulfing and embalming her senses. Then . . .

    . . .freefall

'A paradoxical romp'
Tor.com

'*TimeBomb* is a rocket of a timeslip adventure, designed to appeal to adults young and old and it most certainly succeeds. . . Well-written, funny, sad and exciting, with a whole load of mysteries and paradoxes to puzzle over, it will appeal to all ages. Long may it continue'
For Winter Nights

'*TimeBomb* was tremendous fun and made for surprisingly addictive reading: I finished the book in one sitting. . . If you enjoy fast-paced, action-driven time travel stories, this book is for you, whatever your age'
A Fantastical Librarian

'A fast-paced, time-hopping thriller. . . *TimeBomb* and its cross-curricular genre could potentially be the answer to secondary school teachers the world over; History, Science and Literature all in one neat, little package'
Sci Fi Now

'Fast paced and incredibly addictive to read. . . I'll definitely be keeping my eye out for the sequel and I'd recommend this story to anyone who enjoys a fast-paced read with plenty of mystery, lots of action and more than a little journeying through time'
Feeling Fictional

'*TimeBomb* was a fast-paced, astounding novel that races in time, weaving into mystery and what lies within time itself. . . *TimeBomb* is a novel you don't want to miss, time-travel fans. It'll leave you wanting to race through time to read the whole trilogy before it's out'
Pretty Little Memoirs

TIMEBOMB

Scott K. Andrews

HODDER

First published in Great Britain in 2014 by Hodder & Stoughton
An imprint of Hodder & Stoughton
An Hachette UK company

First published in paperback in 2015

1

Copyright © Scott K. Andrews 2014

A CIP catalogue record for this title is available from the British Library

ISBN 978 1 444 75208 3

Printed and bound by Clays Ltd, St Ives plc

Hodder & Stoughton policy is to use papers that are natural,
renewable and recyclable products and made from wood grown in
sustainable forests. The logging and manufacturing processes are expected
to conform to the environmental regulations of the country of origin.

Hodder & Stoughton Ltd
Carmelite House
50 Victoria Embankment
London EC4Y 0DZ

www.hodder.co.uk

This book is for Kitty, who came up with the idea for the cover, and who is the bravest, cleverest, funniest, kindest daughter a father could wish for.

Part One

Four decisions and their immediate consequences

1

New York, America East, 2141

It was only when she reached the top of the staircase and burst through the door on to the deserted roof that Jana decided to die.

She'd died once before and it wasn't so bad, but she'd hoped to avoid doing it again for a while.

She scanned left and right, searching for some sliver of hope; a skylight, a fire escape, some form of cover, a discarded crowbar to use as a weapon. There was nothing. All she could see were the flat, featureless slabs of reconstituted rubber that formed the skyscraper's top seal. At the far edge of the roof was a small concrete lip beyond which rose the skyline of New York, shimmering in the heat.

The skyscraper was an old twentieth-century construction, forty storeys high. Once it had dominated the skyline, but now it was dwarfed by the looming organic skytowns that twined sinuously up into the cloud base.

Even so, it was quiet on the roof. The noises of the city didn't reach up here. Jana knew the membrane windows of the skytowns masked hives of furious activity, but here it felt tranquil and deserted.

She was easily visible from a thousand offices. Should anyone glance down at the city for a second, they would be able to see Jana, hands on knees, gasping for breath, sweat-drenched, scared and alone in the middle of a flat, black roof. Would anyone spare her a second glance? She was standing at the heart of one of the most densely populated cities on Earth, but she felt entirely alone, just as she always did.

A shout broke her reverie.

'Up here, the roof!'

Jana straightened and began to walk towards the edge. She felt a sudden calm at the certainty of what was about to happen. There was something liberating about having no choice.

She actually smiled as she approached the edge and looked down at the city streets so far below. Traffic was backed up along Broadway again, but the cabs and buses flew serenely in their dedicated lanes, speeding above the general traffic, untroubled by the congestion at ground level.

There in the middle distance she picked out the old stone buildings that ringed Central Park, the prosperous sector of town that she called home; a ghetto of lawyers, technocrats and bankers. Her mother would be there now, working on her speech for tonight's big event.

Jana wondered whether her mother would hear about her death in time to cancel. She imagined her standing on the podium in front of the serried ranks of cameras and dignitaries, mid-speech, as an aide walked on to the stage nervously and whispered in her ear. Jana saw her mother's face crumple and blur, her knees weaken as she slumped forward against the lectern in shock.

A nice thought, but it was more likely she'd show some of that famous stony-faced resolve.

After all, she'd make sure that her daughter would only be dead for a month or so.

'There she is.'

Jana raised her head and glanced over her shoulder. Three young men had emerged on to the roof behind her. She turned to face them, the backs of her calves pressing against the cold concrete of the roof lip.

She'd not had a good opportunity to study them during the pursuit. She'd never seen them before, but twenty minutes earlier they had leapt at her out of an alleyway and tried to bundle her into a waiting car. She had struggled free and run. A number of times she'd thought herself safe, but each time they'd caught up to her again. Now, trapped at the edge of a roof, there was nowhere left for her to run.

The men all carried improvised weapons. The one on the left, with the scar on his cheek and the shock of bright red hair, brandished a thick metal bar. The one on the right, the short one, wielded a wide-blade knife. The middle one, the tall leader with the cold sneer on his thin lips, had a chain dangling from his left hand.

'Who are you?' Jana shouted. 'What do you want?'

They fanned out and began to walk towards her, panting with exertion after the long pursuit.

'Remember our orders,' said the leader to his mates. 'She wants the head intact.'

She'd been assuming they were a gang from the favelas, hunting for rich kids on a day trip to the big city, but this odd statement caused her to reconsider. Some mysterious woman wanted her head? She spent a second trying to make sense of this, but couldn't, so dismissed it as a problem for later.

Much later.

When the three youths were within a few metres of her Jana grinned. The one with the scar paused, unsure how to respond, but the other two kept coming and he soon resumed his advance.

Smoothly, without taking her eyes off her would-be murderers, Jana stepped up and back on to the thin ledge. The leader stopped dead and put his arms out to indicate that his friends should stop too. They did so.

The leader cocked his head to one side, curious, sizing up Jana's resolve. He looked uncertain. He had thought he was in control here, but now it seemed that his cornered prey had seized the initiative.

Finally, he spoke.

'You haven't got the guts,' he said.

So Jana smiled, spread her arms wide, closed her eyes, and leaned back into space.

She felt her feet leave the concrete and the wind buffet her back, roaring in her ears. Her stomach felt hollow and her senses told her she was cutting through the updraughts of the city that was rushing to meet her.

But she didn't hit the ground for a hundred and twenty-eight years.

Cornwall, England, 1640

Theodora Predennick failed to stifle a yawn. She wasn't accustomed to rising so early. Being dressed and busy in the pre-dawn gloom felt unnatural. All her life, summer and winter, she had been woken by the first rays of the rising sun, and had retired to bed as the skies above her village turned black.

Her grandmother had warned her about the things that

6

walked abroad after dark: goblins, werewolves, fair folk, and girls with wickedness in their hearts. Good girls were safely tucked up behind stout wooden doors come sunset. Dora had always been a good girl.

Her new dress pinched at her ribs. She adjusted the wretched thing to try and reduce the chafing as she worked the lump of dough on the table before her, kneading and pounding the mixture into submission.

The logs on the huge kitchen hearthstones crackled and spat as the damp bark was scorched away. The newly dried wood began to catch alight, billowing fresh smoke up the chimney and casting a warm glow that lightened the gloom.

When Dora was satisfied that the dough was ready she set it by the fireplace in a cloth-lined wicker basket so it could rise in the spreading warmth. It was time to light the fire beneath the baking oven.

She had just lifted the iron tongs, intending to prise a log from the main fire and use it to spark the smaller one, when she paused. Had she heard something?

No. Not at this hour. The master was still abed and cook wasn't likely to rise for some time. She'd only been working at Sweetclover Hall for a week, but she already had a good sense of the daily rhythm. At this time she was invariably the only person awake. She must have imagined it.

She leaned forward, the heat licking at her skin. She prised the tongs open and grasped a burning log in the metal jaws.

Once more she froze. There it was again. She was sure she'd heard it this time. She bit her lip nervously. What to do?

The horizons of Dora's life were not wide. She had travelled beyond the borders of her village only twice. Once, when she was five, to visit her paternal grandfather as he lay dying in a neighbouring village, three miles to the south. The only other time had been last week, when she'd left home to enter service here.

She hadn't wanted to leave. She had begged her father to change his mind, but he stood firm. Dora was fourteen now, a grown woman, he said. It was time she made her way in the world. Did she want to stay stuck in Pendarn tending goats for the rest of her life?

Dora had wanted to do exactly that, but her parents wouldn't hear of it. They'd secured her a position as scullery maid at the big house and she was to start immediately.

Who knew, with some dedication and luck she might be cook herself one day, her mother had told her. Imagine that, a Predennick cook at the big house! Her mother's breast had swelled with anticipated pride as she waved her tearful daughter goodbye.

Everything that Dora had experienced since then – every sight, sound, smell, texture and taste – had been fresh and new. Some people would have responded with excitement at the novelty, but not Dora. She longed for the comfort of familiarity and the safe, reassuring sameness of the life she had left behind. She was not curious about much of anything.

And yet, perhaps all the newness had inspired her; perhaps she was becoming confident of her ability to cope with the unexpected; perhaps she was just foolish. But as she stood in front of the fire, straining to hear what she was sure was the moan of pain drifting through the dark, deserted corridors, she made an uncharacteristic decision.

She lit a candle, and decided to investigate.

Kazik Cecka was cold, wet, tired and hungry when he finally decided to stop running and find somewhere to rest.

The cloudless night was full-moon bright, the raindrops picked out in flashes of silver, and the air was fresh with the first chill of autumn. Kaz pulled his tattered jacket tight and considered his options.

He was miles from the nearest town, in open countryside. He could see a copse of trees on the other side of the field, a dark interruption in a horizon which stretched away as far as the eye could see; undulations of ploughed fields and pasture.

He had hoped that by now he would see the welcoming orange glow of a small town or village, but there was nothing; if there was a town nearby, the clear skies and full moon were swamping its light pollution and keeping its location a secret.

Sighing, he decided that the copse offered his best chance of shelter. He trudged across the field, avoiding the sleeping cows. At least he was wearing the new Gore-Tex boots his father had bought for him before their fight, so his feet were warm and dry. Unlike the rest of him.

This was not the adventure he had been hoping for when he'd run away from home.

Not for the first time he replayed the afternoon's events in his head, questioning his actions, wishing that just this once he'd managed to keep his cool and not shoot his mouth off. But even as he chided himself for his temper he found his pulse quickening and the sense of injustice and anger rising inside him again.

It wasn't fair. He'd worked hard in the orchards all day, every day. He'd allowed himself to be exploited and abused, and had never complained about the hours, the accommodation, the flea-ridden mattress and the harsh, cheap vodka. To then find that his wages were docked to pay for the food he was given, food not fit to serve to pigs and which could only have cost a fraction of what the farmer was taking from his pay packet to cover it . . . it was too much for him to bear.

A week's worth of beaten-down resentment, simmering anger and carefully nurtured scorn had burst out of him in a furious tirade directed at his employer. The farmer had shrugged and smiled the condescending smile of someone confronted by a powerless underling. It was that smug grin that had finally pushed Kaz too far.

He wouldn't deny that he'd enjoyed holding the farmer down in the mud and forcing the pigswill down his throat, but he had to admit that it wasn't the best choice he'd ever made. He'd been run off the farm at the barrel of a shotgun.

Now here he was, far from home, nowhere to sleep, no money in his pocket, and no passport; that had been confiscated by the farmer when he'd arrived in Cornwall ten days ago.

It was fake anyway. His father had the real one in safe-keeping. The man who'd organised the whole thing, a minor gangster in the small Polish town Kaz called home, had provided him with a new identity to get him into the UK. It would have taken three months' work to pay off that debt.

He stopped walking as a terrible thought occurred to him. The gangster would reclaim that money somehow. If he stayed on the run, there was a good chance he would go after his father, adding whatever rate of interest he chose.

Kaz cursed his own selfishess as he realised that it wasn't just himself that he'd let down. As angry as he was with his father, he didn't wish him any harm. But what could he do about it now? He dismissed the thought. He'd worry about that tomorrow.

He jogged to the edge of the trees, trying to get his blood pumping. An English boy might have worried about spending the night outside in such weather, but Kaz had spent many winters in parts of the world where the temperature regularly sat below zero for months at a time. He was unconcerned by the idea of a slight frost.

As soon as he walked under the canopy of the trees, he noticed the copse was not what it seemed. Once through the first layer of trees he found himself in the ruins of a formal garden. In the shadows he could just make out the ghostly impressions of old walkways winding between wildly over-grown hedges which loomed over him in the darkness. A crumbling stone statue stood forlorn in the basin of a long-dry fountain, wreathed in ivy. And rising above it all, the three turrets of an old mansion.

Kaz pushed through the thick undergrowth until he saw a glint of metal in the darkness ahead. He stepped forward cautiously and was confronted by a tall chain-link fence that weaved in between the brambly hedges.

He peered through the fence and was able to make out the silhouette of the house beyond the perimeter. It was huge and old, but it appeared derelict. Had it not been for the shiny new fence he'd have thought the house long forgotten.

Nonetheless, an abandoned house in the middle of nowhere was too big a stroke of good fortune to ignore. He was about to start climbing the fence when he noticed a gap at ground level where the wire had broken apart. He could fit through there, easy.

Had he not been so cold, tired and preoccupied by his

earlier actions, he might have paused to wonder why a brand-new fence had a hole in it; he might have examined the hole more closely and noticed that the links had been cut deliberately; he might have wondered whether the hole was in fact an invitation, or a trap.

But he didn't.

He slithered through the opening and approached the moonlit house thinking only of dryness and sleep.

The man in the security centre nudged the joystick, guiding the CCTV camera to follow the boy's progress towards the building.

He'd been sat in the Portakabin for months waiting for the boy to arrive, and he almost couldn't believe the moment was finally here. He felt a rush of adrenaline and shifted nervously in his seat. He'd waited a long time for this.

The boy had no idea at all what was waiting for him inside those walls. The security guard did, and felt sorry for him. He knew what it meant, what it would cost, and who would die if he let the boy set foot in that house.

He could still change his mind. He could pick up his torch and run out after the boy, scare him away. Or, perhaps, give him shelter, share a cup of coffee, send him on his way at dawn. He could do that. He could change everything.

He sat back in his chair and took another sip of tea. No, it was too late to second-guess himself now, way too late. He'd made his decision, he had to abide by it.

He watched on the monitor as the boy stepped across the threshold of the great house and was swallowed by the waiting darkness.

2

Dora cracked open the heavy oak kitchen door, poked her head out into the stone-flagged, wood-panelled corridor, and listened intently.

The silence was absolute. Again she doubted her ears, but as she was about to withdraw she heard a soft rustle of fabric and a low moan. It was hard to be sure, but it sounded like a woman.

She felt a thrill of fear.

In the village they spoke of Lord Sweetclover in deferential tones of respect. No one had a bad word to say about him. He was good-natured, front and centre at all the big festivals of the year, everything a lord of the manor should be. True, there had been some concern when his father died a few years back, rumours that the young master was wayward and wanton, but he had assumed the role without complaint and had done nothing to bring disgrace to the district.

But here in the house there were whisperings amongst the staff. No one knew Dora well enough yet to confide any details to her, but there'd been enough knowing winks and slow, meaningful nods of the head from the stable boy, gardener and kitchen maid. She was aware of an undercurrent of disapproval and caution. The master, she had surmised, was not as lily white as everyone believed; he had just decided to be more discreet once he had assumed the title and its responsibilities.

She had seen him only twice, when she'd taken platters into the dining room. He was a tall man in his mid-thirties, dark haired with a hint of grey at the temples; heavy browed, with deep brown eyes and a fine, square jaw. Somehow all the fine features, which should have rendered him rakish and handsome, failed to fit together as they should. The impression he gave was of solidity rather than panache.

Still, he was unmarried and Dora, unworldly though she was, was not entirely naïve. She had little doubt that he rarely took to his bedchamber alone unless he desired the solitude. Dora thought it likely that he took liberties with the kitchen maid, probably Mary, the coach master's daughter, and possibly even Cook.

However, he did not flaunt his conquests, and nobody seemed to find his behaviour outrageous enough to require their departure. He was lord of the manor, and rank had its privileges.

Now here stood Dora, in a dark corridor lit only by the candle she held, hearing the moans of what sounded like a woman in pain emanating from the open door of the undercroft.

Her every instinct was to close the door and go back to the baking. This was not her business and it could only lead to trouble. Imagine her parents' disappointment and shame if she were sent back to the village in disgrace, dismissed for prying into the affairs of her betters.

On the other hand, they would not want her to stay in a house serving a master who might place Dora's virtue, or even her life, in danger. She held the lowest position within the household. If the master were to take a fancy to her and drag her down into his undercroft to share the fate of the poor woman whose moans now disturbed the silence of the house, she would be powerless to stop him.

She had to find out. It was probably her imagination running away with her, but it had never so much as strolled before so she was quite surprised to find it running, especially at this ungodly hour.

Maybe Cook had got up early, gone down there for some wine and slipped on the stairs.

That was it. Only explanation that made any sense.

Satisfied that she had hit upon the truth, Dora stepped confidently through the undercroft door and peered down the steps.

And screamed.

The security guard was suddenly aware that he was not alone. A tiny creak, the softest of rustling, a gentle shift in the lean of the Portakabin.

'Hello,' said a soft voice in his ear. 'I wondered how you were going to do this.'

The security guard swivelled in his chair. The figure before him was short and slender, clothed entirely in black, even the head and face. Only a small slit allowed him to see his visitor's eyes. The handle of a sword poked up behind their shoulder. Ninja-chic.

'I applied for a job,' he said. 'Seemed the best way. Keep a low profile. Hacked the system, got myself posted here. Sat and waited. It's been fun, if I'm honest. I've actually lived in one time and place for three months. No one hunting me. I lived a normal life for a while. Followed a soap opera. Even dated a bit.' He slapped his thigh, as if providing a full stop. 'Over now, though. He's here. It's starting.' He considered the black-clad figure curiously. 'Surprised to see you. Checking up on me?'

'Just passing through. Making sure things go as they should.'

'Oh, I see,' said the security guard with a small laugh. 'You're my back-up.'

'Something like that.'

The shadowy figure leaned forward to read the security guard's name badge. 'Steve. Hmm.'

'What?'

'I never took you for a Steve.'

The visitor turned to the screens. Kaz was visible on one of them, picking his way through the overgrown garden to the hall. 'So. Everybody's on their way.'

'He tripped a pressure alarm about five minutes ago,' said Steve. 'A team's already en route.'

'I'll get out of your hair, then. Good luck.' The black-clad visitor stepped out of the Portakabin and was swallowed by the night.

'You too,' said Steve, more to himself than to his already departed guest.

Then he put the kettle on, made another cup of tea, took a sip, thought again, tipped it out the door onto the soft earth, pulled a small flask out of his jacket pocket, poured a large measure of whiskey into the paper cup, drank it in one, then poured another and resumed his seat, ready to watch the fireworks.

Jana was expecting a bone-shattering impact and a long silence. Instead, a second or two into her fall, she felt a tug upwards.

16

Her first thought was that it was a freak gust of wind momentarily slowing her descent, but the tug increased. It felt as if the gravity that pulled her down was fighting an opposite force that wanted to pull her skywards.

She opened her eyes and gasped. She was hovering in mid-air, surrounded by a halo of coruscating bright red sparks, like some kind of human firework.

Instinctively Jana activated her ENL chip, intending to scan the quantum physics database for anything that could explain the impossible phenomenon that hovered above her. The chip at the base of her skull responded with a treatise on eating habits during the English Civil War of the seventeenth century.

Jana was so surprised by this that it took her a moment to realise that the world around her was darkening, as if a huge cloud was blocking out the sun.

She hadn't made a sound as she'd fallen to certain death, but she screamed in terror as the darkness deepened and she felt her body being crushed by forces too strong to resist. She only stopped screaming when blackness entirely filled her sight, blotting out the sky, and then . . .

She was lying on a hill, cool grass in the crisp morning air. Bright blue sky, birdsong, the buzz of insects. She heard a noise above her so she sat up and raised her hand to shield her eyes from the sun. Squinting, she could see a plane – no, a missile, a huge missile – arcing down from heaven, trailing fire and smoke, screaming towards the Earth and then . . .

Hot, bright sun, sound of surf, dry air in her nose, sand underfoot, the eyes of a lizard regarding her with listless, heat-sated lethargy. It flicked out its tongue at her. Unsure what to do, she flicked her tongue out in response and then . . .

In a crowd, jostled and shoved by hot sweaty bodies. Smell of stale beer and cigarettes. Loud noise, almost deafening, screech of electric guitar, flash of coloured lights, big screens above her displaying a man in a gold lamé suit smoking a cigar and wearing red plastic devil horns, and then . . .

A clean white room, sterile and silent but for the soft hum of air conditioning and electric lights. A door flung open and a tall, fat man in a white lab coat running towards her, shouting, 'Take my hand, quickly, take my hand.' Reaching out to the man and then . . .

A street. Ruined buildings to her left and right, sound of gunfire and explosions. Impossible butterscotch sky. A tank, hovering above the rubble, floating towards her through the smoke. A hand on her shoulder, turning to face . . . herself, with a gash across her forehead and blood in her eyes. 'You'll be all right,' she told herself. 'I can't tell you how or why, but you'll be all right. I promise. Oh, and—' Then . . .

Freefall . . .

Dora had witnessed plenty of awful things in her life.

There was a man in her village with a gaping wound on his neck that had oozed pus since before she could remember. Her grandfather had a tumour on his face when he passed away, as big as his nose. Her younger brother had died after a tiny cut on his leg had become infected, and an infection had taken him from the world in the slowest, cruellest way possible.

Dora had seen all these things and accepted them as normal. Deformity and sickness did not disturb her. She had a strong stomach.

But the woman on the undercroft stairs wasn't sick, she was *ruined*.

She was covered in terrible burns. Her clothes had melted into her skin, and one of her legs hung down over the stone steps at an angle that told of numerous broken bones. She was barely breathing.

But that wasn't the worst.

Her right arm reached out towards Dora as though grasping for aid, but the other was withered and bent, and it was blurry, faded, as if seen through water. One second it was there, the next it was transparent, then it was back again.

The woman was not only entirely beyond repair, she also wasn't entirely there.

Dora had no idea what to do. She couldn't imagine what could have happened to this poor woman, or how she had found her way to the undercroft. It was plain that no physician could save her.

If she shouted for help, the master may come running. But what if he had done this terrible thing? And what, then, might he do to her?

She stood in the doorway, looking down at the woman, frozen. Then she heard the noise of a door opening upstairs, and footsteps on the landing above her. Her scream had woken the house.

'Dora,' gasped the injured woman, as if squeezing out the syllables was the hardest thing she'd ever done.

Dora felt helpless. She peered more closely, trying to reconstruct the ravaged face. Was it someone she knew? The footsteps above reached the top of the main staircase.

Dora scurried down the undercroft steps until she reached the prone figure.

'Mistress, pardon me, but what can I do to help?'

The woman reached her hand up and grasped at the air.

'Hand . . .' she wheezed.

So Dora, eager to give comfort to the dying woman, fought back her revulsion and reached out to take the offered hand. But before she could make contact, a spark of crimson fire leapt from the woman's fingers, arcing between her and Dora and then . . .

Dora was suspended in mid-air on a bright sunny day, screaming in alarm as she fell onto a cushion of bright fabric, the likes of which she had never seen before. She bounced clumsily back up into the air, her skirts flapping and her arms waving. Then back down again and a series of lessening bounces until she sprawled in a heap and looked up into the eyes of ten startled children, all in their stockinged feet, wearing the strangest garments she had ever seen. 'Big kids aren't allowed on the bouncy castle,' said one prim, outraged little girl. And then . . .

Sprawling on the floor of a chamber hewn from rock – large, silent, ice cold – was she in a cavern? A grey half-light picked out floor-to-ceiling racks of cocoons, each containing the blurred outline of a person. There were thousands of them, stretching away into the darkness. She rose to her feet and saw movement in the distance – three tiny figures, so far away. They were waving. She raised her hand to wave back and then . . .

Water, shockingly cold, up to her neck. She sank beneath the surface before she could even take a breath. Her clothes dragged her down into the dark, suffocating depths. She thrashed and struggled, and broke the surface with her face. She caught a glimpse of a large boat under sail, a warship or a privateer, perhaps. She sank back beneath the water before she could call to it. She fought her way up again, her face breaking the surface for a second time. She managed to raise one arm out of the sea and wave at the distant ship, but the cold and the weight of her dress were too much. She sank again, fast. She felt her ears pop, felt the pressure increase on her as she realised she was about to die. Animal panic pulled open her mouth to try and take a breath to ease the fire in her lungs. And then . . .

Lying in a puddle, gasping like a landed fish on the floor of a clean white room, sterile and silent but for the soft hum of unseen engines. There was light without fire and warmth without sunlight. Breathing hard now, wild eyed with terror and confusion, Dora cried aloud when the door opened and a tall, fat man in a strange white jacket came into the room. He walked forward slowly, anxious not to startle her. He reached out. 'Take my hand. Take my hand and everything will be all right.' But even through her fear she wasn't going to make that mistake again. She scrambled back against the wall, gabbling refusals and protestations. Her back hit the hard wall and then . . .

Awful, deafening noise. A huge explosion next to her and she was sprawling in rubble, crying and screaming and begging for it to stop. Hands on her shoulders, pulling her backwards. She struggled but then there were hands on her feet, and she was lifted bodily into the air and carried away. Dumped on the ground behind a low brick wall. Bangs and crashes and strange, devilish humming. She coughed as the foul smoke and dust clogged her wet nostrils and frantic, gasping lungs. Hands on her face, forcing her to look up into the bright blue eyes of a young man with close-cropped black hair. Over his shoulder she could see a dark-skinned girl carrying some type of musket. She had a nasty wound across her forehead that leaked blood down across her face. 'Calm down, Dora, breathe,' said the boy. 'It's OK. You're all right. It's a lot to handle first time. I remember. But you need to concentrate, you'll only be here for moment. I need you to listen, yes?' Dora nodded, shaking. The boy's accent was strange, foreign.

'Don't.' Yelled the dark-skinned girl. 'You mustn't tell her . . .' But she was interrupted by a series of small explosions that drew her attention away. She raised her odd musket and began shooting beams of light at unseen attackers.

The boy bit his lip, worried, but continued speaking. 'There is one thing you need to know.' He leaned forward, as if to whisper in her ear, but then . . .

Darkness, night-time, winter cold made worse by wet clothes. Firelight through trees and the soft chanting of human voices. She did not know what language they were using, but it was not English. She ran forward, hoping for aid, but found herself standing on the edge of a clearing facing a burning pyre. Tied to a post in the centre of the conflagration was a young woman who screamed and screamed as the flames licked up her legs and her dress caught fire. The crowd stood singing songs to the dying victim; Dora presumed they sang in hope of speeding her to salvation from her wickedness. She couldn't believe what she was seeing. The witch's face was the same face that Dora had seen looking back at her in the mirror a hundred times. The witch was her! Dora screamed in mortal terror as she watched herself begin to burn. The crowd turned, saw her, cried in horror at the impossibility of it, and then . . .

Freefall . . .

* * *

22

Sweetclover Hall sat shadowed and sullen amongst its copse of trees. Its windows were boarded up and flaps of plastic patched the holes in the roof, preventing the worst of the weather getting inside, but apart from that the house appeared unloved and forgotten.

Had there been a nicely printed guidebook to tell Kaz the history of the building he was walking towards, he would have learned some very interesting things indeed. He might even have thought twice about entering. But there was no one and nothing to warn him about the house's bloody and mysterious past, so he pushed open a rust-hinged door and walked across the threshold without a second thought.

The room that had once been the beating heart of the manor lay under a thick layer of dust and cobwebs abandoned by spiders that had moved on in search of richer pickings. The furniture had been removed long ago. Only the presence of a brick baking oven built into the chimney breast revealed the room's original function.

Kaz sniffed the air. The house smelt of mould and damp and crumbling plaster. Still, it beat sleeping on the cold, wet earth. He walked across the room, brushing away the cobwebs that snagged his face and hair, and pushed open a thick oak door into a wood-panelled corridor.

The bright moonlight barely penetrated this far into the house. The thick darkness and utter silence would have been enough to give most people pause, but Kaz was practical and unsuperstitious. He didn't believe in ghosts and wasn't afraid of the unseen things that lurked in the gloom. He knew that the scariest thing this house was likely to contain would be a few rats, scurrying around beneath rotting floorboards.

He moved deeper into the decaying building, not noticing

a cellar door on the right, secured with a padlock. Neither did he register the tiny red light in the far corner of the ceiling, hidden behind layers of cobwebs, that denoted the presence of an active infrared camera transmitting his every move back to unseen eyes.

At the end of the corridor stood two tall, wide doors. They were warped and stuck, half open. Kaz squeezed through the opening into a large room, lit by a beam of moonlight that cut across the blackness through a gap in the window boards. This would do.

In one corner of the room a dim grey mound revealed itself, on closer inspection, to be a pile of discarded curtains. They were musty but Kaz arranged them into a makeshift mattress and lay down.

He was bone tired, emotionally drained, unsure what tomorrow would bring. The only thing he knew for certain was that he would be better able to face his problems after a good night's sleep. Having identified that as his top priority, he banished all thought from his head and closed his eyes.

He opened them again immediately as the room crackled and burned. A circle of firework-bright crimson snapped into existence near the ceiling and spat out a young woman, who crashed to the floorboards with a heavy thud.

The fire vanished as quickly as it had appeared. Silence and darkness reclaimed the room. The only evidence that something unusual had occurred was the fading patterns that danced on Kaz's retinas, and the swirls of disturbed dust that billowed in the single shaft of cold, blue moonlight.

Kaz's exhausted body had been sinking into sleep but now it flooded with adrenaline. He leapt up and stood ready to defend himself from . . . what? He forced himself to take a few deep breaths and relax. He wasn't under attack, not as far as he could tell. But what had just happened?

A groan from the centre of the room reminded Kaz that he was not alone. He ran to the girl, who lay on the floor. He reached out to touch her, but as his fingertips approached her they crackled with sparks of crimson, and he leapt back in alarm. The sparks vanished.

'What . . . happened?' gasped the woman on the floor.

Kaz had no idea how to answer that, so he said nothing.

The woman slowly raised herself up on her arms and glanced around the dim grey room. Kaz could see that she was dressed in a plain shirt and trousers. When the woman noticed Kaz she jumped, startled, and quickly tried to rise to her feet, but her legs gave way and she crumpled to the floor in a heap. She swore.

Kaz felt he'd better say something. 'I am called Kaz. What is your name?' was the best he could come up with.

'Yojana,' replied the heap in an American accent. 'Sorry, no, Jana. My name's Jana.'

'Hello, Jana.'

Jana managed to raise herself again but this time she went for the less ambitious option of sitting up.

'Hi,' she replied.

Before either of them could start asking the questions that were forming in their minds, there was another burst of vivid scarlet light. They both scrambled backwards to clear a landing space for the dripping-wet girl who dropped from nowhere with a piercing scream and crashed in the spot vacated by Jana only a second before.

Once again the fire vanished as quickly as it had appeared. Dust billowed and swirled in the moonlight.

25

Then the two main doors groaned in protest as they were forced inwards. A tall man stepped forward, framed in torchlight, looking down at the three figures sprawled on the floor.

'Welcome to Sweetclover Hall,' he said. 'We've been expecting you.'

The wet girl looked up, apparently recognising the man's voice. 'My lord?'

'Hello, Dora,' said the man. 'Welcome back. You've been away for a very, very long time.'

Kaz smiled to himself; maybe he'd found the adventure he'd been hoping for after all.

Steve the security guard leaned forward and grabbed the CCTV control, zooming in on the face of the man in the doorway. He was a tall man in his early forties, dark haired with thick streaks of grey at the temples, heavy browed, with deep brown eyes and a square jaw. Solid was the best word to describe him.

He could see the man's mouth was moving so he turned up the sound.

'. . . sure they don't touch each other. We move them in separate vans. Quickly.' Four men in generic security guard uniforms entered the room, grabbed the three protesting teenagers and bundled them outside.

As the dust settled in the now silent room Steve saw a small flash, like the glint of moonlight on the blade of a sword.

An external camera displayed three black vans with their rear doors open. Steve watched the captives being forced into them. Jana wasn't putting up much of a fight, and Dora seemed cowed by the unexpected presence of her lord and master. Kaz punched the man carrying him hard in the stomach, but his burly escort barely even flinched.

The van doors slammed and the engines revved. Steve didn't stay to see them drive away. He was already pulling on his coat and reaching for the keys to his motorbike.

The black-clad figure stood in the shadows of the treeline and watched Steve roar away on his motorcycle, then vanished in a flash of red fire.

3

Soft. That was good. She liked soft. Warm, too. Nice.

Dora nuzzled down into the pillows, comfortable and cosy in the seconds of amnesia that accompanied her waking. She felt odd. There was a pain in her arm and an ache in her head. What had . . . ?

She froze rigid. She felt the panic rising in her again but she forced it back down. She was warm, in a bed, although a softer bed than any she'd slept in before. That implied safety, at least for the moment.

Keep calm, Dora, she told herself. Take a moment to compose yourself before you open your eyes. You may not be alone. This thought led swiftly to the realisation that she was naked, which led to an involuntary cry of alarm. So much for remaining composed.

She admonished herself. Of course she had been undressed, her clothes had been wet through. To leave her in them would have caused a chill or worse. Whoever had undressed her – and she shied away from considering the possibility it had been Lord Sweetclover – they had done her a kindness.

The room was silent except for a strange background hum, similar to that she had detected in the clean white room with the tall, fat man. Was that where she was? From the way her cry had rebounded from the walls she could tell she was in a small chamber unlike any she'd known before; the sound lacked the reflected warmth of wood panelling, the cold reverberation of plaster, or the dull absorption of wattle and daub.

Her head, poking out from under the bedclothes, allowed her to establish that the room was pleasantly warm. The air was dry and had a strange, subtle odour that she was unable to identify.

She feared what she would see when she opened her eyes but there was nothing else for it, so that's what she did.

The walls were plain white, smooth and featureless, the floor a chessboard of black and white squares. The light came from a long, glowing, buzzing cylinder that neatly bisected the ceiling; one more impossible thing for Dora to contemplate. She gave an involuntary gasp as she saw the fourth wall of the room. It was a single sheet of the most flawless, unmottled glass she had ever seen. She could see no doors. She was trapped.

The bedclothes were not what she was accustomed to. The pillowcase was fine cloth, like thinly spun wool but softer, and instead of sheets and woollen covers there was one thick blanket draped over her. It was light and airy but still warm. Most odd. It, too, was plain white. She could see a chair beside her bed. The smoothly curved greyness of it was totally alien to her, but a chair is a chair, that much she could divine. The clothes draped across it were similarly extraordinary, but at least someone had left her some. That was an encouraging, generous gesture.

Eventually she decided to accept the offer implicit in the clothing-draped chair. She sat up in bed, careful to keep the strange, thick blanket pulled high to preserve her modesty.

A buzzing above her head caused her to glance up. A small black box was pivoting down to stare at her with its beady black eye. If Dora had known what a CCTV camera was, she would never have climbed out of bed, scurried over to the chair, grabbed the clothes and run back to the safety of the bed. But she was only concerned in case someone appeared at the glass wall.

The clothes were a mystery to her. The black undergarment was tiny and edged with lace, the white blouse fitted and buttoned, the thick woollen smock a bright red that seemed to hint at wantonness. At least the drab grey skirt she had been provided with reached all the way to the floor. She had little clue what to make of the complicated wire and canvas garment, although its form gave some hint as to its function. She tossed it back onto the chair suspiciously. It did not seem to her that it would be a comfortable thing to wear.

She dressed under the bedclothes, then tried and failed to get to grips with the laces on the shoes that had been provided for her. She was accustomed to slip-on footwear, so she eventually discarded them in favour of stockinged feet.

She stood in the centre of the featureless room, nervous and uncertain. The floor felt cold and dead beneath her feet. The black and white squares weren't stained wood, as she'd supposed, but neither were they tiles of clay or stone. They had a slightly sticky feel to them, as did the chair.

She did not like this unnatural place. She did not like these clothes, the noise and the taste of the air. Most of all, she didn't like being caged.

As she stood there, Dora found her anger. It helped her focus her thoughts for the first time since she'd stood in the kitchen holding the fire tongs what already seemed like a lifetime ago. She was still afraid, of course, but now she was annoyed as well. And as her brother and parents could attest, in spite of all her natural meekness, humility and stay-at-home unadventurousness, Dora was very formidable indeed when she was angry.

Which is why, when the glass wall began to rise into the ceiling with a hum, and Lord Sweetclover stepped into the room, he was smacked in the face by a bra.

'My dear Dora,' he said, bending to pick up the bra, 'is that any way to say hello to an old friend?'

With so many things to be confused and angered by, Dora didn't stop to wonder at the unbecoming familiarity of Sweetclover's tone.

'Where am I?' was all Dora could think to say.

'Home. Where else?' Sweetclover turned and walked out of the room, across the corridor that faced it, and stood beside a window set into the plain white wall. He turned back to Dora and smiled. 'Come and see.'

Dora tentatively followed him but stopped short, unwilling to come too close. Sweetclover stepped aside. Dora approached the window and gasped at the view that greeted her.

She was on the third storey, looking across a mad confusion of buildings and roads. The details were overwhelming. A million little impossibilities blurred her vision.

She gritted her teeth and concentrated on one recognisable landmark. There in the centre of all this confusion stood the church in which she had been christened. Sweetclover was right; this chaotic, unreal modernity was her sleepy village of Pendarn, transformed.

Mud tracks replaced by a smooth black surface; horse-drawn carts supplanted by shiny, coloured boxes that rolled along on wheels with no identifiable means of propulsion; a small collection of thatched dwellings swept away by endless rows of brick houses, and metal and glass blocks that towered higher than any spire. The huge village green, utterly gone.

'But . . . how?' she asked.

'Time, Dora. Nothing more. Just time.'

She looked up at Sweetclover, eyes wide, helpless, her anger and fear draining away to be replaced by numb incomprehension.

He gently took her arm.

'Come with me, I'll explain everything, I promise. But first we need to perform a few simple tests.'

He led her down the hall to a thick metal door, punched a key-code into a beeping panel, and steered her through into the infirmary.

The doctor was waiting.

'Name?'

Kaz stared at the interrogator sitting across the table from him.

'Name?'

Kaz smiled at the man and shook his head.

'NAME?'

Kaz stuck his tongue out and blew a raspberry at his interrogator, which earned him a slap.

'Kazik, tell me your name.'

Kaz let out a short laugh and flashed the man a look that told him exactly what he thought of his absurd demand.

The man leant forward, calm and reasonable.

'Listen, Kazik, don't make this any harder than it has to be. You're a long way from home. No one knows where you are. No one is coming to find you, nobody cares. If, heaven forbid, you were to suffer some kind of accident in this room, no one would ever know. Another illegal immigrant gone underground, probably selling drugs somewhere. You'd just be a footnote in a file in some bureaucrat's computer.'

Kaz shrugged.

The man licked his lips as he sat back in his seat.

'All right,' he said, nodding to the other man in the room, the one with the truncheon. 'Knock yourself out.'

Then he got up and left the room, closing the thick, sound-proofed door behind him.

Kaz braced himself for a blow, but it never came. Instead there was a rising hum of power from the next room and then his mind unfolded like a flower in bloom and he began to tell his life story to the table.

Jana knew it would be pointless to resist.

She took one look at the operating table, the array of instruments laid out in the shiny metal tray beside where her head would soon be resting, and knew what they were planning to do. She knew that it would be quick and painless, and that she would survive the procedure. She saw no advantage to putting up a fight.

Plus, there were five of them and one of her.

She remembered what the well-dressed man had said on the roof, something about wanting her head intact. Now she understood why.

She lay down on the operating table, face first, and felt the doctor's cold hands probing at the nape of her neck. Then the prick of a needle, and oblivion.

*　*　*

Steve removed his helmet and placed it on the warm leather seat of his cooling motorbike. He ruffled his flattened hair, took a long, deep breath and considered his next move.

The complex of buildings stood across the road from him, gleaming white in the soft, early morning light. From the outside it could easily have been taken for another anonymous light-industrial building in some barren enterprise park in the suburbs of a small market town. Only the high fence, topped with coils of razor wire, the guards in smart, military uniforms with batons, tasers and hungry-eyed Dobermanns, and the security checkpoint at the main gate gave any indication that this was far from an ordinary building.

A large sign proclaimed this to be the headquarters of Io Scientific, a private research and development organisation.

He activated his eye-mods and zoomed in on a figure that had just appeared at a third-storey window. It was the girl, Dora. He watched her face change from confusion to recognition to astonishment as she gazed at the landscape.

He didn't have much time.

He pulled off his thick leather gloves and laid them beside his helmet, then he unzipped his biker jacket and reached inside. There was a tiny click, as if a switch had been flicked. Steve shimmered for a second, blurring and changing. Then he snapped back into focus.

Except now he looked exactly like Lord Sweetclover.

He began walking towards the main gate.

4

As the ENL chip was removed from her neck, it bestowed upon the sleeping Jana a vivid bright flash of memory that was not, strictly speaking, her own. Her brain, dulled by anaesthetic, was unable to shut the memory down, to divert her thoughts. As she lay there floating in the darkness she relived, in a split second, an afternoon from ten years ago. It was not a normal memory, though. This was far more real and vivid than a simple recollection; less remembrance than reliving. Her numbed body could touch, smell, hear and taste the things that she – no, not she, the other one – had felt on that cold, wet afternoon.

The rain is heavy and cold, but Yojana doesn't mind a bit. Although only six years old she has already realised that her daddy's time is a rare and precious commodity. She does not see him at all during the working week, for she is tucked up in bed before he returns from the office, and he is already at the gym by the time she is woken to begin another day at school.

Yojana sees her mommy a little more often; she makes it home in time to read her a bedtime story most week nights. But from Monday to Friday, Yojana's life is run by her nanny – a young woman so lacking in personality that Yojana has nicknamed her 'the clone' – and a selection of teachers who range from 'lovely' to 'smells-like-poop'.

The weekends are rarely better. Normally at least one of her parents has a conference to attend or a foreign trip to take. Yojana can count on the fingers of one hand the number of days she has spent with both her mom and dad, doing something fun as a family. But sometimes, when one parent is at home on a Sunday or Saturday, they carve out a little time for her. She doesn't mind what they do – cuddle up and watch a movie on a winter's day, read a book together, play a game, even help her with her school work. When those rare moments of time come around she basks in their undivided attention. It makes her feel special. The smile she is wearing, even in the cold September rain, is evidence of that.

He father, balanced above her on an old wooden stepladder, throws down another handful of fresh, ripe plums. Yojana catches them in a bucket which is now so heavy with harvested fruit she can't lift it above her waist.

Some of the plums are overripe and have split in the bucket. The sweet smell of them is almost worth the cold and the wet. Her daddy smiles down at her and tells her it is OK to go inside now. She turns and hurries across the lawn towards the kitchen door.

(Deep in her numbed mind, future Jana tried to stop the young girl crossing the threshold, tried to summon songs to sing or sheep to count – anything to stop the relentless unspooling of unwanted recollection. She did not want to go where this memory was taking her, but she was helpless.)

Dropping the bucket on the floor, Yojana kicks off her rainboots. She does not bother to pick them up and place them neatly on the step as her nanny has taught her. She is too excited for that. They spin wetly across the floor tiles, instantly forgotten. Yojana hears the creaking of the ladder in the garden as her daddy climbs down from the tree. She reaches up and strains with all her might to reach the jug with the sharp knives in it. She is forbidden to touch these, but she has seen her daddy use the small knife to cut the soft plum flesh from the hard stone within and she wants to try. She also remembers him telling her never to bite into an uncut plum, as they often harbour maggots and other larvae which may not otherwise be seen.

She has grown a lot in the last few weeks and her fingers just reach the knife, enough to pull it free of the block so it falls to the wooden surface within reach. She grasps the metal handle and steps backwards from the kitchen counter, turning towards the bucket, already leaning forward to grab a plum.

As she steps backwards, her foot rests on one of her discarded boots and, slick with rain on the polished tiles, it slips away, throwing Yojana's balance off. She falls forward heavily, banging her chin on the tiles. She feels her teeth crack. She opens her mouth to cry but no sound comes out.

Her vision becomes blurred, her hearing muffled. She can see Daddy's feet running towards her, hear his voice shouting, as if underwater. She only vaguely registers him lifting her up off the ground.

Why do her fingers feel wet and sticky?

Jana cried out as, with one hard tug, the doctor pulled the chip free. The doctor assumed it was a cry of pain.

He was right, kind of.

. . . what time do you call this Kaz, I know, just like a cheap sitcom, right, and dad just looks at the clock and says nine, why what time do you call it, and mum doesn't laugh, so I go upstairs and put my records on and drown out the arguing, because there's always arguing, and then it's the morning and I've fallen asleep on the floor again and Mum is shaking me awake and calling me useless and lazy and there's dad behind her telling her not to be so mean to me and she turns and snarls, like a cat or something, and they start again so I shout at them to stop and they kind of do but there's a sullen silence all through breakfast until I can get out of there and head to school and it's a Thursday so I meet up with Tahmina on the way and we chat about stuff and there's the call to prayer in the distance and the sky is a beautiful deep orange and her eyes are like, well I don't know what they're like but they're amazing, and I try to kiss her and she slaps me so that sort of sucks and I don't know what to do so I laugh and pretend I was joking and then I see her looking past me at the road and I follow her gaze and I see this car that's kind of following us and it speeds up as I look at it but as it passes I see her brother looking at me and he looks really pissed and I think oh shit, and I turn to Tahmina but she's turned and walked off so I run after her and I'm talking and she turns and says Kaz what do you think you . . .

Sweetclover had thought this through. He knew that Dora would be disorientated and scared, so he had instructed the doctor to conduct the simplest examination possible and to use only manual instruments. Of course, the girl had never seen a stethoscope or a blood pressure pump, but they were likely to be far less frightening than an ECG or an ultrasound.

When Sweetclover had made his decision earlier in the day, the doctor had reluctantly agreed to the conditions but had muttered something about 'the bloody Stone Age' under his breath as he'd left the meeting. Now, as Sweetclover watched him trying to persuade the girl to offer her forearm so he could take a blood sample, he wondered whether the doctor hadn't been right all along. It probably would have been simpler to keep Dora sedated and conduct the examination before she awoke. But something about this proposal had made him uneasy; it was a violation that he could not in all good conscience support, and while his wife would probably have overruled his objections, she was not here at present. He had no such qualms about the other two prisoners, but would have been unable to explain why. Perhaps he felt a lingering duty of care, perhaps he felt solidarity with someone from his own time, perhaps he felt guilty about what had transpired in 1645. Whatever the reason, he was determined to treat Dora with kindness.

'It will not hurt, Dora,' he said, trying to be reassuring as he ignored the doctor's scornful look. 'Think of the syringe as a mechanical leech, nothing more. It will suck out a tiny drop of blood and then we will be done and can have some lunch.'

Dora did not look convinced, but she stopped resisting and held out her arm, biting her lower lip nervously and screwing her eyes closed as the doctor extracted the necessary. Sweetclover found the look of triumph in the medical man's eyes off-putting even though it was his orders that were being carried out.

'Thank you,' he said. 'You may go.' The doctor nodded and scurried away to his lab. He knew the importance of the blood and the tests he was about to conduct and he obviously couldn't wait to get started.

'Come, my dear, let us eat.'

Sweetclover held out his hand and Dora unclenched her fist, opened her eyes and took it, grateful for his kindness.

He knew she would not be so pliant if she knew the truth.

Jana opened her eyes but the light hurt too much so she screwed them tightly shut again. The pain at the base of her skull was sharp and insistent but it was nothing compared to the hot knives that twisted in her brain with the slight movement caused by her every breath.

She had grown accustomed to the migraines that accompanied hot weather, but this was worse even than the worst of those. Zigzag lines flashed and danced in her vision even when her eyes were closed. The fingers of her left hand were numb and cold.

She experienced a flash of total fear. What if they'd removed the ENL chip incorrectly? Could they have done some permanent damage to her spine? In spite of the pain she wriggled her toes and then tested her limbs one by one, grateful when even her numbed fingers responded.

Among its many functions, the now absent chip could act as a delta wave emitter, counteracting the migraines. She felt sluggish and spaced out when it did its work but it was better than hiding in a dark room with a cold compress on her head, trying to make the pain go away by force of will.

She desperately needed time to think, to calmly and logically puzzle out what had happened to her, but the migraine left no room for anything else. So she stayed where she was, eyes closed, trying to stop the agony from driving her mad.

At least the memories had stopped.

*　　*　　*

. . . and then there's dust and smoke and glass everywhere and I look for her but I can't see anything, really and there's noise like you can't believe, screaming and sirens and the sounds of things falling over and crashing and cars and more screams, so I start to shout out 'Mother! Father? Where are you?' but nobody calls back so I know that they're either dead or wounded but certainly unconscious so I wipe the dust from my eyes with the back of my hand and my eyes are watering but it's the dust not tears and I try to get my bearings and I see a car on its side next to me, blue Audi, and on top of it is a big black lump which I realise is the engine block of another car, broken and charred, and I think 'car bomb' which makes sense and I've seen things like this on YouTube and I know it's going to be grisly because the news doesn't show you what it's really like, doesn't show you the body parts and the blood because people don't like to see that while they're eating their tea, but I've seen it online so I know what I'm going to see but I don't want to see it because who knows if the blackened arm that I trip over is my father's or my mother's but I have to find them so I shout again and I begin working my way through the smoke and chaos hoping that I will find them alive and then I do actually trip, but it's a leg not an arm, and I can taste blood in my mouth and I scramble to my feet quickly, repulsed and flailing and then I see Dad's backpack in the road and the straps are shredded and he's not there, and then a shoe I recognise and I run to it, and then a siren, really close and then . . .

Dora wasn't really hungry. Her usual diet consisted solely of bread, cheese, meat and seasonal fruit and vegetables, so she was unprepared for the place Lord Sweetclover called the 'canteen'.

'I am sorry, I should have thought. I am careless, forgive me,' he said as he noticed her confusion. 'I forget, sometimes, that we have travelled so far.'

Dora did not know where to begin. She was slowly becoming accustomed to the unnatural light, the strange permanent rugs that were stuck to the floor, the perfection of the glass windows which would not open, and the ever-present hum of the 'aircon', but the large room that lay before her was so bewildering that the fight-or-flight reaction she was working so hard to quell threatened to send her scurrying away in search of a nice, dark cupboard.

To her left stood a large metal sideboard containing three shelves upon which were arrayed a collection of bright colours and shapes that she could not interpret. A cold breeze wafted from it. Ahead of her was a metal table with depressions in the surface within which some foul-smelling orange stew bubbled underneath hot lights. There were other cabinets and tabletops as well, but she found that focusing on one or two things at a time helped control her unease.

Lord Sweetclover laughed softly and although he turned a kindly countenance towards her, Dora found that she did not entirely trust his benevolence.

'Let me help you,' he offered.

Dora nodded and bit her lip.

'This' – he indicated the top shelf of the cold cabinet – 'contains drinks made from crushed fruit. They are called smoothies and they are most pleasing. The shelf below contains sandwiches. A sandwich is composed of two slices of bread with some cold meat or cheese pressed between them. It is a staple food of this time. So you see, although the containers and presentation are confusing to you, things have not changed so very much – fruit, bread, meat and cheese. Would you like me to make a selection for you?'

Dora nodded once more.

'I suggest something simple,' mused Sweetclover as he reached into the cold cabinet and handed her a bottle that was made of a kind of light, flexible glass. 'A berry smoothie, nothing controversial there. And how about a ham sandwich?' Dora accepted the strange triangular box, which was made of a kind of stiff paper.

'Ah, but you must have some dessert,' said Sweetclover with a smile that implied this was the best bit. He reached onto the lowest shelf and pulled out a slab of something hard wrapped in paper. 'This is called chocolate, Dora. Trust me, it will change your life.'

'Thank you, my lord,' mumbled Dora, determined to be gracious and grateful despite her uncertainty.

'I shall have the curry, I think,' said Sweetclover, stepping forward, taking a plate from the hot light-table and scooping some of the strange orange stew onto it with a shiny metal ladle. He then led her through a doorway into a large room filled with round tables surrounded by more of the smooth grey chairs. He chose a table and they sat.

'We have the place to ourselves,' he said. 'It is a Saturday, so there is only a skeleton staff on site.'

Dora struggled to grasp his meaning, but kept her lips shut tight as she sat, awkward and uncertain, staring at her meal. She considered the bottle. There was no cork or stopper so she had no idea how to open it, but she was determined not to ask for help. If she could not divine the means of access to so simple a thing, then she would be doomed in this strange place. Not for the first time, she told herself to concentrate and think.

There was a cap of some sort at the top of the bottle's short neck. She could tell by its different colour and texture that it was not part of the bottle's body and was thus removable. She grasped it and pulled, but it did not pop off. Undaunted, she looked more closely and registered the inclined horizontal lines that ran around the bottle's neck. She had never seen a screw in her life so it did not instantly occur to her to turn the cap, but as she looked at the lines she realised what she had to do. She took hold of the cap and, with a firm hand, twisted it off. Her smile of triumph gave way to embarrassment when she realised that Lord Sweetclover was observing her closely.

'Try some,' he said.

Gingerly, Dora raised the bottle to her lips and took a sip. It was overpoweringly sweet, and the texture was thick and unusual. It was also unnaturally cold, which she found disconcerting. But she could tell that she had not been lied to; it was indeed only fruit. Reassured, she turned her attention to the sandwiches. The thick paper container yielded far less willingly to enquiry and after a minute of turning it over in her hands Dora decided that the best course of action was to grab a corner and tear. The box ripped open and the sandwiches flew into the air. Sweetclover chuckled as Dora scrabbled to catch them.

'I do not think it kind to laugh at me,' said Dora, her frustration and embarrassment bubbling over into an act of defiance that only that morning she would never have thought herself capable of.

She carefully put her sandwich back together and took a bite. It too was so cold it made her teeth ache, and there was a taste to it that was slightly unnatural, as if it had been seasoned with some strange herb. But she chewed and swallowed.

'I promised you an explanation,' said Sweetclover, laying down his fork on his empty plate.

'Are you a witch?' asked Dora, the words slipping out from her sandwich-full mouth before she had consciously thought them.

Sweetclover smiled. 'Do you know what technology is, Dora?'

She shook her head.

'It is another word for machines,' he said.

Dora still did not know what he was talking about. He sighed and then said, 'A wise man once said that you can make machines so complicated that they look like magic, but if you don't know what a machine is, even Clarke's Law isn't going to help.'

Dora took a mouthful of sandwich and chewed slowly, waiting for Sweetclover to try again. When he did not, she decided to take the initiative.

'My lord, you told me that the village has been changed by time. How much time?'

'Three hundred and seventy-three years have passed since the morning you disappeared from Sweetclover Hall,' he replied.

Dora could see that he was studying her closely, gauging her reaction as he said this. Some instinct told her that a display of weakness would be dangerous so instead of screaming that this was impossible, or crawling into a corner and crying – both of which seemed like reasonable responses to her – she nodded once, sagely, as if she had just bitten a tree apple and found that it was ripe for harvest.

Her father had told her tales of Merlin and Arthur when she was younger, and Dora remembered the ice cave in which the great wizard was frozen for eternity.

'Did I sleep for this time, or was I frozen in ice?' she asked.

If she was pleased that Sweetclover was impressed by her composure, she did not allow her satisfaction to show on her face.

'Neither,' he replied. 'You travelled here directly. How can I explain . . . when you cross a bridge from one riverbank to another you travel from land to land without actually needing to swim the river itself. You passed over a kind of bridge from then to now without having to live through the intervening years.'

Dora considered this. 'A magic bridge that I could not see?'

Sweetclover smiled and shrugged. 'If you wish. But a bridge nonetheless.'

'Good. For a bridge may be crossed in both directions, may it not? I can go home again.'

'Ah, I'm sorry to say that no, you cannot. The bridge has a toll gate on this bank and neither you nor I have sufficient coin to pay for passage back across.'

'Magic coins?'

Sweetclover noticed a hint of a smile on Dora's face and realised she was, ever so gently, teasing him. 'Something like that.'

Dora took another bite of sandwich. Sweetclover waited patiently for her to process his answer and formulate her next question.

'Who was the woman in the undercroft?' she said eventually.

'You will meet her presently, for she is quite recovered. In fact, this is really her building, not mine. When you encountered her she had also just crossed the bridge but for her it was a much longer crossing, from many years to come, and she had been wounded by the journey. In your kindness you tried to offer assistance but when you touched her it propelled you across the bridge in turn. I must confess that I do not under-stand how or why.'

'A woman from centuries forward travels across a bridge in time and then, by her touch, sends me across the bridge to this strange place. Yes?'

'Yes.'

Dora laughed. 'You are jesting with me, my lord. For surely this woman is a witch. You speak of spells and magics. Well, I will be strong in the face of them. I will pray for deliverance from this evil.'

As she delivered this rejoinder, Dora had been peeling the paper from the slab of brown stuff and, without even thinking about it, she took an absent-minded bite. Upon which all thoughts left her head and her eyes widened to the size of saucers.

'By the lord, this is wonderful. What do you call this?'

'Chocolate.'

Dora took another huge bite. Finally something new which did not fill her with dread. If this strange and alien world had such a thing as chocolate in it, then perhaps it was not the hell she feared.

Sweetclover laughed. 'I told you it would change your life.'

Dora murmured her assent through a mouthful of melting cocoa, all her questions temporarily forgotten.

So the explosion took her completely by surprise.

5

. . . and the wind is blowing really hard so I am worried the plane is going to crash as we land but we don't and so I am back home in Poland for the first time in ten years and as soon as the doors open I feel the cold and I look back at my dad as he struggles with the bags and then . . . and then . . . and then . . . what the . . . ?

Kaz felt the table shake as he stopped speaking. He heard a deep, resonant rumble vibrating through the structure of the building. Even in his confusion, as his mind tried to process what had just happened and reeled in response to the onslaught of unexpectedly detailed memories that had poured from his lips, dry and bleeding after his monologue, his sense memory identified the shock wave of a bomb.

It was not an unfamiliar sensation to him.

His immediate instinct was to rise to his feet and hurry towards the site of the explosion, to see if he could offer assistance to anyone who might have been hurt by the blast, but his vision was blurred, his hands and feet were numb and he found it difficult to think straight. He still had no clue what was happening to him, why he'd been taken prisoner, where he was, what kind of machine had forced him to spew his life story, and why the people holding him were so interested in the first place. But answers could wait. If someone was bombing this building, it meant there would be distraction and confusion, which meant he had a chance to escape.

The guard who had remained in the room had already opened the door and was peering out into the corridor beyond. A deafening klaxon began to sound, which was a relief to Kaz as it masked the noise of his chair scraping on the floor as he pushed it back and tried to stand. His limbs felt lumpen and unresponsive, but he forced himself to concentrate and move slowly while the guard's attention was elsewhere. He knew he might not have much time; he reckoned the blast must have shut down the machine that had been forcing him to speak, but he didn't know how long it would stay off. Maybe it was rebooting or something and any moment he would start talking again.

'Oi, Jim, what's going on?' shouted the guard at the door, trying to get answers from a fellow guard who was running past.

Kaz heard the shouted reply. 'Dunno, some sort of explosion. Stay with the prisoner.'

Jim's footsteps echoed away as the guard turned to look back at Kaz, who had managed to lift the chair above his head but hadn't managed to cover the ground between him and the door. The guard smiled and raised his gun.

'I don't think so. Sit down, sunshine.'

Kaz felt foolish, standing there in an empty room with a chair over his head. He had no choice but to place the chair back on the floor and sit down again. He grinned and shrugged. 'Can't blame me for trying.'

The guard advanced towards Kaz, his face making it clear

that he could and would do exactly that. But before he could administer the slap that was so obviously imminent, the door swung open to reveal the man who had been in charge at the house, the one the young girl had called 'lord'.

'Leave us,' said the man.

The guard turned on his heels, snapped to attention, and smartly stepped outside. He was pulling the door closed behind him when the klaxon stopped blaring and a voice echoed across the PA.

'All guards remain at your posts,' announced the voice. 'There has been an explosion but it is outside the compound, I repeat the explosion is not within the compound. It is either a coincidence or a diversion, so remain vigilant.'

The guard paused, the door still half open. 'Hang on,' he said. 'That was . . .' He turned to look at the newcomer, slowly raising his gun as he began to realise that something here was not quite right.

'Yes, that was my voice,' said the man. 'Confusing, isn't it?' Then there was a flash of light and the guard crumpled to the floor. The man then grabbed the guard's feet and pulled him inside the room. As the man leaned out of the doorway, scanning the corridor outside to make sure he was unobserved, Kaz reached down and snatched the guard's gun.

When the man closed the door and turned back into the room, Kaz was aiming the gun square at his chest.

'This is the central laboratory, the most secure place in the building. You will be safe in here,' said Lord Sweetclover, already turning to leave.

Dora did not want him to go, but she would never have thought to question his decision, or beg him to stay.

50

Sweetclover barked as he passed the young guard who stood inside the door. 'You, what's your name?'

'Simon, sir.'

'You guard this door with your life, Simon, understand?'

The guard – little more than a boy really, thought Dora, as she noticed his wispy moustache – straightened his posture and barked, 'Yes, sir.'

Sweetclover left the room through the two swing doors without looking back at Dora. She heard the doors lock shut.

Left alone with a strange boy in a strange room, Dora paced restlessly, scrutinising instruments and computer terminals, never touching anything but wishing that she could. One wall was lined with strange glass cabinets, their frosted interiors containing shelves laden with glass tubes; another featured a huge mirror which hung alongside a large metal door with a kind of wheel set into the middle of it; the bulk of the room was taken up by long tables. In one corner stood a chair, adorned with leather straps and metal appendages. This was the only thing in the room which caused Dora to shudder. It did not seem to her that anything good would befall a person who found themselves strapped into such a contraption.

'Who are you and what is going on?' asked Kaz.

The man shook his head and smiled, unintimidated by the gun. 'Same old Kaz,' he said, almost fondly. He slowly put the backpack over his shoulder.

'How do you know my name?'

'There's no time for small talk. The bomb won't keep them occupied for long. We have to move quickly and quietly. I'll explain later. All you need to know is that I'm here to help and you have to trust me.'

Kaz shook his head. 'I don't have to do anything.'

'Look, I understand,' said the man. 'You're confused and angry, you don't know what's happening and you want to run. I get it. If I were in your shoes, I'd feel exactly the same way. But the truth is that without my help you have absolutely no chance of escape. They'll pick you up, put you back in front of the mind probe, let you finish your story and then, when they've got everything they need, they'll kill you.'

Kaz stepped forward and rested the cold metal gun barrel against the man's forehead. 'I don't believe you. This is some kind of trick. You're the man who brought me here, why would you let me go?'

The man's face blurred and shimmered. Kaz recoiled in horror as he found himself standing face to face with . . . himself.

'Chameleon shroud,' said his doppelgänger as his face shimmered again, this time turning into that of Dora. 'It's a disguise, see? I'm not Sweetclover, the man who brought you here, but if I look like him, these guards will follow my orders. I can simply march you straight out the front door, get it?'

Kaz was beginning to waver. 'So who are you, then?' he asked as the man shimmered back into Lord Sweetclover.

'You'll find out soon enough,' he said. 'For now, can we go, please?'

After a second's consideration Kaz nodded. 'Don't suppose I have any choice.' He lowered the gun.

'Don't suppose you do.' The man stooped down and began rifling through the guard's pockets.

'Is he dead?' asked Kaz warily.

The man stood, holding a chipped key-card. 'OK, we have three things we need to do before we can leave. First, we need to get the recording from the mind probe. We can't let them keep your life story, it'll cause too much disruption. Second, we need to find the chip they've taken from Jana. Then we need to round up the girls.'

'I have no idea what you're talking about,' said Kaz. 'Can you at least tell me your name?'

The man smiled. 'You can call me Steve.'

The real Sweetclover was feeling a lot less cheerful as he surveyed the wreckage of what looked like a very expensive motorbike, strewn across the road outside the complex's main gate. Around him stood five short men in heavy black riot gear – Kevlar helmets and chest plates, black uniforms and heavy boots. They carried very big guns and their faces were obscured by mirrored visors on their helmets, but their uniformity went beyond their clothing and equipment.

Unlike the rest of the guards, these five stood motionless as if reserving their formidable power for when it was most needed. All roughly the same height and build, they stood with exactly the same posture. Even a person accustomed to facing riot police would have found these men unusually unsettling, their lack of individuality a physical manifestation of something sinister and repressive.

Sweetclover turned to the gatekeeper, who was eyeing the five riot guards nervously. 'And nobody's approached the gate since it blew?' he asked.

'No, sir,' replied the twitchy gatekeeper.

'And there's nothing on any of the perimeter cameras, all the other guard posts have checked in?'

'That's correct, sir.'

Sweetclover shook his head, puzzled. 'Then why blow it

up, if it's not a diversion? Motorbikes don't just spontaneously combust.'

The gatekeeper cleared his throat and nervously offered an opinion. 'Perhaps it's a warning, sir?'

Sweetclover shook his head, annoyed. 'Of what? No, while we're standing here gawping at this wreckage somebody is doing something they don't want us to know about. Check the perimeter again. And you' – he gestured to the riot guards – 'come with me.'

Sweetclover turned on his heels and began walking back to the main building followed by the five hulking soldiers, who, although not marching, still walked in step. After a few paces, Sweetclover stopped dead.

'Unless . . .' He turned back to address the gatekeeper. 'Has anybody come through the gate in the last half an hour?'

'No, sir.'

'Not a delivery van, or a courier of any kind?'

'No, sir, you were the last person through the gate.'

Sweetclover nodded and turned back to the building, took one stride, paused and turned back again.

'You mean when I returned with the prisoners two hours ago in the vans?'

Now it was the gatekeeper's turn to look puzzled. He shook his head. 'No, sir, when you came through twenty minutes ago. On foot.'

Sweetclover was running back towards the complex before the gatekeeper had finished talking.

The sound of five pairs of heavy boots running in perfect unison echoed off the cold, white walls behind him.

Steve swiped the card through the reader, tapping his foot impatiently as it processed the card's ID. Before the door had slid even halfway open, he had turned sideways and slipped through into the room beyond. Kaz followed quickly, keeping his eyes on the corridor as he backed inside, making sure they weren't discovered.

The door closed behind him and Kaz turned to see a darkened room with a huge array of electrical equipment ranged across one wall. Lights and monitors flickered, needles vibrated in semicircular dials.

'What's that?' he asked Steve, who had rushed to the bank of machinery and was typing a series of commands into a keyboard.

'Mind probe,' he replied as he typed. 'Built from scratch using local equipment. Local in time, I mean. A normal mind probe, one from the period in which it was invented, is about the size of a small briefcase . . . ah, got it.'

The machinery whirred and clicked and a small solid-state hard drive popped out. Steve grabbed it, threw it on the floor and shot it with the stubby light gun he had used to disable the guard earlier. The drive smoked and buckled as its destroyer looked up at Kaz and smiled.

'One down. Now they have no record of your memories. Your family is safe. For the time being.'

Kaz didn't think he had any shock left in him, but these words sent a fresh chill through his bones. 'My family? What you talking about?'

'No time. Come on, next we need Jana's chip.'

But as Steve hurried back to the door, Kaz held out a hand and stopped him. 'They were going to use this information to hurt my dad?'

Steve nodded, impatiently. 'Only as a way to hurt you. But they can't because the drive's fried. As long as we don't get ourselves recaptured by standing around chatting when we should be running, you're both safe.'

Kaz shook his head. 'That's not what I meant. What about the guard who was there? He heard everything. When he wakes up he can report what I said.'

'Don't worry about him,' replied Steve, dismissively. 'He won't be telling anyone anything. Now can we go, please?'

As Steve pushed past him and swiped the card to reopen the door, Kaz realised that Steve had never answered his question about whether the guard was dead.

'Split up,' yelled Sweetclover as he burst through the main doors into the lobby. 'Sweep the building floor by floor, room by room. If you find the impostor, radio in but don't wait for back-up. Engage and destroy on sight.'

The five faceless drones walked smoothly, without hurry but also without pause. They broke apart and kept moving in different directions without conferring, moving and thinking as one. As they walked away a thought occurred to their master.

'I shall remain here at the main desk until contact is made,' he shouted. Then, more quietly, 'Don't want to get myself shot, do I.'

'What is a labratree?'

Simon the guard looked confused, though whether he was puzzled by the question, or by the fact that it had been asked at all, was hard for Dora to say. 'I'm sorry, miss?' he replied, his voice rich with an accent that Dora found strange but not unpleasing. Wherever he was from, it was far from Cornwall.

'This place. His lordship said it was the "central labratree". I do not understand what those words mean.'

'Um, well, it's a laboratory,' said Simon, confused by her confusion. 'Where they do science and stuff.'

'Séance? Ah, I understand,' replied the girl with a firm nod of the head designed to make her seem resolute and sensible rather than terrified and confused. 'This is a place of magic.'

The guard laughed. 'Might as well be, for all the sense I can make out of it.'

Dora decided that she liked Simon and, realising that the lab was not going to reveal any of its secrets to her, she turned her attention to him.

'Where are you from?' she asked bluntly as she sat on a stool close to the door where he stood, no longer at attention.

'Dulwich, miss.'

Dora shook her head. 'I do not know this place. And I am not your mistress, my name is Dora.'

'Um, Dulwich's in London. So I'm a Londoner, I reckon.'

'London.' Dora spoke the name as if it were a curse. For some of the boys in her village – and some of the girls too – London had signified excitement and adventure. Her older brother, James, had run off to London on his fifteenth birthday and nothing had been heard of him since. But for Dora it had represented everything she wished to avoid. He father had once told her of a visit to the capital that he had made when he was a young boy, seeking his fortune. To hear him tell it, London was a squalid place of filth, disease and moral decay. It was also populated by strange peoples from around the world, which Dora supposed explained the boy's aspect. She had heard of blackamoors but Simon was the first she had ever encountered. She resisted the urge to approach him and touch his face and hair, feeling that it would be rude to give in to her curiosity.

'I have never been to London,' she said. 'What is it like?'

Simon shrugged. 'Like it is on the telly really. My part of town was banged up, yeah. No money, lots of drugs and gangs and shit. But, you know, it's home. My mum and my sis are still there. It's all right, I s'pose. But when I got this job, I can't lie, I was happy to get out.'

Dora made a mental list of all the things she had not understood about Simon's answer and began to work through them one by one.

'What is telly?' she asked.

As they approached a lobby that marked the junction of two wings of the building, the man disguised as Lord Sweetclover shoved Kaz back against the wall and raised a finger to his lips. They heard heavy footsteps echoing down the corridor ahead of them. Kaz held his breath, desperate to make no sound as their unseen pursuer stalked them.

Steve reached down and grabbed the gun Kaz was carrying. Kaz held on tight and scowled his refusal to let go, but Steve whispered, 'Play prisoner.' Kaz reluctantly relinquished the weapon, which Steve shoved in his pocket before grabbing him by the shoulder and pushing him forward, out into the lobby and plain sight.

The footsteps had been made by a short, wide man encased head to toe in riot armour. Upon noticing Kaz and Steve, the guard stopped dead and turned to regard them from behind his mirrored visor. There was a predatory stillness to him that made Kaz deeply uneasy.

'Good,' said Steve, pushing Kaz ahead of him towards the stationary sentry. 'You can help me get this prisoner to a secure location . . .'

The bluff didn't work. Kaz saw the guard's arm begin to

rise, registered the heavy gun it held, realised that there was a good chance he was about to die and felt a huge surge of fear-fuelled adrenaline coursing through him. His stomach felt empty, his head felt light. Fear paralysed him. Then he felt Steve pushing down on his shoulder, understood what he was being asked to do, forced himself to relax and crumpled to the floor in a heap.

There was a flash of light above his head. Before he could gather his wits, Kaz was being dragged back to his feet and hurried past the twitching guard, who lay sprawled against the wall, his gun lying useless in his outstretched hand. Steve paused and pulled the guard's helmet off. Upon seeing the guard's face he nodded, as if confirming something to himself.

Kaz didn't know what he would have expected to see beneath the helmet, but it certainly wasn't a bald head and face covered in elaborate indigo tattoos. The guard's eyes were open, staring sightlessly at the ceiling.

'Down here, quickly, we haven't much time,' said Steve as he handed the gun back to Kaz. 'My disguise doesn't seem to be fooling anybody.'

Kaz ran after Steve and the gun almost fell out of his hand, so badly was it shaking with excitement and fear.

'Can't we make a break for it?' he gasped.

'I told you, no,' replied Steve as he skidded to halt outside a heavy door. 'We need the chip and the girls.' He swiped the card, the door slid open and they slipped into a stairwell. Steve led them up the stairs at a run.

They were two storeys up when they heard a door crash open somewhere below them. Heavy footsteps echoed upwards. Without breaking his stride Steve reached into his backpack and pulled out a small round object, about the size of a casino chip. He stuck it to the wall. Kaz noticed that it shimmered and vanished as he passed.

They reached the next landing and Steve again swiped the card in an entry coder and pushed Kaz through a door, this time into a long corridor lined with windows on one side and glass-walled cells on the other. The door closed behind them and Steve broke into a run. Kaz followed suit. As they reached the final cell there was a muffled explosion from the stairwell they had just ascended. Kaz looked back at the door and saw smoke and dust billowing upwards behind the glass.

Kaz turned back and saw that Steve had opened the cell and was now kneeling by the single bed it contained, shaking a sleeping girl. Crimson sparks flashed around the pair of them as he did so. Kaz recognised her at once.

'Jana,' Steve was saying urgently into the girl's ear. 'Jana, wake up, you need to wake up now.'

The girl moaned and stirred, rolled over and tried to bat him away.

'Has she been drugged?' asked Kaz.

'And worse,' replied Steve. He pulled a syringe from his backpack and, in one fluid move, popped off the plastic cap and delivered its content into Jana's jugular.

That woke her up fast enough. She roared in pain, sprang up in bed and began pounding on Steve's head and face with tightly curled fists, yelling all the time. Red fire arced and spat in the air each time she made contact. It took Steve a few moments to get a grip on her wrists and restrain her, but eventually he stopped the onslaught. For a second they faced each other, she sitting up on the bed, fists raised, he kneeling at the bedside, restraining her, preventing her from hitting him any more.

So she head-butted him.

Steve reeled back, his nose spraying blood, but he still held her wrists tightly so she tumbled out of the bed on top of him. They sprawled in a jumbled heap on the black and white tiled floor, a penumbra of crimson fire surrounding them like an electric halo.

This bastard's grip was too tight to escape, so Jana decided to keep up her assault another way. She opened her mouth wide and snapped forward, intending to bite off his ear. But before she could crunch the cartilage she felt strong hands around her waist and she was lifted onto her feet. More red sparks flashed in the air around her. The man on the floor let her go. Jana turned her attention to her new assailant, but stopped as she recognised the boy from the old house.

'Please stop,' he said. She wrestled herself free of his grasp and stepped backwards into clear space, adopting a fighting stance. She didn't have the first clue how to fight, but they didn't know that. Jana had long ago learned that a posture of defiance was always better than one of submission.

'Jana – it's Jana, isn't it?' said the boy. 'We met before.'

She nodded, wary, keeping her eyes on the other man, the one who had kidnapped them, who was rising to his feet looking very annoyed indeed.

'OK, listen, Jana,' said the boy. 'Like you, I have no idea what is going on. I don't know where we are, I don't who anybody else is and I don't know why they're doing this to us. But this guy' – he indicated his companion – 'is trying to rescue us. I think.'

'You don't sound very sure,' Jana replied.

The boy shrugged and held out his right hand, offering her

the gun that lay within it. 'I'm not. But we can ask for an explanation later. There are security guards with big guns trying to catch us, so I say we get out of here. Yes?'

Jana eyed the gun suspiciously. It was old and crude, heavy, metal and alien to her. She could not deny she would feel safer with it in her hand, but she had no idea how to use it. She looked up at Kaz, trying to work out the angle, the trap she was missing. But try as she might, she couldn't get a handle on the situation. Reasoning that it was better to be armed and confused rather than merely confused, she took the proffered weapon and nodded.

'Great,' said the boy. 'I'm still Kaz, this is Steve, but I don't think that's his real name and it's definitely not his real face. And you're Jana, yes?'

'Have they already removed the ENL?' snapped Steve, before Jana could answer the boy's question.

Jana's left hand flew to the back of her neck where it found a patch of gauze. She ripped it off and felt a raw, puckered wound, glued shut. She nodded, which pulled at the wound, causing a flash of hot pain that made her wince.

The man cursed under his breath and reached into his backpack, pulling out another gun, which he handed to Kaz.

'What's this?' asked Kaz, handling the strange device warily. The way he held it told Jana it was heavier than the revolver he had just given her, although it had no metal components that she could see. It looked like porcelain, cream coloured, smooth and featureless. There was a trigger, barrel and handle, but instead of a hammer there were two dials sticking out of each side, like the volume controls on an old radio. Jana recognised it as laser weapon, not that dissimilar from the ones used in her time. Which meant this Steve character could be from the future, like she was.

Steve snatched the gun away from Kaz, adjusted the two dials, pressed a small button on the top of the barrel, and handed it back. 'Point and shoot. I've set it to non-lethal, OK?'

'But . . .'

'Give it to me,' said Jana impatiently, offering the revolver back to Kaz. 'I know how to use one of those.'

They swapped weapons. Jana felt the cold weight of the laser and smiled. This was more like it.

'Are we done?' asked Steve impatiently. 'We have very little time. We need to get to the central lab. That's where they'll be running the analysis. We need to get that chip back at all costs. I'll lead the way. Kaz, bring up the rear. Shoot if you see any guards.'

Without waiting for agreement, Steve ran out of the room. Kaz shrugged at Jana again and indicated that she should go ahead of him.

Seeing no other choice, Jana raised the gun and ran.

63

6

'I do not understand. You say that if you were to walk down one of the streets in your town wearing any garment coloured blue, a gang of boys would attack you with knives?'

'Yeah.'

Dora shook her head in frustration. She was certain there was some deeply buried religious or philosophical grievance behind such territorial aggression, but she could not get Simon to explain it to her. 'But why they would do this? Is the colour blue a symbol of a particular religious sect? Do the boys who wear red pledge their allegiance to a different church?'

She was certain this would prove to be the explanation; surely the blues were Catholic and the reds were Protestant. Simon shook his head, as confused by her suggestion as she was by his answers.

'Nah. 'Sjust territory.'

'So the dispute is political. Either Reds or Blues claim their territory for a foreign power. Are they Spanish puppets?' Dora did not understand how they could be Spanish agents without being Catholics, but she was determined to try.

Simon laughed at her, which made Dora blush with

embarrassment and annoyance, even though she knew his laughter was not unkind.

She pouted, folding her arms crossly.

'Calm down, I'm not taking the piss,' he said. ''Sjust funny. Look, it's real simple. The Dully White Gang own my part of town, the Kingswood Estate. They hate the Ninerz from Norwood. They don't want them on their patch, causing trouble, trying to cop off with their sisters. If everyone stays in their territory, there's no trouble, is there.'

'But you said that sometimes innocents are hurt.'

'Well, yeah, if you're thick enough to go walking down Kingswood with a red scarf on or summat then yeah, you're gonna get stuck. But that's your lookout. Shoulda done your homework.'

Dora sighed, finally accepting that the situation Simon described was as arbitrary at it had first appeared. 'This lacks all sense,' she said. 'Were such gangs to arise in my village, the boys would be soundly whipped on the orders of the magistrate and that would be an end to it.'

Now it was Simon's turn to look astonished. 'Whipped?'

'Yes,' replied Dora, matter-of-factly. 'On the green, for all the village to witness their shame. The oldest Watkins boy sought to force himself upon little Milly Allan three weeks ago. He was in the stocks for two days and then received thirty lashes upon the post. I wonder that your magistrates do not lock these gang boys in the stocks and let the local citizens put them in their place.'

Simon shook his head in wonder. 'Where did you come from, Duchess?'

'Cornwall,' replied Dora with a mostly successful attempt at haughty pride.

Somewhere in the depths of the building there was a muffled explosion which rattled the glass tubes in the cold cabinets.

'What was that?' asked Dora, belatedly remembering her predicament. She had been enjoying her conversation with Simon.

'Sounded like another bomb,' said Simon, as he pulled a short black pistol from a leather pouch on his hip. Dora had never seen such a weapon before, but it was sufficiently similar to a flintlock for her to guess what it did.

'Simon,' asked Dora, eyeing the weapon nervously. 'Are you my protector or my gaoler?'

The boy bit his lip nervously, momentarily betraying his youth and inexperience. 'Bit of both, I reckon, Duchess, if I'm honest.'

This answer did not reassure Dora one little bit.

The weapon felt comfortable in Kaz's grasp.

He'd never fired one in anger, but that didn't mean he was unfamiliar with guns. He had grown up around soldiers, and even though his parents had disapproved, he'd always been able to find a squaddie willing to let him take a few shots on the range when they weren't around. His parents insisted that Kaz should pursue his studies, get qualifications, find a safe job somewhere, even as they travelled the world dragging him from one war zone to another. Their lives were full of danger and excitement, but they told him every day that he mustn't be like them, they wanted better things for him than that. Do as we say, not as we do. The hypocrisy of it had infuriated him, so he had trained in secret, finding allies amongst the troops, willing to teach him to shoot, to fight, to plan and strategise.

Then his mother died, and everything changed. His father

had brought him back to Poland, tried to build a normal, stable life. But neither of them had taken to it. Undone by grief, they had fought almost constantly, until eventually his father had threatened to put Kaz into a Catholic boarding school that would fence him in with rules and regulations, curfews and timetables, the tedium of routine. He'd run away at the first opportunity. It hadn't been difficult, not after the preparations he'd spent his life making. And now here he was, eight weeks later, being pursued through a building in a strange country, outnumbered and outgunned.

He knew it was stupid, but he couldn't help it – he was enjoying himself. He was surprised to find, though, that he wasn't entirely sure he had it in him to actually shoot anybody.

The girl ahead of him, Jana, seemed to harbour no such doubts. A couple of times they almost ran into the riot guards, and each time she let off a few shots in support of Steve's more focused fire. She did not hit any of them, but it was not for want of trying. To Kaz, Jana did not seem to be enjoying herself. She just seemed really, really angry. He was glad she was on his side.

The guns she and Steve were using did not fire bullets, but projected a single beam that shot out like an extending tape measure and then switched off. It seemed more like stabbing than shooting. It buzzed when it fired, like a crossed wire in a light fitting, sparking and live.

They hit a long corridor, the longest yet. It stretched out ahead of them, its numerous side corridors offering a world of cover for potential attackers. It was silent and deserted but Steve slammed to a halt so unexpectedly that Jana and Kaz barrelled into each other. There was a momentary scrabble for balance.

67

'What is it?' asked Kaz.

'Those doors at the end, that's the lab,' said Steve softly.

'Come on then,' said Jana, pushing forward. Kaz grabbed her shoulder to hold her back. She angrily shook herself free and turned to scowl at him.

'I think he's about to say something like "it's too quiet",' said Kaz.

Steve nodded as a clatter of footsteps echoed around them. There were definitely guards behind them, and almost certainly guards waiting for them in the side corridors up ahead, ready to cut them down in a crossfire if they attempted to run the gauntlet to the lab.

'If we can get through those doors and secure our position, we'll only need a few minutes,' said Steve.

'For what? Won't we be stuck in there?' asked Kaz.

Steve smiled knowingly. 'Oh no, we've got an escape route. We could leave right now, but we can't abandon Dora, and we must retrieve Jana's chip at all costs.'

'Think fast, because those guards are getting closer. I say we run,' said Jana, tensing as if to sprint. But before she could take off there was a massive unified stamp, as if a battalion had stood to attention. A phalanx of riot guards stepped out ahead of them, two from each cross-corridor entrance. Kaz found the unnatural synchronicity of their movement chilling.

He turned as if to run back the way they had come, but a group of four guards rounded the corner of the corridor behind them.

They were trapped.

It would have surprised Kaz to learn that Jana felt afraid.

Not the almost-fear she had felt on the rooftop as she had

leaned out into the crosswinds, but proper, bone-deep terror of death. She'd been feeling it ever since she had been rudely awoken in her cell and, after a moment of disorientation, remembered that her ENL chip had been removed. That chip was her ticket to immortality, the safety net that made her invulnerable. It was because of the chip that she had been so devil-may-care throughout her short life, so reckless that only the craziest of her classmates had anything to do with her. Jana, they all knew, was willing to push it one degree more – swim that bit further from the shore, take a corner a few mph faster than the car was designed to handle.

It made her fun to be around. And dangerous.

More than once a classmate or friend had been injured trying to emulate or impress her. The pattern was always the same – they'd try to push things as far as Jana but, at the last minute, realising how much of a risk they were taking, they would lose their nerve and try to pull out of whatever mad death-spiral they had committed themselves to. There was a look they got in their eyes as they recalculated the odds, Jana had seen it many times, a mixture of fear and surprise. She wondered if that was what she looked like now, as she stood trapped by an army of faceless kidnappers in a building farther from home than she had ever thought it possible to be.

The secret, she had learned, was to follow through, to never back out once you'd committed to a course of action, no matter how risky. Whatever danger you were in, it was always more dangerous to second-guess yourself at the last instant.

Gripping the gun tight in her right hand, she forced herself to wait. Normally she would have taken charge, but not today. Instead she looked to the man called Steve and said, 'What do we do now?'

Steve paid her little attention. He was assessing the forces arrayed ahead and behind them. The guards stood there, unmoving, implacable, penning them in but in no hurry to disarm or capture them. Their immobile calm was terrifying.

'Come on, what are you waiting for?' yelled Kaz.

The guards did not respond in any way to his taunt.

'They're waiting for Sweetclover,' said Steve, almost absent-mindedly, his gaze now fixed firmly on the lab doors at the end of the corridor before them. 'He wants to be in at the kill.'

'You said we could leave right now if we wanted,' said Jana, alarmed at the tremble in her voice.

Steve nodded. 'But I may have a better idea.' He glanced down at his watch, then turned to face Jana and Kaz. 'When the bomb goes off, stay focused on me,' he said. 'We need to hold hands to form a circle and you must, absolutely must, empty your minds of all thought.'

Jana didn't even know how to begin to respond to such a bizarre order, so she decided to go with it.

'OK,' she said.

'What bomb?' asked Kaz.

'Not a place, not a time in your life, not a person. Nothing, understand?' Steve continued. 'Think of the colour white. Empty, blank, void. Can you do that?'

Jana nodded. Kaz just looked confused. 'Um, I'll try,' he muttered.

'Hello there.' It was Sweetclover. He had stepped out into the corridor ahead of them, about halfway to the lab door, flanked by guards. He was waving and smiling. 'I must say, you are the most handsome terrorist I've ever met. Dashing, too. When this is over we really must share grooming tips.'

Steve did not smile as his doppelgänger made jokes.

'You can drop the disguise now,' Sweetclover continued, his fake smile fading away. 'It's not fooling anybody any more and I would so like to look you in the eye.'

Jana slowly slipped her gun into her pocket so that her hands were free. She caught Kaz's eye and, with a glance, indicated that he should do the same. He gave an almost imperceptible nod and did so. He reached for her hand but a single red spark arced between their outstretched fingers and he whipped his hand away again. If Sweetclover noticed this, he gave no sign of it. His attention was focused tightly on Steve.

'You did Kaz no favours, you know,' Sweetclover was saying. 'By destroying the recording you merely ensured he'll have to go through the mind probe again. I imagine he'd prefer to avoid that, wouldn't you, Kaz?'

'Screw you,' Kaz shouted, an act of defiance that finally earned him a smidgen of respect from Jana.

Sweetclover tutted and shook his head. 'Such manners. When I see your father, I'll have to tell him the kind of man he raised.'

Kaz balled his fists and took a step forward but Steve held out his arm, not touching the boy, but blocking his way.

'Calm down, Kaz. He's playing with you,' he said. Then he whispered to them both, 'Look at the lab door and get ready.'

Jana squinted down the corridor. She could see silhouetted figures moving behind the frosted glass windows of the central lab doors behind Sweetclover.

'I suppose you want us to lay down our weapons and come quietly?' asked Steve.

Sweetclover shrugged theatrically. 'Do or don't, makes no odds to me. Either we kill you here and now, or you surrender and let us put you on ice until we're ready to do it properly. Your call.'

'But why?' screamed Jana, finally allowing her own frustration to boil over. 'Who are you? What is the point of all this? What do you want?'

'Oh, Jana. Dear sweet Jana. What would be the fun if I told you that? Let's say we had history, you and I. But we won't have had soon.'

Jana shook her head as he mangled his tenses. 'What does that even mean?' she yelled, more in confusion than anger. The shadows behind the lab window drew her gaze. Someone was holding up a hand, pressing it to the glass with their fingers spread wide.

'Five,' muttered Steve.

The thumb bent inwards under the palm.

'Four.'

The hand was withdrawn and a shadow seemed to hurry away from the doors.

Jana unfurled her own tight fists and got ready to grab the hands of Steve and Kaz.

'Three,' whispered Kaz, taking up the countdown.

'Guards.' At Sweetclover's bark, all the guards raised their weapons.

'Two,' muttered Jana and Kaz in unison, raising their hands.

'Hands above your heads, I think,' shouted Sweetclover. 'We don't want anybody—'

Before he could finish his sentence, the lab doors blew off their hinges in a ball of flame and spun down the corridor, cutting down the row of guards. The blast wave toppled many more, and Sweetclover himself was engulfed in smoke.

Shots rang out ahead in the confusion.

'Now,' yelled Steve as the smoke reached them, shielding them from the view of guards both ahead and behind. Jana reached out and grabbed Kaz's hand, lighting up the smoke with red fire from within. Her hand tingled where it touched his, like static electricity or the feeling of pins and needles you get when the blood returns to a numbed limb. Then both she and the boy leaned forward to take Steve's outstretched hands as they did their best to empty their minds of all thought. Steve grasped their fingers tightly and the world exploded in a riot of firework red. Jana felt a familiar lurch in her stomach, the same as she had felt when she had vanished in mid-air above New York. She realised immediately what was happening.

She closed her eyes and forced herself to relax, surrendering to the pull of whatever force it was that had snatched her away from certain death once already.

And the world reshaped itself around her.

7

Kaz had seen the two girls appear in mid-air, but in many ways that had been the least unexpected thing to happen to him since he had fled the farm in search of a bed for the night. Since that first flash of red fire he'd been granted no time for reflection, no opportunity to consider the events of his day, the things he had witnessed or the things that had been done to him. He had spent the last twenty-four hours reacting to events he did not understand, hoping that at some point everything would become clear to him and he could begin to take an active role.

But as his hand found Jana's, and he felt the tingle in his fingers, he realised that things were only going to get stranger. When Steve grabbed his other hand and completed the circle Kaz felt such power flowing through him that his vision, already fogged by smoke, blurred even more and began to speckle with tiny firework flashes of red and white. He was unsure how much of this was real and how much a result of trauma from the shock wave. He was part of a circuit, power flowing in through his right hand and out through his left.

Smoke. Confusion. Fire. The low whine in the ears that follows a concussive blast. Dust in the eyes and the taste of blood and iron on the tongue.

These things were not new to Kaz. So as he stood in the corridor, grasping for the hands of his companions as the shock wave of the explosion rolled over him, he could not empty his mind as he had been instructed. Instead he was overwhelmed with memories. The sensory onslaught pulled his thoughts back to an earlier time and place, and that time and place came rushing forward to greet them.

His stomach lurched, his head swam and everything changed.

Unfortunately, it changed into something familiar.

Shouts and screams, a cacophony of various sirens. The smoke that engulfed them was different; dirtier, mingled with earth and metal and something else, something organic. The sterile smell of a clean bomb in a clean corridor was replaced by cheap nitrate explosive and scorched blood.

Kaz didn't trust his senses. He knew where he was but he was equally sure that he couldn't be here. He had been in a corridor in some kind of secret research establishment, penned in by weird gunmen and holding hands in a doomed gesture of defiant solidarity with two people he didn't know. There was no way he could have instantly been transported from there to here.

Even in his confused state his mind checked and corrected itself – from there and then to here and now. Another flash of thought: have I gone mad? Am I reliving my past as some kind of retreat from reality? Is this all only trauma?

'Crap. Where are we?' That was Steve, who loomed out of the smoke, still holding tight to Kaz's hand and shouting through the tumult.

'I . . . I don't know.' That was Jana shouting back, still grasping his other hand.

Kaz did not reply even though he knew full well where and when they were. Partly he stayed silent because he did not trust himself to say anything coherent, partly because he refused to accept the evidence of his own senses.

He knew that he was going into shock, but he also knew that this realisation didn't help him.

'Over here, let's get under cover.' Steve's shouts sounded like whispers through fog as he pulled Kaz. He in turn held tight to Jana and dragged her along behind him, out of the smoke.

The light was diluted and milky, even outside the dusty smoke, but gradually shapes and forms appeared as if out of a thick mist. A grocer's stall, boxes overturned, fruit split open and strewn everywhere across a slab pavement and a roughly tarmacked road. An arc of pulped tomatoes and oranges was splashed across whitewash. A third stain, deeper and darker, mingled with the juices that oozed slowly down the wall.

Someone ran past them, knocking Jana off her feet. Kaz let go of Steve and bent down to help the girl up, his peripheral vision registering a man running with a young woman held in his arms, motionless and limp, her long brown hair swaying in rhythm with her lifeless limbs as the man pressed on in search of aid.

Kaz saw Jana's lips move and understood that she was thanking him for helping her up, but all his ears delivered were sirens and whine.

For the next minute, as Steve ushered the two teenagers away from the smoke and confusion of the recent explosion, all Kaz's mind registered were tiny details, as if the totality of what was happening to him had become too large for him to comprehend.

The way the red and white of the ambulance lights refracted within the haze of smoke.

The look on the face of a man in army uniform running towards the scene of the blast.

A wrought-iron balcony, ripped from an outside wall, twisted and broken in the street, surrounded by shattered plant pots and dying roses.

A discarded shoe he recognised.

He hurried on, pulled away from his memories, blindly stumbling through the wreckage of his past.

The world returned to Kaz a piece at a time.

First the cold, sharp fizz of Coke sucked mechanically through a straw that had been placed between his lips.

Then the gradual fading in of sound as the whine subsided. Sirens in the distance, the hubbub of conversation, the tinny echo of a TV. The ambience of a local café.

Then the pungent, spicy aroma of falafel and kebab, so familiar and comforting.

Then the hard feel of wooden slats on his back and buttocks. He was sitting at a table.

Finally the worried faces of Steve and Jana, two people he neither knew nor trusted but who offered the only continuity available to him. He locked on to Jana's eyes and used them as an anchor to pull himself back up into consciousness.

She was the one holding the bottle of Coke up to his lips. He reached up and took hold of it for himself.

'Thanks,' he said.

He took another gulp and allowed his swimming senses to settle down, told himself to focus on facts, to think his way through the shock. He knew exactly where he was, and when. He just didn't know how or why.

'Welcome back,' said Steve, not unkindly.

'How long?' muttered Kaz.

'You've been zoned out for about half an hour,' said Jana, more brusquely.

'Sorry.'

Steve shook his head. 'First time's disorientating for everybody, but making your first jump under fire and ending up in the middle of a war zone, especially one that's so personally traumatic . . . it's enough to make anybody check out for a while.'

'Steve's told me where we are and why. I'm sorry.' Jana's offer of condolence was forced and awkward, as if she knew she had to say something but really wanted to get it over with so she could move on to more important things.

'I know where we are,' said Kaz, his tone of voice indicating that he didn't quite believe it. 'This is Beirut, 2010. The day my mother died.'

Steve nodded. 'The last time and place I imagine you would want to revisit.'

'But how?'

'That is a much longer story, and one we don't have time for yet.'

'The highlights, then.'

Steve shrugged. 'I was attempting to jump us a hundred metres north and ten minutes into the past. Into the laboratory. That way we could grab Dora, and I could plant the bomb to cover our escape. Unfortunately, when the explosion occurred it triggered your memories of this day, so instead of my mind leading us to the lab, yours brought us here. Your memories were so strong I couldn't steer us.'

'So we, what . . . travelled in time and space using the power of thought?' replied Kaz after a moment's consideration. 'That's stupid.'

'He's telling the truth,' said Jana. 'This was my second trip. You saw me arrive after my first. Back at that old house, remember?'

'Dora too,' said Steve. 'Both Dora and Jana came adrift in time for a moment and ended up at Sweetclover Hall in 2013. You were already there, Kaz. And so were Sweetclover and I, both waiting for your arrival. He so that he could capture and interrogate you, me so that I could rescue you.'

Kaz shook his head, refusing to accept this explanation. He tried to put everything in order, to examine the evidence and make it fit with his experiences to provide an explanation, but nothing seemed to gel.

'OK, if I believe that time-space travel is possible, then where and when are you from?' He looked at Jana.

'Yojana Patel. Born eighth August 2123 in New York, Eastern Protectorate. You?'

'I am Kazik Cecka, born twelfth December 1995 in Kielce, Poland. You're really from the future?'

'No; you're really from the past,' she replied.

Kaz turned his gaze to Steve. 'And you?'

'I plead the fifth,' said Steve with an apologetic shrug. 'It will all become clear eventually, but for now I have to remain enigmatic. Sorry. Look, there'll be time for a full explanation later but basically, you two can travel in time. Dora too. There's a reason for that, but it's complicated and not terribly important right now. What is important right now is that there are people who want to capture you because of things you haven't done yet. They want to stop you doing them, to change their history, and your futures. I'm trying to stop them.'

'Not good enough, we need more,' said Jana. 'Who is after us?'

Before Steve could answer, a fat, sweaty man wearing a greasy apron slapped three plates of food down in front of them with a grunt. Kaz reached for a wallet, but of course he had none. The man saw what he was doing and waved him to stop.

'You have just been blown up, son,' said the man, business-like. 'Food's on the house.'

Kaz thanked the man, who waved away his thanks as he had waved away his attempts to pay, as if vaguely insulted by them. He returned to the counter and joined his friends, who were watching the news coverage through a flurry of shouts and gesticulations.

'What is this?' asked Jana.

'Kebab,' said Kaz, realising that he was starving. Jana's face told him that she had no idea what he meant. 'Lamb, salad, dressing, hummus, flatbread. It's good,' he said, through a mouth already half full. 'Spicy.'

Jana eyed the plate with deep suspicion.

'Don't they have kebabs in the future?' said Kaz with a first hint of good humour.

'Not like this we don't,' was all Jana would say. She reached down, lifted the pitta bread pocket gingerly and sniffed it once before taking an exploratory nibble. She pulled a face but chewed, swallowed and took another.

For five minutes they sat in silence, eating their food, trying to order their own thoughts as the sirens wailed in the distance and the men in the corner argued loudly about who was trying to blow them up.

The sounds and smells of the café were as alien to Jana as the lab canteen had been to Dora.

The sirens had died down now, and the commotion at the scene of the explosion was muted and distant enough to be drowned out by the ongoing discussion at the café counter and the drone of the TV.

The light also seemed strange to Jana; diffuse and creamy, laced with steam, smoke and spice. All Jana's innate prejudice about the Long Island favelas were rearing up in her head. She was sure that at any moment she would be robbed by a feral gang of wild-eyed junkies dressed in rags. The café owner's brusque generosity confused her far more than it relieved her. Had she wandered into such a place back home she wouldn't have lasted five minutes before her wealth, education and social superiority would have gotten her into more trouble than she could have easily talked her way out of. She may have been reckless, but there were some risks even she wouldn't take lightly.

Jana tried not to think about the journey the food had taken to her plate. She seriously doubted the meat was properly vat-grown, and the mess of grease and food stains on the waiter's apron told her way more than she wanted to know about the conditions in the kitchen.

But the boy Kaz seemed relaxed. He had spoken to the café owner in the local dialect and was wiping his lips already, having practically inhaled his kebab. This was not his home but he felt comfortable in this place, knew its ways.

As he dropped his paper napkin on to his plate Jana decided to trust him, at least for now. He was as confused by all that was happening as she was, so he made a natural ally.

The older man, who was eating more slowly, his eyes constantly watching the street for signs of discovery or attack, did not inspire her trust, no matter what he said he had done.

His motives were unclear, his true objectives mysterious. She did not think he was a threat right now but it was clear that he was working to a strategy, and that could mean that she and Kaz were allies of convenience only, pawns that he would use until he needed them no longer. She simply did not have enough data to make a judgement and refused to rely on instinct, which she did not trust. It was safest to withhold trust, so that is what she did.

When they had all finished, the greasy man returned with coffee and honeyed pastries, which Kaz told her were called baklava. The drink was hot and strong, although a thick layer of grounds floated on the surface, which took her by surprise and made her spit and sputter.

'Like this,' said Kaz, leaning over and stirring it vigorously until the vortex sucked the grounds to the bottom. 'Now let it settle for a minute and it'll be OK to drink.'

Jana thanked him, aware as she did so that her thanks were curt and unfriendly. She did not like looking stupid and could not help her resentment showing.

It was Steve who broke the silence.

'We need to try again, to get back to the lab . . .'

Jana shook her head firmly. 'Oh no. You owe us some answers.'

Steve considered for a second. 'You will travel in time a lot. It will get easier for you to do so, and to navigate your journeys. Your enemy is a woman named Quil. And you have friends in . . . no, no that would be too risky.'

Jana waited for him to continue, but when it became clear he was done she snorted derisively. 'That's it?'

'I could tell you more,' said Steve, sounding apologetic. 'I could tell you it all. I could tell you exactly what action to take at every step of the adventure you're embarking upon – but if you fail to remember my instructions and freeze up at the wrong moment, or worse, misremember them and take the wrong action, I risk unravelling the chain of events that led me here.'

'So this is all the help we get?' asked Jana. 'You rescue us from the bad guys and then send us on our way?'

'Afraid so,' said Steve. 'If I tell you the future, I basically take away your free will. It's your choices, taken freely in the heat of the moment, that have enabled me to come back and rescue you at this point in your timeline.'

'And I am grateful about that,' said Kaz, looking pointedly at Jana, who took the hint and gave up her interrogation with a frustrated shrug.

'I need to rescue Dora and get you to the cavern,' said Steve. 'That's when you can take stock. Until all three of you are together and safe, you can't begin to take control of the situation, start to become the people you need to be.'

'More riddles,' sighed Jana. 'Why is this girl so important, anyway?'

Steve leant forward and folded his hands together on the table, clearly trying hard to contain his impatience. 'For the moment your ability to control your travels is limited,' he explained. 'You will get better, stronger, but right now the only way for you to travel is if you are all together, in physical contact. You need Dora, and she needs you. The only reason we were able to jump here is because I made up the third member of the party.'

'There's one more problem,' said Kaz through a mouthful of pistachio honey. 'I'm eighteen, Jana is about the same, yes?'

'Seventeen,' said Jana, reluctant to admit that she was younger.

'OK, but that other girl, Dora, she's only, what, fourteen maybe? And where's she from? I think she's from the past.'

'She's from the sixteen hundreds. About the time of the English Civil War,' said Steve.

Jana decided to chime in and back Kaz up. 'OK, so how is she going to cope with all this?' she asked. 'I can handle myself. Kaz here looks the part if nothing else. But do we really need a kid like that trailing after us, especially if we're being hunted by persons unknown?'

'Oh yes,' said Steve with a self-consciously enigmatic smile. 'You really do.'

'Enough with the man of mystery act,' said Jana. 'From now on it's either yes, no or no comment, right?'

'Whatever you say, Yojana,' said Steve.

She recoiled as if she had been slapped. 'Don't call me that. No one calls me that. I'm Jana.'

'Yes, ma'am.'

Jana stared at him hard, her lips pursed. 'Right. You go wait outside for a minute, I want to talk to Kaz alone.'

Both Steve and Kaz seemed surprised by this, but after a moment Steve nodded, pushed back his chair and walked out of the café.

Jana turned and considered the boy. If what Steve was saying was true, she and this guy, Kaz, were going to be allies, maybe even friends. He was tall and fit, with short brown hair and bright blue eyes set deep in his square head. He looked tired and confused. She tried to get his measure. Was he a fighter or a quitter? She was sure she'd caught flashes of excitement, even enjoyment, on his face when they were being chased

84

through the labs earlier, and he'd watched their backs. But if they were to be allies, she needed someone with a cool head, not some excitable idiot who thought he was immortal. Plus, he hadn't fired a shot, so how much use was he, really? She wasn't sure about his reliability in a crisis, but she was sure that as little as she trusted anyone, she trusted Kaz more than Steve.

'What do you think?' she asked him.

'I don't know,' he said, shaking his head wearily. 'I haven't a clue what's going on, and he's not telling us everything. I haven't had time to think, I've been reacting since I got to that damned house.'

This boy wasn't a leader, decided Jana. He wasn't a panicker, but he wasn't the one to take the reins. She was relieved. That meant she didn't have to challenge him for control.

'I think we need to do as he says, for now,' said Jana in her firmest voice. 'If what he's saying is right, then soon it'll just be you, me and this history girl. We can start to make plans then, work things out. For now, I think we have to let things play out his way.'

Kaz seemed relieved. 'All right.'

Jana was satisfied. He'd caved almost immediately. She'd read him right, he was a follower not a leader, which made things easier for her.

'Then let's go collect our friend and get on with it,' she said as she rose from the chair.

Kaz thanked the men at the counter, and the owner gave him another dismissive wave. Then they stepped out to the street, grasped each other's hands and reached out to take Steve's.

* * *

When the café owner looked back, his eyes drawn to the window by a flash of red, the three strange customers had vanished. He grunted as he levered himself off his stool and went to collect their plates.

When he returned to the counter he knocked on the small door that led to the storeroom at the back.

'They're gone,' he said.

8

For a girl who would only that morning have described herself as lacking in all curiosity, Dora was being surprisingly inquisitive.

It was as if, having made the decision to investigate the noise in the undercroft, she had opened some kind of door in her head and all the questions in the world had come tumbling out.

'Look, I've told you already,' said Simon. 'I don't know how electricity works, right? You plug something into the socket and switch it on, yeah?'

'So all of these things – the cold cupboard, the tube of light, the thinking boxes – they all receive magic power through the holes in the walls. And this makes them go?'

'The fridge, the lights and the computers all run on electricity, yeah. But it's not magic.'

Dora smiled patronisingly and shook her head at the boy's obstinacy. 'It is an invisible power that flows through lines beneath the earth. What else would you call it but magic?'

'Fine.' He threw up his hands. 'It's magic. Whatever. Power stations are big buildings full of witches and wizards doing spells. For definite.'

Dora folded her arms and gave a curt nod. This was an explanation she could accept. But his countenance betrayed his deceit. 'You are saying this to make me be quiet, are you not?'

Simon closed his eyes and bowed his head. 'Oh God, make it stop.'

As if on cue there was a blinding flash of crimson fire and three figures materialised in the far corner of the laboratory.

Dora didn't miss a beat.

'Ha,' she said, pointing at the new arrivals. 'What explanation have you for this, if not magic?'

Simon was not listening any more. He had drawn his sidearm and was focusing intently on Kaz, Jana and Steve, who were orientating themselves to their new surroundings with varying levels of ease.

'Don't move,' he shouted.

'Simon,' said Dora firmly, as if scolding a naughty child. 'Put that weapon down at once, can you not see that our Lord Sweetclover is amongst them?' She walked forward to offer support to the disorientated time travellers, completely blocking Simon's shot. She did not see the resigned shrug her guard gave as he holstered his pistol, or the weary shake of the head as he tried to work out how he had ended up following the orders of this absurd girl.

Three people appearing out of thin air did not strike Dora as cause for panic. She had seen enough magic today that such events were beginning to seem commonplace.

The boy was looking at the laboratory in wonder, shaking his head incredulously.

'That was incredible,' he said.

The young woman had less time for gawping. Dora saw

her take a businesslike inventory of the room and its inhabitants before turning to Lord Sweetclover.

'How long?' said the girl.

Sweetclover glanced at his watch. 'Five minutes. Right now Kaz and I are breaking you out of your cell two floors above. We have to hurry. Kaz, you talk to Dora. Jana, and you,' he gestured towards Simon, 'help me lay these charges.' He reached into his pockets and pulled out four small grey discs. He handed two to the girl he had called Jana.

'Yes, sir,' said Simon, although his face betrayed his alarm and uncertainty.

'My lord, may I ask what is happening . . .' asked Dora, but he ignored her question. The boy put himself in her way and steered her to one side.

'Hi,' he said, smiling. 'My name's Kaz, we've not been properly introduced.'

Dora was suspicious of this young man and of the frantic activity of her lord, Simon and the other young woman, but she was not about to forget her manners.

'I am Dora,' she replied primly. 'Pleased to meet you again, sir.'

The boy laughed and Dora wondered why it was that young men seemed to find her so amusing today.

'Please, no sirs,' he said. 'I am just Kaz.'

Dora was not certain that she wished to be so informal with this strange boy, but he appeared to offer her no choice in the matter. In the absence of anything else to do, Dora defaulted to questioning him, ignoring the little voice at the back of her mind that meekly suggested the prudent course would be to try silence for a while.

'What are they doing?' She indicated his companions and

Simon, who was obeying Lord Sweetclover's orders but looked extremely dubious about doing so.

'Preparing our escape,' replied Kaz.

'But . . .'

Kaz held up his hand to silence her and she clamped her mouth shut. 'There's not time to explain everything, but you, me and Jana,' he indicated the other girl, who was sticking things to the door frame, 'have all travelled in time.'

Dora scowled. She knew this full well.

'Jana is from the future,' Kaz continued. 'I am from this time, you are from the past. See?'

'That girl is from the future?'

'Yes.'

'But this is the future.'

'No, this is the pres . . . oh, what's the use. Yes, this is your future. She is from even farther into the future. You see?'

Dora nodded slowly.

'OK, good. So, this place is a laboratory run by very nasty people who want to lock us up, maybe even kill us.'

This Dora could not accept. 'You are mistaken, this place is overseen by my Lord Sweetclover, who has taken great care of me.' She turned to Sweetclover. 'My lord, this boy maligns you.'

'Two minutes,' said Lord Sweetclover, handing another small grey chip to Simon, who was looking more and more uneasy.

There were loud bangs in the distance.

'There is a battle approaching,' she said, as the first hint of fear broke through her confusion and disdain.

'Wrap it up, Kaz,' said Lord Sweetclover, standing back to admire the placement of the strange grey chips arranged around the door.

'OK. Listen.' Kaz leaned forward and placed his hands on Dora's shoulders, staring intently into her eyes as if trying to convince her by force of will. 'Here's what will happen. In a minute we are going to blow that door off. Then you, me and Jana will join hands and travel somewhere safe. Once there, we can talk, and I promise we will tell you everything we know. But right now, I need you to trust me.'

Dora was inclined to like the boy. His eyes were kind and his words were persuasive. But she did not know him, and she was nobody's fool. She turned to the one person in the room she did trust.

'My lord?' she asked.

'Do as he says, Dora,' said Lord Sweetclover. 'You will have your answers soon enough.'

Dora regarded Sweetclover curiously. Something about him was wrong, but she was unable to put her finger on what it was. She could see that Simon was also becoming wary of him.

Everybody watched as Sweetclover hurried over to a large metal door that had a kind of small wheel set into it. He began to spin the wheel left, then right, then left. To Dora his actions looked random and silly, but after a few turns he grabbed a handle and pulled it down, causing the door to give a mighty click and swing open.

He vanished inside for a moment then emerged and threw a small container to Jana.

'Yes,' said the girl as she cracked the container open and pulled out a small black square which she slapped onto the back of her neck. Dora heard a soft sucking sound as Jana's body gave a single massive shiver, then she stood upright, her eyes blazing. 'Oh, that is so much better,' she said. 'Thank you, whoever you are.'

'You're welcome,' said Sweetclover. 'And this is for you, Kaz.' He swung the backpack off his shoulder and tossed it to the boy, who strapped it to his own back without a word. Then Sweetclover stepped forward and placed his open hand on the window in the door with his fingers splayed out.

'Five,' he said.

'Step away from the door.'

Dora looked around to see Simon, weapon drawn and aimed at Lord Sweetclover.

'Simon, no,' she said.

Lord Sweetclover closed his thumb.

'Four.'

'I don't know who this guy is or what's going on here, but this isn't my boss,' said Simon.

'Three.'

There was a loud crash and Simon crumpled to the floor to reveal Jana standing behind him, a large metal tray – now dented by Simon's head – held high.

'Hold hands, now,' yelled Lord Sweetclover. Jana dropped the tray and ran over to Dora, grasping her right hand tightly. Kaz stepped forward and grasped her left. A familiar red fire began to spark and flame in the air around them.

'Where shall we think of?' he yelled.

'Two,' was the only reply he received.

'No,' said Dora, and she tried with all her might to pull her hands free.

There was a deafening roar as the door exploded and flew outwards into the corridor beyond.

Jana and Kaz still held Dora's hands tightly and she saw, through the flashes, Lord Sweetclover raising his strange weapon and firing out of the door into the smoke beyond.

'But where are we going?' said Kaz urgently.

The red fire around her grew brighter and stronger. Dora felt a familiar, terrible emptiness in her stomach and knew that she was beginning to slip away from this place. She cried out again in protest, but there was nothing she could do. The room began to blur and fade.

And just before it winked out of existence she saw Lord Sweetclover jerk and shake, arcs of blood spraying from the holes that appeared in his chest and belly. He staggered under the force of the attack and his face began to blur and shift. Finally, all she was able to make out was the way his mouth formed a perfect O of surprise . . .

. . . and then darkness and cold and the faint drip of water . . .

. . . and a scream.

Simon snapped awake.

There was deafening gunfire, smoke and a bright red flash of light through the haze which silhouetted three figures that were there one moment and gone the next.

Between him and the silhouettes was something far more shocking. His boss, Henry Sweetclover, was flying backwards through the air, blood spraying from a series of bullet wounds across his torso.

Simon reached for his gun, and then . . .

93

9

The darkness was absolute.

Jana pulled her right hand free of Kaz's and then, using the hand she was still holding as a guide, she estimated the location of Dora's face and delivered a hard slap. The screaming stopped and Dora's hand pulled itself out of hers. Jana wished she could see the hysterical girl's face. She would be able to tell a lot about her character if she could see whether her reaction was shock or outrage.

'Did you just slap her?' Kaz's voice seemed ghostly and disembodied, issuing from the stygian gloom.

'Yes she did,' said Dora.

Jana smiled. Outrage, then. That was good, it indicated some strength of character underneath the terror. She could work with that.

'I am sorry, Dora,' said Jana, although she was anything but. 'You were hysterical. Are you both OK? No wounds from shots or shrapnel?'

There was a pause as both Dora and Kaz checked themselves for injuries, then they both indicated that they had none.

'Where are we?' That was Dora, skirting along the edge of hysteria again already.

'Steve said something about a cavern,' explained Kaz. He then gave a short yell, which echoed back at them tenfold. 'And this place is big, dark and cold, so . . .'

'He knew we were coming here,' said Jana. 'Kaz, check the backpack. He's probably given us flashlights or something.'

Jana heard the rustling as Kaz unslung the pack, unzipped it and began rummaging around inside. A moment later there was a soft click and there he was, holding a small gas lamp, grinning, haloed by his own frosted breath.

The lamp was small but it cast a powerful glow, highlighting the crannies and crevices of the rock that enclosed them. They were definitely underground, in a huge space the size of a cathedral. Stalactites hung from the arches of the roof, high above them, like spears waiting to fall. Dumpy stalagmites dotted the floor, which sloped away to the right. Powerful as the lantern was, it did not entirely reach the edges of the space. Shadows and phantoms danced at the periphery of their light-made world.

Jana took everything in with a glance then turned her attention to working out the implications.

'OK,' she said. 'That lantern's gas powered. Kaz, are there any spare canisters in the pack?'

The boy rummaged again and then shook his head.

'That means we're on a clock,' said Jana. 'We need to use the time we've got light to find a way out of this place.'

Kaz tipped the rucksack upside down and its contents scattered onto the damp rock. Dora gave a squeal of delight and thrust her hand into the pile of stuff, grabbing a bar of chocolate which she greedily unwrapped and began to devour. Jana did not scold the child – at least this way she was occupied and silent.

Jana joined Kaz in his examination of the bag's contents

as Dora perched herself on top of a stalagmite and watched, the sounds of her chocolate feast loud and distracting; she chomped with her mouth open.

The pile of stuff contained three woolly hat, glove and scarf combos, which Kaz distributed. There were shoes and socks for Dora, and fleeces for both the girls. Kaz helped Dora master the laces after she and Jana had wrapped themselves against the cold that was beginning to numb their extremities.

There was also one pair of binoculars and three plastic boxes, each containing a packed lunch composed of ham sandwiches, water, apple and biscuits. Jana shook her head in wonder. 'It's like he's packed for a school trip.'

There was also a compass and a sharp hunting knife and leather sheath, which Kaz attached to his belt without asking – a unilateral decision which made Jana scowl even as she chose not to challenge it.

'Pop the lunches back in the bag,' she said. She wasn't hungry, but she spent a moment trying to remember when she had last eaten. She was shocked to realise it had only been fifteen minutes since she'd been sat in a café in Beirut eating wild meat and flatbread.

There was a scrunching sound as Dora balled up the chocolate wrapper and dropped it on the ground.

'I think I have been here before,' said the girl.

'What?' asked Kaz, astonished by her claim.

'When I crossed the bridge of time I was briefly waylaid in different places before I returned to Sweetclover Hall,' explained Dora primly. 'This was one such.'

'Don't be ridiculous,' snapped Jana. 'If you had been here, you would not know it because it would have been too dark for you to see.'

Dora folded her arms and pouted. 'I do not like the way you talk to me.'

Jana realised her mistake; she had not taken the time to introduce herself to the youngest member of their party. She forced herself to smile, even though she felt sure they did not have time for such chit-chat.

'I am sorry, Dora. This must all be so confusing for you. My name is Jana, pleased to meet you.' She held out her hand, but the girl only scowled at it.

'In my time,' Jana explained patiently, 'we shake hands as a sign of greeting and friendship.'

Dora's face darkened further. 'So do we,' she said, keeping her arms firmly folded.

Jana withdrew her hand with as much dignity as she could muster, aware that Kaz was trying, unsuccessfully, to conceal his amusement.

'We should tell our stories,' suggested Kaz. 'If what Steve said is true, we will be spending a lot of time together. Our survival could depend upon trust, but we don't know each other at all.'

'Shouldn't we be spending our limited light trying to find a way out of this place?' said Jana.

'Do we need to?' he replied. 'When we want to leave, we all join hands and think of somewhere else.'

Jana reluctantly conceded the point.

'So,' Kaz continued, 'I think the best thing we can do is tell our stories. For me, the last twenty-four hours has been very confusing. I want answers. Maybe we can help each other, yes?'

'I think he speaks sense,' said Dora.

'Fine,' said Jana, trying not to sound too petulant. She did not like being ganged up on and saw no value in wasting their precious light chatting, but she could see that this was not the best time to assert her authority. She and Kaz both perched themselves on lumpy stalagmites, and the boy placed the lantern on the ground in the centre of their little circle.

'I'll go first,' said Jana, determined to retain a little initiative. 'My name is Jana Patel. I was born, as Kaz already knows, in 2123. I am an American citizen, from New York.'

'Sorry, I do not understand these names,' said Dora, seemingly genuinely apologetic at interrupting. Jana sighed. This was going to take a long time.

'And that's when I landed at your feet.'

'Wow,' breathed Kaz after a moment of silence.

'Let me save you some time,' said Jana. 'No, I don't know who the men were who chased me. Neither do I know why. One of them did say that "she" wanted my head intact, but I don't know who they were referring to. I'm just an ordinary girl.'

'Sorry, but you are not ordinary,' said Kaz. He instantly realised that he had outraged the girl from the future and tried to explain himself better. 'Who jumps off a skyscraper?'

'What is a skyscraper, again?' asked Dora.

'Very tall building,' explained Kaz for the second time.

Jana dismissed his question with a wave of her hand. 'It was the only option.'

'Most people would have put up a fight.' Kaz shook his head, still confused by her explanation. He didn't know whether to be impressed or terrified by the disregard she seemed to have for her own life, and the dispassionate way she described her decision to take it. He found her calm, logical explanation disturbing. Were all people from the future this emotionless, he wondered? He briefly pictured a world of robot-like people, all emotion purged from their lives, some kind of dystopian future from a sci-fi film. But he dismissed the idea. Nothing in her story supported that vision of the future. He was convinced that her detachment was uniquely hers, a personal quirk.

'Explain that thing in your neck,' he said. 'You said it was a "back-up". What do you mean?'

Jana indicated Dora, her face a patronising mask. 'Happy to, but she won't understand a word of it, no matter how many times we stop to explain.'

Dora stuck her tongue out at Jana.

'Maybe not, but try,' replied Kaz.

'You have the internet in your time, yes?'

Kaz nodded.

'Mobile phones? Wireless connections?'

Kaz glanced at Dora, who had turned her attention to a nearby stalagmite which she was investigating with exaggerated lack of concern.

'Yes,' he agreed. 'We have that stuff.'

'Good, well my ENL chip is basically a wireless internet connection. It interfaces with my brain to give me full online access at all times.'

'ENL?' asked Kaz.

'Embedded Net Link.'

Kaz considered this. 'How do you access information without a screen?'

'Most people use special glasses that beam the information into your retina,' explained Jana. 'Kind of like a screen. But that's the cheap option. If you've got more money, you can have your auditory and visual cortexes wired up so you can see and hear whatever you want to access. And then, if you've got even more money, you can interface your memory.'

'How does that work?'

'Impossible to explain the sensation to someone who's never experienced it. It's kind of like you ask a question in your mind and the answer pops into your head, like a memory, like you learned it at school.'

Kaz shook his head in wonder. 'I have so many questions.' He registered Jana's look of both tiredness and warning. He took the hint. 'We haven't got time, but quickly: you have the best version of this chip thing, right?'

Jana nodded.

'So you are super-rich or something?'

'Or something,' Jana replied curtly.

'OK, so what do you mean "back-up"? Back-up what?'

'If you're really, really super-rich,' she glanced at Kaz, 'or something, you can set the chip to transmit all brain activity, in real time, to remote servers. That way, if something happens to you, you've got a back-up of yourself, of your personality and experiences, stored away in case of accidents.'

Kaz thought about the implications of this for a moment but in the end he shrugged and decided to let the questioning lie for now. 'So many questions,' he said again. 'Last one: what use is the chip to you if you're not connected?'

'There's some internal storage on the chip itself,' said Jana. 'Not much, a couple hundred petabytes. Pitiful really. But you can take some stuff with you when you go offline.'

'Anything in it that will help us?'

Jana's forehead creased in puzzlement. 'Weirdly enough, there may be. I found it full of stuff about seventeenth-century England earlier today, but didn't put it on there. I think maybe it was hacked sometime last night, but I can't be sure.'

'How about you, Kaz?' interrupted Dora, her examination

of the limestone concluded. 'Can you tell us your history in a way that a peasant like me can understand?'

'Yes,' said Jana, much to Kaz's surprise. 'You know enough about me for now. What's your story?'

Kaz shrugged. 'My story is not interesting, like Jana's.'

Dora folded her hands in her lap and gave him a smile that told him she would find anything he said utterly enchanting. He tried not to smile at how obviously this annoyed Jana.

'All right. Um, my name Kazik Cecka, born 1995. I grew up travelling with my parents.' He stopped for a moment as the memories of the explosion, so shockingly fresh and vivid, washed over him again. When the moment passed he glanced up to see Dora looking concerned. Jana just looked impatient.

'I travel with my father to where he works,' Kaz went on. 'But last month we had a big fight and I ran away from home. If you can call it home. I came to England to work on a farm in Cornwall, but conditions were bad and the farm owner was a bastard. So I walked out. I was looking for somewhere warm to sleep, I found the old house, you two – BOOM! – arrive out of air.' Kaz shrugged, apologetic that his story was so simple. 'You know the rest.'

'That wasn't boring at all,' said Dora sweetly, with a snide sideways glance at Jana.

'Interesting, though,' said Jana. 'You're the odd one out here, Kaz. Dora and I were both snatched from our own times for whatever reasons. You weren't. But according to Steve you also have the power to travel in time. One more question we need an answer to – why did Dora and I travel through time but you didn't?'

Remembering Steve reminded Kaz of yet another question he'd been pondering earlier. He focused on Dora.

'When we were prisoners, they took Jana's chip out,' he said. 'I think they did that to get her memories. At the same time, they connected me to some kind of machine that made me tell my life story. They were gathering intelligence about us. What did they do to you, Dora?'

Dora bit her lip and thought hard. 'Lord Sweetclover made me wear these silly clothes, gave me some very strange food . . . oh, and a doctor stuck a metal leech in my arm and sucked out some of my blood.'

'That doesn't fit the pattern,' said Jana curiously.

'Hang on,' interjected Kaz. 'Dora, you knew Sweetclover from your own time, yes?'

Dora nodded. 'He was older on this side of the time bridge, but yes.'

'So have you known him your whole life?'

'I do not know him at all. His family have lived at the hall since before I was born, but his sort don't mix with the likes of me.'

'But you come from a nearby village, yes?'

'Yes. Pendarn.'

Kaz turned to Jana. 'So he does not need her story. He knows it already.'

'But why the blood?' asked Jana. 'They didn't take any of mine . . .'

Kaz interrupted. 'How do you know? You were unconscious.'

Kaz could see she was surprised to have missed something so obvious, and to have it pointed out. He thought maybe his question had garnered a smidgen of respect, but he sensed that getting her to like or trust him was going to be hard work. She did not seem the kind of person who made friends easily, or at all. But by proving himself to be clever, asking the right questions, he was slowly making headway.

Dora coughed, pointedly. 'Don't you want to hear how I crossed the bridge of time?'

Kaz turned to Dora, who sat prim and straight backed with her hands folded in her lap. 'Absolutely,' he said.

'Then hark, for this is a tale most strange and terrifying . . .'

'And thus was I magicked across the years.'

For the first time since she had met the bossy brown-skinned woman, Dora felt she had her complete attention.

'You saw us on your journey? Jana and me?' asked Kaz.

Dora nodded.

'I wonder . . .' said Jana slowly. 'Dora here encounters a strange woman from the future who's been injured by being thrown back in time. Steve told Dora that the operation at the lab was being run by the same woman. I was attacked by guys who said "she" wanted my head.'

'You think it's the person Steve told us about?' asked Kaz. 'What was her name?'

'Quil,' replied Jana. 'I think maybe you met our enemy, Dora. A time traveller who was controlling events in Kaz's time and mine. And you say she knew your name?'

Dora nodded. 'She did.'

'That's suggestive. I think . . .' began Jana, but Dora was tired of listening to what Jana thought.

'It seems to me that we are all victims of circumstance,' said Dora. 'Neither Jana nor I chose to cross the time bridge, and poor Kaz was unfortunate enough to witness our arrival and was taken prisoner as a consequence.'

Dora registered Jana's surprise at her understanding. Good.

She was determined to prove to this boyish future-woman that she was not as stupid as she seemed to think. She went on.

'We have all three been unable to make decisions for ourselves until this moment. Now we find ourselves free. Nobody is hunting or chasing us, locking us up, sticking us with needles or telling us what to do. I think it is time for we three to decide what we *want* to do.'

'She's not wrong,' said Kaz. He gave her a warm smile, which Dora gladly returned. She liked this man. He was kind and patient. 'But there are too many questions,' added Kaz. 'Until we know more, how can we be sure that anything we do will not make things worse?'

'I agree with Dora,' said Jana, much to Dora's astonishment. She tried not to look too triumphant. 'We've all just been reacting. We have to take control of this situation.'

'OK,' conceded Kaz. 'How?'

What Jana did next took Dora entirely by surprise. 'Dora,' she said, 'what do you think we should do?'

So astonished was she by Jana soliciting her opinion that it took Dora a moment to gather her thoughts and formulate a response.

'I believe that we should join our hands again,' she said. 'I will think of my home. We can cross the bridge back to my village and then we can ask Lord Sweetclover about the woman in the undercroft.'

Jana turned to the boy. 'Kaz?'

He nodded. 'It seems a good place to start.'

Jana clapped her hands together and smiled, although Dora thought the expression did not sit comfortably upon her normally stern countenance. 'We have a plan.'

'I think we do. But listen,' said Kaz seriously, making eye

contact with both of them in turn. 'We have to trust each other, OK? We are a team. We look out for each other. Yes?'

'I agree,' said Dora, smiling.

'Me too,' said Jana. 'But if you suggest a group hug I'll puke.'

Before Dora could enquire what a 'group hug' was, she noticed something that made her jump to her feet and point into the darkness.

'I told you,' she said. 'I told you I had been here before. I recognise this place.'

The murk had lightened. There was soft, dim light in the cavern now. Dora had been so focused on their conversation that she had not noticed. The far end of the cavern was swimming gloomily into view and there, exactly as she remembered, was a wall of strange cocoons.

'Stasis pods,' said Jana, her voice full of wonder. Dora did not think she would ever tire of seeing Jana surprised.

'What?' asked Kaz.

'Hibernation units, used for long-term deep space travel,' Jana explained.

'That means we're in your time, or close,' observed Kaz.

The light, which seemed to be emanating from the very rock itself, was spreading, the edges of the cavern sketched out of shadow by its gradual progress. As the light moved, more serried ranks of the glass cocoons were revealed set into the far walls of the cavern. There were thousands of them, row upon row, stacked as high and as far to the right and left as she could see, more swimming into view with each second.

There was a bright flash of crimson in the far recesses of the cavern to their left. Dora turned to see a tiny figure in the distance, barely visible in the lengthening twilight.

'That's me!' she said. 'I remember this!' She waved and shouted. 'Hello, me!'

The figure waved back and then vanished in another flash of violent red fire.

Dora turned to Jana and folded her arms defiantly. 'See, I told you I had been here before. And you didn't believe me.'

Jana barely had chance to apologise – a muted 'Sorry' – before Kaz interrupted.

'They're moving,' he said, pointing to the cocoons. Dora squinted and sure enough there was an impression of movement behind the glass.

'I don't know about you,' continued the boy, 'but I really, really don't want to be here when they wake up.'

'Me either,' agreed Jana.

Dora's heart sank as she realised it was time to leave. She should have been excited about going home, but she found she was more afraid of the journey itself. After a second's consideration she decided she was even more afraid of the cocoons and their strange inhabitants than she was of another journey across the magic time bridge.

She held out her hands. 'I shall think of my home.'

By the time the cocoons opened – all at once, with a single massive crack and hiss of released air – the three travellers were long gone.

First Interlude

'You are not a very good interrogator.' The woman leaned back in her chair, a half-smile dancing on her lips.

The interrogator, sitting across the table from her, said nothing. The woman studied him. About forty-five, she thought. Sagging chin, slight bulge at the waist, thinning hair. He wore a wedding ring, so somebody found him attractive. Or did once, anyway. His skin was pallid and grey, his teeth off-brown. He wore no uniform, preferring an anonymous grey suit, white shirt, blue tie combo that completed the picture of a man who was in every sense middling; middle-aged, middle-rank, middle-England. A functionary, a bureaucrat.

His small grey eyes, though, told a different story. They lacked all pity. He looked at her as if she were a specimen beneath a microscope. The woman harboured no illusions. The interrogator's appearance was a façade, part of his act.

'I think,' she said, pursing her lips and considering him with exaggerated care, 'that you were the kind of boy who liked pulling the wings off flies. Burnt ants with a magnifying glass. Maybe graduated to cats and dogs. Lots of pets go missing in your neighbourhood when you were young, did they?'

The interrogator stifled a yawn.

'Oh,' said the woman. 'Am I being predictable?'

The interrogator inclined his head slightly as if to say 'sort of'.

'Sorry. I'll try harder.'

The interrogator widened his eyes as if to say 'go on, then, surprise me'.

'Really? Is this the act? Sit there and let me talk? A bit of body language – that's your big play?'

The interrogator gave an almost imperceptible shrug.

The woman shook her head. 'I think I'd almost prefer the mind probe.'

The interrogator smiled and shook his head.

The woman cursed inwardly. He knew about her defences. Someone had betrayed her. She'd known that already, of course. She wouldn't be stuck in this anonymous room, buried deep within a top-secret high-security building in an out-of-the-way part of an insignificant country, if she hadn't been betrayed.

She'd known there was a chance of capture. It was an outside chance, certainly; unlikely without inside help. But the possibility had always been there. So she had taken steps. There was a device implanted deep within her brain. Tiny, barely detectable even with the strongest scans. Booby-trapped, impossible to remove. If anybody subjected her to a mind probe it would heat instantly, boiling her brain inside her skull. Keeping her secrets safe.

Whoever had betrayed her had known about it, tipped them off. That narrowed the list of possible suspects.

Not that that did her any good. Yet. She'd have to escape and rejoin her forces before she could ferret out the traitor. And right now she had no idea how she was going to do that. They would mount a rescue attempt, she was sure of that. All she could do was play for time. Which brought everything to a very simple point – she had to endure interrogation for as long as possible.

Looking into the cruel eyes of the man sitting across from her, she didn't fancy her chances.

'You have been betrayed,' he said. His voice was thin and high. Punctilious.

'No, really?'

'I wonder, do you know who betrayed you?'

'I could hazard a guess.'

'I don't think you could.'

The woman shrugged. 'It's academic anyway.'

'Far from it. But we can shelve that for now. I have been given a list of questions. I am not to leave this room until I have answers to each and every one of them.'

'Then you'll die here.'

He actually seemed amused by her defiance. 'Oh, very good,' he said, smiling.

'You have two options,' said the woman briskly, leaning forward, folding her hands before her on the table. 'You can torture me until I break.'

'Not my preferred choice, but it's on the table.'

'I'm not an idiot. I know I would break. Everyone does, eventually.'

The man nodded once. 'In my experience.'

'So then it becomes a race. Can you break me before my forces track me down, storm this building, and slaughter every last one of you?'

'Nobody is coming to rescue you.'

His calm certainty was chilling, but she refused to let her discomfiture show.

'Your other option is leverage,' she said.

'A subtler approach. More reliable, I find.'

'Which raises the question – what leverage do you think you can you bring to bear on me?'

The interrogator held his hands out wide as if to say 'what do you think?'

'I have no children,' said the woman. 'No husband or lover. No family at all. Your armies are on the run, so you can't threaten to strike at my home. It's too well defended. You don't have a thing on me.'

The interrogator smiled. She really wished he'd stop doing that. 'You'd be surprised how left-field a person's weakness can be. I once broke a man by threatening to have his favourite singer killed. He'd never met her, didn't know her at all. She was just a face on a screen. But he worshipped her. His apartment was practically a shrine to her. Spilled his guts the second I slapped her photo on the table.'

'I never was a big music fan.'

'No, you didn't strike me as the type.'

'So?'

'So you are sure we can have nothing,' said the interrogator. 'No leverage at all. You've dedicated yourself so completely to the cause that there is nothing and no one you give a damn about. No one and nothing for us to threaten.'

The woman sat back in the chair and folded her arms, triumphant.

'If that were true, it would be a pyrrhic victory, don't you think?' he said. 'What would you do if you won? What would be left for you? Who would you go home to when you've burnt down the capitol and stuck the president's head on a spike? Who would you celebrate with? Your generals? Oh, they follow your orders, but I don't think they like you very much.'

'I'm not important,' said the woman firmly. 'Never have been.'

'It's all about the cause?'

'It's all about the cause.'

The interrogator smiled and shook his head. 'You are good. The best, I think, that has ever sat across the table from me. Your control is admirable. Uncanny. Even among the Godless, you are uniquely adept.'

The woman winced inwardly at his use of *that* word, but she knew it had been said for effect and did not reward him with a reaction.

'If I did not have the evidence that you were lying,' he continued, 'I would swear that you were telling the truth.'

'There is no evidence,' she replied. 'I'm not lying.'

The interrogator nodded slowly. 'So how do you explain this?'

He clicked his fingers and a holo-screen flickered into life above the table between them. It took a moment for her to focus on the picture that floated before her, and when she had worked out what she was looking at her only response was confusion.

'What's that?' she asked, looking through the image to the interrogator who sat beyond it.

The interrogator's eyes narrowed. He seemed genuinely perplexed.

'You know exactly what it is,' he said. But he was good at his job, and he had read her reaction perfectly. He could see her confusion was genuine.

She refocused on the picture. It seemed to show her sitting

at a café table, holding hands with a man she had never seen before.

'Sorry,' she said, shrugging. 'Not a clue. Wherever, whenever this was taken, I wasn't there. That's not me.'

'I suppose you weren't here either?'

The picture changed. Now it showed her and the mystery man walking by a river, again hand in hand. She could see the cathedral Notre Dame in the background. Paris.

'Or here?'

A picture of her kissing the man in the lobby of a hotel.

'Or here?'

A picture of a far more intimate nature, taken in a hotel room.

The woman could make no sense of what she was seeing. The interrogator clearly thought these pictures were genuine. He thought he'd found out her big secret, a lover. But she knew they were fake. She had no lover. The man in the photos was a stranger. He wasn't even her type. Did she even still have a type? It had been so long since she'd allowed herself any kind of personal connection, she was no longer sure.

Which raised the question – where had these pictures come from?

A sudden, shocking possibility occurred to her. Her mind raced as she calculated the odds, explored the possible ramifications. After a few seconds she laughed.

The interrogator did not like that at all.

'What is so amusing?' he snapped.

'You think that's me.'

'We took DNA from the bedsheets. Conclusive.'

'Unless she's another Godless.' She emphasised the word, allowing a momentary flash of disdain to show.

The interrogator shook his head. 'No. The mark-up was yours. It's you.'

'Then I win,' she said.

'Excuse me?'

'I win,' she said again.

'I do not understand.'

'No, of course you don't. But OK, let's say I believe you. Let's say you did take these photos, and the tests were right. It was me with this man doing . . . that stuff.'

'We did. It was.'

'And do you have him in custody? Are you going to wheel him in here and hold a gun to his head until I answer all your questions?'

The interrogator shifted uncomfortably in his seat.

'Ah, I see. You thought that I would lose my nerve when I saw these pictures. Thought I would be so desperate to protect him that I'd spill my guts. But you don't know who he is, do you? You tested his DNA and it came up blank. He's not on the system. Thought you'd give it a shot with me, anyway. But I don't know who he is. You see, I haven't met him yet.'

'Explain.'

'Your tests were probably right. That probably is me in the picture with whoever that man is. But not yet. You're showing me my future. And if my future involves long romantic walks in Paris, well then. I win. This war. This struggle. I win.'

'These photos were taken weeks ago.'

The woman shrugged, but kept smiling. 'I believe you. But it hasn't happened for me yet.'

The interrogator was genuinely flustered now. The woman could see this was not something he was accustomed to.

'So, let me get this straight,' he said. 'You're saying . . . what? That at some point in the future you will travel back in time?'

'Looks that way from where I'm sitting.'

'That is your explanation? Time travel?'

'Hey, don't knock it till you've tried it.'

'But . . .'

He was interrupted by a frantic knocking. The interrogator leaped out of his seat and hurried to open the door.

The woman could not see who had knocked on the door, but she did see the point of a sword burst from the interrogator's back, hear the sigh as his last breath left him, see the sword retract through his torso, see his lifeless body topple sideways to the floor.

For a long, stunned moment she stared into the eyes of the person with the sword who stood in the doorway. And the eyes were all she could see, for above the black clothing was a balaclava with a single slit for the eyes.

The woman rose to her feet. 'Who are you, and how do we get out of here?'

The black-clad figure stepped into the room and then to one side. Five people, all dressed the same as the first, hurried in. Once they were all inside, one of them bolted the door. Another overturned the table to clear the centre space. Ignoring the woman, four of the newcomers ran to the four corners of the room. Each laid a small grey disc on the floor and then ran back to the centre of the room. All six of them formed a circle around the woman, joining hands to enclose her in a protective ring.

'We've not left enough time,' muttered one of them, female by her voice.

'Of course we—'.

The charges went off and the floor dropped away beneath them.

They fell a short distance and landed flat inside a dark echoing space. The woman's ears rang, her eardrums stunned by the force of the explosion.

She heard a faint muffled cry of 'Scatter' from one of her rescuers, and she was dragged away from the wrecked floor. She looked up and saw a square of light above her; the room they had just blown their way out of.

Another of the team, a man, yelled something as he crouched in the middle of the recently fallen floor. The woman thought she made out the word 'quantum', but that was all. He had a piece of apparatus in his hands; a tangle of metal and wires that looked like nothing the woman had ever seen.

The persistent ringing of a distant alarm began to penetrate her blast-deafness. The woman supposed that was coming from the room above, as the people in the facility realised they had been infiltrated.

There was a brilliant flash of light from the centre of the dark space and an image of a massive room with doors leading off in many directions seared itself onto her retina before the flash faded to be replaced by a steady glow from the apparatus.

The hands that had dragged her clear of the rubble now spun her, and the woman found herself face to face with one of her rescuers; the one with the sword.

'Who are you?' she shouted.

Her rescuer pulled the balaclava off, held the woman's head firmly between their hands, stared into her eyes and mumbled something she couldn't quite make out above the sirens and the fading ring of the explosion in her ears.

115

Then everything went horribly wrong.

The woman had been in combat before. She had been blown across rooms by explosions, felt bullets and laser beams fly past her, had been in situations where it seemed every second could be her last. She was accustomed to the sensation of time slowing down, of seconds elongating endlessly as the moment of crisis approaches.

But this felt nothing like that.

This felt as if time was literally slowing down. And only for her.

The six rescuers stood frozen like statues as the woman surveyed the scene before her.

The wreckage of the interrogation room floor lying in a square of light cast from above.

The body of the interrogator, broken and bloodied, sprawled half on the floor of the room he had died in, half on the floor that lay beneath it.

The strange apparatus that glowed, and the bubble of coruscating light that was expanding from it so very slowly, swallowing up the rescuers one by one.

The face of the mysterious person in black.

The shadowed outline of the huge subterranean room they now stood in the centre of.

And then a slow, deep rumble from above. The woman looked up and saw, to her complete horror, the ceiling of the interrogation room begin to split apart in a slow billowing cloud of concrete dust. She thought she glimpsed, within the chaos of debris, a shiny metal point descending towards them. To the woman, in her crazy slowed-down state, it seemed as if a missile was gently pushing its way through the solid building.

It was directly above her. In less that a second it would

smash into them, obliterating them entirely. She knew what it was and she screamed inwardly at the scale of the betrayal the missile represented.

The edge of the bubble of light had reached her. All the others were now ensconced within it.

She turned and moved towards them, entering the light, presuming that it offered some kind of protection, that this apparatus was part of a complex rescue plan and the light represented a shield to protect them from the fate that literally hung over them.

The woman was halfway into the bubble, the line that marked its limit bisecting her lengthways, when time resumed its normal speed.

The missile smashed into her.

But instead of oblivion, silence, death, there was instead a violent flash of red and then . . .

. . . she was staring into her own face, a shimmering curtain of light between herself and herself. She reached up a hand to touch her mirror image's face and then . . .

. . . freefall.

She felt bones breaking as she crashed into a hard black surface. She looked up, eyes wide, breath coming in sharp, ragged gasps, at the massive wheeled vehicle that bore down on her. She raised her unbroken arm to her face and screamed and then . . .

. . . freefall.

Hitting wood this time, on the same side of her body that had borne the brunt of the previous fall, grinding already broken bones, splintering some that had escaped the last impact. She cried out, pushing against the wooden floor with her one good hand. She looked up again, feeling splinters in her fingers, the roll and swell of the deck beneath her feet, seeing the white of billowing sails above her head and the bright blue sky beyond. She heard a cry of alarm, but could not tell where it came from. Had someone called her name? She smelt smoke, pungent and acrid. She took another breath and her lungs filled with it, choking. She coughed violently, each cough causing her broken bones to scrape together, agonisingly. She rolled with the pitch of the deck. She tried to turn her head to see, but as she did so a terrible pain shot through her neck and she felt herself passing out, but before she did there was a tremendous explosion, flames engulfed her, she screamed but could make no sound, and then . . .

. . . freefall.

Total darkness. Complete silence. Hard rock beneath her, smooth and even, slimy and wet. Had she been unconscious? She could not say. Every part of her hurt. Her skin, her lungs, her head, her bones.

'Hello?' Her voice was a pitiful screech.

Echoes.

'Hello?'

She jolted. Had she been asleep? Unconscious again? She did not know, she could not tell. With no light or sound to judge the passing of time, she was cut adrift from it. From herself. She did not know how long she lay there. Every now and then she would shake, but did those moments mark her waking or her sleeping? Did they signify that she was drifting in and out of consciousness?

Her thoughts were disjointed and fractured. Betrayal. Destruction. Failed rescue. Her own face, and that of another, framed in black. A name. A picture of a man she did not know, but who looked at her with a lover's fondness. A weapon.

Vengeance. The supercilious smile of a grey man in a grey suit. Thirst. Hunger. Jolt awake. Flash of red. And always pain. Total pain, engulfing and embalming her senses. She was the pain, the pain was her. Then . . .

. . . freefall.

A terrible impact as she fell on to hard stone steps, the edges of each one digging into her, forcing the edges of her broken bones farther apart. She tried to scream but she was no longer capable. All that came out was a soft moan. The kind of noise a broken soldier makes in the moments before they succumb to their wounds.

Oh no, wait, that was a scream. Was that her? She saw shapes emerging from the darkness. No, not her. A girl in an old-fashioned dress standing on the steps above her. The face was familiar, but she could not tell from where. Her memories were hopelessly jumbled.

'Dora . . .'

Had she said that, or was it the girl? She couldn't be sure. She reached out with the arm that hurt least.

'Hand.'

Then a bright flash of red, and merciful senselessness.

Part Two

The Pendarn Massacre

10

Cornwall, England, 1645

Richard Mountfort swallowed his last mouthful of cheese and glanced up at the darkening sky. He was out of provisions and out of time. If he wished to delay his mission any longer, he must turn thief or coward, and he knew he could never be either, no matter how scared he was.

The woodland here was beautiful, alive with squirrels and deer, birds and insects. Had he the time he would have taken out his commonplace book and spent a happy day sketching the local flora and fauna with charcoal, making notes and observations on their habitat and habits. The study of the natural world was his passion and his palliative, but there was little time to indulge such gentle study in time of war.

He took his bearings from the setting sun and rose to his feet, brushing leaf mulch off his cambric trousers and straightening his smock. To a casual observer he looked like a simple farmhand. It was a disguise that had served him well, allowing him to make his way across two counties unmolested by the enemy. But his final destination was within two hours' walk, and no subterfuge, no matter how well rehearsed, would disguise his true intent if he were caught now. He would have to rely on stealth, cunning and the cover of darkness as he made his approach.

He took a deep breath, took one step forward, and froze in horror as a young man stepped into view from behind an oak tree, as casual and unconcerned as could be. The man wore the distinctive colours of Parliament's army; his hand rested upon the hilt of his sword, which remained in its scabbard at his hip.

Richard's mind raced as he tried to gather his wits, but the surprise had been so complete he knew his alarm had been plainly visible upon his face.

'Oh, you gave me quite a start, good sir,' he said.

The parliamentarian did not acknowledge Richard's comment in any way. He remained still, face impassive, hand on sword. He was a young man, probably about twenty years or so.

'I was on my way home, if you'll excuse me,' continued Richard, unnerved by the calm stillness of the soldier. He bowed his head and turned to walk away. He had gone three steps, long enough that he had almost begun to think he was getting away with it, when the soldier said quietly, 'Your voice betrays you.'

Richard stopped, but did not turn to face the soldier. 'Excuse me?' But he knew the game was up – the soldier spoke with the thick accent local to this part of England.

'Your voice,' said the soldier. 'You do not speak as a Cornishman speaks.'

Richard turned then. 'I was not born in these parts. I am a London man, born and raised.'

The soldier raised a single eyebrow. 'A city pauper come to work the land? If that truly be the case, then you are a most uncommon creature.'

'I am as you see me, sir. A working man on my way home.'

'From where?'

'The fields where I labour.'

'Whose fields?'

Richard cursed inwardly. This man really was a local. That would explain how he had tracked him and approached so silently – he knew these woods and the villages that bordered them. Richard realised that any lie he told would be instantly discovered. But to come so close only to be caught at the last minute would be intolerable. Richard stretched, faking a yawn. As he drew his arms down he reached behind him to take the knife from his belt. Before he could grasp its handle, the point of the soldier's sword was brushing the soft flesh of his throat.

'I do not think so,' said the soldier. 'I was born in Pendarn, two miles yonder. You were the unluckiest of spies to have me come across you this day. Many of my comrades would have believed your story. But not I. You are a Royalist spy, taking intelligence to the Sweetclover estate.' It was not a question, and Richard did not give any indication of a response – he was too busy trying to think of a way out of the situation. The other man's sword hopelessly outmatched his knife, even if he were able to reach it before the soldier opened his throat.

The only thing on his side was that the soldier appeared to be alone.

'You calculate your chances of escape, or of overpowering me,' said the soldier. 'They are not good.'

Richard shrugged, smiling ruefully, and then turned the shrug into a jump backwards, his arm reaching behind and grasping the knife handle. As he brought the knife around, the soldier stepped forward and, with one casual swipe, opened a foot-long gash upon Richard's chest. He gasped at the sharpness of the blade which parted cloth and flesh as easily as air, but he did not pause. He dived sideways, rolling in the leaves and coming up on his knees, arm raised. He let the dagger fly purely on instinct, but though his aim was true his choice of target was fatally flawed. The blade bounced off the soldier's shiny silver breastplate and fell, useless, to the forest floor.

'Alarum!' cried the soldier. 'Spy!'

Within a minute a group of three more parliamentarian soldiers burst into the clearing, drawn by their comrade's cries. Richard could see that these were men who had marched long and fought hard. There was something in their eyes that spoke of compassion worn down and extinguished by hardship; these were not men to look to for kindness or reason.

Richard knew that all was lost. As the soldier stepped forward, he held his arms out at his side in surrender. His best hope now was that his captor would take him back to the parliamentarian camp for interrogation.

The bakery oven was cold.

Dora's relief at their arrival, her cry of recognition and joy as the crimson fire faded to reveal the familiar interior of her home, had faded also as she had registered the silence. There was sunlight streaming through the window, so the room should be hot, the oven blazing, the air full of the warm, comforting aroma of baking bread.

Instead the oven was cold and empty.

'Something is wrong,' announced Dora as soon as the three time travellers regained their balance.

'Is this not your home?' asked Jana as she examined her surroundings.

'My father is a brown-baker. We bake every day,' said Dora, the words rushing out of her. She gestured to the white clay oven that dominated the wall beside her, a long wooden paddle standing beside it alongside sacks of flour. 'The embers from last night's fire should be drying the wood for today's bread, but the oven is cold and there is no wood within. If the sun is up, the oven should be full and hot.'

Dora took a deep breath, but Jana shook her head before she could cry out for her parents.

'Don't,' she warned. 'We don't know what's going on here. If something is wrong, then it could be that Quil or her servants have got here first. Let's not announce ourselves until we have to.'

'I needs must find them,' said Dora, her voice betraying her rising panic.

'And we will,' said Jana. 'Kaz, what can you see outside?'

Kaz had moved to the small mullioned window and was peering out. 'The sun is low, some mist, so it's morning. Autumn or spring, maybe. Can't see much. Few other houses, no people. Seems quiet.'

'It was summer when I left,' said Dora, trying hard to keep the edge from her voice. 'So we have either arrived early or late.'

'Do you ever remember a day when you didn't bake?' asked Kaz.

Dora shook her head.

'Then we're probably late,' he said. 'But how late?'

'Dora, what's the layout of this house?' asked Jana.

'Layout?'

'The rooms, how many?'

Dora was puzzled by the question. 'There is this room, and

127

there is the room upstairs,' she replied slowly, as if talking to an idiot. How else would a house be constructed?

'Perhaps they still sleep,' said Dora. She hurried to the simple wooden staircase that ran up one of the walls. As she climbed the stairs she was aware of Kaz ascending behind her. When she reached the top Dora could see there was nobody home. The single room was not large, so Dora instantly registered the changes, and she felt a deep thrill of fear.

'There is but one bed,' she said.

'Which means . . . ?' asked Kaz.

Dora was already across the room, rummaging in a pile of clothing that lay by the bed. She recognised the garments, and the tears that had already been welling in her eyes began to roll down her cheeks as she realised what they meant.

'These are my father's. There are none of my mother's garments here. My mother . . . my mother must be dead,' she said.

There was a flash of sparks from her shoulder that made her jump. She turned and saw that it was Kaz, reaching out to comfort her.

'You don't know that, not yet,' he said.

Dora shrugged his hand away, wiped her eyes and looked up at his kind, concerned face. It had the same look the older version of him had worn when she had encountered him on her first trip through time, and she was surprised how safe it made her feel. She nodded.

'You are right, of course,' she said, sniffing.

Kaz bent over and picked up a shirt. It was canvas, old and patched, with many stains. 'Dora, do you recognise this shirt?'

Dora held out her hands and Kaz passed her the garment. She examined it and found that she did.

'Yes, this is Father's.'

Kaz smiled. 'So we know that if we are late, we've still arrived within the time that your parents own this bakery. That's good. Can you tell anything else from this shirt? Did it have these patches?'

Dora understood what he was trying to do and nodded, impressed by his cleverness. She examined the shirt closely. There were two new patches across the belly, where the heat of the oven tended to scorch the material if Father was careless removing the loaves from the oven.

'No, there are two new patches,' she said. 'And they have been sewn here by my mother's hand. Her needlework is very precise. The fabric is thinner too, more worn.'

'OK, so using the shirt to help you guess – how long since you were here?'

Dora thought for a moment then said, in a whisper, 'I think perhaps three or four years.' She felt despair rise within her again. 'What will they think has become of me? They will think I have run away, as James did.'

'James?'

'My brother. Fled to London on his fifteenth birthday. It near killed my mother. And now, oh, what must they think?' A sudden, terrible thought occurred to her, and she caught her breath. She looked up at Kaz, desperate for him to dismiss her fears. 'What if she could not bear the loss? That would explain her absence from this room. Oh Lord, what if she died of a broken heart? Or worse . . .'

'You're jumping to conclusions, Dora,' he said, trying to calm her. But she could see on his face that he thought she might be right. She felt heavy sobs building up in her breast, but she forced them down.

'We must find my father,' she said, trying to sound resolute but knowing she sounded like the scared child she was. She hurried back down stairs, where she found Jana reading a piece of paper which she held up as Dora approached.

'What year was it when you left, Dora?' she asked.

'The year of Our Lord sixteen hundred and forty,' she said.

Dora took the paper and examined it. The words meant nothing to her.

'Then you've been gone five years,' said Jana. Her voice lacked any of the sympathy that had warmed Kaz's. She was simply stating a fact, and although Dora knew enough by now to realise that Jana was not trying to be unkind, she felt a sudden surge of anger at the girl's detached calm. She dropped the paper to the floor and held out her hands.

'We must try again,' she said.

'Try what?' asked Kaz as he came down the stairs behind her.

'To cross the bridge of time. We must go back to 1640.' Dora grabbed his hand as he reached the floor and felt the tingle in her palm as the fire of time crackled and sparked.

Kaz did not pull his hand free, but he looked unconvinced and did not hold his other hand out to Jana, who anyway was backing away from them both and shaking her head.

'I don't think that's a good idea,' she said.

Before Dora could shout at her, Kaz asked, 'Why not?'

'Why do you want to go back, Dora?' Jana asked.

Dora was furious that she even had to answer such a stupid question. 'I thought you were supposed to be wise. Because,' she said slowly, as if addressing an imbecile, 'my parents must think I have abandoned them and my mother may be dead as a consequence. If we go back we can correct this, make sure it does not happen . . .'

'That won't work, Dora,' explained Jana, visibly working to remain calm and patient. 'Now that we've seen this' – she gestured to indicate the house and its contents – 'we know that this is what happens.'

Quick as a flash, Dora darted forward, dragging Kaz with her left hand and reaching for Jana with her right. Jana skipped sideways.

'Dora, think about it,' she said. 'We don't know how time travel works. It's not exactly precise. If we try and jump again, isn't it equally likely we'll end up five years early?'

Dora lunged for Jana again, still pulling Kaz behind her. 'I have to try,' she shouted, but Jana stepped back again, keeping herself out of reach.

Then Dora felt Kaz gently but firmly extracting his hand from hers. She turned and grasped his forearm with her right hand, but he prised her fingers free and stepped away.

'I'm sorry, Dora, but I think she's right,' he said. 'We're close enough. We should get to Sweetclover Hall.'

Dora felt hot, angry tears welling in her eyes and stamped her foot in fury. 'Then curse the pair of you,' she shouted as she ran out the front door into the early morning mist.

'Let her go,' said Jana as Kaz made towards the door. Kaz didn't slow down, so Jana stepped in front of the door and barred his way. 'Don't be stupid,' she said. 'We're wearing the wrong clothes, we speak the wrong dialect. We've both got the wrong damn skin. Go outside like this and the first person we meet is likely to lynch us.'

Kaz stopped, his face only a few inches from hers. Jana

held his gaze and saw for the first time how much anger there was in this boy, and how hard he was working to control it.

'She's alone and scared. We have to help her.' He spoke slowly and clearly, enunciating each word in his effort to avoid shouting.

'And we will, but not like this,' said Jana, carefully modulating her tone to sound placatory rather than bossy. Looking into the furious eyes of this boy, she was beginning to realise that bossing him around had probably worked earlier only because he was in shock after their trip to Beirut. Now he was beginning to find his feet, which meant she needed to recalibrate the way she handled him if she wanted to remain in control of the situation.

She bent down and picked up the leaflet that Dora had thrown away, unscrunched it and smoothed it against her belly before handing it to Kaz. 'You should read this,' she said, keeping her tone neutral; it was a suggestion not an instruction.

He took the heavy paper and scanned it. 'So?' he said when he had finished, impatient to resume his pursuit of Dora.

Jana consciously stifled a weary sigh. This was going to be harder work than she'd anticipated. 'So it's 1645. The height of the English Civil War.'

Kaz shrugged. 'So?' he said again, and this time Jana had to prevent a roll of the eyes. She obviously didn't entirely mask her impatience, because he continued, 'I never studied that. Why would I? Why did you? You're an American from the future, why would you learn about an ancient civil war?'

'OK, fair point,' said Jana, even though she thought exactly the opposite. What did it matter whether they knew the specifics of the situation or not? It was a civil war, for God's sake, a society tearing itself apart, brother against brother. The levels of suspicion, hatred and violence waiting for them outside that door were unlike anything she had ever encountered and she wouldn't have been ashamed to admit that it scared her, if she'd thought admitting it would be in her interest. But as self-evident as this was to Jana, she could see Kaz hadn't reached that understanding yet, so she spelt it out for him, trying as hard as she could not to sound condescending. She knew that if he felt patronised she'd lose him in an instant.

'My chip is full of English Civil War stuff,' she explained. 'Politics, people, dates of skirmishes and battles, details of the society and culture. I know everything there is to know about what's waiting for us outside, and trust me, this is a very dangerous time to stand out from the crowd. There are armies roaming the land picking fights almost at random, sweeping through villages and towns and stripping them bare. Forcing men to join up and fight. Forcing women to keep them . . . entertained. Then there are the religious zealots who think pretty much everything is ungodly and must be destroyed, and the civilian militias who organise to protest against the war and protect their homes but who end up just as brutal as the armies they're opposing. It's a mess, Kaz. The most violent period in Britain's history.' She stopped, as something occurred to her. 'In fact, it's the perfect time and place for someone like Quil, someone out of time, to lay low and hide.'

'But Dora . . .'

'Needs our help and protection, yes. But we'll need hers too. The second we step out that door we enter a war zone, so we need to be careful.'

Jana judged that she had calmed Kaz enough to take control again, so before he could protest she grabbed his hand and pulled him upstairs.

11

Dora ran from her house out into the cold, fresh mist of a winter morning and was immediately struck by the silence.

Pendarn was a small village, humble and unambitious, but the sun was up and there was no rain or snow, so there should be people going about their daily tasks. There should be chickens scratching in the dirt, Farmer Weth grazing his sheep on the green, children running around and getting into mischief.

Instead there was only stillness.

The mist was beginning to burn away as she ran on to the village commons. She stood there, wiping her eyes and turning round and round, watching and listening for the slightest hint of life. The smithy was locked up, furnace and forge unused. There were no horses tethered to the water trough. The stocks were empty. Dora found herself remembering the world she had seen through the window of the lab in the future. The grass beneath her feet would, she knew, be covered with buildings and streets. Somehow the village felt different to her because she knew what would become of it.

She tried not to think about the pamphlet that Jana had shown her. She could not read, but the picture had been easy to understand. It had shown two men in some kind of uniform, one with a baby held high, impaled on the end of a pike, the other standing, holding another child above the head of a kneeling woman, about to dash its brains out on the ground before her. The image filled her with horror and dread. There was great violence abroad in England, this much was clear, though whether the threat came from within or without, be it rebellion or popish invasion, she could not tell.

As Dora stood in the deserted heart of her home village, her imagination offered terrible visions of what could have befallen her friends and family. Try as she might, she could not banish them.

Then she caught the faintest hint of sound. An echoing murmur of distant conversation. Without hesitation she ran towards the source of the sound – the village church – desperate to see a familiar face.

She raced through the lychgate and ran up the path to the solid oak door of the ancient building. The hubbub of conversation was clearly audible now. She paused at the door and then thought better of her haste. Were she to enter this way, there would be little chance of her remaining unobserved. Until she knew exactly what she was walking into, she preferred caution. So she stole around the side of the church to a small door at the rear of the building. She gently pushed it open and slipped into the gloomy narthex, a screened-off area at the rear of the church from which penitents could observe the daily worship they were forbidden to join.

It took a moment for her eyes to adjust to the half-light, as there were no candles burning, but soon she could make out what seemed to be the entire population of the village. The relief she felt was so powerful that she felt her knees go weak and she sat for a moment behind the screen, catching her breath.

The villagers were milling around near the pulpit at the far end of the nave, talking softly, as if afraid of being overheard. No candles, hushed voices; Dora realised that they were hiding. But from who, or what? Seized by a sudden apprehension, Dora rose to her feet and stepped back up to the screen, straining to overhear.

She recognised most of the people who congregated at the far end of the church, but their fear was palpable. How would they react to the sudden reappearance of a girl missing for five years but now returned, not aged a single day, and dressed in the strangest of garments? The vision of herself, strapped to a stake, with fire licking at her legs, rose up in her mind, and she shuddered at the thought that perhaps it was her own kin, mad with fear and suspicion, who would fall upon her and offer her to the flames as a witch. As much as she wished to fly to the arms of those who knew her, to beg them for news of her parents, she resolved to stay hidden until she could establish exactly what was happening.

She did not have to wait long. Parson John, looking older and more tired than Dora remembered, took the pulpit and gestured for silence.

'Friends,' he said, his voice tremulous and cracked. 'We have known for some time that this was approaching, but we have been too divided amongst ourselves to determine a course of action. As a consequence, we find ourselves unprepared.'

'The menfolk should have fled,' shouted one woman, who Dora recognised as Goodwife Bamford. 'That way they could not be pressed into service and could return when it was right, to tend the livestock and crops.'

'They did that at Wych Cross,' countered a tall man, who Dora could not make out. 'And we all know what happened there. The womenfolk were sorely abused and half the village burned.'

'Yet they all live still,' replied Goodwife Bamford, folding her arms resolutely. 'In Low Ercall, the men remained and resisted. They lie cold now, and who will protect their families as winter draws in?'

'Friends, please,' pleaded the parson. 'We have argued too long and now we must decide what to do. The war is at our doorstep. I took it upon myself to dispatch a messenger to Sweetclover Hall . . .' There was a smattering of derision from the crowd; murmurs of 'you'll get no help there' and 'curse him', which astonished Dora. When she had left – which she had to keep reminding herself was not yesterday but five years previously – nobody would have dared speak ill of his lordship openly. 'I dispatched a messenger to ask for help,' continued the parson, raising his voice slightly to push through the murmurs of discontent.

'And what did your messenger find?' asked a voice in the crowd.

The parson bowed his head and answered softly. 'The door was barred and he could not gain admittance.'

Perhaps it was the parson's obvious distress at reporting this news that prevented the outcry Dora would have expected. Instead a sole voice spoke out. 'He has turned his back on us.'

Dora gasped in delight as she recognised her father's voice, but she still prevented herself from running forward and declaring her presence.

Her father continued, walking up the pulpit steps to address the village. 'We knew he would. Since he married, rarely has he shown his face outside his walls. He has made his position clear. He considers this war none of his concern.'

'He is too busy preparing his next black mass to honour the devils he worships. And your wife seems quite content to accept his protection,' spat hatchet-faced old Goodman Squeer. Dora's heart leapt again. That was why her mother had been absent from the bakery – Jana and Kaz had been right, she was not dead, she had taken a position as baker at Sweetclover Hall.

'I will ignore your ridiculous accusation of sorcery,' replied her father, his voice dripping with cold contempt. 'It is founded on gossip and rumour.'

'Rumours begun by your wife,' pointed out one old lady.

Dora saw her father's shoulders sag, but he regained his composure and continued. 'My wife spoke out of turn and now recants her slanders,' he said. 'Lord Sweetclover does no more than we seek to do, to remain apart from this conflict, minding his own business. I, for one, see no blame in that. My point is, if we run, then our village and our womenfolk will likely be plundered by the army as it makes its way to Lostwithiel. If we stay and offer no resistance, our pantries will be emptied, our church defiled, and the men of fighting age will most likely be pressed to arms. I see no alternative but resistance.'

There were more murmurs of dissent, but no open challenge, so Dora's father spoke on. 'I know you have heard of the Clubmen who rose up against this war in Shropshire last year, and of the Woodbury Declaration, in which the Clubmen of Worcestershire set out their opposition to this war and those armies that prey upon decent, honest working folk. I have a copy of it here.' He held up a piece or paper and handed it up to Parson John. 'Parson, would you read out, please, the sentence that you marked for me.'

The parson unfolded the paper and began. 'We, our wives

and children, have been exposed to utter ruin by the outrages and violence of the soldier; threatening to fire our houses; endeavouring to ravish our wives and daughters, and menacing our persons.' At this point he paused for effect, letting the details of their coming plight sink into the minds of the restive congregation. Then, enunciating clearly, issuing a call to arms, he continued, 'We are now enforced to associate ourselves in a mutual league for each other's defence, to protect and safeguard our persons and estates by the mutual aid and assistance of each other against all murders, rapines, plunder, robberies, or violences which shall be offered by the soldier or any oppressor whatsoever.'

The words echoed around the interior of the church and Dora admired, not for the first time, the parson's skill as an orator.

Her father stood and surveyed the crowd, waiting for the echoes to fade before taking up the sermon. 'And so must we, men of Pendarn. We must arm ourselves and stand firm against those who would seek to pull us into their war. I know there are those among us who favour the king, and those who favour Parliament. I know there are those who find the reforms of Archbishop Laud – the altar rail, the coloured glass windows and crosses of our church – offensive to their faith. But our differences matter not in the face of the destruction of our homes, our families and our livelihoods. We must set aside our quarrels and make common cause. This is not our war, but we must fight to keep it so.'

Dora's head spun. This was no foreign invasion, it was a civil conflict between Parliament and the Crown. How such a thing had come to pass, she could not begin to imagine, but the idea that her country was tearing itself apart filled her with deep dread.

She looked at her father, standing upon the steps of the pulpit, and she marvelled. He had always been a man of firm convictions but he had been content with his lot in life. He made good bread that fed his family and neighbours. Although not a man given to much discussion of spiritual matters, he had once confided in her that he thought his work was holy. 'Feeding the people around us is a Christian calling,' he had told her. He had taken such pride in his work, such pleasure in the process of mixing and kneading, shaping and baking the loaves. He had seemed entirely at home in his bakery. She had never seen him as the kind of man to seek attention or leadership. Yet here he was, speaking treason to the whole village with a zeal she did not recognise.

One thing was clear to Dora – the world had changed much in the five years she had been absent, and her father had changed with it.

Before he could continue his oration, Dora heard a sound which added to her sense of growing unease.

'Listen,' the parson said, holding up his hand for silence. The distant noise was unmistakable.

'Horses,' came a terrified cry from a woman in the crowd, and there was a cacophony of frantic voices, all asking for guidance or trying to propose a course of action.

Dora kept her eyes focused on her father and the parson. She noticed they gave each other a nod, as if agreeing to enact some prearranged plan. The parson spoke quickly and firmly, his voice cutting through the hubbub with the authority of a lifetime spent asserting his will from the pulpit.

'Able-bodied men remain here, women and children to the crypt.' And, grateful for the direction, the women began herding their children towards the door at the side of the altar. The parson climbed down from his pulpit, shook hands with Dora's father once, and then shepherded them underground.

'Gather round,' said Dora's father, and the thirty or so men did. Dora corrected herself once she got a better look at them; in fact about half of those who remained were little more than boys, and of the men, five were well beyond fighting age. But all stood ready, hanging upon her father's words.

'Take these,' said her father, handing out scraps of white cloth. 'And wrap them around your arms. Then go to the altar. You'll find a pile of weapons hidden there. Select one. The parson and I agree that they can defile the church if they wish. We must go to ground. We only resist if they plunder our homes.'

Of all the amazing and awful things that had happened to her in the last day, nothing had made Dora feel so despairing and helpless as watching the men of her village prepare themselves for battle. As they hurried out of the vestry door, away from the approaching soldiers and the village green, there was a loud smashing sound as a heavy rock crashed through the large stained-glass window that lit up the church from above the altar. The men at the vestry door had all turned to see, almost in spite of themselves, and so they all witnessed a second and then a third stone come flying through the glass, sprinkling the church floor with coloured shards and strips of redundant lead. Then they turned and fled. The vestry door closed at the same instant the main church door was flung open. A steady stream of soldiers poured through the door into the church and set about destroying the interior with a passion that mystified Dora.

There was a large wooden cross hanging by the altar. The soldiers pulled it from the wall and smashed it on the ground, cheering as they did so. A mural of the saints that adorned the east wall, which Dora had studied for so many hours as a child she could draw it blindfold, was daubed over with whitewash. The fact that the soldiers had come prepared to perform this task astonished Dora. More stones were hurled through the stained-glass windows.

Dora watched the destruction and thought her father wise to let the invaders give vent to their violent urges upon the signs and symbols of the church first, although what offence a mural, a wooden cross and a stained-glass window could have afforded them, Dora was powerless to guess.

Eventually the iconoclastic orgy began to abate and the soldiers drifted outside again.

When the last man had left, Dora stepped out from behind the screen, surveying the broken glass, shattered cross and defiled wall in horror before hurrying out of the church door into the sunlight.

The mist had burned away and the sun hung higher above the horizon, but there was still a chill in the air. Dora saw the soldiers making their way through the lychgate back to the village green, upon which were gathered a large collection of men and horses. Worried about being spotted, Dora crouched low and hurried away from the path towards the trees which lined the east side of the churchyard. Once safely hidden from view she made a beeline for the village boundary. Running as fast as she could, she cut back in through one of the fields and approached the bakery unseen. But as she re-entered her abandoned home she was horrified to find it empty again. She called out for her friends as loudly as she dared, but there was no reply.

Kaz and Jana were gone.

She stood there for a moment, dumbfounded and clueless. Where on earth could they have fled to? Had they been taken by the soldiers?

For a few seconds she was frozen with indecision. Her mother was three miles distant in the hands of a man Dora knew was not at all that he appeared to be. Her father was about to do battle with a far superior force. Her friends were nowhere to be found. She was in the right place but the wrong time, wearing both the wrong clothes and a face that everyone who knew her would find impossibly young. And as much as she tried to banish the image from her mind, she knew that whatever decision she made next would inevitably bring her a step closer to the fire of a witch's death. She felt tears welling in her eyes as she contemplated the hopelessness of her situation but she blinked them back and took a deep breath. All she really wanted to do was climb upstairs, crawl into her father's bed and hide.

'Stop it,' she hissed, clenching her fists, willing herself to think clearly. She had never been the kind of girl who talked to herself before, but in a day of changes this was one that she was willing to accept without argument. 'There must be something you can do,' she implored herself. Nothing sprang to mind.

As she stood there, fighting to conquer her indecision and fear, the door to the bakery swung open to reveal a soldier, silhouetted in the sunlight, a sword hanging casually from his right hand.

There was nowhere for Dora to run.

12

'Strip,' ordered Jana when they reached the top of the bakery stairs.

Kaz was so astonished by her curt instruction that he stood there dumbfounded.

'Come on,' she urged him, unzipping her fleece and throwing it on the floor.

So many thoughts ran through Kaz's head that he felt dizzy. 'Um . . .' was all he could muster.

'Are you blushing?' asked Jana, displaying the first signs of genuine amusement he'd seen from her.

'No,' he snapped back, painfully aware that the heat given off from his cheeks was probably equal to that of a two-bar electric heater.

Jana stepped forward, reached up and pinched his cheek, smiling up at him. 'I hate to admit it, but that's actually kind of sweet.'

Now she was showing signs of affection. What was going on?

'Hey.' He brushed her hand aside. 'What . . .' but again, he ground to a halt.

This time Jana actually laughed. Kaz couldn't decide which was more surprising – that she had done so, or that it sounded so nice.

'You are actually, genuinely speechless, aren't you? Oh, you are priceless,' she said.

Kaz tried again to spit out a sentence, and again failed. 'Look, I don't know what you think . . . I mean . . .' He stopped himself, for he realised he was so befuddled he was speaking in Polish. He was amazed when Jana answered him.

'Relax, you lunk,' said Jana, pulling off her T-shirt to reveal a simple black bra. 'Even if you were my type – which you absolutely are not – then this would hardly be the time and place, would it?'

'You speak Polish?' he asked.

Jana looked as surprised as he was. 'Apparently I do,' she replied in perfect Polish. 'Never did before, but my chip apparently has Polish now.'

'OK, so then, um, what . . .' Kaz cursed himself again. Even in his native language he was stammering like an idiot and couldn't get his words together. It was taking all of his considerable willpower not to stare fixedly at Jana's chest.

Jana did not help by arching her back and smiling broadly.

'Yes, that's right, these are my breasts,' she said. 'I am a girl. We all have them. Which, right now, is a bit of a problem. So I'm going to need you to ignore your embarrassment – or any other feeling you may be feeling – and come over here and make them go away for me.'

'You are strangest girl I've ever met,' said Kaz, pleased that he had finally managed to construct and articulate a coherent sentence.

'I'll take that as a compliment,' replied Jana. 'Now, take the sheet from the bed and rip a strip off, about a hand's width should do it.'

Shaking his head in confusion, Kaz did as he was told. He

leaned down and pulled the rough linen sheet from the bed. It tore with surprising ease and he turned back to Jana holding a long strip of linen.

He gave a cry of alarm and averted his gaze. The bra was now on the floor, too.

Jana laughed again. 'Kaz, listen, this is the seventeenth century,' she said. 'I am a foreigner with brown skin. That's bad enough. But I'm also a girl. The chances of me lasting a day out there without being arrested as a spy, accused of being a witch, or taken off and raped by some soldier who's been on the march too long, are about zero. In fact, I'd lay good money that all three could happen simultaneously. My only chance of moving freely in this time period is to become a boy. Luckily my hair is already short, and my breasts, as you would see if you weren't studying your shoes so intently, are A cup. Which means that one good, tightly bound piece of linen and a baggy shirt are all I'll need to remove at least one of my problems. So would you please try and forget that you're a teenage boy for a minute, and come over here and help me bind these bad boys up.'

Kaz nodded once, swallowed hard and told himself that she was right, he was being silly, her plan was sensible and logical. That didn't entirely quell the potent mix of mortification and uncomfortable excitement he was feeling at finding himself alone with a half-naked girl, but it did at least allow him to muster the self-control necessary to look up and walk across to Jana, who was standing with her hands on her hips.

'Do you not feel even a little bit embarrassed standing there like that?' he asked as he held up the linen strip and handed it to Jana.

'Not even the littlest bit,' she confirmed as she pulled the linen across her chest and held out either end.

146

Kaz walked behind her, took hold of the ends of the linen and pulled it tight. He absolutely refused to pay attention to the soft warmth of her skin as his fingers brushed against it.

'Nudity taboo's stupid. The body is just biology,' she said. 'Nothing special. The only reason you're in such a fluster is because you're eighteen and basically suffering from hormone poisoning. It's not your fault, you'll grow out of it.'

Kaz pulled the linen even tighter and began to knot it against the curve of her spine. 'Hey, you're actually younger than me,' he said.

'Yeah, but I'm a girl,' she said, as if stating the most transparently obvious of all possible facts. 'We're just, y'know, better.'

He gave a final, slightly vindictive tug, and finished the knot, then he stepped back. 'Done,' he said.

Jana stepped forward, grabbed one of Dora's father's discarded shirts, pulled it over her head and turned back to Kaz, arms out wide. 'What do you think?' she asked. 'Will I pass?'

Forced to consider her appearance seriously for the first time, Kaz was alarmed to notice that he found her very attractive indeed. In a defiant, bossy, American kind of way.

'I don't think so,' he said, shaking his head. 'Your face is very . . . girly. You just look like a girl with very small breasts. Sorry.'

Jana sighed. 'It'll have to do. You've got to remember that this is a different time. People here are very set in their gender roles, there's not a whole lot of androgyny in seventeenth-century rural Cornwall. The people we meet are far more likely to think that I'm a very effeminate boy. I'll have to lower my voice slightly, though,' she said, doing exactly that. 'Now your turn. You've got to ditch the modern clothes, you'll stand out like a sore thumb.'

Jana was already pulling down her trousers, so Kaz was grateful for the distraction as he collected together all the garments he could find. Dora's father was a total slob, and the few items of clothing he had were scattered randomly across the floor.

He found another shirt, one pair of leather trousers and a kind of smock thing made of rough cloth. He held the trousers up to his legs and then threw them to Jana.

'Too small,' he explained. 'I'll stick with jeans.'

Jana considered him as she pulled the trousers on. 'Lucky they're black, not blue,' she said. 'Rub some mud over them when we get outside, it should do unless we get a close inspection.'

Kaz held the shirt up and recoiled as he was hit in the face by a potent whiff of old sweat. 'Wow, stinky,' he said, pulling a face.

'Mine too,' said Jana. 'No showers here. No soap either. Just the manly musk of unwashed baker.'

Kaz pulled off his jacket and jumper, but left his thermal top on; it was white and would be hidden by the shirt, which he pulled over his head and left untucked at the waist to help disguise his jeans.

'This thing is too small,' he said, throwing a jerkin to Jana. 'Dora's dad is tiny.'

'So is Dora,' replied Jana as she tried the jerkin on. 'People are smaller in this time. Actually, I hadn't thought of that. You're going to look like a giant.'

Kaz felt stupid in his jeans and smelly shirt, but then he realised there was another problem. 'Shoes,' he said. He scoured the room again, but found no footwear at all.

'He probably only has one pair, and he'll be wearing those,' said Jana. 'I think I'll be OK. My leather boots will probably pass, once I get them nice and muddy. But yours . . .'

Kaz looked down at his bright blue Gore-Tex walking boots and shook his head. 'No way,' he said. 'These were a present from my dad.'

'We are so doomed,' said Jana, shaking her head but still seeming to Kaz as if she was more amused than scared.

Kaz laughed at the ridiculousness of their situation. He knew that he and Jana were acting recklessly, dressing up and playing at undercover spies, but he didn't really care. 'Are you enjoying this as much as I am?' he asked.

'Are you kidding me?' she replied. 'I woke up this morning and the most exciting thing I could think of to do was give my bodyguards the slip and play hooky from school. Now I'm hundreds of years in the past, disguising myself so I can go mingle with soldiers and peasants as I make my way to a fortified manor house in search of a woman from the future who wants to kill me. Call me insane, but it sure beats hanging out at the mall.'

She and Kaz smiled at each other, a moment of shared excitement that was broken when Kaz heard the distant rumble of hooves. He could see that Jana heard it too.

'Come on,' she said, heading for the stairs.

'Wait,' he replied. 'Sooner or later we're going to jump back to the future and I don't want to be walking around looking and smelling like a seventeenth-century peasant.' He began bundling up their discarded clothes and shoving them into the backpack as Jana impatiently tapped her foot and peered out of a dusty window, trying to see what was going on outside.

'We can't carry that around with us, you know,' she said, over her shoulder.

'We can bury it in the woods, collect it later. Shall we put the guns in it?'

Jana pulled a face that told him exactly what she thought of that idea.

'OK, we keep the guns.'

'I can't see much, but I think there are soldiers on a patch of grass outside,' said Jana as Kaz joined her at the window.

'Village green, I think,' he said.

'What's that?' asked Jana.

'Oh, something you don't know.'

She scowled at his sarcasm, so he explained. 'A patch of common land at the centre of the village, used for keeping animals and playing cricket. England still has them in my time.'

'Thank you,' she replied frostily. 'Come on, let's go take a look.'

They hurried downstairs. While Jana cracked the front door open to get a better look at the new arrivals, Kaz nipped out the back door and found a pile of leaves in which to hide the backpack. Having stashed it safely, he joined her at the front door.

'Roundhead troops,' she said, with the brisk functionality of a TV voice-over. 'Forces loyal to Parliament. They're often Puritans, fundamentalist Protestants. They'll defile churches that display anything they think smacks of Catholicism, and be that bit harder on the population of a village or town that tolerates such a church.'

Something about the calm, dispassionate way Jana imparted this information gave Kaz a chill. She was regurgitating it from a chip in her head, not speaking from her own learning or experience. He thought it made her seem slightly robotic, a million miles away from the cocksure, amused girl who had

150

teased him only minutes before. She was a mass of contradictions. One moment funny and excited, the next cold and inhuman. He found himself wondering how much of her warm, approachable self had been an act, carefully calculated to make him like her.

The sound of smashing glass snapped Kaz's attention back to the soldiers.

'That'll be the church windows. Stained glass, at a guess,' said Jana.

'Forget that,' said Kaz. 'What about Dora? The village is deserted. What will they do if they find her?'

'Nothing good,' muttered Jana. 'You're right, we have to try and find her before they do.'

'They're coming,' Kaz observed, pointing to a group of three soldiers who were walking towards the collection of houses that included the bakery. 'They'll go house to house.'

Jana shut the door and turned. 'Out the back,' she said.

They slipped out the back door and began to work their way around the perimeter of the village, checking houses as they went, staying ahead of the Roundhead soldiers, hoping against hope that Dora hadn't done the obvious thing and run straight for the church.

Dora came running from the opposite direction and re-entered the bakery mere seconds after Jana and Kaz moved out of sight.

13

Dora balled her fists, ready to fight back if the soldier tried to force himself upon her, as she expected he would.

She forced defiant words through her tightly clenched teeth. 'I warn you, I will not submit easily.'

The soldier stood there, seemingly as surprised as Dora. Then he took a single step forward, crossing the threshold of the bakery, his features sharpening as he emerged from the sunlight.

'I would expect no less of you, Dora,' he said, his voice deep and rich.

He stood there, examining her face and clothes, puzzled but stern. For her part, Dora stared hard at his face, trying to make sense of its odd familiarity. There was a strong chin hidden underneath the straggly beard of early manhood; the grime accumulated from a long military campaign caked high cheekbones and framed piercing green eyes. In a flash, she recognised him.

'James?' she said, amazed.

The soldier nodded, and Dora ran forward and flung her arms around her long-lost brother.

It took her a moment to realise that he was not hugging

her back. She awkwardly relinquished her grip and stood back to regard him more closely. 'You have changed so much,' she said as she examined his face, his height, the broad expanse of his chest and his thick arms. 'You are a man now. And a soldier.' She smiled, teasingly, even though she instinctively knew he would not respond with the easy smiles of his younger self, the boy she remembered from long childhood days spent playing in the fields and forests.

'I am,' he said. 'You also have changed, sister. Though not as much as I would have expected.' There was a note of suspicion in his voice that made Dora uneasy.

Dora took a step backwards. She had been so overwhelmed with surprise and joy at seeing James that she had forgotten her strange clothes and inexplicable youth. But James had last seen her when she twelve years old, and while the changes that two years' growth had wrought were slight enough to give him pause, she was still older than when he had last seen her. She hoped that would be enough to quell his doubts.

'I know,' replied Dora with a nervous smile and a kind of apologetic shrug. 'I was grievous ill three years ago. It is only through the grace of God that I survived, but it withered me and I have not grown as I ought.' It was a desperate lie, but James nodded, seeming to accept her story.

'I am saddened to hear it, Dora. You are well now?'

Dora did not think he sounded especially sad, and the cold calm of his response served only to increase her nervousness.

'I am.'

James surveyed the bakery. 'It is smaller than I remember.' There was no fond nostalgia here. His tone of voice conveyed both surprise and contempt. He returned his gaze to Dora. 'Where are our parents?'

'I . . . I do not know,' she stammered. 'I have returned from Sweetclover Hall this past hour. I am as vexed by the village's desertion as you.'

James reached forward and grabbed her arm roughly. 'The hall? You've been at the hall?'

The urgency in his voice told Dora that she had made a mistake. She had thought her lie a good one, but the force of his grip told her otherwise.

'James, you're hurting me.' She wriggled but he did not relinquish his hold on her.

'These garments you wear, are these new fashions brought in from Spain?' Now his voice was colder still, full of hatred and fury. 'Do the Royalists at the hall consort with popish agents? Is that what my home has been brought to?'

His grip was very tight now, and Dora squealed in pain as she struggled to free herself. 'James! Let me go!' she cried.

James turned and dragged Dora out of the door and into the street, even as she writhed and kicked.

'Any sign?' he called as he emerged.

'No, sir' and 'All empty' came the shouted replies of two other soldiers who were working their way down the street, checking the houses for occupation.

James stopped and turned again to Dora. 'No more lies, sister,' he said. 'Where are they?'

'James, I swear to you, I do not know,' shouted Dora. 'Now let me go.'

Her brother's only response was a hard slap across the face that momentarily stunned her into silence. Her eyes watered and her ears rang as he dragged her towards the green. She stumbled along behind him, barely keeping her footing, trying to make sense of what was happening.

154

Throughout her ordeal in the future, Dora had longed to return to her own time. In Pendarn she knew the rules, knew her place, how things worked, what people expected of her, how to behave and how not to. But ever since she had crossed the time bridge back to her old home, she had found things even more confusing. The total strangeness of her experiences in the future was somehow less disorientating than the world turned upside down to which she had returned. The familiarity of the setting, and her knowledge of the people, made the unchar- acteristic fear and cruelty far more upsetting than anything she had seen in the future.

She had escaped inexplicable danger and returned to her place of safety only to find that it was every bit as perilous as the future she had fled.

As her feet dragged and tripped across the thick, dew-wet grass of the green, Dora realised that her home had been taken from her. She was vaguely aware that this required a response from her, that she needed to decide how she was going to cope with a world now lacking in all certainty and kindness. But she needed time to gather her thoughts, and that was not to be allowed her.

'Sir, there is but one inhabitant remaining in the village,' she heard her brother say as he stopped abruptly, and she struggled to orient herself. 'She is the baker's daughter and claims she has lately returned from Sweetclover Hall to find the village deserted.'

Dora's vision cleared as she found her balance. She was on the green, surrounded by soldiers. In front of her stood a tall man, his hard grey eyes reflecting the glint of sunlight from James' metal breastplate. His bearing and position amongst the soldiers told Dora he was their commanding officer.

From the depths of her confusion and shock, Dora pulled a hard kernel of anger. 'Baker's daughter?' she spat, outraged, into her brother's face. 'James Predennick, I do not know what has befallen you since you left home, but when our parents . . .'

She was not allowed to finish her diatribe, silenced by another ringing slap from her brother's gloved hand. He released his grip on her arm as he struck, and she lost her footing, tumbling to the ground at his feet.

As her senses reeled again she heard the officer, muffled as if through a blanket, say, 'The girl is your sister?'

'In blood only, sir,' replied James. 'Her garments and her lies betray her popish corruption. I only give thanks that I departed this place before I, too, could be sullied.'

Looking up, Dora saw the ghost of a smile flit across the officer's lips. 'I do not think, Corporal Predennick, that the devil himself could have corrupted one as zealous as you.' The hint of mockery seemed not to register with her brother.

Carefully, fearful of losing her balance and toppling over, Dora regained her footing. She resisted the urge to hold her cheek, which she could feel was already swelling from the blows, because she did not wish to seem weak. Ignoring her brother, she turned to the officer and curtsied as best she was able.

'Sir,' she said, trying to quell the tremble in her voice. 'My brother, who has been a stranger to his brethren for many years, is mistaken.'

James raised his fist once again, but this time the officer raised his own hand and gestured for him to stand down. 'What is your name, girl?' he asked.

'I am Theodora Predennick, sir,' she replied, not quite able to prevent herself flashing a hateful glance at her brother as she did so.

'Dora, in what respect is your brother in error? You must own, your garments are passing strange. What say you to his charges of popery and falsehood?'

Dora thought furiously and began to spin a yarn.

'I no longer reside in Pendarn,' she said. 'I married a tailor from Lostwithiel two years ago and have resided there since. The clothes I wear represent his artful craft – he is a most creative cutter of cloth. Yesterday I rode to Sweetclover Hall to visit my mother, who works in the kitchens there. This morning I journeyed on to Pendarn to visit my father, who still resides herein. I found the village as you see it. This strange vacancy is as great a puzzle to me as to yourselves.'

The officer considered her curiously for a moment. 'You have been to the hall?' he asked.

Dora's heart sank as she remembered that it was this admission which had triggered her brother's ire only minutes earlier. Had her senses not been so scrambled by his beating she would have remembered. 'Indeed, sir, I have.'

He stepped forward, his eyes fixed hard on hers, narrowed with intent. 'And how found you the lord? Was he well?'

'He is not one to mix with the likes of me, sir. I saw him not.'

'We have been sent to ascertain the allegiance of this lord of yours. This very morning your brother brings me intelligence that suggests he is at the heart of a Royalist plot.' The coldness of the officer's voice scared Dora more than the violent fury of her brother.

'I know not his politics, sir,' she replied, casting her eyes to the ground. 'It was my mother with whom I went to visit, not her master.'

'A godly woman would not cross the threshold of such a place,' said her brother, his voice low and threatening.

'My corporal refers, no doubt, to the stories of witchcraft that swirl around Sweetclover like vile miasma,' said the officer.

Dora's blood chilled at the uttering of that word. 'I have heard no such stories,' she said.

There was a low murmur from the crowd of soldiers who stood around them, watching the interrogation. They obviously did not believe her.

'Corporal,' barked the officer, turning his attention to James. 'When you were a child, did your mother ever show signs of witchery?'

Dora looked up at the boy with whom she had shared a childhood, the big brother who had kept her safe from bullies, the boy she had adored and loved only a few years earlier. She saw not one ounce of the kindness she had known in him. This absence, more than the words he spoke next, were what shocked her to the core.

'Once, when I was a boy, I fell and hurt my leg most grievous,' he said. 'A gash, deep and poisoned. My mother mixed a poultice which, when applied to the wound, did rid it of poison and allow it to heal.'

No longer able to restrain herself, Dora raised her hand and inflicted her own blow upon her brother's cheek. Before he could retaliate, the officer stepped back and shouted, 'Bring forth the prisoner.'

Dora was gripped from behind by one of the other soldiers, her arms pinned at her back. 'Keep still, witch,' hissed the soldier in her ear.

The crowd of soldiers parted to reveal a man dressed in the clothes of a farm labourer, his hands and feet bound with rope, his face a blurred mass of bruises and swellings. His tatty shirt was red with blood. He limped forward at the point of a soldier's sword until he stood before Dora and her brother. The officer reached out, grabbed the man's shirt and casually shoved him to his knees. The prisoner was so weak it took hardly any effort at all.

'Dora Predennick, meet Richard Mountfort,' said the officer. 'He is a Royalist spy who was unlucky enough to encounter your brother last night.'

The prisoner looked up at Dora and, despite his pitiful condition, he nodded a greeting. She thought he tried to smile but it was hard to tell, his face was so badly beaten.

'Richard, this is Dora,' the officer continued. 'She is at best a Catholic whore, at worst a witch.' He clapped his hands together, as if an idea for an amusing game had just occurred to him. 'Come, let me show you both something.' Without waiting for an acknowledgement, he spun on his heels and strode away, the crowd of soldiers parting around him as he walked.

Dora found herself being pushed in the officer's wake, but at least she was still upright. She saw Mountfort being dragged across the ground by a rope that had been looped around his wrists. Dora lost track of her brother in the crowd.

She was now so rigid with fear that she had almost stopped thinking entirely. All anger forgotten, all hope abandoned. She allowed herself to be pushed forward, a sick feeling building inside her as the certainty of her fate dawned on her.

When she was roughly pulled to a halt she was standing at the foot of the large oak tree that dominated the far corner of the green. The officer stood underneath one of the huge boughs, his hands clasped in front of him.

'Corporal, the ropes, if you will,' he shouted. The crowd of soldiers was growing rowdy at the prospect of entertainment.

James stepped forward and threw a rope over the bough. The officer caught it and quickly, with an ease that spoke of an action many times practised, fashioned a noose.

Meanwhile the soldiers dragged Mountfort to his feet beside her. Dora wanted to reach out and help steady him, but the soldier who held her had a grip of iron.

The officer called for silence and the hubbub faded away. 'You.' He pointed to Mountfort. 'You were taking secret intelligence to the hall. Perhaps news of reinforcements? Were you to warn them of our arrival? Tell them to prepare for a siege? Or was it that you were going to beg for their intervention? What hellish armies would have spewn forth from that place had you delivered your message? And you.' Now he pointed to Dora. 'In your wanton garments. All of Cornwall knows the stories of the black mass that is performed at Sweetclover Hall. By your own admission you have been keeping company with the infernal denizens of that cursed place. What devilry did you enact? What have you done to the people of this village? Did you sacrifice them to Satan, hagsdaughter?'

Mountfort did not protest, but Dora most certainly did. But as she loudly proclaimed her innocence she heard the desperation in her voice and fell silent, shocked at the stark terror apparent in her own pleas for clemency.

The officer then gestured for the men who held Dora and the spy to drag them to the foot of the tree, beneath the bough over which James was throwing a second rope.

'I will give you each a chance,' the officer said, his voice quieter now, as he fashioned the second rope into a noose. 'The first one to confess, entirely and completely, to their sins, to fall at my feet and beg the forgiveness of our merciful Lord, to offer up their accomplices and familiars, shall be spared the rope.'

The officer gestured again. Dora and Mountfort were forced to their knees side by side. Dora cried out in fear as James placed the noose around her neck.

'James,' she said, staring into his eyes in a fruitless search for any sliver of the brother she had once loved. 'Why would you do this? I am your sister . . . James.'

He turned away with a cold sneer as the rope scratched the soft flesh of her bare throat. Dora felt hot tears run down her swollen cheeks. If there was no pity to be found in the heart of the boy who had shared her childhood, what hope could there be anywhere in this awful mirror image of the safe, secure village she had once called home?

Dora tried to focus her thoughts, to banish despair and think of possible escape, but despair had driven all rational thought away. She looked across at Mountfort, who caught her gaze and this time definitely smiled. First he shook his head, wincing at the effort it took, then he nodded to her. He would not break his silence, and she understood that he was giving her the chance to save herself at his expense. Faced with the unexpected opportunity, Dora didn't even pause.

'I confess,' she said, hating her weakness and cowardice as she did so, but also unable to prevent herself clinging desperately to the slim chance of survival. More than anything, she realised in a moment of sudden clarity, she wanted to live. She felt a deep rush of self-loathing race through her as she understood that, right at this moment, there was nothing at all she would not do in order to stay alive.

She had not thought her will would be so easy to break.

'You are right,' she said. 'Sweetclover Hall is infested with sprites. Demons and ghouls that serve a fearsome witch named Quil. She has enchanted Lord Sweetclover and his servants and she bends them to her will.' The words poured out of her, almost as if spoken by someone else. She gave full rein to her darkest imaginings and fashioned them into words designed to both save herself and condemn a brave man to death in her stead. She cried as she testified, each word feeling like a thorn in her flesh, mortally wounding herself in the name of base salvation. 'If you approach the hall you will be beset by goblins of all sorts – those that fly and swim and crawl, those that breathe fire and those that will chill your blood to ice in your veins. They made me dance with them only this last night, and suckle a black goat that walked upon its hind legs and did sing lullabies composed of the stolen screams of babes bedevilled by succubae.'

The crowd of soldiers began to cry out in alarm, to step away from her in fear. Dora rose to her feet, the noose still around her neck as she cried and shouted and raved of the devil and all his works. For a moment she detected horror in James' eyes, but then it was gone, replaced by cold indifference and superiority.

When finally she had finished, Dora fell to her knees again and buried her face in her hands, weeping hysterically.

'Hang the spy,' the officer said.

She looked up to see Mountfort being dragged to his feet, but her view was swiftly blocked by the officer, who walked over to her and held out his hand. She reached up and took it, and he hauled her to her feet, looped the noose off her head and pulled her in close to him.

'As for you,' he said. 'You shall languish in the church this night, and we shall hang you at dawn.'

With a contemptuous leer, he threw her to the ground again and walked away. A circle of soldiers enclosed her, and many hands reached down to carry her away as she screamed for mercy that she knew would not be offered.

Behind her, she heard the gruesome rattle of the spy's final, desperate breath as he was hauled skywards.

14

Thomas Predennick did not consider himself a brave man, and
he certainly did not consider himself a violent one. But he was a
proud man. Proud of his home, the value of his labour, the place
he held within his community. With his wife and children gone,
these were the only things left in which he could take pride.

The loss of James, seven years before, had not been unexpected. The boy's eyes had always been wide and excited at the
promise of adventure. As much as he tried to deny it, Thomas
had known that his son would leave as soon as he was able.
In his darkest moments, when the night was still and there was
nothing to distract him from his thoughts, he could admit his
own guilt – that he had tried so hard to keep the boy close, to
groom him for a baker's life, that he had driven him away.

But the loss of Theodora two years later had unmanned
him entirely.

His daughter, whom he had adored utterly and without caveat,
had always been a homebody. She was not timid or foolish, but
she lacked the adventurous spirit that had pulled James away.
Thomas had taken comfort in the knowledge that even though
he had lost a son, his daughter would stay close to him for the
rest of her days. He had looked forward to grandchildren. He

knew she hadn't wanted to take the job at Sweetclover Hall, but it was only three miles yonder, an easy walk on a sunny day. Yet it seemed that much as he had underestimated his son's lust for adventure, so he had underestimated his daughter's determination to stay at home. The best explanation anybody could provide for her disappearance was that she had run away from the hall at night, intending to return home, and been waylaid on the road by persons unknown. Robbers or vagabonds, gypsies perhaps. Thomas knew that she would have fought them but he knew also, by her absence, that she must have lost the fight. She was dead, of that he was certain, and it was his fault, for it had been he who had insisted she take the job at the hall.

In the year after her disappearance, Thomas had barely spoken to a soul. He baked his bread and wandered the woods and fields, the paths and byways, searching for a sign, a clue of any sort to the fate of his little girl. He found nothing. Eventually his wife, Sarah, locked deep in the well of her own grief, lost patience with him. She cultivated the opinion that Dora had not run away. She became certain that some fate had befallen her at the hall itself. Thomas could not believe it; certainly the lord had strange ways, but there had never been gossip or stories about him that indicated the kind of dark purpose Sarah suspected. Still Sarah clung tight to her suspicions. She became possessed by the idea that Lord Sweetclover himself must have done their daughter wrong. Eventually the tension came to a head in a furious argument and Sarah had spoken the words she had been holding in for so long. She screamed into his face that Dora's fate was his fault. So Thomas, unable to form words that could express so much guilt, did something he had never done before. He raised his hand and struck his wife.

She left immediately and never returned.

Thomas only discovered his wife's refuge a week later when he did a favour for the miller and took the monthly delivery of flour to Sweetclover Hall; he found her there, in floury aprons, ready to take receipt of the sacks. If he would not investigate Dora's disappearance, she told him, she would. With that cold rebuke she turned her back on him. To the miller's surprise, Thomas had offered to deliver the flour every month thereafter.

For six months she refused to talk to him, and Thomas sank even deeper, this time taking solace in the only thing that could help stem, briefly, the tide of guilt – strong drink. The days, weeks and months blurred into one long haze until, one day, he just . . . stopped.

He did not know how he managed to stop, or why. He just did. Had he been a man of deep conviction he might have concluded that he had been touched by the mercy of a divine God. In reality he simply reached a point where he had to choose between grave and granary, and he chose the latter. From that day he had not touched anything stronger than small beer, and he'd resumed an active role in the civil and social life of the village. While there were plenty of people who judged him harshly for the dissolution of his family, plenty more were willing to offer understanding and forgiveness. He kept delivering the flour; she gradually began to be civil to him, but nothing more.

Three years later, he was a respected elder of the village, his opinions given weight by the experience of loss and grief that he had borne. He found what little contentment he could in this newly garnered respect, but it did not dispel the shame he felt, and he would trade it all in an instant for the companionship of the family he had lost.

Now, with the coming of the war, he had sworn to protect

the families of his fellow villagers in a way he had not been able to protect his own.

'We shall circle the village,' he said as he led the men of Pendarn through the graveyard to the woods that marked the settlement's boundary. 'There is a good vantage point on Potter's Hill. From there we can observe the soldiers unseen.'

The men murmured their agreement as they hurried into the half-lit woods.

'And what provocation shall be sufficient to spur us to action, Thomas?' asked Squeer.

'If they look set to burn our houses, then we have no choice but to intervene,' he replied firmly.

'Or if they find the womenfolk,' added young Henry Chandler, who awkwardly brandished a sword as long as he was tall.

'We need have no fear of that, son,' said Thomas, trying to sound more certain than he felt. 'They are well hid.'

The sound of smashing glass and the crash of splintering wood echoed through the trees from the church behind them as the men moved with silent, practised ease through the undergrowth, skirting the south side of the village, heading for high ground.

They had not gone far when Thomas spotted motion ahead. He stopped and the men behind him did likewise, following his lead. Thomas knelt down and squinted, trying to identify the source of the movement. A moment later he caught sight of two figures moving stealthily through the woods ahead of them. He could not make out much detail but their gaits were unfamiliar, and he already knew exactly where every inhabitant of Pendarn was this day. Whoever these two were, they were strangers, keen to remain unseen.

He turned back to the men and addressed Squeer. 'Edward,

take everyone up to Potter's Hill,' he instructed. 'I'm going to track these two, see who they are and what they want.'

'On your own? Is that wise?' questioned the thin-faced man.

'I can handle myself,' Thomas reassured him with a smile, brandishing his cudgel. 'Look at them. They wish to remain hidden, so I think they are not with the soldiers. Perhaps they are spies for the Crown. If so, they may be able to render aid to us, to help us drive out the invaders. They warrant investigation, but meanwhile you must follow our original plan. If you are forced to attack, I will hear, and will come with haste if able.'

Squeer held out his hand, and Thomas took it. 'Good luck, Thomas.'

'And to you.'

The men of Pendarn stole away through the trees as Thomas forged ahead, stalking the two strangers who in turn stalked his home. He was not a hunter by nature but he had grown up in these woods, playing hide-and-seek almost as soon as he could walk. He could be as stealthy as the most practised poacher. His quarry were not as adept. To Thomas' ears they fair crashed through the woods like a herd of bulls, though he doubted their noisy progress would be heard by the soldiers on the green. Keeping his distance, Thomas watched as they nipped out of the woods and tried the doors of each village house in turn, checking briefly inside then leaving and closing the doors behind them before skulking back into the woods and moving on to the next dwelling. Were they searching for allies or enemies?

Eventually his patience wore thin. He could see no weapons about their persons, and although the taller of the two was freakishly tall, they moved like children rather than adults. From their clothes he could tell that they were boys, although the gait of the smaller one had initially led Thomas to identify him as a girl. He did not think they posed an immediate threat, but he was curious and wary. Thomas hurried swiftly into the deeper woods and cut ahead of the two strangers. Selecting a good wide oak behind which to hide, he lay in wait.

When the tall one came alongside the tree, Thomas lunged forward and tripped him. The boy fell hard onto the ground with a muffled cry of alarm and surprise. Thomas stepped out and confronted the smaller stranger, all the while keeping his cudgel in plain view, close to the fallen one's head.

'Stay down, son,' he said, keeping his eyes fixed on the smaller one, who had taken a step back and spread his arms in the universally recognised sign of submission.

'If you say so,' came a strangely accented voice from the woodland floor. Thomas was immediately suspicious. This was no Englishman.

'Who are you, and what are you doing skulking around my village?'

The smaller one answered, at first in a high voice but then, after a clearing of the throat, in a deeper. 'We are . . . huhh-huggh . . . we are strangers to this land, good sir, but we offer you no threat.'

Another foreigner, but with a brogue far removed from the tall one's.

'Where do you come from, then?' he asked.

'I am lately voyaged from the New World,' said the short one. 'And my companion is from, um, Poland . . . ?'

'You say that as if you are not sure,' said Thomas. 'Tall one, hail you from the eastern lands?'

'Uh, yes. I do. Long story. Can I get up now?'

Thomas swiped the cudgel through the air before the tall one's face. 'OK, I'll stay here,' he said.

Thomas gestured for the short one to step forward. As he did so he stepped into a shaft of sunlight and Thomas was surprised to note the girlish aspect and dark skin of this slender boy. 'The New World, say you?'

'Aye,' said the girlish boy. 'I am a savage of that land. Hence my dark skin, and strange accent.'

Thomas nodded. ''Tis true you look and speak most oddly. What shall I call you, savage? And what brings you to Pendarn?'

'My name is Jana. And Pendarn is but a way-station on my journey to visit the lord of Sweetclover Hall.'

'What business have you at the hall?' asked Thomas sharply.

Jana shrugged apologetically. 'Sorry, can't tell you that.'

'Can I get up now?' groaned the tall one. 'My arse is wet.'

Thomas stepped aside and let the tall one rise to his feet.

'Thank you,' he said, as he brushed leaves and moss from his trousers. 'I'm Kaz.'

'So it's Kaz from Poland, and Jana from the New World. Hiding in the woods by my village, inspecting the houses, who knows why, on their way to a secret meeting at Sweetclover Hall. That is the matter?'

'Pretty much,' said the small one.

'Yes,' agreed the taller.

Thomas regarded the curious strangers closely, and as he did so his eyes widened in surprise.

'I could ask you about the strange footwear that adorns your feet,' he said, gesturing to Kaz's bright blue boots. 'But I would perhaps do better to enquire as to how and why you are both wearing my shirts.'

'Ah,' said Jana, pulling an embarrassed face. 'That's, um . . .'

'Your shirts?' interrupted Kaz urgently. 'You are the baker?'

'I am. Thomas Predennick,' replied Thomas, his confusion

nothing to that which he felt a moment later, when Jana asked, 'Dora's father?'

At those words the world spun around Thomas' head and a thousand thoughts raced through his mind. The most obvious being that these thieving vagabonds must be the ones who had stolen his daughter away. If that be the case, and if they referred to her in such terms, then she must be alive and in their company. He felt his knees buckle a little, but he regained his composure sufficiently to ask, haltingly, 'What know you of my daughter?'

'Wow,' said Kaz after a moment's silence.

'Right?' Agreed Jana.

Thomas clenched his fist tighter around the handle of his cudgel and raised it slowly into the air. 'For God's sake speak the King's English, and tell me what you know of my daughter,' he said again, struggling to get the words out.

'Your daughter is alive and well,' said Jana, obviously choosing her words with great care. 'Dora was with us only half an hour ago ago. She ran off into the village looking for you.'

All the questions he needed to ask, all the anger and fear and joy that were mixed up inside him so that he did not know whether to cry or shout or dance, were all swept aside in an instant by what happened next.

There was a roar from the direction of the village green, as of a group of assembled men cheering.

Then a piercing scream. He recognised it instantly.

'Dora,' said Thomas.

He lifted his cudgel high and ran out of the woods towards the noise, with no thought to the consequences.

15

'Oh crap,' said Kaz.

'Come on,' yelled Jana. Without waiting for acknowledgement she ran after Thomas. She could hear Kaz's heavy footsteps behind her as she broke from the treeline and scurried between the houses on to the lane that ran through the village. Thomas was ahead and to her left, racing for the green.

'Get your gun ready,' she shouted to Kaz as she pulled the laser out of her pocket. She hared after the determined baker, who, she was certain, was about to get himself killed. As she rounded the final cottage the village green spread out before her. To her right was a huge oak tree around which crowded a gaggle of soldiers cheering as a struggling peasant was hauled off the ground by the rope around his neck. Ahead of her, three soldiers were dragging Dora towards the church, which sat on the far end of the green. Dora was screaming and crying as her feet dragged behind her. Thomas was halfway to the men, cudgel still raised. They had not yet seen him.

Jana made a lightning calculation of the odds. If Thomas could silence the three soldiers quickly enough, there was a chance that the main body of men, distracted by their lynching, would not realise Dora had been freed until they made good their escape. She checked the gun was still set to its lowest measure. At this power it worked like a taser, delivering an electric charge that would disable rather than kill. She did not have any compunction about killing the soldiers, but she did not want to use up the charge needlessly.

There was a yelp from up ahead and Jana raised her eyes to see one of the soldiers stumbling away from Dora, nursing his wrist. Jana smiled. Good on Dora; she'd bitten him hard. Thomas, who was nearly upon them, took advantage of this distraction and ran straight at the wounded man, swinging his cudgel in a huge arc and smacking the soldier square on the temple. The soldier never even saw his assailant. From ten metres away Jana heard the wet crack as the cudgel connected and the soldier collapsed in a heap.

The two other soldiers dropped Dora and stepped away as she sprawled on the grass between them. One drew a sword, the other a pistol. Jana raised her own weapon and fired, taking the swordsman out of the equation with a single, precise beam. The soldier with the pistol stood dumbfounded. He had only one shot in his weapon, and two attackers bearing down on him. He did the sensible thing and ran as hard as he could. Unfortunately he ran back towards the lynch mob, yelling at the top of his lungs. Thomas took a swing at him as he ran past, but the soldier dodged easily and kept going, shouting for aid.

Jana took careful aim at the fleeing soldier but her concentration was broken as Kaz ran between them, reaching Dora before Thomas. He scooped her up and kept running, almost without breaking stride. Thomas fell in behind him, cudgel still raised. Jana thought it likely he'd fell Kaz if he got the chance so she gave chase, letting the other soldier run.

She did not look around to see what was going on at the oak tree, but she could picture the soldier's arrival, the realisation that they were under attack, the hue and cry that would come after them in mere seconds. Thinking fast, she turned and dropped to one knee, spinning the gun's setting to maximum. She could see some members of the crowd at the tree turning to look in her direction, but not as many as she had feared, because the peasant's death throes were so entertaining. She could make out his legs, kicking and wriggling as his airway was slowly crushed and the process of strangulation began.

Jana used her eye-mods to zoom in on the lynch mob. She took a deep breath, released it and squeezed the trigger. A bright white beam of light crackled from the gun and held steady, like an impossibly long knife. She swept it slowly to the right, cutting through the rope that held the struggling man. He tumbled to the ground and the soldiers gave a roar of disappointment. The angle was so fine that Jana accidentally let the beam slice into the oak tree. Neatly bisected, the top half of the tree slid sideways and then tumbled to the ground, bursting into flames as it did. The huge mass of burning foliage and thick, heavy oak fell onto about half the crowd of soldiers, who found themselves pinioned beneath exploding branches. There was an awful lot of screaming.

Those soldiers not trapped and burning milled around waving their arms, wishing to free their comrades but unable to brave the inferno.

Jana released the trigger, rose to her feet and ran after Thomas, Kaz and Dora, who had now almost reached the sanctuary of the church. She had bought them some time, she only hoped it would be enough.

If she was secretly enjoying her second gunfight of the day, she made sure to give no outward sign of it.

In the doorway of the church, Dora pushed Kaz and her father away. She did not want anybody near her. She felt unclean, disgusted with herself and the world. She wanted to bathe in scalding oil but knew not even that could wash away the shame of what her own base fear and cowardice had made her do, or burn away the knowledge of the unfeeling monster that had replaced the brother she still, somehow, loved. A distant, disconnected part of her mind knew that Kaz and her father were trying to help, but she could not use that knowledge to guide her actions; it was as if she had been reduced to something feral and desperate.

She felt arms trying to enfold her, a voice, familiar and deep, saying her name over and over again, but she screamed and kicked and pushed the arms away. Jana ran up to them, panting.

'I bought us some time,' she said, smiling and waving back at the green.

Dora saw the burning tree, the crowd of men milling around it. She also saw a group of ten soldiers hurrying across the green towards them, swords and pistols drawn.

Her gaze fell upon something she could use. She held out her bound hands and nodded to Kaz, then at the knife sheathed on his belt. Kaz understood and cut her free.

Before the ropes even hit the floor, Dora grabbed the gun from Jana's hand, turned and flung herself past her momentarily stunned companion. Barely conscious of what she was doing, unaware of the frantic pursuit of her friends, still crying out loud in fear and humiliation, Dora ran to the lychgate, raised the gun and pulled the trigger.

The bright white beam lanced forward across the village green, burning into empty space. Then with one swift move, screaming in rage, Dora swept the beam across the green like a searchlight.

With a single, dreadful cry of agony, the ten soldiers who were running towards her fell to the grass.

In twenty pieces.

He had built his career on luck, but Richard Mountfort was pretty sure that it had finally run out. As the rope began to bite he desperately looked to the edges of the green in hope of rescue. His interrogation had been short but simple. The soldier who had captured him, whose name he had learned was James, had not wasted time with questions. He had got straight on with the urgent business of kicking, punching and, shortly thereafter, cutting the truth out of him.

Mountfort had little intelligence to offer. He had been sent by the king to sound out Sweetclover, to see whether he would join the fight. Rumours of black magic had reached exalted ears, and it was whispered that the king would dearly love to recruit a wizard to his cause. Mountfort had never reached the hall, so he could not tell James whether Sweetclover was for Parliament or the king, nor could he confirm or deny the stories of devilry. His ignorance made James angrier, and for a while Mountfort had been sure that the next cut would end him. When James' superior officer had finally intervened, Mountfort had initially been relieved. Now he knew he had been saved only so he could provide sport and entertainment for the blood-thirsty mob that crowded around as he was hauled skywards by his neck.

He had always thought he would die in bed or battle. Being

strung up from a tree in a muddy, out-of-the-way Cornish village was about as ignominious an end as he could imagine.

The rope pulled tight, pressing hard against his throat. A second later he was dangling, feet kicking desperately for purchase that would not come, as his vision faded and the roar of blood in his ears blotted out all sound.

Then there was a flash of heat from above him and a crunching impact as he tumbled back to the ground. His hearing faded back in as he took desperate breaths and tried to gather his wits. He lay, floundering like a fish on a beach, hearing the hubbub of disappointment and confusion generated by the soldiers who had, only moments before, been looking forward to his execution. The word 'witchcraft' featured prominently, and Richard wondered whether the girl he encountered before his aborted execution had indeed turned out to be a witch. Maybe she had interceded to save him. If that were so, he would gratefully pledge allegiance to Satan and all his sulphurous hordes, for nothing he could imagine would ever be as welcome to him as the sweet breeze at the back of his throat.

He had begun to consider his next move when there was a tremendous crash and the screaming began. He looked up to see that the tree trunk now ended in an angled lateral line about ten feet off the ground. The top half of the tree was lying on the green, burning fiercely even as it pressed down on a horde of dying soldiers. Before he could work out what to do next, the nearest soldier fetched him a crippling kick to the gut with his mud-encrusted boot. Mountfort felt all the air he had so gratefully gulped down expelled forcefully again as he doubled over in agony. The kicks came thick and fast, raining down on him as he curled up and raised his arms to protect his head. He felt a rib crack as one particularly hefty blow caught him.

Once again he felt his senses begin to slip away and he thought ruefully that he had exchanged one pathetic death for another.

Then, miraculously, the kicking stopped as a thick bough of burning oak crashed to the ground beside him, showering him with sparks.

He cracked open a swollen eye and found, to his amazement, that he was no longer surrounded by men determined to kill him. In fact he seemed to have been entirely forgotten. Behind him stood the oak tree, blazing like a beacon, surrounded by soldiers who sallied forward to try and pluck their friends from the fire before retreating with their eyebrows singed.

Realising that, against all odds, he had been presented with a chance to escape, Richard held his bound wrists out and leaned forward until the rope was positioned above the flames that rose from the burning bough. He cried out as the fire licked his skin, but after a moment the ropes fell apart and he pushed himself away from the conflagration. Ignoring his searing flesh, he undid the rope around his ankles, jack-knifed himself upright, and took off as fast as he could away from the fire, making for the safety of the church. Oddly, there was already a group of soldiers ahead of him, racing, swords and pistols drawn, in the same direction. He glanced beyond them and saw a group of people approaching the church. It seemed that this small group of soldiers was pursuing these escapees, while the remaining men were doing battle with the fire. Abandoning the church, Richard broke right and headed for the cottages. If he could reach them, he could perhaps find a horse and make his escape.

He ran hard, his lungs burning. His chest ached as the broken ribs ground against each other with every agonising step, but he did not slow down until he reached the lane that ran through the cottages away from the green. Finally he reached the shelter of the structures and allowed himself to glance back. He was not being pursued.

Thanking God most fervently, he hobbled away from the green.

But as he did so he heard marching feet ahead of him. He looked up to see a line of ten men, short and stocky, dressed head to toe in what looked to be black-dyed leather. Their hair had been coated with thick, coloured pastes and teased up into spikes, and their faces were etched with complex indigo tattoos. They carried weapons that he did not recognise – small, white pistols with no obvious flintlocks. When he tried to look into their eyes, they did not acknowledge him; all he saw were the reflected flames of the burning tree.

His mouth dropped open in astonishment as they began walking towards him in eerie unison. He spun on his heels and ran to the door of the nearest house. Finding it unlocked, he pushed through the downstairs, out the back door and made his escape into the woods. A few moments later he heard a new and strange sound rising above the commotion of the fire. It sounded like the screams of hell itself, but it was cut short, stopping abruptly in a manner most chilling.

Richard ran on without looking back.

16

Strong hands grasped Dora's shoulders and she fought to throw them off. She kneeled on the hard, cold ground, weeping uncontrollably, the gun forgotten, discarded by her side. She could not say why she wept, whether for shame at her cowardice, for the loss of her brother's love and its replacement with cruel zealotry, or for the innocence she had lost when her panic and grief had led her to strike down ten strangers in cold blood. She was absent of all conscious thought, a fourteen-year-old girl reduced to a storm of overwhelming emotions trapped in a shaking, traumatised shell.

The hands moved away from her shoulders and she felt them encircle her, beneath her knees and arms, lifting her. Even in her state she knew that they were the arms of a friend, although she could not have said who. She allowed herself to be carried back into the church. She was still racked by great, heaving sobs as she felt the arms embrace her, turning the act of carrying into a hug. She looked up through her tears into her father's eyes. She had not realised he was there, and the thrill of mixed joy and terror as she met his gaze broke through her fugue and returned her to the world. For he was crying too, into her hair. His sudden, raw emotion collided with her own and cancelled it out in the simplest way possible; it gave her someone to look after.

She returned his embrace, hugging him tightly and saying over and over, 'It's all right, I'm here. It's all right.'

Once Thomas and Dora were safely through the door, Kaz closed and bolted it. He turned to Jana, who was examining the gun she had reclaimed from where Dora had discarded it.

'We can't stay here,' Kaz told Jana, reverting to Polish. 'The fire won't keep them occupied for long, and once this church is surrounded we'll be trapped.'

Jana shrugged, her attention focused on the weapon. 'Let them surround us,' she said. 'All I need to do is go up the church tower with this and they'll be running or dead within seconds. They can't hurt us, Kaz, relax.'

'Wouldn't it be easier to go out the back door? Or do you enjoy shooting people?' replied Kaz, feeling the anger rising at Jana's glib assuredness. 'We've been here an hour. We were going to keep a low profile, remember? Sneak about under the radar, work out what was going on before showing ourselves. And what have we managed to do? Kill a bunch of soldiers by dropping a burning tree on them, and turn a fourteen-year-old girl into a mass murderer. Stop looking at that gun.'

Kaz snatched the weapon from Jana, dropped it to the floor and stomped on it hard until it cracked, sparked and spilt a foul-smelling liquid.

Jana, astonished and horrified by what he had done, pushed him in the chest aggressively. He staggered backwards.

'You moron,' she yelled, fists clenched, visibly restraining herself from punching him in the face. 'What did you do that for? That was our one advantage.'

'Enough killing,' he replied, feeling as though he were about to boil over with rage.

'Great,' said Jana, sarcastically. 'Let's hope those soldiers feel the same way, yeah? 'Cause if they don't, we're screwed.'

A particularly guttural sob from Dora's dad interrupted the escalation of Kaz's temper long enough for him to force a few deep breaths. He clenched his fists, turned on his heels and stalked away from Jana. He had to get away from her.

'I'm going to climb the tower,' he said over his shoulder. 'See what's happening outside.'

Dora was also fighting her feelings. They were too confused and powerful to make sense of. She found herself bouncing between joy, shame, fear, anger and guilt moment to moment. She took comfort in the strong warmth of her father's embrace, but after a few seconds she unfolded herself and set her feet back on the ground. Then she gently took his arms and prised them open, holding his hands as she stepped back and smiled up at him.

'I'm back. Do not fret. All will be made clear to you, I promise,' she said, amazed at the sight of her strong, silent father tear-stained and sobbing. He was beside himself. Dora swallowed her sobs. Her feelings didn't matter, she had to take care of her father. 'But not yet,' she said. 'Our situation is perilous and you do not yet apprehend the full seriousness of it.' She was about to tell him about James, but looked into his eyes and found she could not bring herself to quell his joy with such horrible tidings. Not yet.

'Where have you been?' he asked. 'Look at you. You haven't aged a day. And what are you wearing?'

She saw no suspicion in his eyes, not like in James'. Her

father felt only wonder and joy. Dora squeezed his hands and smiled reassuringly. 'Later. First, we must evacuate this church. Get the women and children from the crypt, it's no longer safe.'

The father she knew would never have taken instruction from a woman, let alone a girl, least of all his daughter. But this man, his personality broken and reassembled by five years of grief and loneliness, saw the wisdom in her words, composed himself, took back his hands and ran to the crypt without even asking how Dora knew the villagers were there. Dora watched him begin to usher the women and children out of the vestry door and into the woods.

'You shouldn't have gone running off like that.' Dora turned to see Jana regarding her coolly. 'Could have got yourself killed.'

'I know,' said Dora, bowing her head. 'I am sorry.'

It looked to Dora as if Jana tried to reward her apology with a smile, but she was so tired and stressed that it came out as more of a grimace. ''S OK,' she said through gritted teeth. 'This whole day's been a headtrip, can't blame you for freaking out. Please don't do it again, yeah?'

Dora nodded.

'Look, we really need to get out of here,' said Jana. 'So we . . . hang on, who are they?' She pointed to the crowd of villagers filing out the back door.

'The women and children of the village,' explained Dora. 'They were hiding from the soldiers, hoping they would pass through if the village was empty. But now I fear this church will be put to the flame and they must flee for their lives.'

'Hey.' Dora turned to see Kaz, breathless and wide eyed, in the door of the church tower staircase. He was gesturing for them to come with him. 'Quick, you need to see this.'

Jana ran ahead of Dora, and together they hurried up the narrow circular stone staircase as quickly as they were able. Ascending past the bells, they emerged on to the roof and joined Kaz at the crenellated battlements, looking down at the village green.

The bisected oak still burnt fiercely but the soldiers were no longer trying to free their friends from the flames; they were long dead anyway. Instead the soldiers were mustered in a line before the flames, facing towards the village. Dora squinted to see what they were doing, trying to see whether James was amongst them. She could not see him, and for the first time she realised he might have perished in the fire. She was glad she had not told her father of his return. Better he believe his son long gone than learn he had lost his soul to zealotry and then been burnt alive.

'What are they doing?' asked Dora, as the soldiers appeared to raise their pikes and muskets.

'Look,' said Kaz, pointing.

'Oh no,' said Jana.

What Dora saw chilled her blood. Ten men in black, their heads and faces a riot of colour, were walking in perfect formation, advancing slowly towards the soldiers. 'Who are they?'

'I think they're the same guys Kaz and I met in 2014, at the labs,' replied Jana. 'Same build, same kind of outfit. They move the same way, too. Not natural.'

'That proves it,' said Kaz. 'Someone from the future is here.'

Kaz was interrupted by a deafening fusillade of musket fire as the soldiers peppered the advancing guards with shot. The soldiers briefly vanished in a cloud of smoke. Dora could only imagine how terrified they must have been when it cleared to reveal all ten of the menacing figures still advancing.

'Why are they here? What do they want?' wondered Jana.

'My guess?' said Kaz. Then he pointed to the neat angled line where the oak tree had been severed. 'They want to find out who did that.' As he said this, he flashed Jana a meaningful look, which Dora took as an accusation.

'But how did they know? Unless they were . . . Oh,' said Jana.

'What is it?' asked Dora.

Jana pointed skywards. 'We're being watched,' she said.

Dora looked up into the sky, heavy with clouds that promised imminent snow, but could see nothing at first. Then she caught a tiny glint of light, high up, and gasped. 'What is that?'

'A drone,' said Jana.

'You're kidding,' said Kaz, shielding his eyes with his hand and squinting upwards. 'How can you see that?'

'ENL chips aren't the only enhancements available,' said Jana, tapping the side of her eye socket. 'It looks knocked together but it's an eyesky. Not standard issue for Cromwell's army.'

'What is a drone?' asked Dora.

'A very good reason for us to get off this roof and into the woods as fast as we possibly can,' said Jana.

'Agreed,' said Kaz.

They were halfway back down the staircase when terrible screaming began to drift across from the village green.

Dora led the way down the staircase, as fast as she was able.

17

Dora held the strange contraption up to her eyes then recoiled in surprise.

'That is wonderful,' she said, examining it closely. 'What is it called?'

'Binoculars,' said Kaz.

'I like it.' Dora's voice was gleeful, making her sound like a fourteen-year-old girl for the first time since they had arrived in 1645. She was scanning the faces of the captured soldiers for her brother, but could not find him. She knew he had not been one of the soldiers she had gunned down, so he either perished beneath the boughs of the blazing oak or he fled to safety at some point. Despite what he had done, Dora found herself wishing fervently that he was safe. If he lived, there was still a chance he could be reasoned with, saved, made again the man she'd once known. She continued to inspect the faces of the terrified captives, checking and double-checking.

She, Jana and Kaz crouched in the undergrowth watching the green. It had been out of their sight for a few minutes as they fled the church and found cover, and in those few minutes the situation had changed dramatically. The soldiers were now all kneeling in a straight line, their wrists bound. The strange men who had overpowered them so easily were asking questions, slapping and punching, kicking and gouging their captives in search of answers.

'I wish we could hear what they're saying,' said Kaz.

'Their captain told me they had been sent here by Parliament to meet with Lord Sweetclover and find out to which party of this war he pledges allegiance,' explained Dora. 'If this woman, Quil, is at the hall, she perhaps thought these soldiers a threat, maybe she sent these strange blue-faced men to deal with them.'

'But Quil's goons arrive to find evidence that some other time traveller has already picked a fight with the soldiers, so now they're trying to gather intelligence about us. Makes sense,' said Jana.

'What will they do if they get no answers?' asked Kaz.

The answer was immediately provided. Dora gasped in horror as the ten strange men began shooting the soldiers with their own muskets and pistols, or running them through with swords and pikes one by one. The tenor of the screaming worsened as they worked their way through the men, as those left alive realised their imminent fate and began to cry and beg for mercy that did not come.

Jana turned to Kaz and whispered something to him in harsh, angry Polish. Dora felt certain it was a rebuke for his destroying the gun, an act that rendered them helpless to intervene in the massacre unfolding before them.

Kaz and Jana turned away after a while, unable to watch, but Dora kept her eyes fixed on the horror, still trying desperately to pick out James.

When the slaughter was finished, the guards released the

soldiers' bonds and scattered the weapons around the bodies, to make it seem as if they had died in battle. Next they set fire to the tree trunk, to disguise the clean line where Jana's laser had cut through it. Finally, satisfied with their work, they made for the woods on the far side of the green.

'They are finished,' said Dora. The other two rejoined her. Jana eyed her suspiciously, uncomfortable that she alone had remained to watch.

'Think they're looking for us?' asked Kaz, watching the guards disappear into the gloom of the woods.

'I think so,' replied Jana. 'Good thing they're heading in the wrong direction.'

'They are not,' said Dora. 'That is the way we must go, to Sweetclover Hall.'

There was a sharp crack behind them and Jana whirled around.

'It is I,' said Thomas, hands spread wide.

'Not good, creeping up on us like that,' warned Jana.

'It worked well enough the first time,' he replied with a smile, handing the backpack to Kaz. 'It was exactly where you said it would be. It is a most strange material.'

'Did you open it?' asked Jana.

'I gave you my word I would not,' he replied.

'Good for you,' said Jana. 'If a backpack amazes you, the Tupperware would have blown your mind. New world. Full of wonders.'

Thomas nodded, aware that he was being made fun of but unable to grasp the joke.

'I heard musket fire and screaming,' he said. 'What's happened?'

'Cleaning up,' said Kaz, inspecting the backpack's contents.

Thomas walked to his side and looked out at the green. 'God preserve us,' he said as he took in the scene.

'Good news is, I think you can take back your village,' said Jana.

'Is everybody safe?' asked Dora, stepping to her father's side and taking his hand.

He nodded. 'The other men were still arguing about whether to intervene when I arrived with the women and children. They are waiting at Potter's Hill.'

'You must rejoin them, and set them to work,' said Dora. 'Dig a pit, bury the evidence, say the tree was hit by lightning. Nobody will be any the wiser. There may be other soldiers in the area, it would not do for them to think our village had perpetrated this atrocity.'

Thomas looked at her askance. 'You speak as if you were not coming with me.'

Dora sighed. 'Father, there is something Kaz, Jana and I must do first. Something important, which I cannot explain at present. You must trust me.'

Thomas tried to find an answer but before he could argue, Dora continued. 'I must to Sweetclover Hall,' she said. 'Mother is there, is she not?'

'She is.'

'I will find her, complete my business, then we shall both come back to Pendarn,' said Dora. 'I promise, we shall return before tomorrow nightfall.'

Thomas cupped her cheek in his hand and smiled. 'My little girl, telling me what to do.'

Dora put her hand over his. 'Never.' She smiled.

'I will not leave you alone, however,' he continued. 'After so long from my sight I fear losing you again. I shall return to

Potter's Hill, give instructions to the others, then bring my monthly flour delivery to the hall. As it happens, I was due there this morning. I shall see you there. I must have answers from you, Dora.'

Dora wanted to tell him not to come, but she could see he was not going to be dissuaded. She realised this might not be a bad thing. If things got difficult at the hall, he could take Mother to safety.

'As you wish, Father,' she said. 'Join us at the hall and I swear you shall have your answers.'

Thomas turned to Kaz and Jana, his face altogether sterner. 'Take good care of my daughter. I shall rejoin you before sunset. God help you if anything befalls her.'

Jana rolled her eyes. Kaz nodded and said, 'Understood.'

Dora and Thomas embraced, then he hurried away. The moment he was out of sight Dora ran as hard as she could, out across the green to the gruesome pile of bodies that lay scattered there.

She estimated she had fifteen minutes before her father reached Potter's Hill and could once again look down on the carnage.

Just enough time to check the bodies to see whether James was amongst them.

Thomas walked away from the three young people, happy and proud. The horrors of the day should have been enough to fill him with despair at man's cruelty and the madness of civil conflict, but seeing his daughter again had released so much emotion it was almost too much for him to bear. The astounding force of his love overwhelmed the horror, made it seem distant and insignificant. His girl was alive and well.

190

Her presence raised more questions than he could formulate, and her manner had changed so much in the last five years that she was almost a different person – slightly broken yet braver and more thoughtful – but it was his Dora, returned to him. He felt certain that nothing could surprise him more than the events of this day.

He hurried back to his friends and neighbours, determined to complete his grim task as quickly as possible so that he could hurry to the hall and be reunited with Dora and his wife, so they could sit by the fire, sup and share tales of the years they had missed. Who knew, maybe this could repair the breach between Sarah and him. Maybe his family could be put back together again somehow. Maybe she would finally forgive him, and maybe then he could finally forgive himself.

He hurried on, lost in his thoughts and dreams until blinded by a flash of red fire directly ahead of him. A loud crackling sound and a stench of burning made him stagger backwards and raise his cudgel, trying to flush the sudden smoke-blindness from his eyes. When his vision cleared he found himself looking down at the young man, Kaz, who was scrambling about in a pile of smoking leaves, breathing hard and looking left and right in confusion.

Thomas did not immediately announce himself. His mouth was hanging open and his pulse was racing. After a moment, Kaz noticed him and the sight seemed to calm him. The young man rose to his feet and Thomas backed away, brandishing his cudgel. 'What witchcraft is this?' he hissed.

Kaz held his hands out to indicate that he was no threat, and stood his ground. 'Mr Predennick?' he asked, as if he was struggling to recognise a man he had seen only moments before.

'You know my name well enough, wizard,' replied Thomas,

struggling to keep his voice level. 'Where is Dora? What in God's name is occurring here today?'

Kaz blinked. 'Today?' he said. 'What day is this? Have you seen me today?'

'I saw you but five minutes ago,' said Thomas angrily. 'As well you know.'

So shocked had he been by Kaz's sudden appearance that he only now registered the true strangeness of the boy's aspect. Kaz was soaking wet, shivering with cold and dressed in different clothes – a white frilly shirt above leather trousers and high black leather boots. His hair was longer too, and there was an unimpressive dusting of furry beard upon his face.

'So this is Pendarn? This is the day we first met?' Kaz sounded desperate, fearful and excited all at once.

'I know not what you are raving of,' replied Thomas, 'but I bade you farewell but five minutes ago, back down this path a ways, as you, my daughter and the boy Jana set off for Sweetclover Hall.'

Before Thomas had finished his sentence Kaz had begun to laugh, loud and throaty with a slight edge of hysteria. He fell backwards into the leaves and sat there, holding his head, laughing and laughing until the water dripping from his hair mingled with tears. Thomas could think of nothing to do but stand and watch as his fearful confusion faded into nervous curiosity.

'I made it,' said Kaz, when the hysteria had subsided. 'I finally made it.'

He looked up at Thomas, wiping his eyes, composing himself, smiling broadly.

'Thomas,' he said. 'Your daughter's in terrible danger. I need your help.'

18

Half an hour later, Kaz, Jana and Dora walked stealthily through the woodlands, following the same route the guards had taken, heading for Sweetclover Hall.

Each of them had taken a sword and dagger from the weapons discarded on the green, shoving them into their belts. Jana had also taken a brace of pistols and bags of shot and gunpowder, explaining that her chip contained instructions for priming them.

Dora had been silent since the green. She had wiped the blood from her hands on the grass, but a dull red stain still lingered on her skin, testament to the gory task she had undertaken. She must have inspected thirty bodies, Jana reckoned, in various states. Dora had told them that her brother was not present but Jana could not divine Dora's feelings on the matter.

While Dora was lost in thought, or possibly shock, Kaz just seemed angry. He stalked along beside Jana, hands in pockets, shoulders hunched, eyes focused ahead. Jana thought maybe he was experiencing a comedown; that the thrill of their adventure had palled once people had started dying.

As the only one of the group who seemed, to her mind, to

be coping well with the situation, Jana took it upon herself to try and break the tension.

She took a deep breath. 'That's amazing,' she said.

Dora and Kaz looked at her quizzically.

'I've only noticed it since we left the village, but the smell, the taste of the air,' explained Jana. 'It's so . . . clean. I shouldn't be surprised. We're hundreds of years before the invention of the internal combustion engine, or even steam power. Pre-industrial air.' She took another breath and smiled widely, not only surprised by the atmosphere, but by her reaction to it. 'Love it.'

'The air in your time was most unusual,' said Dora. 'It had a taste of . . . I cannot describe it, but it did not seem natural to me.'

'Pollution and air conditioning,' said Jana. 'Air that has been filled with fumes and then scrubbed clean again.'

'It was not pleasant,' replied Dora, pulling a face. 'But this is normal. This smells of home.'

'I can't imagine what it would be like to grow up somewhere so clean,' said Kaz.

'This is Carroty Wood,' she said. 'James and I would play here when we were children.'

Jana was only half listening, because she had become genuinely involved in what had been conceived as a distraction. Now she tuned into the sounds of the woods and was astonished all over again.

'The birds,' she said. 'Is this chorus usual?'

Dora nodded. 'Do you not have birds in your time?' she asked.

'Not like this, not in New York.'

Dora considered for a moment and said, 'That is sad, I think. They sing sweetly and taste good.'

Jana was shocked. 'Taste good? You eat songbirds?' She had thought there could be nothing more revolting than wild meat, with all its parasites and imperfections. But the idea of tiny wild birds, captured, plucked and stewed, made her feel ill. Just like that, the magic of her new surroundings vanished, replaced by reality, harsh and practical.

'Do you have predators in these woods?' asked Jana quietly, remembering that long-extinct animals like wolves and bears were still roaming the land at this point in history.

'No.' Dora laughed.

Jana felt a flush of embarrassment and allowed the conversation to falter, but Dora seemed a little less spaced out, and Kaz had managed to speak without growling. Job done.

'This is where it all started for me,' said Kaz as Jana forged ahead of them. 'I was lost at night, on the other side of woods, when I found Sweetclover Hall. It is derelict in my time, as you saw, but I broke in to find shelter. I'd only just got inside when you and Jana dropped in.'

Dora considered her companion. His skin was light brown, his accent strange and his name unfamiliar to her. 'Kaz, where do you come from?' she asked.

'I was born in Poland.' He registered Dora's look of confusion. 'It is a country east of Germany.' Still confused. 'Which is east of France.'

Dora nodded slowly. 'That is very far east.'

Kaz laughed. 'Yes. Well, my father is Polish, so is my passport.'

'Pass port?'

'Official document that tells where you come from. In my time everybody must have one if they want to travel to other countries.'

'I see, continue.'

'My mother is Iranian.' Kaz noticed Dora's confused look. 'Sorry, in this time it's called Persia. She is Persian.'

'So you come from two different countries,' she said, shaking her head in wonder. 'Are the people of Poland brown?'

Kaz smiled. 'No, but the people of Persia are.'

'And which language do you speak?'

'Polish and Farsi, which is the language of Persia.'

'And English.' Dora smiled.

He nodded. 'I also have some French, Spanish, a little bit of German and Russian.'

'How is it possible to hold so many tongues in your head? Do you not become confused?'

'Sometimes.' He laughed. 'We travelled a lot. My father is kind of a soldier.'

'And he took you with him on his battle campaigns?'

Kaz shook his head. 'No, he is a peacekeeper.'

'I do not understand. He is a soldier who keeps the peace? Like a nightwatchman?'

'Sort of. In my time, armies sometimes go to countries where there is war and stop the fighting while politicians talk and try to fix things.'

'Soldiers who fight for peace, not conquest,' said Dora. 'It seems to me that your world is upside down. And you travelled with him to these places, even as a child?'

'My mother was a journalist, so she . . .' Kaz registered the look on Dora's face. 'You don't know what a journalist is, do you?'

Dora shook her head.

'OK. Her job was to travel to interesting places, find out what was going on there and write about it so people at home could read her reports and understand what was going on.'

Dora was incredulous. 'This is woman's work?'

Kaz nodded. 'So she followed my father around the world, reporting on conflicts he was trying to end. She couldn't go home because in my time Iran is not a great place to be a female journalist, and she wouldn't stay alone in Poland because she would have died of boredom. She was very passionate about her work, about trying to change the world. So she followed my father, and I followed with her.'

'And because of this you grew up in many different lands?'

'All over the world. A year here, a year there.'

'That sounds very exciting.'

'It was,' agreed Kaz.

Dora considered this. 'If you had asked me yesterday, I would have said that was the most awful thing I could imagine. All I wanted was to stay in Pendarn and raise goats.'

'But now?'

'Now, I do not know.' She shrugged. 'I have seen much in one short day. I do not know if I could go back to a settled life, even if I were to be allowed. Which I suspect I will not be.'

'You don't know that.'

Dora looked at him sideways. 'You talk about your mother in the past,' she said.

'She died.'

'That is very sad. How old were you?'

'Your age. Fourteen. After she died my father took me home to Poland and we stopped travelling. But after that things were not so good between us. I suppose he was only trying to protect me, but it was stifling so I ran away and now here I am.'

'Losing someone from your family is not an easy thing,'

said Dora, laying a hand on Kaz's arm. 'I had two brothers. Little Godfrey, who was born after me. He was a sweet boy, kind and funny. I loved him so much. He had the most delightful laugh. But he died. Then James, my older brother, ran away without a word some years later.'

Kaz looked across at Dora and smiled sadly, but did not say anything further. They walked together in companionable silence.

'Please tell me,' said Dora after a short while, 'what is a "headtrip"?'

19

There was snow in the air; Sarah Predennick could tell that from the dense, low clouds on the horizon. For all the inconvenience it brought – the frozen toes, the struggle to get provisions delivered from the nearby villages and towns, the tiny fissures in the roof that widened and cracked as the snow thawed, and the cascades of meltwater that poured through them when the sun returned – she still felt a flutter of excitement at the prospect. Even now, at forty-two years of age, she had not entirely lost the girlish thrill the sharp white light of a snow-covered landscape gave her.

This year there was another reason to welcome the prospect – it was harder to wage war in winter. A good, deep snowfall would halt the armies in their tracks for a while. It would be a temporary respite, she knew that well enough, but any delay was welcome. Any pause increased the chances, however slim, that cooler heads could prevail and further hostilities could be avoided. Surely a period of enforced reflection would cause Cromwell's troops to realise their folly and turn away from their godless battle with the king. One long, harsh winter would restore the natural order: such was Sarah's hope.

So as she stood at the scullery door, her back warmed by

the fires within, her face nipped by the frosty air that insinuated its way past her to battle with the heat of the ovens, she welcomed the coming deluge and the serenity she hoped it would deliver.

But she still wished her husband would get a shift on. He should have been by an hour or more ago with the delivery of flour. She strained her eyes, trying to pick out the telltale wobble of his cart as it clattered its way up the track to the house, but try as she might she could discern no movement. Where was he? He was the most punctual man she had ever known, some would have said punctilious, but she valued reliability. And whatever his faults may be – and the good Lord knew they were many and varied – no one could accuse him of failing to take his duties seriously. At least, not since he had forsworn strong drink.

Try as she might to avoid it, a flicker of hope flared in her breast. Maybe he was late because Dora had returned home at last. She pictured him on his cart, rattling out of the village, passing a girl walking in the opposite direction. Maybe he gave a cry of recognition, maybe it was she who cried out, but recognise each other they did. He reined in the horses and jumped down from the cart to sweep his long-lost daughter in his arms, crying with joy as she wept too, begging forgiveness for abandoning them so callously and running away to seek excitement in London.

It was a bitter-sweet daydream, but after a moment Sarah dismissed it with a shake of her head. Dora was gone, that was that. All the wishes in the world would not bring her back, but Sarah could not help pining for her. The fact of her absence was a cruelty that tugged at Sarah's heart, no matter how much time passed.

Sarah dismissed the maudlin thoughts that so often followed her more benign daydreams. Dora had left home at the first opportunity, run away like so many girls before and so many surely to come, probably to London. What fate had befallen her, Sarah would never know. She would simply have to bear the pain of her loss.

She no longer believed Lord Sweetclover responsible for Dora's disappearance. She couldn't imagine what had made her think he was. It was obviously untrue, and the memory of her suspicions made her guilty. At one point she had even believed that there was witchcraft in this house, but now the rumours she had spread caused her nothing but shame. It was so kind of Lord Sweetclover to forgive her. He really was a lovely man, and so trustworthy.

She shook her head again, as if nagged by a passing thought that had slipped from her grasp, then turned away from the doorway and stepped back into the warmth of the kitchen, ready to begin preparing breakfast. There was nothing unnatural going on at Sweetclover Hall. There was no crisis, only a late husband and a lack of flour. Anyway, she could always get a loaf from the freezer. The toaster had a setting for frozen bread, so you'd never know.

She paused at the threshold and turned back, squinting at the horizon one last time. What she saw made her shiver far more than the ice in the air.

A thin skein of smoke was rising into the low clouds.

She gasped and her hand flew to her mouth before she turned and ran into the house, shouting the alarum.

Sarah's greatest fear had been realised.

War had come to Pendarn.

* * *

Lord Henry Sweetclover was woken by Sarah's cries. There was a dull ache in his head, his bones felt heavy and old, his mouth gummy and foul. He reached over to the other side of the bed, but found it cold. This wasn't unusual. His wife was an early riser and normally left him to sleep away the morning. Last night's revelries had been particularly drunken and energetic, so he had expected that she would break her habit and lie in with him as she sometimes did on those occasions when the wine flowed freely. She had proved herself immune to most things, but a hangover was not one of them.

He rubbed his forehead, which made bright flashing lines appear behind his eyes, so he stopped that, groaned and rolled over, burying his face in the pillow, trying to blot out the noise.

He wondered what could have made his wife rise early after such a night. He thought back, trying to recall whether she had given any indication as to her intended business this day, but he could bring nothing to mind. Except, now he thought about it, she had seemed slightly out of sorts earlier the previous day. Her demeanour had worsened throughout the afternoon such that he was sure he was due a long evening of silent reproach and frosty disregard. He was pleasantly surprised when she produced the cards and the wine as the sun was setting, and even more pleased at what followed after. But on reflection there had been an edge to her revelry. A hint of determination, recklessness, enforced jollity covering some deeper worry. He dismissed the thought. She was a woman. Who knew what went on in her mind. Her moods and fancies were as mysterious to him as the sun and the moon, and he knew no good could come of trying to understand her.

Anyway, what had he expected, marrying a witch?

Footsteps clattered across the floorboards on the landing

outside but Sweetclover ignored them. The few remaining servants knew what kind of reception to expect if they knocked on his chamber door before midday, so he was confident he would be left alone.

He pulled the pillow up over his head for a second before some halfwit began banging on his chamber door.

Sweetclover growled his frustration, lifted first the pillow then his head, and bellowed, 'Cease your infernal banging or be hanged.'

The banging stopped. Grunting, Sweetclover lay down his head again. Before he could muffle it with the pillow once more, a voice called tremulously through the door.

'My lord, the mistress instructed me to tell you that you are required in the reception room. She said it was most urgent.'

That was another disadvantage to marrying a witch, he thought ruefully – the servants are more afraid of her than they are of you.

'I shall remember this, Oliver,' Sweetclover yelled as he threw off the covers and shuddered at the sudden cold. 'I can always find another stable hand, don't you worry. It would be the tiniest inconvenience to have you filleted and fed to the pigs.'

He immediately regretted yelling, as his head pounded in response. He swung his legs out of the bed and reached for the flagon of water he kept by his bedside. His wife assured him that hangovers were made worse by something called dehydration – which he understood to mean, basically, being thirsty – and had recommended water as the best remedy. He also unstoppered the glass bottle of pills that she had provided him, and swilled a couple down. He loved these tiny medicines, for they made his headaches disappear in a manner most miraculous. Another advantage of being married to a witch – her potions, poultices and pills made life considerably easier.

'Oh, and tell Goody Predennick to put the coffee on,' he shouted, hoping that Oliver was still within earshot. He was rewarded by a distant yelp of 'yes, m'lord'. A good cup of coffee was worth the pain it took to yell the instruction.

Wincing, he shuffled across the carpet to the new water closet, sloughing off his nightshirt as he did so. Then he stepped into the stone bathing cubicle, pulled the chain to start the water flowing, and took a nice, hot shower. Of all the innovations his wife had brought to Sweetclover Hall, this was his favourite. At first he had been suspicious of her desire to wash herself each day. He had thought it at best unnatural, at worst unhealthy, and he enjoyed the ripe smell of a comely woman. But his wife had insisted that he take a shower every morning, and anoint himself with strange foaming substances designed to cleanse the skin and rid him of the odours that came naturally to a healthy man. He had resisted at first, but gradually he came to appreciate the sensual pleasure of hot water, the pink freshness of his skin and the invigoration that came from an early morning deluge.

But the most important consideration was that his wife had made a daily shower a condition of intimacy. He did enjoy intimacy.

He stepped from the shower, dried himself with a piece of fresh linen, and applied the various unguents and perfumes that his wife provided. Then he enacted the other ritual upon which she insisted – he used a brush covered in a strange-tasting poultice to massage his teeth and gums until they felt smooth and clean. He found this process far less agreeable than the shower. The feeling of minty foam in his mouth made him want to gag but he had to confess that on mornings such as these it felt good once it was done, even if the process of doing it was fundamentally unpleasant. He spat out the foam and rinsed his mouth with water from the basin.

By the time he re-entered the bedchamber he was starting to feel almost well. He dressed quickly. His wife had tried to persuade him to adopt a different mode of dress, but this had been one step too far. The strange trousers and shirt she'd had their tailor prepare had not felt right to him, and she had smiled and shrugged and said OK. He suspected this was because he remained the public face of the family. Whereas she never left the grounds, he was very occasionally required to travel to Lostwithiel or Portsmouth, where strange clothes would only draw attention to his business, which she insisted remain as secret as possible.

He emerged from his bedchamber and followed the smell of coffee down the grand stairs and into the kitchen. Here he found Goody Predennick fussing over the moka pot. A small, round, mousy woman, she was an efficient and affable cook but her appearance belied an iron spine, and her curiosity regarding her daughter's disappearance had made her trouble-some for a while. His wife had seen to that, though.

'What cause had you for such loud alarums, Goody Predennick?' he asked brusquely as he helped himself to a slice of buttered toast. His hangover prevented him trying anything more substantial.

She turned, startled by his arrival, and bowed apologetically. 'Beg pardon, m'lord. There is smoke rising from Pendarn. I fear the war has reached us.'

Sweetclover walked to the door and peered out, munching thoughtfully as he noted the column of smoke that rose to meet the low, dark clouds three miles yonder. He became aware of the cook at his side, peering anxiously past him.

'And I thought I heard musket fire, sir,' she said.

Sweetclover felt a thrill of nerves in his already upset stomach. He gingerly laid the half-eaten piece of toast on the kitchen table as he spun on his heels and walked away without a word. He had been expecting this, of course. Even a land-owner as minor as himself was required to take sides these days. He had kept a very low profile for the last few years, staying at home with his wife, putting the story about that he was the model of domestic bliss, trying to stay out of it all. The truth was that he did not much care for politics or religion. Never had. He had always been rich and lazy, much to the disgust of his late parents. Until he met his wife, his philosophy had been a simple one: he fulfilled all his responsibilities assidu-ously, but nothing more. As long as he was able to hunt, drink, play cards and dally with the ladies, he was content to let the rest of the world go hang. But he had known for a while that eventually some army or another would turn up and demand to know where his loyalties lay. To that end, his wife had made preparations. He found, as he walked to the grand reception room, that he was more excited than nervous. The army's arrival provided a possible explanation for his wife's peculiar mood. She had the sight, after all. She must have foreseen the coming war and decided to deal with her nervousness in her uniquely agreeable way.

He no longer found the world of glamours, spells and sigils unusual, so he wondered what special surprises she had in store for any force that should besiege them.

He did not envy any army foolish enough to try.

20

'You need to tell me if anything looks different to when you were last here. Anything added or changed, anachronistic,' said Jana as Dora raised the binoculars to her eyes.

'Anachro . . . what?'

'Anachronistic. It means out of time. Things that shouldn't be here yet, stuff from the future.'

'Then why did you not say that?'

Jana was already assessing Sweetclover Hall and its grounds. The three-storey building was beautiful and relatively new, the height of seventeenth-century fashion. There were two huge wings jutting forward on either side of a connecting frontage which was topped by a clock tower. There were also towers at the point of intersection between the wings and the central block, making a symmetrical pattern of three spires that marked the main points of the house. From her vantage point, hidden within the woods, Jana could see that the grounds were not as well kept as she would have expected. The house was bordered on all sides by huge ornamental gardens, but they looked overgrown and unkempt. A fountain stood dry; topiary shapes, which had once been animals, had grown untrimmed until they seemed like mutant monsters; the entrance to a maze had grown so narrow that even Jana would have to squeeze through sideways.

'Whatever he's paying his gardener, it's too much,' she said.

'Those gardens were his father's passion,' explained Dora, still studying the hall. 'He died a year before I came to work here. They were magnificent then, but I see the son does not share his father's enthusiasm.'

Jana had checked the building twice but could see no evidence of security measures.

'The stables and stuff, is that round the back?' she asked.

Dora nodded. 'I can see nothing out of the ordinary,' she said, handing back the binoculars.

'Me either,' agreed Jana. 'Which makes me more worried about what we can't see. We need to find a way into that house unseen.'

'You think too much,' said Kaz, who was lying in the leaves next to them. 'We see no guards, no cameras, the house is quiet. I say we go to the back door and ask for Dora's mum.'

'Great idea,' replied Jana. She had been hoping Kaz would come out of his funk, but now he had, his impulsive excitability was bubbling up again. She found it incredibly annoying. 'Why not knock on the front door? Ask to see the big man?'

'Stop squabbling,' snapped Dora, rising to her feet. 'What a pair. There's no need to do either. Follow me.'

Dora led Jana and Kaz back into the woods. They walked a short distance until they came to a small bank of earth, overgrown with ivy and brambles.

'Help me clear this away,' said Dora as she rolled up her sleeves and began pulling the undergrowth from the bank.

Jana and Kaz looked at each other, shrugged, and joined in. Within a couple of minutes they had uncovered a small, square wooden door.

'Let me guess,' said Kaz. 'Hobbits?'

Jana slapped him on the arm but smirked.

'This is the ice house,' explained Dora. Seeing that her companions were none the wiser, she explained. 'In winter, they collect the ice from the pond and lay it down in here with straw, to use in the summer.'

'OK. But how does that help?' asked Kaz. 'I'd love a cold drink but . . .'

'There is a tunnel that runs from inside the ice house to the undercroft of the hall,' said Dora. 'If we can get this door open, we can sneak inside and nobody will know.'

Kaz stepped forward and examined the door. About four feet high, it was made of heavy oak. There was a round handle which he tugged, but the door didn't budge. He turned and shrugged. 'Stuck.'

Jana gently pushed him aside. 'Leave this to the experts,' she said, sorting through the various pieces of pistol kit attached to her belt. First she selected the powder horn, popped open the metal stopper on the thin end, and poured the black contents into the keyhole. Then she took a strip of cloth, which she explained to Kaz and Dora was patch material, normally used to help a musket ball sit safe in the barrel. She rolled it into a thin taper and inserted that into the keyhole too, to act as a fuse.

'Now I have to prime the pan,' she said, biting her lip as she poured a measure of gunpowder into the pan on her pistol. 'No powder or shot in the barrel, though. Don't want to make too much noise.' She grinned at Kaz and Dora, and gestured for them to stand back. Then she placed the pan of the pistol next to the makeshift fuse, drew back the flintlock and pulled the trigger. The pan flashed as the powder ignited, setting fire

209

to the fuse in turn. Jana stepped back and shielded her eyes as the fuse burnt down and, with a soft thump, ignited the powder in the keyhole.

'Try it now,' she said.

Although the hinges had almost rusted shut, the door swung open on the first tug. It gave an awful grinding squeal as it did so. They stood silently for a moment, waiting for someone to come and investigate. When no one did, they relaxed.

'*Voilà*,' said Jana smugly, taking a bow then rearranging her gun belt.

'Come on,' said Dora, leading the way by squeezing through the narrow gap into the cold, damp interior of the brick-lined ice house. Kaz pulled the gas lamp from the backpack, clicked it alight and followed. Jana brought up the rear, pulling the door closed behind them.

Damp straw squelched underfoot as Kaz shone the lamp around the room, which was a perfect sphere. There was a hatch in the roof, and another door on the wall opposite the one they had entered through.

'Where's the ice?' wondered Dora.

'Maybe they don't need it any more,' replied Kaz as he walked over to the interior door. 'They have drones and laser guns, I think maybe a fridge is not beyond them.'

'I know what a fridge is, that's one of those cabinets that keeps things cold,' said Dora, pleased with herself.

'You got it. How would it be powered, though? Batteries, maybe? No solar panels on the roof, no wind turbines . . .' Kaz stopped when he noticed Jana had stopped walking.

'OK, you know what?' she said. 'The more I think about drones and guards and massacre, the more stupid walking into this place seems.'

'What do you mean?' asked Kaz.

'I mean, what kind of security system is watching us now? What chance they're waiting for us? And are we really sure this is right thing to do?'

'We agreed . . .' began Dora, but Jana cut her off.

'We did,' she said. 'Before Pendarn Green. This Quil is very ruthless, and probably expecting us.'

'You have flintlocks,' said Dora.

'And they have lasers. And big, scary guard men with blue faces.' Jana shrugged. 'I don't know what I'm doing here. What are we doing?'

'One minute you want to confront our enemy, the next you want to run away and hide. Will you please make up your mind?' said Dora.

'Hey, look, I'm only seventeen, OK?' she said. 'Not a ninja. You're not a spy, either. You're a fourteen-year-old girl who should be in school. Kaz is . . . I don't know what he is. Dropout. Farmhand. Loser. But time-travelling James Bond? I don't think so.'

'Hey!' said Kaz.

Jana stared at her feet, Dora pouted.

Kaz had been expecting something like this. Nobody could witness what they had and not be affected by it. He was feeling a little shaken himself. He had expected a freakout from Dora, but she seemed to still be in a kind of delayed shock – articulate and helpful but somehow dead behind the eyes. Kaz had no doubt that a meltdown was coming but it didn't seem imminent. He was kind of impressed by the girl's emotional stamina. It took a lot of courage to go sifting through a pile of dead bodies the way she had. So it was Jana who was losing her cool instead.

'Do you have an alternative suggestion?' asked Kaz.

There was a long pause before Jana reluctantly said, 'No.'

'Look, I understand the cold feet, really I do. But back in the cavern, you were right. Yes, we've seen something horrible, but it hasn't changed the fundamental situation. We need to stick together and hold course. I think we're way past the backing-out point. We could hold hands now and . . . what? Where would we go? We can only travel together. We know there are people waiting for us in my time. And I'd be amazed if those guys who attacked you on the way to school were a coincidence, so we've got to assume they're waiting for you in your time, too. So yeah, going in here is risky. But really, what choice do we have?'

Jana studied him for a moment, then swore loudly and colourfully. 'I hate this,' she said.

Kaz punched her in the arm. 'Hang in there, champ,' he said, 'we're nearly there. Can you get the door?'

Jana walked towards the internal door and reached for her powder horn. This lock was equally easy to break but the hinges were even more rusty and it took the combined strength of all three of them to pull it open wide enough to slip through. Kaz went first, holding the gas lamp. Dora and Jana followed. The tunnel was low and narrow, lined with stone and with an arched ceiling that dripped dank water on their heads as they crept down it.

'No one's used this for years,' said Kaz as he led the way. 'How did you know about it, Dora?'

'My brother and I would play in these woods when we were younger. We weren't supposed to go this far from home, but on long summer days we used to take the chance. We found the ice house one day, unlocked. It was magical. We played a game here in which we pretended to be exploring the ice cave wherein Merlin was frozen. I played Morgaine and James . . .' She trailed off.

'What exactly happened with James, back in Pendarn?' asked Jana after a moment. 'You told us he was one of the soldiers, but . . .'

'I do not wish to talk about my brother,' said Dora firmly.

'As you wish.'

They continued walking through the damp, dark tunnel, the only sound their feet on the cold earth. After a few minutes they came to another locked door. Jana squeezed her way past Dora and Kaz then performed her gunpowder trick once more.

They pushed through into the undercroft of Sweetclover Hall.

Second Interlude

Cornwall, England, 1640

Sweetclover was floating in the hinterland between wakefulness and sleep when he heard the scream.

Screams were not uncommon in his house, but he preferred it when they emerged from his bedchamber, and were accompanied by laughter or moans of pleasure. This scream was high, loud and piercing. He sat upright in bed, blinking himself awake.

'Did you hear that?' he asked.

The coach master's daughter, who lay beside him, snored softly.

Sweetclover fancied the scream had the timbre of the new scullery maid's voice. He could not recall her name but she was young and comely. If she were in some distress, it might not hurt for him to come to her aid. He liked to make a good impression upon young ladies.

Sweetclover jumped off the bed, pulled a gown about himself, and hurried to the door. He grabbed a sword from his sideboard as he left the room, just in case.

The corridor was cold and the floorboards creaked beneath

Sweetclover's feet as he made his way to the top of the staircase. He peered over the balustrade, but could see nobody. He thought he heard a distant sound, as if somebody was speaking, but he could not determine its origin.

He began down the stairs and had reached the landing when a bright flash of brilliant red illuminated the entire stairwell. Sweetclover raised his hand to shield his eyes as he felt a flutter of fear. That was no earthly light. Fearing witchcraft, he paused on the landing for a moment, uncertain. If his house was under attack, it was his duty to defend it. His father had always drilled it into him that duty was not to be neglected. So he raised his sword and ran down the stairs, following the fading glow to its source, which seemed to lie down the corridor to the kitchens.

When he reached the undercroft door, which hung open, he heard a soft rasping sound drifting up from below. He leaned through the doorway and peered down the stairs, sword held out before him ready to give any scheming witch a taste of cold iron. There was a single candle lying on its side on the top step, still burning. In its dim light he made out a figure lying motionless on the steps. There was something odd about her, but he could not see clearly. He stepped through the doorway and onto the top step, bending down to pick up the candle.

The shape of the prone figure was womanly. The tattered remains of her burnt clothes were smouldering and the arrangement of her limbs told of many broken bones. Her face was so badly burnt he could discern no familiarity in it. Her chest rose and fell almost imperceptibly, her breath drawn in with only the greatest of effort.

This strange woman, who had no place in his house, was

dying, and there was nothing Sweetclover could imagine that would save her.

He stood there considering her for a moment, utterly bewildered as to his next move. Then, as if on cue, there was a second violent red flash, this time at the foot of the undercroft steps. Sweetclover stepped back and shouted in alarm as the unnatural light burnt his retinas. He raised his sword again and peered down the stairs, his vision slowly returning as the scorchlight faded.

'Boy, you gave me a shock.'

The woman who had spoken bled into Sweetclover's sight as he blinked away his temporary blindness. She was tall, with dark brown hair that cascaded past her shoulders. She wore trousers of a most uncommon fashion; cut straight and narrow, they accentuated the length of her legs and the womanly curve of her hips. Above that she wore a red velvet jacket of the kind a pageboy in a fashionable London salon might wear, above a simple white blouse.

Her height, dress and unexpected arrival were not the most unusual aspect to this visitor – her face was entirely covered by a plain white mask, broken only by two ovals for her shadowed eyes and a row of smaller holes denoting a mouth.

She peered up the stairs at Sweetclover and shook her head in a manner that seemed overfamiliar and fond. 'Honestly, Hank, you are a sight,' she said in an accent that Sweetclover did not recognise.

Sweetclover stood, facing this frankly terrifying witch over the soon-to-be corpse of another woman, barefoot, in a gown, unkempt and fresh from his bed. He brandished his sword and adopted his most impressive baritone in an attempt to salvage some dignity.

'Begone, witch, from this place,' he said.

There was a long pause, then the woman snorted and began laughing. 'Oh, man,' said the woman, bowing her head, her shoulders shaking. 'That's . . . I don't have the words. Priceless.'

'I said begone,' he said again.

The woman shook herself once and took a deep breath to stop her laughter, then strode up the stairs to the woman who lay between them. She looked the woman over and gasped in what seemed to Sweetclover to be both horror and revulsion. 'My God, look at me,' she whispered.

Ignoring Sweetclover, who stood directly above her, still waving his sword, the woman in the mask pulled a strange object from her pocket. Like a thick black plate, it was six inches in diameter, with vicious-looking spikes pointing up from the edges. The masked woman turned it so that the spikes pointed down and she slapped it hard into the unconscious woman's back. The woman spasmed once and cried out, but did not regain consciousness. The disc began to hum softly and the woman's breathing became easier and more regular.

Then the masked woman looked up and said briskly, but not without a hint of amusement, 'My name is Quil. I am a witch, but I'm friendly. Please don't be disturbed by the mask, but as you can see' – she gestured to the unconscious woman on the steps – 'my face is badly burned. I am going to ask you to help me now, and because underneath it all you are basically a lovely guy, kind to small animals, that sort of thing, you will do so without complaint.'

Sweetclover found himself lowering his sword and mutely nodding. Was he bewitched? Had she cast a glamour upon him?

'No,' said Quil, as if reading his thoughts. 'I have not put a spell on you. You're just the kind of guy who'd rather help a stranger than run her through with a big sword. Now, I've stabilised my condition. Could you help me carry me down . . . no, that's confusing you, isn't it? Please help me carry this poor woman – who is obviously not me – downstairs.'

Quil grabbed the woman's ankles and looked up at Sweetclover expectantly.

Sweetclover didn't know what to do. His head was swimming. 'I, um . . .' was all he could manage.

'Come on, Hank, time's short,' said Quil impatiently.

'My name is not Hank,' he said, still trying to retain some measure of dignity. 'It is Lord Sweetclover.'

'Your first name is not Lord. It's Henry. And where I come from, Henry is Hank. But right now this lady is dying and unless you want to try and explain a dead body as well as a missing scullery maid, then you'd better help me get her downstairs.'

Not really knowing why he was doing it, Sweetclover dropped the sword and reached forward, grabbing the prone woman by the wrists.

'One, two, three, hup,' said Quil. On her mark they lifted the woman into the air and began to negotiate their way down the small, narrow staircase.

'Why are we taking her into the undercroft?' he asked as he walked off the bottom step. 'If she is ill, she would be better in a bedchamber, where she can be attended to.'

Quil did not answer, merely steered them through the first chamber into a second. Sweetclover did not like to come down here. The house, built by his father, had been completed the year before he was born. Sweetclover had grown up here, but it had not been a warm or comforting place. The huge structure had taken years to settle and dry, so the home of his childhood had been alive with creaks and moans, sharp cracks and soft architectural sighs.

He had never felt quite at ease within its walls, his young mind full of ghostly imaginings. To him, it seemed a haunted place. His father had dismissed his boy's superstitious fears.

'This is a new house,' he would say. 'It has not yet had the opportunity to accumulate ghosts.'

Then he would add, 'Unless it's your mother. And I doubt she had the gumption to come back and haunt us.'

Sweetclover's father had never forgiven his wife for dying in childbirth. In his eyes it had proved that she lacked backbone, a deficit he often pointed out in his only child.

But as uncomfortable as the house made Sweetclover, it was nothing compared to the fears the undercroft provoked. It had been off-limits to him throughout his childhood. Used to store provisions of all sorts, it was not considered a safe place for a child as fond of running into, jumping off and bouncing around amongst things as he was. But one day, when he was six years old, a careless servant had neglected to lock the door and he had slipped down the stairs into the subterranean chambers with a single candle.

He had not been down here since that day, when he had run, screaming, out of the darkness.

'Through here,' said Quil briskly. Sweetclover, still amazed both that he was being bossed around and that he was acquiescing, did as he was bid.

They carried the prone woman through an arch into one of the long vaulted chambers that ran the length of the east wing. As they left behind the last of the illumination that bled through from the stairwell, Quil loudly said, 'Lights.'

Sweetclover cried out in alarm as the chamber was flooded with bright white light. He managed not to drop the woman, but he stopped dead and squinted, his retinas seared by the sudden shock.

'What sorcery is this?' he asked, fearfully.

'Damn,' swore Quil, almost to herself. 'Sorry, sorry. I keep forgetting you don't know this stuff yet. Um, look, this is going to be very weird for you, but I promise I will explain later. There is nothing infernal about my magics.' She said the phrase in an oddly stilted way, as if the sentence construction felt odd on her tongue.

'All magic is the work of the devil,' he replied.

'Then you're really going to hate this next bit,' replied Quil. 'Door.'

A strange noise began to emanate from the far wall. It started as a low hum that made the dirt on the floor jump about, then it rose in pitch and volume until a loud squealing filled the air.

'Banshees,' said Sweetclover, but still he held the woman tight by the wrists. The simple fact was that he was afraid to hurt her if he dropped her. His care for a wounded innocent overrode his fear.

'I know that noise,' he said, as it faded back into a hum. 'When I was a child, I came down here once. I heard it then.'

Quil nodded. 'Yeah, sorry about that. Gave you quite a fright, didn't I?'

'You? Impossible. This was twenty-five years past,' replied Sweetclover, but he could hear the fear in his voice.

'No, that was me. Sorry.' Quil shrugged apologetically. 'Had to get the lab installed while your dad was building this place. Took me months. The amount of money and time I spent bribing the builders, making sure your dad and you were out of the way when the main construction went on. Worth it, though. Popped back a few years later to check the work was all done properly, there you were creeping around, heard me open the door, caught a glimpse of me, ran off like you'd seen a ghost.'

Sweetclover searched his memory for the vision of the ghost he had seen in the undercroft as a child. In his mind she was a formless grey thing, surrounded by light.

A patch of stonework in the far wall wobbled and vanished, revealing a large oak door. Above the door was a bright light source that shone into his eyes.

And yes, looking at Quil, silhouetted against that light, he had a flash of memory, a single image clear and crisp, not fuzzed by years of half-remembrance and nightmare. It was her, in outline, turning to look at him as he dropped his candle and made to run.

'Lay her down,' said Quil. Sweetclover did so.

With the woman lying on the floor between them, her chest barely rising as her shallow breathing seemed to fade yet further, Quil used a large key to unlock the door.

She turned back, reached down to grab the woman's heels and looked up at Sweetclover expectantly. He stood for a second, trying to decide whether to run for his life. Eventually he bent down and took the woman's wrists, knowing that his curiosity about the door was overwhelming his good sense.

They lifted her again and Quil led them into an antechamber that he had never known existed.

The ceiling and walls were the same as the undercroft outside, but there were the strange sources of light placed on the wall at regular intervals, illuminating the room in a way that Sweetclover had never seen before. It lacked the soft warmth of flame-light; instead it was sharp, harsh and cold. It did not seem to him to be a welcoming sort of light.

The chamber was long and wide. Sweetclover estimated that it must run some way out into the grounds, extending far beyond the walls of the house.

It was filled with strange cabinets and tables covered in instruments and apparatus that spoke to him of alchemy.

Quil led them to a bed and together they laid the stricken woman, still unconscious, upon it.

'Thanks, Hank,' said Quil, and then she ushered him away from the bed and began to work. He stood watching as she took tubes and wires from the various cabinets that ringed the bed, and connected them to the woman. She flicked and touched the cabinets and one by one they began to glow and hum, displaying strange signs and pictures that he could not interpret.

Quil worked quickly and efficiently. Although Sweetclover had no idea what she was doing, it was clear to him that she was well practised in her dark arts.

She cut away the clothes, working gently around those areas where they were burned into the woman's flesh; she placed a kind of mask across the woman's face and connected it to another softly humming cabinet. Eventually Quil stepped back from the bed and turned to face him. Her posture spoke of tiredness, but her impassive stone face betrayed nothing.

'She'll be fine for now,' said Quil. 'I could do with a sit-down and big glass of wine and then, I promise, I'll try and explain all of this to you.' She gestured to the huge chamber and its baffling contents.

Sweetclover considered her for a long moment, and then

said, 'Very well. But be warned, if you try to bewitch me, I shall vanquish you.'

'Oh, Hank, I have every intention of bewitching you. And I do so love to be vanquished.' He couldn't see her face, but he would have sworn that she was smiling as she walked past him and out the door.

As he watched her go he noticed, for the first time, how alluring her womanly figure actually was.

He followed behind her, trying to choose between the hundred different emotions fighting to dictate his actions. He was certain of only one thing – his life would never be the same again.

Part Three

The Battle of Sweetclover Hall

21

'Hmmm, musty,' said Jana with fake relish as Kaz shone the lamp around the cool, damp undercroft. He had to stoop so his head didn't brush against the low ceiling. They stood in a small chamber which marked the intersection of three long barrel vaults which stretched away into darkness; one straight ahead, one to their left, another to the right. Each vault was packed to the brim with barrels and wooden chests, leaving only narrow aisles through which the three of them could pass. Standing in the chamber, they had a choice of three directions.

'Eeny, meeny, miny, mo . . .' began Kaz, but Jana strode off straight ahead without waiting for him to finish.

Dora hung at his shoulder. 'What was that rhyme you were reciting?' she asked.

Kaz shook his head at Jana's impatience, and started after her. 'It's a counting rhyme,' he explained as they walked. 'You use it to help make difficult choices. Like if you have three ways to go, you . . .' Kaz became aware that he was talking to thin air. He turned to see Dora standing behind him, her head cocked to one side as if listening intently. Dora held up her hand for Kaz to stop walking.

'Hey, Jana, wait,' said Kaz. Jana stopped and turned back to join him, tutting at the delay.

'Can you hear that?' asked Dora.

Kaz could hear nothing. He glanced at Jana, who shrugged.

'It is like the strange humming sound I heard in the central labratree in the future,' explained Dora.

Jana listened again. 'Ha,' she said. 'I'm so used to the constant background hum of electrical stuff, I didn't notice it.'

'To me, it does not sound natural, and it is not a sound this undercroft should be making,' said Dora firmly.

'Generator?' asked Kaz, but Jana shook her head.

'No, something else,' she said. 'It seems to be coming from underneath us.'

Kaz knelt down and placed his palm flat on the floor. There was an unmistakable vibration, soft and distant. 'There is something down there.'

'That proves it, then,' said Jana. 'Whoever was controlling those blue-faced heavies in Pendarn, and that drone, must be based in this house.'

'The woman whose touch sent me across the time bridge?' asked Dora.

Kaz nodded as he stood up. 'Quil,' he said. 'So now we're here, what do we do?'

'Dora, I think you should go and find your mother. There are some steps up ahead.' Jana pointed to where she had been heading moments earlier. 'See what she can tell us. She lives here, she must know something. We'll explore down here.'

Dora did not need telling twice. She eagerly pushed passed Kaz and Jana, hurrying for the steps.

'But be careful,' said Jana, to her back. 'Meet back here in an hour.'

'I will,' said Dora as she climbed the steps without a backward glance. A few moments after she vanished from view Kaz heard the creak of a door opening and closing as she entered the house above.

'What are we going to do?' he asked, happy to be able to slip back into his native Polish now that he and Jana were alone.

'We're going to open that door,' said Jana, grinning wildly and pointing to a wall.

Kaz stared at the blank wall, then back at Jana. 'Huh?'

'Look right,' said Jana.

Kaz did so, and saw the undercroft stretching off into darkness, piled high with barrels on both sides, leaving only a narrow aisle down the middle. 'What am I looking for?' he asked.

'Now look ahead,' said Jana.

Kaz turned, his patience wearing thin. Same thing – corridor, barrels, steps in the distance.

'Now look left.'

And sure enough, there was a break in the barrels, leaving a roughly door-sized section of wall exposed for no apparent reason.

'That,' said Jana, both smug and excited, 'is a secret door.'

'Secret door?'

'I know! Isn't that great!'

Kaz rolled his eyes. In an instant Jana had switched again, from calm leader to overexcited teenager. 'I could spend a lifetime hanging out with you and still have no clue what you're going to say next,' he said, shaking his head in amazement.

Jana batted her eyelashes, put on a sultry voice, and said, 'Sounds like the beginning of a beautiful friendship.'

Kaz couldn't formulate a sensible response. What he wanted to say was 'please make your mind up – either be analytical or overexcited, distant or flirty – but please please please stop switching from one to the other every few minutes'. What he ended up saying was, 'You're doing my head in, you are.' Which was some way short of the mark, but would do for now.

'What can I say?' Jana shrugged, her eyes sparkling with amusement. 'I'm a complicated dame.'

'Door. Secret one.'

'Right.' Jana nodded. It seemed to Kaz that she made a conscious decision to switch back to business mode and as she did so her posture, body language and facial expression changed instantly. It was as if she became someone entirely different. For the first time it occurred to him that maybe, just maybe, this girl wasn't entirely healthy in the head. Her behaviour posed too many questions for him to be entirely relaxed around her.

She stood staring at the door for a long minute as Kaz waited impatiently for her to do or say something. But she just stood and stared at the wall, as if she was going to make it turn into a door by force of will. After a while he said, 'Well?'

'I'm cycling through the spectrum; give me a moment,' said Jana.

'So, what, you can see ultraviolet and stuff?'

'The eye-mods can do all sorts of things. Zoom in to microscopic level, night vision, infrared and some more exotic stuff. They can override the visual cortex entirely if you want. Close your eyes and watch a movie in your head. If we ever end up in my time, I'll treat you to a set.'

Kaz was not sure that he particularly wanted to be able to watch films in his mind, but he didn't say so.

'Ah-ha,' said Jana. 'Hologram.'

She stepped forward and pushed her arm through the stones. Kaz gasped as her hand disappeared. She pulled it back instantly and then turned to him.

'OK,' she said. 'So there's probably some kind of password or gesture control to switch off the hologram. Luckily, we don't need that.'

'What do you . . .' but he didn't get a chance to finish his question, as Jana grabbed his hand and dragged him through the hologram after her. He flinched and raised his free arm to protect his face as he was pulled towards and then through a wall of not-really solid rock. He was relieved he managed not to yell.

The world went blurry and indistinct as he walked through the hologram, then snapped into sharp focus as he found himself standing in a doorway. In front of them was a heavy oak door, dotted with metal studs that held a criss-cross pattern of iron bands in place. It looked very solid, but it stood ajar. Beyond the door Kaz could see a large chamber. It had stone walls and a brick vault ceiling like the section of undercroft they had just left, but this new area was illuminated by light bulbs strung along the wall at regular intervals. He could not see much more through the half-open door, especially with Jana standing in front of him.

'Am I going to ask the obvious question, or are you?' said Kaz.

'Be my guest,' replied Jana, peering around the door to see what lay beyond.

'Who leaves a big secure door lying open?'

'Someone who doesn't think anyone can see it because of the hologram,' said Jana, slowly, as if talking to an idiot.

'In which case, why make it such a strong door?' said Kaz.

Jana turned back and glared at him for a moment before admitting that maybe he had a point. 'You think this is an invitation?' she asked.

'Or a trap,' he replied. 'For someone who can see through holograms.'

Jana shrugged impatiently. 'Or maybe someone just forgot to close it,' she said as she pushed through the doorway.

Kaz turned the lamp off, stashed it in the backpack again, and followed Jana. 'If I get mind-probed again,' he said as he caught up with her, 'I am blaming you.'

The chamber was wider and taller than the tunnels they had just left, so he was able to walk without stooping. He examined one of the light bulbs that were strung along the wall. It was a large glass ball with a zigzag vertical filament inside, intricate and beautiful; old-fashioned by his time, but insanely futuristic in 1645. The bulbs were strung together by a line of cable which hung off hooks in the wall. It was a strange mix of old and new technology. When he surveyed the rest of the room the sense of things being cobbled together grew stronger. Near the far wall stood a row of large wooden chests, entirely in keeping with 1645, but in the centre of the room stood a table with a Mac computer on it – not the shiny smooth white products of his time, but an old, beige box with a rainbow Apple logo on the side. The monitor, however, was something way beyond the machine it served – an oblong sheet of light which hung in the air above the desk, displaying an old screensaver of a starscape. The table was solid oak, the kind of thing Kaz would have expected to find if he ventured upstairs into the hall proper, but the chair was one of those wooden standing chairs that you loop your legs into and kind of perch on. The design was from the future, but when he examined it more closely he could see that it was freshly made and had what looked like hand-turned wooden features, presumably put there by a seventeenth-century carpenter working to a plan that had no right existing yet, unable to grasp the concept of minimalist interior decoration and believing that any round piece of wood should be shaped into something elegant.

A series of holographic screens, Kaz reckoned twenty at least, hung in an array in front of a long stretch of otherwise bare wall. He studied them closely. Three displayed what appeared to be real-time readouts of temperature, pressure and electrical output – monitoring some kind of generator? Some other monitors displayed images he couldn't identify without context – a pool of water, some kind of furnace. Most of the rest showed scenes from around the house, better quality than the CCTV he was used to, but obviously from surveillance cameras that served the same function. One showed an aerial view of a country track down which a column of soldiers were trudging; he presumed that was the feed from the drone. Were those soldiers heading this way?

'Come look at this,' called Jana. She had perched on the computer chair and was using a keyboard to scroll through various forms of information. Kaz peered over her shoulder, but could make no sense of any of it.

'What am I looking at?' he asked.

'I'm not completely certain, but some of this stuff looks like . . .' She stopped scrolling when she found a document labelled 'temporal displacement – theories and practice'. 'Now that's more like it,' she said, smiling.

But Kaz wasn't listening to her. 'Scroll back,' he said.

'No, come on, this is the good stuff,' said Jana, beginning to read the document.

'It can wait.' He shoved her roughly aside.

'Hey,' she said, but Kaz ignored her. He leaned over her shoulder and pressed the back button, scrolling back through the contents until he found what he was looking for. It was a collection of thumbnail images that had caught his eye.

'Make these bigger,' he demanded.

Jana was looking daggers at him, but Kaz was not bothered. He was sure of what he had seen. Eventually Jana spat 'Fine,' and pressed a few buttons that made the screen zoom in. The thumbnails increased in size until they could make out the faces of the people in the photographs.

'Oh, crap,' said Jana, when she realised what she was looking at.

'Yes,' said Kaz simply.

He was looking at photographs of himself, Jana and Dora. Photographs that he knew hadn't been taken yet. There he was, holding a huge gun, running towards the camera, shouting. Jana, covered in dust, a livid gash across her forehead, dripping blood into her eyes. Dora, older, hard faced, snarling. And more images, a dizzying array of soon-to-be hims, not-yet Doras and someday-maybe Janas.

After the shock had worn off, Jana mused aloud, 'No timestamp on the images, and the filenames don't give anything away. We have no idea when or where these were taken.'

Kaz leaned forward and pointed to a picture of Jana crouching behind a partially collapsed wall. 'Look at the top right of that picture.'

Jana zoomed in and whistled softly. A small patch of sky was visible above a jumble of sandy-coloured buildings. It had a brownish tinge to it like nothing Kaz had ever seen before.

Kaz and Jana exchanged a look but neither vocalised what they were thinking – it was so outrageous.

Jana moved the focus down so they could examine her face. 'It's hard to tell through the grime and the, um, blood, but I look about the same as I do now, yeah?'

Kaz nodded. 'Yes. Do you recognise the gun you're carrying?'

'Nope. Nothing like that in my time.'

They both stared at the photo for a moment, taking in the implications.

'Try that one,' said Kaz, pointing to another thumbnail. But before Jana could pull it out and enlarge it they heard a distant voice calling, 'Hello?'

Jana nearly toppled off the seat as she jumped in surprise at the unexpected interruption.

'Where did that come from?' she asked, unfolding herself from the seat.

'Hello?' came the voice again. 'Is there someone out there? Is that you, Hank?'

Kaz looked in the direction the voice had come from and saw a door in the far wall. 'Over there,' he said. He and Jana hurried to the door, but she held up a hand to stop him rushing right in.

'We have no idea who is on the other side of this door,' she said.

'Sounds like a woman,' replied Kaz.

'Still think this was a trap?' asked Jana.

Kaz shrugged. 'Let's find out.'

He pushed the door open gently and stepped into a large room at the centre of which sat a grand wooden bed. On it lay a woman. The bed was ringed by machines, many switched off. Some appeared to have been brought from the future, others seemed to be the best possible seventeenth-century equivalent of medical equipment not yet invented. A wooden pole held a bladder of some kind – literally, an animal's bladder, Kaz suspected – from which a thin tube snaked into the patient's arm; a primitive drip. A strange metal and wooden contraption with a big internal wheel could perhaps have been a sort of dialysis machine, he thought. The ECG was genuine, though, and the heartbeat of the bedridden patient was traced in glowing light on its cathode ray monitor screen, strong and healthy. There were other instruments and contraptions arranged around the room on tables and chairs.

Although lying in bed, the woman was dressed for outside, even down to a pair of sturdy boots, and her trousers had numerous bulging pockets. She also had some kind of helmet on, completely enclosing her head. It was red and polished smooth, as if made of plastic or ceramic. It hummed softly, and there was a little green light blinking near the neck, indicating that it was doing whatever it was supposed to be doing.

'Hello?' she asked again. Her voice was strong and clear, but she spoke English with an accent Kaz had never heard before. There was a bit of American in it, he thought, but something else that he couldn't quite pin down.

'Should we speak to her?' said Kaz.

Jana shrugged.

Obviously perturbed by the lack of response, the woman reached up a hand to grab a cord that hung from the ceiling. At the end of the cord was a small switch with a red button on it, the kind they had in hospitals so the patient could call for a nurse. Kaz leapt forward, determined to stop her raising the alarm. The backpack slipped off his shoulder as he dived across the bed and grabbed the woman's hand. He was conscious of Jana shouting at him to be careful, but he couldn't hear her properly because of the roar in his ears. He immediately realised

236

his mistake and tried to release his grasp, but it was too late. He heard the woman cry out as he was engulfed in red fire and the room began to fade around him.

Just as Dora had been, he was flung into time by the touch of the woman from the future. And he was powerless to stop it.

Jana watched in horror as both Kaz and the woman on the bed glowed and vanished. The release of energy was enormous; screens flared, machines sparked and shut down in a storm of mini-explosions. Jana was thrown backwards and slammed into the wall. She pulled herself upright and then sat there, senses reeling, wondering what she was supposed to do now.

22

Sarah worked the soft dough on the wooden tabletop, her hands mechanically going through motions she didn't even have to think about any more. Push, fold, add some water, push, fold, add some flour. The tactile squish of dough between her fingers felt like safety. The fire warmed her back, and the smell of the slowly roasting chicken that hung on the spit above it made her mouth water. As long as there was bread to make, and chicken roasting above an open fire, she could pretend that her world was the same as it had always been, that the war was still far, far away from her door. When she judged the dough ready she placed it in the cloth-lined wicker basket and left it to prove. She rubbed her hands to remove the clinging specks of gooey dough and flour, then wiped them on her apron as she turned to see a silhouette in the internal doorway and gave a small yelp of surprise.

'Ooh, you gave me quite a . . .' She trailed off in amazement as the silhouette stepped forward and she saw her daughter's face for the first time in five years.

Sarah's eyes went wide and then rolled back up into her head as she gasped in surprise and her legs began to crumple beneath her. Dora darted forward but she was not fast enough to catch her collapsing mother. A man Dora had not noticed was close enough, and fast, too. He had been sitting at the kitchen table, Dora's view of him obscured by her mother. His chair crashed to the floor behind him and he grunted with effort as he lunged forward just quickly enough to get his hands beneath Sarah's shoulders and ease her gently to the floor.

It took Dora a moment to recognise her mother's rescuer as her fellow captive from the green. He looked up at her, did a double-take and then smiled.

'It gives me joy to see you again, young lady,' he said. His voice was croaky and raw; a side effect of his botched hanging.

'And I you, sir,' replied Dora, kneeling beside her mother, who lay still. 'She is quite insensible. I fear my appearance was too great a shock for her senses to bear.'

'It would be best to leave her to recover her wits in her own time,' said Mountfort. 'Waking people from such a swoon can result in great distress.'

Dora looked around the kitchen for something soft to place beneath her mother's head. As she did so she registered a number of items that seemed similar to the kind of things she had seen in the future, including a silver machine with two slots in the top and a cable running from the base, a box with a glass window beside a panel of numbers, and a tall white cabinet that was surely a fridge. Filing these anomalies away for later investigation, she spotted a spare apron hanging by the door, rose to collect it, then folded it into a makeshift pillow. She handed it to Mountfort, who placed it beneath Sarah's head and rose to his feet as Dora resumed kneeling by her unconscious mother.

'May I ask why your arrival occasioned such alarm?' he asked as he righted his chair and sat down again.

'It has been many years since my mother has seen me,' explained Dora. 'I think she believed me dead.'

She looked at her mother's face. There were many new lines, especially on her forehead and around her eyes. They were not lines worn by countless smiles, but betrayed years of frowning worry. Her hair, once so brilliantly blonde, was now almost entirely grey. Dora guessed that her disappearance was the most likely cause of such marked changes in her mother's countenance. This thought brought her father to mind. So fraught had their reunion been that she had not fully registered the changes time had wrought upon him. Now she thought back on it, he too had been aged prematurely by the last few years, his eyes deeper set, his hairline in full retreat across his scalp. She felt tears come to her eyes but wiped them away immediately, unwilling to let Mountfort see her cry.

'I must thank you for your kindness towards me in Pendarn,' she said, careful to keep her voice from wavering.

'You are most welcome,' replied Mountfort. 'I had no wish to die, but I was unwilling to purchase my survival at the cost of your own. I am a soldier, of sorts, and a violent death is likely inevitable. But a girl such as yourself has no place at the end of a hangman's rope.'

'It was kind of you,' replied Dora. 'I am ashamed of the spectacle I made of myself. I would not have you believe that the things I said were true.'

Mountfort laughed. 'I have seen many strange things in my life, not least this day, but even I have not yet witnessed – what was it you said? – a black goat walking upon its hind legs singing lullabies composed of baby screams. You have a most creative imagination.'

Dora was mortified to hear her desperate lies memorised

240

and repeated. 'I would be grateful if you would forget what I said, or at the least never refer to it again,' she said.

'As you wish,' he replied with a gracious nod. 'We were not, I believe, formally introduced when last we met. My name is Richard Mountfort, humble servant of the Crown, and your good self.'

He gave a small, seated bow.

'Dora Predennick,' said Dora. 'Scullery maid of this house. Once. Now I do not know what I am. Let us say I am a traveller and leave it at that.'

'A woman of mystery. How delightful.'

'How came you to be sharing this kitchen with my mother?'

'I was on my way here when I was apprehended by those ruffians and accused of being a spy, correctly as it happens,' he explained. 'Once I had gained my freedom I resumed my course and made for my intended destination – this house, and the hospitality of your fine mother's kitchen. I carry an urgent message for your master. One of the servants has been dispatched to inform him of my arrival. While I wait at his pleasure, your mother kindly furnishes me with food, drink and good company.'

Dora appraised her new friend. She reckoned him to be mid-thirties, with black hair and dark eyes that sparkled with a gentle, lascivious wit. His lips were thin, but curled up at the edges in a permanent sardonic grin. He gave the impression, she thought, of being an honourable libertine. His hair, moustache and beard were wild and unkempt, as if he had taken his disguise as a peasant a step too far; Dora knew many farm labourers, and they generally had more self-respect than to traipse around looking as if they had been dragged through a hedge backwards. This was a well-to-do man playing at dress-up, and none too well. Dora found the combination of artless pretend, base cunning and flirtatious charm oddly attractive. She did not consider him an immediate threat. In fact, he might make a useful ally. She would never trust him, but she was not sure she would ever trust anybody again, not after what had happened to James.

'The young man who apprehended you,' she asked urgently. 'Did you see what became of him?'

'The whelp?' Mountfort's voice dripped contempt. 'I think perhaps I saw him running for the woods when the blue-faced devils began their advance.'

Dora felt a surge of relief. That meant he was probably still alive, which meant there was a chance he could be turned from the path he had taken.

'Did I hear right . . . he is your brother?' asked Mountfort.

Dora nodded. 'He is. James.'

'I would think you glad to see him burn, given how shamefully he used you.'

'I would have thought so too,' agreed Dora. 'But I find that I cannot wish him ill.'

'Foolishness,' said Mountfort shortly. 'Do not let it cloud your judgement should you encounter him again. There was no spark of human kindness left in that boy, and family loyalties mean little nowadays.'

Sarah gave a soft moan and Dora, who was holding her hand, clasped it more tightly.

'On the contrary, sir,' replied Dora. 'They mean more now than they ever did.'

His face betrayed his scepticism. 'Sentiment will get you killed,' he said.

'I would be grateful if you would not mention James to my mother when she wakes,' Dora said. 'She knows nothing of his current whereabouts or affiliations.'

Mountfort nodded graciously. 'As you wish.'

Dora leaned forward and softly called her mother's name, stroking her hair as she did so.

Sarah's eyes flickered open and for a moment they roved, senseless, before focusing on her daughter's face.

'Mother, it is your daughter. I have returned,' said Dora, now unable to stop the tears from welling over and running down her cheeks.

'Dora?' muttered Sarah, her drowsiness fading into excited disbelief. She sat up and pulled Dora into a soft, floury embrace that smelt like childhood. For the second time that day, Dora held a parent as they wept for joy. This time there was nobody chasing after her, so there was little opportunity for Dora to dodge the barrage of questions her mother fired at her. All she could do was try to make her mother the centre of attention.

'You've had a shock, Mother,' she said, trying to help Sarah to her feet. 'Come, sit down.'

But Dora's attempts to cluck and fuss her mother into momentary quiet were an abject failure. Sarah brushed her daughter's hands away and rose to her feet unaided.

'Sweet child, I am not a cripple nor a halfwit to be cosseted so,' she said as she arranged her clothes and straightened her hair. It seemed to Dora that her mother's immediate shock and joy were already beginning to shade into anger at her daughter's unexplained five-year absence. Dora wasn't surprised. She had little choice but to take a seat and endure the interrogation, pointedly ignoring Mountfort's obvious amusement.

Sarah sat herself in a chair directly facing Dora and reached out to take both her hands. 'Now, child,' she said, 'you must tell me where you have been.'

'I . . .'

'And no stories, mind. I am a grown woman. I know the ways of the world and although you still look exactly like the girl who left, five years have passed and you are a woman now too. So be honest with me. Was it a man?'

Dora answered 'Yes' even before she had consciously decided to lie. But once the word was out of her mouth, she was sure she had done right. The last thing her practical mother would accept was the truth. Dora was still not sure she accepted it herself – the events that had overtaken her since she had last stood in this kitchen increasingly seemed like some kind of fever dream. Were it not for the out-of-time kitchen appliances that sat so incongruously amongst the copper pots and pans, she would almost be able to believe she had imagined it all.

Sarah tutted and shook her head. 'You silly, silly girl,' she said. 'I thought it must be. Well, what is his name?'

Dora hated lying, but she gritted her teeth and willed herself to do so. 'Kaz,' she said eventually, silently begging her travelling companion's forgiveness for dragging him into her deception.

'Kaz? What kind of name is that?' exclaimed Sarah.

'He is a traveller from the east. That morning he passed by the house and knocked on the kitchen door in hope of provisions.'

Sarah pursed her lips and regarded Dora sternly. 'Did he force his affections upon you?'

'Oh no, nothing like that.' Dora felt awful as the next lie passed her lips. 'He . . . he stole my heart with a glance and we ran away in search of adventure.'

Mountfort sniggered, but the double daggers flashed at him by two generations of Predennick women silenced him instantly.

Sarah shook her head wearily. 'Am I a grandmother?' she asked after a moment.

'No,' replied Dora, trying but failing not to sound outraged.

'Oh, I see. He has deserted you.'

'He has not,' scolded Dora, unsure why she was so annoyed on behalf of a mostly imaginary lover. 'He is nearby. I returned this day because it was not possible for me to return earlier. I did not wish to leave without saying goodbye but . . . oh, I do not know what I can say to you. I am sorry for the pain and worry I have caused, but please believe me, it was not done cruelly.'

Sarah withdrew her hands from her daughter's and sat more straight in her chair. 'Well, it is not only me to whom you must apologise. For a time after you left Lord and Lady Sweetclover were suspected of involvement in your vanishing. There was much gossip abroad, and their names were blackened for a time.'

Dora was surprised that her mother was accepting her lies so easily, but even more so by the sudden change of focus to Lord Sweetclover. Especially since the conversation she had overheard in the church had led her to believe that it was Sarah herself who had spread such stories.

'Gossip, Mother?' she asked.

Sarah nodded primly. 'Wicked lies were spread. I never believed them. I knew that they could never be guilty of such a crime.'

Dora would have accepted 'I felt in my heart that you couldn't be dead' or 'I dared not believe such a fate had befallen my beautiful girl'. But 'I knew Lord Sweetclover was too nice to murder you'? That did not sit well with Dora at all. She struggled to construct a suitable rejoinder, but something about her mother's eyes brought her up short.

'Mother, did you not, perhaps, spread such tales yourself?' she asked.

Sarah's face was a picture of outrage. 'Most certainly not!' she cried.

In a flash, as if someone had switched on one of those instant electrickery lights, Dora realised that her mother was not in her right mind. Dora had never been able to lie to her mother, and nor had anybody else; she had been too quick witted for that. Yet now she was accepting Dora's clumsy deceptions with the easy faith of the truly stupid. What's more, she was bowing and scraping to her social superiors with a subservient zeal that Dora did not recognise, and seemed unable to remember actions that her old neighbours had referred to in Dora's earshot earlier that day. Her mother had never been anybody's lapdog, nor had she ever been scatterbrained. Dora realised someone must have bewitched her mother to be more easily led, less curious and assertive; someone who had played tricks with her memory. Dora decided to play along.

'You speak of a Lady Sweetclover?' she asked.

Sarah leaned back in her chair and folded her hands, her preferred attitude for a good gossip. 'Oh yes. The kindest lady I have ever known. She met Lord Sweetclover shortly after you disappeared. Well, I should rather say after you left, now that we know what became of you. I must own, I greeted her less amiably than I should have. The thought shames me.'

Dora was incredulous but saw an opportunity to obtain useful information. Playing on her mother's bewitched pliability, eyes wide and innocent, she guilelessly began asking pointed questions.

'But Mother,' she said, 'it is not like you to be so unwelcoming. What was it about the mistress that caused you to act in such a way?'

Sarah leaned forward, conspiratorially. Dora was aware that

Mountfort was doing the same, but refused to make eye contact with him lest his grin of amusement break the concentration she required to keep a straight face as she dissembled so.

'Well, there was an accident many years ago. Milady is badly burned. Disfigured, in fact. She wears a mask made of stone to hide her features, walks with a mighty limp and covers her baldness with a wig. I, foolish flibbertigibbet that I be, surmised that she was a witch who had, by use of infernal magics, escaped a burning stake and taken refuge here, enchanting Lord Sweetclover to fall in love with her despite her disfigurement. My belief was that she had done away with you, perhaps because she considered you a potential rival for Lord Sweetclover's attentions. And I did not stint to spread this scandalous rumour to all and sundry.'

'Mother!'

'I know, sweet child. All I can say in my defence is that I was not of sound mind for a period of time after your departure. Eventually the mistress sought me out and, while she would have been justified in sending me away, even taking action against me, she instead explained her situation and showed me, by her kindness, how wrong I had been in my opinion of her.'

'She sounds a most patient and understanding mistress,' said Dora.

'Oh yes, she is the kindest lady I have ever known.'

The repetition of this phrase was not lost on Dora.

'And what exactly was her situation? How did she come by those burns?'

'An overfilled bed warmer set her sheets alight. It was a miracle she survived. And it is a miracle that Lord Sweetclover should be able to love her in the state she is in, but love her he most assuredly does.'

Dora could not help wondering whether Sweetclover had been bewitched by Quil, much as her mother clearly had. But something about the way he had spoken of his wife in the future made Dora think otherwise. Unlikely as it seemed, perhaps they truly were in love.

'You must apologise to both of them for your impulsive abandonment of your station,' instructed Sarah sternly. 'Perhaps, if you are sufficiently abject, they may agree to let you resume your post. Would you like that, my dear? To work alongside me in this kitchen?'

Dora could think of nothing she would detest more.

'Certainly, Mother,' she said. 'If you would introduce me to them, I will provide a full explanation and apology.'

Mountfort rose to his feet. 'I am sorry, ladies,' he said. 'Fascinating as this discourse is, I can wait for this tardy servant no longer. I must seek out the lord of this house and relay my message. If you will excuse me.' He bowed to each of them in turn and left.

As soon as he was gone, Dora explained that she would go with Mountfort and take the opportunity to apologise to Lord Sweetclover for her disappearance. Sarah tried to stop her, told her she would do better to wait here and let her handle it, but Dora would not be turned aside. Leaving her mother with a promise to return shortly, she hurried out in pursuit of Mountfort. Following the sound of voices, she scurried down the corridor towards one of the rooms off the main entrance hall. She crept up to the door and discovered she could hear what the two were saying. Lord Sweetclover was rebuking Mountfort.

'. . . for my servant to fetch you to me in good time. I do not take kindly to being interrupted in my private chambers by a man unannounced and, regardless of his claims to the contrary, seeming to be no more than a common farmhand.'

'My apologies, your lordship,' replied Mountfort, affecting a moderately convincing tone of genuine contrition. 'But the intelligence I bring is most urgent.'

There was a long pause. Dora imagined Sweetclover considering Mountfort disdainfully. 'Very well,' said Sweetclover eventually. 'Say your piece.'

'My lord. I am an agent of the king. Tasked with bringing you both a warning, and a request.'

'Out with it then,' snapped Sweetclover.

'First the warning, your lordship. There is a large parliamentarian force marching upon this house even as I speak. They believe you to be a Royalist sympathiser and will demand a statement of allegiance from you. If you do not swear to their cause, and allow them to billet their soldiers here to prepare for the forthcoming battle which is sure to occur in or around Lostwithiel in the coming weeks, then they will take this house by force.' He fell silent, as if waiting for a response. After a few moments, when none was forthcoming, he pressed on. 'Secondly, the request.' Mountfort cleared his throat and Dora could tell by the changed tone of his voice that he was nervous. 'Reports have reached the court of witchcraft and magic being performed in this house. Your sovereign would like to know whether these stories hold any truth.'

A long pause, and then, 'And if they do?'

'Then I am tasked with asking whether you would be willing to lend your particular skills to the king's cause.'

Another pause and then a rising tide of laughter from Sweetclover. He laughed long and hard for at least a minute until he caught his breath. 'The king wishes me to use magical powers upon the soldiers of Parliament's army?'

'If such would please you, sir.'

'This is most strange, think you not, my dear?'

Dora gasped as she realised that Sweetclover's wife was also in the room. 'It is so, husband,' came a female voice. Dora could not tell whether it was the same voice that had called her name before its owner had flung her across the years, for it was muffled. Dora remembered that Lady Sweetclover wore a mask, which would explain the strange muted quality of her voice. This, Dora felt certain, must be Quil.

'I am able to set your mind at rest on one matter,' said Quil. 'The force you describe was earlier today destroyed utterly by a cadre of men loyal to this house.'

'Do you mean the soldiers in Pendarn, milady?' asked Mountfort.

'I do.'

'Unfortunately, I regret to inform you that they were merely a scouting party. A far larger force is right behind them. But I must thank you. If not for the intervention of your . . . unconventional militia, I fear my life would have been lost. The arrival of your men provided the opportunity for us to escape.'

'I am glad of that, at least. But perhaps you can answer one nagging question,' said Quil.

'If I am able, milady.'

'The oak tree on the green. It had been cut through at an unusual angle. And there were bodies by the church, which seemed to have been sliced in half. Can you shed any light on this?'

'I regret that I cannot,' said Mountfort. 'I was hanging by the neck when the tree collapsed and began to burn. My attention was focused strictly on my imminent demise. As for the bodies, I did hear a terrible scream, but I was fleeing in the opposite direction at the time, so cannot testify as to its cause.'

Dora could not be sure what happened next, but she fancied she heard Quil give a groan, and then Sweetclover began expressing concern, telling her to sit down. Had the woman suffered a dizzy spell?

'I am quite all right, Hank, stop fussing,' said Quil. But she sounded far from well. 'If you gentlemen will excuse me, I have to attend to something urgently.'

Dora heard footsteps hurrying towards the door. She had no time to make it back to the kitchen, so desperately looked around the hall for a place of concealment. Seeing nothing behind which she could hide, she hurried to the door of the room that sat on the other side of the entrance hall and slipped inside. She heard the door to the opposite room swing open, and footsteps moved away down the corridor.

Dora risked peeking around the door, but she was too late to catch a glimpse of the elusive Quil. She could hear Mountfort and Sweetclover talking still, and decided it was time to return to her mother and get her away from Sweetclover Hall. With luck they could intercept her father on the way here with the flour delivery and make their escape before the house was attacked. As quietly as she could, she slipped back into the hallway.

Moments later she burst into the kitchen. Her mother was taking a jug of milk from the fridge as if doing so were an entirely normal thing for a seventeenth-century servant.

'Mother, come quickly,' Dora shouted breathlessly. 'We have to leave. The hall is about to come under attack.'

Sarah turned to her daughter, jug in hand, bemused. 'Beg your pardon, dear?' She did not seem particularly alarmed.

'Mother, come on,' urged Dora, stepping across to her, prising the milk jug from her grasp and replacing it in the fridge. 'The forces of Parliament bear down upon us and we must flee for our lives.'

Sarah shook her head and smiled. 'Oh, don't be silly, dear. His lordship and her ladyship will allow no harm to befall us. Sweetclover Hall is the safest place in the whole of England. Besides, I couldn't leave now – the bread's nearly proven and I need to pop it in the oven.' She spoke to her daughter as if addressing a foolish girl afraid of spiders.

'Mother,' said Dora, stepping forward and putting a hand on her mother's arm, 'when was the last time you left the hall? Stepped outside, visited with neighbours in Pendarn?'

Sarah looked at Dora as if she were mad. 'Leave the hall? Heavens, child, why on earth would I ever want to leave the hall?'

Rescuing her mother was going to be even harder than Dora had expected. Sarah pulled away and began to rub flour on her hands preparatory to lifting the dough from the proving basket, carrying on as though her long-lost daughter were not begging her to escape, as if no attack was imminent. For a moment Dora seriously considered knocking her mother out and dragging her away, but Sarah was a round, matronly woman and Dora thought it unlikely she'd be able to pull her farther than the threshold. She tried desperately to think of some other inducement, some story that would exert a strong enough pull on her mother to get her from the hall.

And then the answer, so obvious, occurred to her.

'Mother, listen. I saw James this morning. In the village.'

Sarah looked up sharply. 'James?' she said.

'James, your son, my brother. I saw him in Pendarn not an hour after sunrise.'

'James?' Sarah said wonderingly, as if it the name were a lost memory, tantalisingly beyond recall.

'Like me, he has returned to make amends to you and Father for the grief he caused by his sudden disappearance. Even now, he waits for us at home. I was sent to bring you to him.'

'James is returned?'

'Yes, Mother,' she said. 'If you would but come with me, our family can be reunited once more.'

Sarah brushed off the flour and stood back from the table. 'James is with Thomas in Pendarn, even now?'

'Yes, Mother,' said Dora, trying not to let her frustration show. The spell that held Sarah in thrall was a strong one, and if the love of a mother for her child could not break it, nothing could.

Sarah's face was a parade of confused emotions. Finally she smiled. 'That is wonderful news, Dora. You must hurry home and fetch them to me. The bread will be baked by the time they arrive and we can have a hearty meal.'

Dora gave a groan of frustration. There was no way she was getting Sarah out of here. She stood still, hands balled into fists, utterly at a loss.

Someone ostentatiously cleared their throat behind her. She turned to see Sweetclover and Mountfort standing in the doorway. Thinking quickly, Dora decided to play innocent. She bowed her head in deference. 'My lord, please forgive my intrusion.'

Sweetclover waved her obsequiousness away. 'On the

contrary, I am the intruder here, in your mother's wonderful kitchen. Is that not so, Mrs Predennick?'

Dora was horrified to see her mother put her hand across her mouth and giggle, girlishly.

'Hello, Dora,' said Sweetclover. 'Welcome back. You've been away for a very, very long time.' The way he said those words forbade any further pretence. His tone was light, but laced with menace.

'You already said that,' replied Dora.

'I beg your pardon?'

'The last time we met, you spoke those very words to me.'

'I think you must be mistaken, young lady.'

'I seem to be mistaken about most things, this day,' said Dora wearily. 'My mother's character, my brother's love, the decency of my betters.'

'Dora.' Sarah's voice was sharp with rebuke.

'Oh, be quiet, Mother,' snapped Dora, her impatience and frustration finally boiling over. 'You are bewitched. It is a plain as the nose upon my face.' She felt almost ashamed as her mother's cheeks bloomed pink with embarrassment and outrage.

Ignoring her mother's confusion and anger, Dora turned to Sweetclover. 'What have you done to her?' she said, her voice full of fury.

Sweetclover regarded her coolly. 'After your unfortunate disappearance, your mother offered her services as our cook,' he explained, his voice calm and even. 'We accepted, but cookery was the farthest thing from her mind. She asked awkward questions and prowled around the house, peering into places where she was not welcome, spreading vile gossip about us to local tradesmen. Eventually it became necessary to perform what my wife terms "behaviour modification". In terms that you will understand, we put a spell upon her to make her more biddable.'

Dora was shocked at Sweetclover's lack of remorse.

'You will change her back immediately,' she said, placing her hands upon her hips and glaring at him.

'I do not understand what is happening,' said Sarah, her voice small and uncertain. Dora turned back to see her mother looking so lost it made her heart ache.

'Mountfort,' snapped Sweetclover, all attempt at charm abandoned and replaced by brisk command. 'Follow me and bring these two with you.'

He spun on his heels and walked away.

'Goodman Mountfort,' said Dora, 'I feel sure you will not partake in this madness. My mother and I must . . .'

But at some point in the preceding ten minutes Mountfort had acquired a sword, which he now drew and levelled at Dora. 'I am sorry, girl, but Lord Sweetclover has pledged aid to the king's cause. Consequently, I am now under his command.' He gestured towards the undercroft door with the blade of his weapon. 'If you two would precede me.'

Dora turned to her mother, who was standing by the kitchen table, hands coated in flour, looking lonely and afraid. Dora reached up and placed a hand on her shoulder. 'Come, Mother,' she said. 'Our master requires our presence. Let us walk together.'

Sarah allowed herself to be led and, at the point of Mountfort's sword, she and her daughter descended the undercroft steps.

23

Reeling from Kaz's sudden disappearance, and that of the mysterious patient whose touch had sent them both spinning off into time, Jana momentarily had no idea what to do next. She sat with her back against the cold stone wall and tried to gather her thoughts. She knew she hadn't got long before she was discovered; if the bedridden patient was being monitored so closely by various machines, it was likely that someone had received an alert when the patient vanished. Deciding that her best course of action was to rendezvous with Dora upstairs, she pulled herself to her feet, grabbed Kaz's discarded backpack and hurried back out into the main chamber, heading for the door. She was halfway across the chamber when she heard the distant clack of footsteps coming down the undercroft stairs.

Desperately she spun through 360 degrees, looking for an exit or a place of concealment. The anteroom she had just left would be the first place someone would search, so she discounted it immediately. The only hiding place it offered was under the bed, and the humiliation of being found cowering there would be intolerable. Her gaze lighted on a door in the farthest corner so she ran towards it. As she approached she realised that it was an elevator. With nowhere else to run, she pushed the button as soon as she reached it, praying that the car didn't have to travel far. Her luck was in, and the door opened immediately. She stepped inside the spartan, functional carriage. It was made of wood, and was lit by a single light in the ceiling. Beside the door was a simple control panel. There wasn't a lot of choice – there were two buttons, up and down. The up was already lit. She hit the down button and the door closed silently. She was thankful for that, and for the noiseless descent that then began; the quieter it was, the greater the chance her descent would remain undetected by whoever was about to arrive in the chamber she had just vacated.

The journey was smooth but slow, so Jana took the opportunity to prime her pistols in case she was jumping from the frying pan into the fire. Allowing the chip to take control of her actions, she performed the task as if she had done it a thousand times. She half-cocked the pistol, pushed the striker forward, primed the pan with gunpowder, locked the striker, poured gunpowder down the barrel, dropped the ball after it, pulled the ram out of the pistol stock and used it to push down a plug of wadding. Then she replaced the ram, fully cocked the pistol, and repeated the process on the other gun. She had just completed her task and adopted a stance with legs apart and her brace of pistols aimed forward ready for firing when the elevator juddered to a halt and the door opened to pitch darkness.

She stood still for almost a minute, waiting for something or someone to come looming in on her from the gloom, but nothing and nobody did. Deciding that she had better get out of the elevator in case it auto-returned to the undercroft, Jana uncocked the pistols, stashed them in her belt and pulled the lamp from the backpack. She clicked it on and stepped out onto smooth, wet rock. The elevator door closed behind her but there was no indication whether the carriage was rising or remaining in place.

The air was cold and damp and even in the feeble light of the lamp, which was beginning to run out of gas, Jana had a good idea where she was. She could see that there were lights strung along the rock wall behind her so she cast about for a switch and eventually found one on the cable itself. She flicked it. As the bulbs flickered into life one by one, she was rewarded with a sweeping panoramic view of a vast cavern. She surveyed the vista, whistling softly at the enormity of it.

She knew where she was.

She lacked the words to describe a space so big. The edges were so distant that she had to use her eye-mods to make out the details of the stasis pods that lined the farthest wall. When she, Kaz and Dora had briefly stopped here to catch their breaths on the way to 1645, they had known it was large, but they hadn't grasped the true enormity of it. The cavern was a huge dome with a floor that gently sloped inwards to the centre where a large rock sphere sat, as if a giant marble had been dropped into the cavern and rolled to the lowest point. As Jana cycled through the spectrum she saw that it was giving off a faint glow of radiation, as if it had been daubed with fluorescent paint.

She used her eye-mods to take measurements and established that the cavern was a fraction shy of two miles wide, almost perfectly circular, with the apex of the dome being half a mile high, exactly above the lowest point. There was a mathematical precision to the dimensions of this cave which demonstrated that it was not natural; this space had been made somehow.

To Jana's left was a collection of wooden buildings that

gave out a hum she could feel through her feet. This must be the source of the vibration they had detected earlier, in the undercroft above. Apart from these buildings, the cavern was entirely given over to thousands upon thousands of stasis pods, which lined the entire circumference of the cavern and were stacked ten high. Jana could see that only a fraction of the pods were occupied, those closest to the elevator door; she reckoned about a thousand or so had people – or whatever – inside them. She was pretty certain that there had been more occupants last time she had been here, so she mentally flagged her previous visit as taking place at some point in the future.

Jana walked over to the wooden buildings and pushed through a simple door into a room dominated by a large polished metal container with doors like a closet or cabinet, about two metres high. It sat in the centre of the floor, humming with power. A collection of cables ran from its base out through holes in the wall. Jana pushed through three similar buildings, all housing the same sort of metal cabinets. She knew what they were – cold-fusion generators. Stable, powerful and, if configured correctly, capable of maintaining the stasis pods for millennia. It would have been possible for Quil to create generators such as these quite easily at any point in history, once she had collected the right raw materials. So that explained how she was generating power in Sweetclover Hall, and what she was using it for. Which only left the bigger question: *why*?

Slipping back into the cavern, Jana walked past the last of the generator buildings to the point where the stasis pods began and examined one carefully. In a conventional pod the cocoon would be made of metal, shaped roughly to mimic the figure of a human being, sealed on top with a strengthened glass cover. But for these pods, the shape of a human had been cut into the rock walls of the cavern itself, and the glass cover had been placed over the top and somehow fused into the rock. The glass was mottled and uneven, definitely not mass produced or brought from the future.

It was an ingenious solution to the problem of time, energy and resources; in the past, Quil would have had less of all, so she would have needed to figure out another way to create the pods. And she had. Even so, it must have taken a team of workers decades to carve all the alcoves, even if the correct tools had been procured from the future to speed up the work.

There were lifetimes of backbreaking effort implicit in the existence of these pods.

Jana knew enough about the science of cryogenics to know that the pods should have been flooded with some kind of gas, but she could see no evidence of it. Perhaps it was just not visible. She turned her attention from the pod to its occupant. Male, short, stout, naked. His face and body were covered with intricate indigo tattoos which, now she could see them up close, were obviously Celtic. She glanced around. All the occupants nearby were similarly decorated. These were Celtic tribesmen from Britain's distant past, frozen in time for – Jana whistled as she realised – about a thousand years. The scale of Quil's operation took her breath away. She had been assuming that 1640 was as far back as Quil travelled, but it seemed she had been active in, around and beneath the site of Sweetclover Hall for at least two thousand years. Building this chamber, equipping it to store warriors and then freezing them down here to wait . . . for what?

She skirted the edge of the chamber for a while, examining the frozen men. In one pod the occupant was clearly dead, mummified by the hermetically sealed cocoon. His tongue was black, his fingers were raw and there were streaks of dried blood on the inside of the glass where he had tried to claw his way free. There was dried spittle on his lips. His cloudy eyes bulged in terror, staring through the rough layers of silicate that separated him from the air he needed. There was no way of knowing how or why he had not been preserved like his fellow tribesmen. Jana shuddered and moved on.

After a while the Celts were replaced by men without tattoos, which made them far harder to date. But assuming they were placed in here chronologically, Jana thought she could see ranks of Vikings, Romans, Normans and many other tribes and ethnicities. All the knowledge, about periods of history, peoples and places that were of no interest to her and which she had never studied, was provided by her chip. She was now certain that it had been hacked before she left home; she had suspected as much when she had discovered it was full of English Civil War trivia. Someone had filled it with the information she would need to make sense of her travels through time – historical info, weapons training, Polish. She could only assume that it had been some ally or other, maybe Steve. Whoever it had been, she was grateful but wished they could have done something more useful, like perhaps warned her to stay at home instead.

Jana decided she had seen enough. There was a small army down here, and room for lots more recruits to come. It was clear that whatever else she was doing, Quil was playing a long, long game. But there was nothing else for Jana to learn.

She returned to the elevator and sat by the door, trying to decide what to do next. She was trapped. There was no way out except back up in the elevator, where there were almost certainly people lying in wait. She felt suddenly hopeless. When she'd fallen through time it had all seemed so exciting, such an adventure. After the cold sterility of her home, her distant parents, the hateful school, the parade of faceless security guards who dogged her every moment of every day, the expectations, the requirements, the arguments and rebellions and all the tedious, predictable stuff that goes with being a teenager, all of it made a hundred times worse because of her parents' political profiles . . . after all that, time travel had seemed like the most wonderful gift she could have been given.

There was no more complete form of escape. Nobody in 2013 or 1665 was likely to say, 'Oh, you're *that* Yojana Patel!' with the normal mixture of curiosity, disapproval and sycophancy that most people oozed when they found out who she was. Lost in time, she could be herself, free of it all.

Plus, it was not only time travel – she'd been given an actual, proper, honest-to-goodness quest! An enemy to confront and travelling companions who, against all odds, she actually liked. She couldn't have imagined a more perfect opportunity to reinvent herself.

But where had it gotten her?

Dora was probably captured, Kaz was gone, and she was trapped in a cave with a creepy sleeping army and a dead Celt.

As she sat against the wall feeling uncharacteristically sorry for herself Jana was able, just for a moment, to be completely honest with herself. To admit that she would trade everything this day had given her for a single loving hug from her mother. A treacherous tear trickled down her cheek, but she hated herself for her weak sentimentality and she felt the familiar fury rising in her again.

Wiping the tear away, Jana rose to her feet and pressed the

button to call the elevator. The doors slid open and she stepped inside, pressed the button to go up, and drew her pistols.

She wasn't going to just sit down here and wait to be discovered. If she was going to be captured, she was going down fighting.

She rose through the earth, ready for war.

24

Richard Mountfort had considered his mission to Sweetclover Hall straightforward, if unconventional; warn of the imminent attack, solicit Sweetclover's help. That the help he was supposed to be soliciting was supernatural seemed absurd to him, but he did as he was ordered. He was a loyal subject and a good spy. His orders stated that if Sweetclover pledged himself to the king, Mountfort was to remain at the hall under Sweetclover's command until Parliament's attack had been dealt with. Afterwards he was to escort him to Oxford, where the court now resided. Now that Sweetclover had agreed to serve the Crown, Mountfort was duty-bound to follow his orders. He had expected these to consist of siege preparations – defences, supplies and so forth. He had not expected to be holding a brave girl and her halfwit mother at the point of his sword, and he was far from comfortable with it.

Mountfort had heard tales of terrible atrocities visited upon innocents during this war. More than once he had stumbled across the aftermath of such events, seen the gruesome evidence of what can happen when a group of armed men feel themselves above the law and seek only to satiate their baser urges on the general population. He had seen victims of slaughter and rape left to rot in the streets of towns and villages once prosperous and peaceable. Women, children, old people and boys so young they should never have been called upon to bear arms, all cut down and abused most heinously. Neither side was exempt from the stain of such sin, so Mountfort knew that one day he might find himself explicitly instructed to participate in such actions by a superior officer. It was one of the reasons he preferred espionage to soldiery – a spy customarily works alone. Nonetheless, he had always sworn to himself that should he find himself present at such an event he would stand in opposition to it, even if it cost him his life. Which is why he felt so uneasy as he ushered Dora and Sarah down the steps into the undercroft. To his way of thinking, nobody would drive people such as these below ground with anything but the foulest of intentions. This, he realised, may be the moment he had been dreading. He only hoped he was adequate to the challenge.

Earlier, when he had entered the drawing room without invitation, Mountfort had found Sweetclover and his wife, to whom Mountfort had never been formally introduced, embracing. She was a tall woman, taller even than her husband, and she wore striking, scandalous clothes – trousers and a shirt. But as tall as she was, she had appeared to Mountfort to be vulnerable in that moment, seeking comfort and support in the arms of her husband. Their relationship had seemed to him, based upon that first momentary glimpse, what he would have considered conventional – strong, solid husband; weak, emotional wife. But when they became aware of his presence, and she lifted her head from Sweetclover's shoulder and stepped away, it was not only the impassive mask that surprised him, it was her posture and attitude, which spoke of command and control. It was she who first demanded to know who he was and why he was intruding upon them, and her husband seemed content to allow her to speak to another man in such an unfeminine manner. It was she, also, who informed him of the attack upon Parliament's forces in Pendarn, as if it had been orchestrated by her rather than her husband. To Mountfort this made little sense. He could not understand how such a mannish woman, who took command with such ease and authority, could at the same time be the feminine creature whom he had found seeking solace in the arms of her husband.

He also struggled to understand Sweetclover. Here was a member of the aristocracy, who had married a woman by all accounts horribly disfigured, who never left the grounds of the estate, wore a mask and unusual clothing, and gave orders with the peremptory decisiveness of a general. Yet Sweetclover did not seem to be the kind of weak-chinned man to marry a harridan who would terrorize and belittle him. Mountfort had met a few of those, and Sweetclover was definitely not the type; Sweetclover's bearing and face bespoke pride and self-confidence, though he allowed his wife to command their militia.

It was, whichever way Mountfort examined it, a relationship that he could not fathom, between two people he found entirely confusing. The only explanation which seemed to make any sense to him was that which Dora had offered – that Lady Sweetclover was an enchantress of some sort. She did not fit his image of such a woman, but then she did not fit his image of any kind of woman, so there was no reason she could not be a witch who had cast a spell upon her household. The idea that it would be her intervention which swung the tide of war back in the king's favour was absurd but he found that he could not discount it entirely.

Now, marching two defenceless, terrified women to

subterranean imprisonment, Mountfort wondered what the cost of such intervention might be, and whether the victory of a just cause, if secured by infernal means, was truly a victory at all.

At the bottom of the stairs Sweetclover held up a hand to halt their progress, then pulled a candle from one pocket and a small box from another. He slid the box open, removed a small splinter of wood from it and then struck the splinter against the side of the box. The wood sparked into flame, which he used to light the candle. Mountfort was agog. 'My lord, what magic is this?' he asked.

'Not magic, Mountfort,' said Sweetclover. 'Simple alchemia. A creation of my wife's.' He held up the candle to light their way. 'Follow me, ladies,' he said.

Dora and Sarah Predennick followed, although Dora flashed Mountfort another look of mixed disappointment and scorn.

'What know you of your wife, my lord?' asked Dora as they walked. 'From where does she hail?'

Sweetclover did not acknowledge the question.

'Let me frame my question differently,' said Dora, undeterred. 'From when does she hail, my lord?'

At this Sweetclover spun on his heels and fixed Dora with a sharp stare. 'Why would you ask such a question?'

Dora stood her ground, meeting Sweetclover's gaze. Sarah stood by her daughter's side, looking bewildered and scared.

'I would ask it, my lord, because I would fain know the answer,' replied Dora. 'I have reason to believe that she hails from years hence. That she has journeyed here across a sort of magic bridge that traverses the river of time. What say you to such an idea?'

'I would say,' he replied, 'that my wife's suspicion of you, which I have hitherto not shared, seems now to be most prudent. You know things that a scullery maid should not. I wonder, does this make you dangerous to us?'

Dora shook her head. 'Not so, my lord. But I fear it may make *you* dangerous to *me*. I only wish I understood why that should be the case. You use my mother and me most ill.'

'And I am sorry for it,' he said, with seeming sincerity. 'But my wife wishes to talk with you, and I wish to attend the conference.'

'I am told that your wife is a woman most dangerous.'

Sweetclover laughed softly. 'That she certainly is, to those who would seek to do her harm. If you pose no threat, you have nothing to fear.'

Dora turned to Mountfort. 'Do you believe that, Master Mountfort? Did you help save me from the noose only to deliver me to a witch who can conjure fire from dry wood and commands a militia most unnatural? A hag who hides her monstrousness behind a mask? A foul creature who . . .' She was prevented from finishing her sentence by the ringing slap that Sweetclover dealt her across the face. Dora cried out and staggered backwards.

'You will speak of her with respect,' snapped Sweetclover.

Sarah also cried out in alarm, and held her daughter's arm to support her. She flashed Sweetclover a look of total incomprehension. 'My lord,' was all she could manage to say.

But Mountfort found his tongue easily. He stepped forward, placing himself between the women and his new commanding officer. 'That will not stand,' he said, raising his sword. 'I will not abide such behaviour.'

Sweetclover dismissively batted the sword away with his

bare hand. 'You will follow orders, Goodman Mountfort, if you seek the glory attendant upon saving the king.'

'There is no glory in wanton cruelty, my lord,' he replied.

Sweetclover sighed and shook his head. 'I knew I was not born to be a leader of men,' he said ruefully. 'I have had one soldier under my command for ten minutes and already he flies to mutiny.'

'Young Goodwife Predennick,' said Mountfort to Dora. 'If you would care to lead your mother back the way we came, I will ensure you leave unmolested.'

'I cannot allow that, Mountfort,' said Sweetclover, but his attempt to recapture his authority was futile.

In a single smooth movement, Mountfort flipped the sword around and smashed the hilt hard against Sweetclover's skull. The lord of the manor dropped like a stone. Sarah screamed and knelt by Sweetclover's side. Dora and Mountfort looked down on her with a mixture of pity and disgust.

'We must away from here,' said Mountfort, taking Dora's hand.

'On the contrary, brave friend,' she replied. 'We must hurry to the aid of my companions. Quickly, help me hide him.' She bent down, took Sweetclover's ankles and looked up at Mountfort expectantly. 'We can hide him behind some of these kegs.' Mountfort reluctantly took Sweetclover's wrists and together he and Dora laid him behind a row of barrels, hidden from view. As soon as this was done, Dora picked up the candle and hurried forward into the gloom.

'Bring my mother.'

Presented with no option but to obey, Mountfort took Sarah's hand – the other was at her lips as she bit her nails nervously – and pulled her along in pursuit. They reached a small chamber that marked the intersection of three vaults – the one they had just travelled along, and two others which snaked away to the left and right. Ahead of them was a small wooden door, partly ajar.

Dora stood waiting for them, peering down the two other chambers, confused. 'This is the door through which we entered, but I can see no evidence of any kind of room in any of these chambers.'

'Who are these friends you seek to aid, Mistress Predennick?' asked Mountfort, placing a hand on her arm to stop her hurrying away. 'Are they girls, such as yourself?'

Dora shook her head. 'They are older than I, but no less victims of Lord and Lady Sweetclover.'

'But you believe them to have been captured by their militia? These men with blue faces who do not fall when peppered with musket balls?'

'It is possible.'

'Then they are lost, miss, as surely as your brother's soul. And so will we be, if we fall into their hands. You said this door was your means of ingress. If so, we should use it now, to flee this devilish place while we still can.'

Dora shook her arm to dislodge Mountfort's hand. 'I will not abandon them. But you are, of course, free to leave on your own account.'

Mountfort stared her down for a moment, but he could see she was not to be turned from her course. 'In which case, I am sorry, but for the sake of your own safety, I must compel you.' Knowing that she was not going to come quietly, but determined to do whatever was necessary to safeguard the wilful girl, he sheathed his sword, stepped forward and grasped her tightly in his arms. She gave a cry of outrage and kicked him in the shins.

'Unhand me this instant,' she said.

Mountfort shook his head. 'You will thank me for this one day, I swear.'

She writhed and kicked, wriggled and pushed, but he was able to drag her to the small door. He stopped dead, however, when he felt her teeth bite softly into his left ear. 'Now now,' he said. 'You wouldn't.'

Her teeth remained clamped there for a few seconds until she released his ear and leant backwards, still in his grasp. 'You are right, I would not. But I would do this.'

For a moment Mountfort did not know what she was talking about, then he felt a sharp agony in his right wrist and looked down to see her holding the candle flame to his flesh. He yelled loudly and released her, springing backwards as the pain shot through his arm.

'You ungrateful cub,' he swore as he blew on the livid red burn. 'I am trying to save your life.'

'I am tired of being rescued,' replied Dora hotly, 'and then being told what to do. I accept your intentions are honourable but your assistance is unwelcome. I thank you for your earlier aid, but the tunnel is there, and I suggest you take it. Meanwhile I would like, if you do not mind, to attempt some rescuing of my own for a change.'

As Mountfort stood there, hopping from the pain in his shins and wincing from the burn on his arm, he decided to acquiesce. He had tried, he told himself. Nobody could have done more. If this girl wished to run towards danger, that was her right. He was about to take his leave when a beam of blinding white light shone down the tunnel and illuminated them.

'Who is there?' came the voice Lady Sweetclover, who he surmised was producing the unnatural light by witchcraft.

Mountfort cursed under his breath. There was no escape for him now. 'It is I, milady, Mountfort. Your husband dispatched me to bring this girl to you.'

'Dora? Is that Dora Predennick?' The voice of the woman behind the light was both surprised and, he thought, angry.

'It is,' said Dora haughtily.

'Bring her,' snapped Quil.

Dora looked back at Mountfort as he unsheathed his sword. Her eyes asked him whether he was still her ally. Churlishly, he gave her no response, but gestured for her to walk ahead of him.

Sarah, who has stood silent and still through all this performance, finally spoke up. 'That's my girl,' she said, seemingly to herself. Mountfort suppressed a smile, and followed the two ladies as they walked into the light that showed the way to their enemy's lair.

25

Dora could have sworn the doorway through which Quil led them had not been there when she looked down this corridor earlier. The large chamber that lay beyond it was filled with the kind of machines she recognised from the central labratree, so she was far less shocked and afraid than her mother, who whimpered and held her hand tightly, or Mountfort, whose eyes bulged in amazement at the floating screens and the soft hum of machinery. There were five of the militia guards standing motionless at various points around the room; the only part of them that moved was their eyes, which followed Dora in a way that made her flesh creep.

Jana and Kaz were nowhere to be seen, so hopefully they were still at large. She cast a quick glance at Mountfort, again trying to ascertain whether their argument had changed his mind about helping her, but he gave her no indication either way.

Dora turned her attention to the enemy she had gone to such lengths to track down. Quil stood about six feet tall, a height which seemed freakish to Dora but which she guessed was not uncommon for women of the future, given Jana's height. She was slender, and dressed in trousers and shirt which flattered her figure. Again, Dora had to remind herself that such attire was common in years to come. Quil wore brown leather gloves and a smooth, white mask. Dora thought maybe it had been carved from some fine stone. There were two wide ovals through which she could barely make out Quil's eyes, and a series of small holes in a line to mark the mouth. Beyond that there was no adornment – no painted eyebrows or rose blushes to approximate glowing cheeks. It was white, cold, hard and impassive. Dora could make out four metal clips, two on each side, from which leather straps snaked behind her head to hold the mask in place. A cascade of brown hair tumbled around the mask, but something about the way it sat made Dora feel sure it was a wig. The only inch of exposed flesh was at Quil's neck, between her shirt collar and the chin of her mask; it looked scarred but not raw. She was an altogether singular sight – broken on the inside, but projecting a proud and confident façade.

Quil held up a hand. Dora and Sarah stopped, with Mountfort behind them, still holding them at the point of his sword.

'I helped you,' said Dora before Quil could begin talking. 'I heard your cry, I came to render aid. I held out my hand to you in your moment of need and how do you repay my kindness? You send me into the future, hold me captive, stick me with needles, steal five years of my life, ruin my parents. And for what? Who am I to you to be used thus?'

For a moment, Dora thought Quil was going to be reasonable; something in her body language spoke of weariness. But the moment passed. Quil crossed the distance between them in two long strides and struck Dora a ringing smack across the face. Dora cried out and staggered backwards into the arms of her mother, who gasped and then began, almost silently, to cry.

'Where is she?' demanded Quil.

'Where is who?' shot back Dora, disentangling herself from her mother and standing tall again, determined not to cower in the face of aggression even though her twice-slapped cheek felt swollen and hot.

'The woman who was in that bed,' snarled Quil, pointing to a door that led Dora knew not where.

'I do not know to whom you refer,' replied Dora. 'This is the first time I have set foot in this room.'

'Then where are your two friends? Yojana and Kazik. Were they down here?'

'I don't know who you're talking about,' said Dora, folding her arms defiantly. 'I have returned here to visit with my mother. That is all.'

Quil stood silently before Dora, clenching and unclenching her fists, her eyes wide with fury. But after a moment she took a deep breath, lowered her head and sighed. When she looked up again she peered closer, examining Dora's face, then held out her hands placatingly. 'How old are you?' she asked. 'How long has it been for you since our first meeting?'

Suspicious of Quil's sudden calm, Dora answered warily. 'I have slept but once since you threw me across the time bridge.'

This answer seemed to shock Quil, who took a step backwards and breathed, 'Once?' in wonder. 'Then this is the first time we have met since that day?'

'It is.'

Quil seemed to consider this for a moment. Dora could never, in her wildest dreams, have expected what Quil said next.

'I apologise for my temper,' the masked woman said. 'You must be very confused by everything that has happened to you.'

Dora did not trust such sudden solicitousness, so she did not relax her defiant stance.

'You did come to help me, of course you did,' Quil continued. 'And I am grateful. I didn't know my touch would send you through time. It was an accident. A side effect of my own journey. I was full of potential and you earthed me.'

Dora did not understand what this meant, but did not interrupt.

'You cannot blame me for the five years you have lost,' Quil continued. 'I have no control over where or when your travels will take you. As for your parents . . . I don't know your father. But yes, I have been forced to modify your mother's behaviour a bit. We needed a cook, and we needed to stop her spreading stories. But I've caused no permanent damage. I used a simple machine from my time, on its lowest setting. The procedure is easily reversed. Although looking at her right now, I'd say she's in shock, so it might be best to wait until she's calmer. Sometimes people who've been conditioned like she has go a bit screwy if they have a big surprise. It'll wear off. Here.' She fished a small packet from her trouser pocket and tossed it to Dora, who caught it. 'Open that up, slap one of the patches on her wrist. I use them for the pain, but it'll put her out like a light. Kindest thing.'

Dora glanced at her mother, who was staring at the floating screens in mute wonder, and decided that some strange medicine might be the very thing. She examined the packet and after a moment's examination realised she needed to peel it open. Inside it she found a patch of cloth, sticky on one side only. She pressed it to her mother's wrist. As she did this, she continued to talk to Quil, whose unexpected civility had left her befuddled. 'You possess a machine that can change the very substance of a person's mind?' she asked.

Quil nodded. 'It's called a mind-writer.'

Dora shook her head in amazement. 'In the future, is everybody's mind constantly being remade, to suit the whims of others?'

'Absolutely, but not in the way you mean.' Quil laughed. 'They only use machines like this on particularly dangerous criminals – serial killers, psychopaths. The nutbags. But adjust the settings and you can use it on anybody. I stole one from a supermax a while back, thought it might come in useful.'

'You say you can use it put my mother right?'

'Certainly. Where is Henry, by the way?' Quil addressed this question to Mountfort, whose sword had not wavered during their exchange.

'He stayed upstairs, milady, something about preparing the servants for a siege,' he said.

Quil nodded, accepting this story, to Dora's relief. 'Dora,' she continued, 'you must understand, my actions towards you are not dictated by what you have done, but by what you will do, you and your two friends. But perhaps the future – your future – is not set in stone. I'd like to try and prevent us becoming enemies at all. So I am willing to offer you a deal. If you swear to me that you will remain here, in this time and place, for the rest of your life, then I will leave you to your own devices. You can have your mother back, and you can go live in your little village and tend goats to your heart's content. Find a man, marry, squeeze out a few kids. Trust me, nothing would make me happier than to never see your face again.'

'Truly?'

'Truly.'

Dora did not know how to respond. She had not known what to expect when she finally met the woman who had been the focus of her fears, but it was not this calm, reasonable offer of truce. 'You are not what I feared,' she admitted.

'I'll take that as a compliment,' replied Quil. 'Do we have a deal?'

Before Dora could answer there was a loud chime from one of the machines. Quil turned to examine one of the screens and whistled softly. 'It seems our parliamentarian friends decided not to bother talking.' On the screen, Dora could see groups of men busying themselves around a row of cannons.

'Is this a picture of what is occurring outside?' asked Mountfort.

'Yup,' replied Quil. 'That's the ridge to the east. It was always the most likely position for them to put their big guns. I don't understand why they haven't come to parley first, though.'

'I know of at least one soldier who escaped the massacre in the village,' said Mountfort, with a knowing look to Dora. She realised he was talking about James. 'If he has provided an account of the attack to the main force, they would have no need to parley. They would know your allegiance already.'

Quil shrugged. 'I'm not allied to anyone. Not in this time, anyway. Doesn't matter,' she said. 'I'm ready for them. Guards, to your stations, as we drilled.'

The five guards spun on their heels and jogged from the room.

Quil busied herself at the computer, talking over her shoulder to Dora and Mountfort. 'It won't be safe for you to leave, not while I repel this attack,' she said. 'Stay down here with me for a while. It won't take long, and then you can get going. Assuming you accept my offer, Dora?'

'I do,' said Dora impulsively, realising only as she said it that she did indeed accept. But then something occurred to her, and she added, 'On one condition.'

Quil stopped and turned to regard Dora. 'And what would that be?' she asked, her voice cold.

Dora remembered the moment on the green when she had noticed a brief expression of horror cross James' face as she had raved of devilry. For a second she had seen a flash of the boy she had known – someone out of his depth and lost. Had she not caught that tiny moment of doubt, she would not have asked what she did. But she had seen it, she knew the brother she had loved was still in there, buried beneath fear and fervour, and she saw a chance to rescue him. 'That much as you altered my mother, you agree to alter my brother too,' she said.

'Brother?' Quil sounded surprised.

'James. The escaped soldier Mountfort just referred to. He is my brother. If I am to return to my family, I would have it as it used to be. He must be changed back into the person he was before the religious zealotry of these Puritans twisted his mind. Can you do this for me?'

Quil nodded. 'Fix the mother, fix the brother. No problem. Assuming he survives the battle, of course.'

'Then we are not enemies, you and I,' said Dora. 'I know not what you do here, or why, but I allow that it is none of my concern. I would much rather be left alone and in peace.'

'You got it.'

As Quil resumed her business with the computer, Dora and Mountfort took Sarah and sat her down against the wall. 'Mother, can you hear me?' asked Dora, gently.

Sarah was staring into space, biting her nails. She gave no indication that she had heard a thing.

Mountfort laid a hand on Dora's arm and she met his gaze. 'Young mistress, do I understand correctly, that you are in fact in no danger?'

'It appears so,' she replied.

'Then I must away from here. Sweetclover will awaken soon, and when he does I shall be in great difficulties.'

'You will take the tunnel?'

Mountfort nodded, so Dora explained how to find the ice house, and the best route he should take to quit the area quickly. 'I thank you, young mistress,' he said as he rose to leave. 'I am sorry for our earlier disagreement, I hope you can accept that I was trying to do the honourable thing by my king and by my country. And I wish you all the best in this strange place.'

Dora leaned forward and kissed him on the cheek. 'Go safely,' she said, before returning her attentions to her mother.

Mountfort smiled and then walked to Quil. 'Milady, I think I would be of best use in the house above, helping repel the attack.'

Quil, fixated on the screens, did not look at him. Her fingers tapping away on a curious instrument before them, a long flat object covered in buttons, each with a different letter painted upon it. 'You'd be in the way,' she said over her shoulder. 'But you could go and get Hank for me, OK? Bring him down here. He should see this.'

Mountfort nodded. 'Yes, my lady.' He walked away, flashing a wink at Dora.

But when he reached the door and placed his hand upon its edge, he stopped in his tracks and gave a soft groan. Dora stared at him, puzzled, as he stood there, frozen in place. After a moment she called, 'Master Mountfort? Are you well?'

He slowly turned towards her and opened his mouth as if to speak, but no sound came out. Instead a thin dribble of blood leaked from his lips. It was only when he stepped forward, unsteady on his feet, that she saw the knife hilt protruding from his belly. Dora's hand flew to her mouth to stifle a scream as Mountfort fell first to his knees and then toppled forward onto his face.

Behind his prone body, which twitched and shook as shock took hold, Sweetclover stepped through the doorway. Dora watched, horror stricken, as he rolled Mountfort over and pulled the knife from his stomach. Mountfort groaned in agony as the blade slid out. Sweetclover used Mountfort's smock to clean the knife, then began to advance puposefully towards Dora.

Dora froze, holding her mother, whose eyes were now heavy with sleep. She could feel her grip on sanity slipping away from her again, as it had done in the church. The horrors of this endless day kept piling up and threatened to bury her beneath them. She had been foolish, trying to rescue Jana and Kaz. They weren't even here, and if they had been, what could she have done? She was a fourteen-year-old girl armed with a candle. It was she who needed rescuing. She was a danger to herself and others, not least poor Mountfort, salty and sneaky, but kind at heart and now dying in a pool of his own blood.

As Sweetclover bore down on her, she made a vow to herself: if only someone would intervene to save her, if only she could survive this day, she would make sure that she never needed rescuing again, for as long as she lived.

26

The elevator doors slid open silently. Jana stood ready, legs apart, pistols raised, teeth gritted in anticipation. But she found, to her astonishment and relief, that although the room was occupied, everybody had their backs to her.

By the computer table and the bank of floating screens stood a woman in an obvious wig. Had to be Quil. Beyond her was Sweetclover, walking towards Dora, who cowered on the floor with her back to the wall cradling an unconscious woman. There was a man lying by the door. Jana thought he was dead till she saw one of his arms twitch. A glint of light drew Jana's gaze to Sweetclover's hand, where he held a vicious-looking knife. She stepped forward, taking aim at Sweetclover's back. She was just drawing breath to issue a command for him to stop when Quil saved her the trouble.

'What are you doing, Hank?' said Quil, rushing to put herself between him and Dora.

Although Quil was now facing in her direction, Jana was masked from her view by Sweetclover. But she wouldn't be for long. She ducked down, hurried behind a nearby chest and peered out at the unfolding drama, ready to intervene if needed.

'That whoreson and this cat beat me unconscious and left me for dead,' Sweetclover shouted.

Quil looked down at Dora, whose hands Jana could see were shaking. 'Is this true, Dora?' asked Quil.

'Yes,' replied Dora, her voice quavering with fear. 'But that was before you and I spoke. We believed he was bringing us down here to imprison or torture us. Poor Mountfort was only trying to save me.'

'Poor Mountfort was an insubordinate wretch who paid for his disloyalty with his life,' snarled Sweetclover. 'How do you intend to make amends?'

Quil placed a hand over the knife and forced Sweetclover's arm down. 'Stand down, soldier,' she said. 'Dora and I have reached an understanding. No need for any more blood here. It's all good,' she said, her tone mollifying and placatory. There was a long, tense moment when Jana thought Sweetclover was going to argue, but finally he sheathed his knife and stalked through a door into the anteroom where the patient had been kept.

Quil looked down at Dora. 'Am I wrong to trust you?' she asked.

'No,' replied Dora simply. 'I only want to go home and be with my family. Please believe me.'

Before Quil could give a response, Sweetclover burst out of the anteroom. 'She is gone,' he yelled, alarmed.

'I know,' replied Quil, impatiently. 'I told you this was going to happen, I just didn't know when. She was well prepared, I made sure of that. She'll be fine. We've got other fish to fry now, OK?'

'But how?' said Sweetclover, bewildered.

'Good question,' Quil replied, kneeling before Dora. Jana had to strain to make out what she was saying.

'If you want me to honour our agreement, Dora, I need a show of good faith,' she said softly. 'Tell me the truth – were Jana and Kaz down here? They're not here now, so you're not betraying them. I already know they must be in this time period. I need to know if they were in this room.'

Jana willed Dora to keep her mouth shut. She did not know what agreement Dora and Quil had reached, but she didn't think it could be anything good.

'I think they may have been, yes,' said Dora. 'I last saw them in the chamber outside.'

Quil cursed loudly as she rose to her feet again. 'Today of all days I forget to lock the door. I'm an idiot, Hank. One of them must have touched her.'

Sweetclover's shoulders slumped and he looked sad. 'Then she is gone forever?'

Quil walked over to him and took his face in her hands. He looked up into her mask as she spoke. 'No, of course not. How many times do I have to explain this to you, you big lunk? She is me. I am her. I never knew how I was blown back in time again. I thought it must have been another random jump. But I took precautions. She's got everything she needs on her person. She'll work it out and start making her way back here, and then you'll meet her again, five years ago when I turn up to help me recover from my first time journey. Capiche?'

Jana could tell by Sweetclover's face that he was having trouble grasping Quil's explanation, but it made perfect sense to Jana. Quil had been blown back in time to 1640, horribly damaged on the journey, and had encountered Dora. But then an older version of Quil had arrived, set her up in the makeshift hospital in the undercroft, and nursed her younger self back to health. The recuperation was still ongoing, five years later when the younger Quil came into contact with Kaz and was blown back through time once more. Right now she was waking up in some prehistoric era and would soon begin a journey back to 1640, building her army in the cavern below as she did so. Eventually, she would catch up to herself and arrive ready to live the same five years in this house for a second time, this time as the nurse to her younger self.

Her mind boggled as she worked out the complexity of Quil's life; it was no wonder Sweetclover was having trouble wrapping his head around it.

'Look, we can go through it again later, OK?' said Quil. 'I'll draw diagrams and everything, promise. But right now we have two pressing problems. First, Jana and Kaz will have been thrown across time when they touched me. But if only one of them made contact, then the other is still here, and there's only one place he or she can be.'

Jana ducked back behind the chest as she realised Quil was turning towards the elevator.

'Down there,' she heard Quil say. 'So I need you to go down and get them for me while I deal with our other problem – the army that is about to attack our home. Can you do that for me?'

Sweetclover did not reply, but he must have nodded because Jana heard his footsteps echoing across the chamber as he walked towards her. Jana shuffled around the chest, keeping out of sight as he entered the elevator. She peeked out as the doors closed and he began to descend.

Knowing it might be her only chance, Jana rose to her feet and aimed both pistols at Quil, who was halfway across the space, walking towards the computer desk. She froze when she saw Jana. After a moment Quil held her hands out wide in the universally recognised posture of submission.

'Hello, Yojana,' said Quil, her voice calm and seemingly unsurprised. 'Sorry, you don't like that name, do you. Jana, then. Hello, Jana.'

'You must be Quil,' replied Jana. 'It's nice to finally put a face to the name. Sorry, mask. I meant mask.'

'Jana.' That was Dora, rising to her feet, smiling.

'Dora,' said Jana coolly, not taking her eyes off Quil. 'What's all this about you and Quil reaching an understanding?'

'She has promised to help me fix my family and then leave me be,' replied Dora. 'She has no quarrel with me, nor I with her.'

Jana couldn't believe what she was hearing. 'Fix your family?'

'She has a machine that can change a person's mind. She used it upon my mother, to make her more biddable. She will reverse what she has done to her, and she has agreed to use it to return my brother to the man he once was. I will have my family again, Jana. That's all I've ever wanted.'

'And what do you have to do for her? What does she get out of it?'

'Dora stays here and lives her life as if she'd never met me,' said Quil. 'It's a good deal for both of us. She gets her life back, and I turn a potential enemy into a friend. Win win.'

'So we can end this whole thing before it even begins, that's what you're saying?' asked Jana.

'Not exactly,' replied Quil. 'It's simple for Dora. For you and me, it's a lot more complicated.'

Jana didn't like the sound of that but before she could ask Quil what she meant, Dora interrupted.

'He is still alive,' she said. Jana glanced over to see Dora kneeling by the man on the floor. 'Help me save him.'

'Mountfort was not part of the deal, Dora,' said Quil.

Dora rose to her feet. 'He is now.'

Quil's shoulders slumped wearily. 'All right, all right, by all means let's focus all our attention on the insignificant local spy and ignore the great big army that is about to open fire on this building. Yes, let's do that. What a *spectacular* idea.'

Jana took a step forward and pointed the flintlocks square at Quil's chest. 'If Dora says that's the deal, that's the deal.'

'Fine,' said Quil through gritted teeth. 'Get him into the sickroom.'

Jana gestured towards Mountfort with the pistols. 'Oh no, I'm keeping you in my sights. You carry him.'

Quil stomped over to Mountfort, leant down and grabbed his hands. Dora took hold of his feet and they lifted him, which provoked a strangled cry of agony from Mountfort. Together they carried him, blood dripping on their shoes as they staggered under his weight. Jana followed, keeping the pistols trained on Quil at all times.

'On the bed,' said Quil. She and Dora laid Mountfort on the covers. Dora took Mountfort's hand and stood by his head as Quil began to work.

'He's lost a lot of blood,' she said as she busied herself in the tray of equipment that stood next to the ECG and animal-bladder drip. 'I have to fix the physical damage before I can transfuse him.' She turned back to the bed holding a small silver device which she laid on the counterpane next to Mountfort, whose smock she then ripped open to reveal the nasty, oozing wound in his stomach.

'Dora,' she said. 'I need you to hold the wound open for me.'

'I beg your pardon?' Dora looked at the blood queasily.

Quil leant across Mountfort and grabbed Dora's wrists, pulled her hands down to the wound, and shoved her fingers deep into Mountfort's belly. Dora squealed and turned white.

'Now hold the wound open so I can get to his innards,' said Quil as she picked up the silver instrument. She bent over the now-gaping injury and inserted the silver tool into the wound. Jana was unable to see exactly what Quil was doing, but the smell of burnt flesh began to waft towards her, so she assumed she was cauterising the internal injuries. The stench made Jana gag, and Dora looked as if she was about to faint. Quil, on the other hand, was a model of calm efficiency.

'You've done this before,' said Jana.

'When you've fought in as many battles as I have,' replied Quil, 'you get good at patching people up.'

'I have a whole world of questions for you.'

'I'm very good at being interrogated. Lots of practice. Fire away,' said Quil, without looking up from her work.

Jana hardly knew where to begin, now that Quil was being so open. 'The woman who was in this bed. That was you, first time around, yes? You've lived the same five years in this house twice over – first as the patient, then as the nurse. That right?'

Quil nodded. 'I wish Hank understood it as quickly as you did. He gets this look when I try to explain time travel to him, like a cat when it sees its reflection in a mirror.'

'Very neat.'

'Thank you,' said Quil, still focused on Mountfort's intestines. 'I kind of had to rescue myself. Nobody else was volunteering for the job.'

'And Sweetclover's your husband. How did that happen?'

Quil allowed herself a quick glance up at Jana. 'That's your question? Everything you could ask me, and you want to know about my relationship?' She shook her head in wonder and returned to her work. 'Honestly, young girls.' She sighed. 'You think I used the mind-writer on him, don't you? I used it to deal with all the servants, and was perfectly willing to use it on Hank. He's useful. He knows this time and this area, he is my public face when I need one. And he's essentially a kind man. Pampered, lazy, indolent . . . but not cruel.'

Dora, her fingers still holding Mountfort's wound open, scoffed.

'OK,' admitted Quil. 'Sometimes he gets a bit ornery. But not often. Anyway, during my first time in this house, as I was recuperating in this bed, he would come down here and read to me. I think I fell in love with his voice. It took me years before I could even open my eyes and take solid food, but for all that time, I heard his voice, soft and deep, like a lifeline. I used it to pull myself out of the darkness. So when I came back here a second time, healed, ready to nurse my younger self, I'd already fallen for him.'

'And he returned your affections? In spite of your disfigurement?' asked Dora. Her voice was sceptical.

'I didn't think he would. I was ready to use the mind-writer on him, like I said, but not for that. That would be . . . wrong. But I didn't need to use it at all. He listened, was patient. I asked him to help me and my younger self, and he willingly agreed. I suggested he read to her, and he was glad to do it. I think he fell in love with the mystery long before he fell in love with me. But the servant girls of this time are, well, enthusiastic but insipid. He had gone to London, more than once, in search of a society wife, but they bored him. Say what you like about me, but I am not boring. Before I knew what was happening, we fell in love. Go figure.'

'But you're . . . y'know.' Jana waved at Quil's mask and wig.

'What, burned to a crisp? I've had time to heal. Pretty much back to normal now, apart from my face and hair. Those require skills I don't have access to yet.' She leaned across and whispered, conspiratorially, 'But I think he kind of likes the mask, if you know what I mean.'

To which Jana could only respond, 'Eeuuw.'

Quil chuckled at Jana's discomfort as she stood upright. 'OK, you can let go now.'

Dora pulled her hands from Mountfort's innards and held them as far from her body as possible, looking for something to wipe them on.

Jana couldn't help but smile. 'Dora,' she said. 'You examined how many dead bodies in Pendarn earlier? You had blood up to your elbows, and now you're squeamish?'

'I did not sink my fingers into their wounds,' replied Dora, wincing.

'Just wipe them on the blanket,' said Quil, who had returned to the instrument tray and was rummaging again. 'Nobody's using this bed any more anyway.'

Jana registered Dora's confusion. 'She means the counter-pane,' she explained, thanking the chip for providing the requisite archaic term. Dora wiped her hands as clean as she was able and once again took Mountfort's hand in hers.

'Can I ask you a question?' Quil said to Jana, returning to Mountfort's stomach and swabbing the wound with some liquid antiseptic. 'On the day you vanished from your life, in 2141, what exactly happened?'

Jana was taken aback by Quil's specificity, and wondered how much she already knew. 'I was sick of being mollycoddled and escorted everywhere by big thugs in cheap suits,' she explained. 'I decided to skip school, hang out at the Science Museum. So I gave the guards the slip, but on the way there I was attacked and chased by a gang of men.'

'Who were they?'

'Don't you know?'

Quil looked up curiously. 'Why should I?'

Jana considered her next words carefully. If she was right, it was a future version of Quil who had sent the men to kill her in 2141, but this Quil didn't know that because she hadn't done it yet. In which case, telling Quil the truth now might be the very thing that inspired her to send those men after Jana in the first place. Jana's head began to swim with the complexity of the paradoxes she was trying to negotiate. Finally she decided to tell the truth and see what happened; it was the best plan she could come up with.

'I got the impression you sent them to kill me,' she said. 'They were after my ENL chip, I think. And they were working for a woman.'

'A woman?' Quil said sharply. 'They said that? They definitely said a woman?'

'Yes,' replied Jana, uncertainly. 'I assumed it was you.'

Quil shook her head firmly. 'Not me. Depending upon how this conversation goes I might try to kill you now. I certainly tried to kill you last time I met you. But on that specific day, at that point in your timeline? Never.'

'Why not?' asked Jana.

'Jana, listen to me,' said Quil urgently, Mountfort momentarily forgotten. 'That day is important. What happened to you is important. More important than you can possibly know. Would you let me take a download of your chip? All the data you've got, the recording of that day and anything still left in the buffer.'

Jana was baffled. 'Um . . .'

'Trust me when I say it could save countless lives.'

She was so confused by Quil's remarkable claim that Jana made a dreadful error and asked: 'Is that why you wanted my chip when you captured me in 2014?'

The instant she'd said it she knew she'd screwed up. She cursed her idiocy. She'd been wondering how they had known to keep Sweetclover Hall under surveillance in the future, and now she knew – she'd just stupidly told Quil when to wait for them.

'That's not actually happened for me yet,' said Quil, obviously choosing her words with great care. 'But there's no reason it has to. If you give me access to your memories, direct from the source, then I can offer you the same kind of deal I offered Dora. There would be no need for us to be enemies. You couldn't go back to your life, I'm afraid. There's no way, it would be too . . . complicated. But together, you and I, we could make history. Right a great wrong.'

Jana realised her mouth was hanging open in astonishment and clamped it shut. 'If I did that, gave you my chip, you'd have to tell me what is going on. What you're doing here. About the army downstairs, the base in 2014, everything.'

'Everything,' nodded Quil. 'Full disclosure. Then, if you decide not to help me, but promise not to try to stop me, you'll be free to go wherever and whenever you want. We can end this little war of ours before it even begins.'

Mountfort gave a low gurgling moan and Quil returned her attention to his wound. She used the silver tool a last time, to burn the flesh closed.

'Think about it,' said Quil, smoke from Mountfort's cauterized wound wreathing her masked face.

Jana was thinking about it. It sounded like a good deal. She had expected Quil to be a cackling super-villain, but the burnt woman was more complex than that: impossible to read, impossible to understand. She spoke about righting wrongs and correcting injustices, and obviously loved her unlikely husband. Jana couldn't see an obviously correct choice.

Perhaps Dora had been right to make a deal with her.

'I will think about it,' she said. 'You've overseen this place yourself. Scavenged the equipment, built what you couldn't get. You're clever. A scientist, I think. So maybe you can tell me – how are we travelling through time? And why us?'

'A scientist,' said Quil wistfully. 'Yes, I suppose I was, once upon a time.'

'What are you now, then?' asked Jana.

Quil shrugged as she stood away from the bed and dropped the tool back in the tray. 'Terrorist. Freedom fighter. Freak. Wife. Take your pick, your mileage may vary. But you asked about time travel. I wish I could give you all the answers. My understanding is theoretical and incomplete.'

'Give me the bullet points.'

Quil busied herself with the drip and the ECG, and began to connect Mountfort to them. She spoke as she worked.

'They found an asteroid out in the Kuiper Belt. It was composed of a kind of substance that messes with time somehow,' she said. 'I spent years experimenting, trying to understand its properties and powers. It changed me. Literally. Some of it was absorbed through my skin, I think, like mercury. Anyway, when the war got really bad, when I thought my forces were going to be utterly defeated, I used the asteroid to make a weapon. The greatest discovery in a century and I turned it into a bomb.' Quil shook her head, as if even she could hardly believe what she had done. 'And of course, as all great scientific mistakes inevitably do, it destroyed its creator. It blew up right on top of me. The explosion threw me back to 1640, burnt to a crisp, and cracked the structure of time, which for the purposes of this explanation you can think of as crystalline. I shattered time itself. Can you imagine such a thing?'

Jana shook her head. 'Not really, no.'

'Me either, and I did it.' Quil laughed mirthlessly. 'I've spent a lot of time down here trying to work it all out; the equations, the mechanics of it. I'm still none the wiser. I hate to admit it, but I think I'm just not clever enough. There is one guy, back in my time, who might have been able to figure it out. When I finally get back there I plan on giving him my findings, see if he can make sense of it all.'

Jana considered Quil's answer. 'But that doesn't answer my main question. How are *we* – Kaz and Dora and me – travelling through time?'

Quil shook her head. 'Beats me. I think, to stick with my analogy, that we're kind of navigating the cracks in the crystal to different times and places. It's a consequence of having been exposed to the raw asteroid.'

'But Dora, Kaz and I haven't been to your time; we've never touched this asteroid thing,' Jana said.

'And that's the great talent of this particular material. It starts working before you are exposed to it. The effect travels backwards down your timeline from the moment of exposure. In a few months of your subjective timeline, you'll be exposed to it. Which means all three of you are heading for the future soon. But I already know that, 'cause I met you there.'

Jana's head was beginning to spin. 'This is so confusing,' she said softly.

'You get used to it soon enough,' said Quil. 'Just accept that you're never going to work it all out until it's over. Go with the flow.' She shrugged. 'It's the only way.' She stepped away from the bed.

Mountfort was now connected. His heartbeat was weak but the ECG showed it to be steady. Quil waved her hands at him distractedly.

'That's the best I can do,' she told Dora. 'I stopped the internal bleeding, patched the wound. He's getting antibiotics through the drip. The shock might still kill him, unless I can find a suitable blood donor. So I'm going to type his blood, then yours and hers, OK?' Quil gestured at Dora.

Dora looked to Jana for reassurance. 'She's going to take a sample of our blood and see if we match Mountfort's blood type,' explained Jana patiently. 'If we do, she can take some of our blood and put it in him. It will save his life.'

Dora's face was a picture of horror and disgust.

'Don't worry,' said Jana, smiling at Dora's primitive fears. 'It's a very common thing in the future. Happens every day. You'll be fine. If you want to save him, we need to do it.'

Dora nodded tentatively. 'Very well,' she told Quil. 'You may take my blood if it will save him.'

Quil walked over to a cabinet and removed a syringe, a bowl and some chemicals in small bottles. She set to work, using the bedside table.

'I have a question,' said Dora. 'What year do you hail from? When did you start . . . everything?'

Quil shook her head, as if Dora had asked a very tough question indeed. 'There are lots of possible answers to that.

The date I was born. The date I first travelled in time. But let's go with May twenty-seventh 2155.'

'And what occurred upon that day?'

'If you keep to our deal, you'll never need to know.'

'Tell me, then,' said Jana.

'If *you* keep to our deal, you can see for yourself. Believe me, it's something you need to experience. Being told isn't adequate.' Quil looked up from the bowl where she had just squirted a syringe of Mountfort's blood. 'Since we're being so open, there's something else I want to know,' she said. 'The boy, Kaz. Who is he?'

Jana shrugged. 'I don't know. Wrong place, wrong time, I think. He was there when Dora and I arrived in 2014. He seemed surprised to see us, so I don't think he was there on purpose.'

'He may not have chosen to be there, but that doesn't mean that he wasn't supposed to be there,' said Quil. 'Someone wanted him to meet you and Dora, you can count on that.'

Jana suspected that someone might have been 'Steve', but she wasn't going to mention him; she'd already given away too much by accident. She was acutely aware that as relaxed and friendly as their chat seemed, she was still holding Quil at gunpoint. Who knew how their talk would have gone if their positions had been reversed.

Quil was about to take a sample of Dora's blood when two things happened at once.

First there was the sound of a huge explosion somewhere above them, the room shook and dust showered from the ceiling.

Then Jana felt sharp, cold steel at her throat.

27

Dora let out an involuntary squeal as the house shook, and then a second louder one when she saw Sweetclover standing behind Jana with his knife at her throat.

'Don't kill her,' shouted Quil as she dropped the bowl of Mountfort's blood. 'We need her alive, Hank.'

Jana was looking at Dora, mouthing 'Sorry' as Quil ran past her out into the main chamber.

There was another heavy impact in the house above and another shower of dust and mortar.

'Up,' barked Sweetclover.

Dora got to her feet.

'Drop the pistols.'

Jana did so.

'Outside.' He pushed Jana forward.

Jana and Dora walked out the door as Sweetclover scooped up the pistols from the floor, then both jumped and turned in horror as a single shot rang out from the sickroom. Sweetclover was standing over Mountfort's bed, a smoking flintlock in his right hand. Dora flew at him through the doorway, hands out, scratching at his face, kicking and wailing. He batted her away with a mighty swipe of his hand and she crashed to the floor.

'You bastard,' spat Jana as Sweetclover strode out of the room. 'He was defenceless.'

He raised the second pistol and pointed it at Jana's right calf. 'Do not test me, wench,' he said, although he sounded more tired than angry. 'My wife forbad me to kill you, but she did not say I could not hurt you.'

'I will see you hang for that,' said Dora as she rose unsteadily, her head swimming from the impact of Sweetclover's blow.

'In case you haven't noticed,' shouted Quil from the computer terminal, 'the house is being bombarded. Could everyone please sit down and shut up while I deal with this? Hank, don't hurt them but don't let them leave. Girls, our deal still stands. Just keep out of my way and let me work.'

There was another concussive blast from above, louder and closer than the last two.

'They are finding their range,' said Sweetclover as he waved the pistol to indicate that the girls should sit against the wall. Dora ran to her mother, who was still unconscious. She rested Sarah's head on her lap and looked up at the bank of floating screens. Jana came and sat beside her.

'Sorry,' said Jana, looking crestfallen. 'I kind of forgot about him.'

Dora wanted to lash out, to blame Jana for Mountfort's needless death, but in truth she had also forgotten about Sweetclover. 'Do not fret, Jana,' she said.

'Is this your mom?'

'It is.'

Jana reached over and placed her hand on Sarah's neck. 'What are you doing?' asked Dora.

'Just checking her pulse. She's fine.' Jana smiled. 'So they brainwashed her, yeah?'

'I do not know what that word means,' replied Dora impatiently. She was getting a little sick of the way future-people spoke to her.

'Sorry. Quil mentioned something called a mind-writer?'

'Yes, a machine from the future. It has made my mother gullible and stupid. She is asleep now, for the alarums and excitements of this day have overwhelmed her senses. When she wakes, Quil has promised to restore her to her right mind.'

Jana looked sceptical. 'I wonder how many of her promises she'll feel like keeping now she's got a gun.'

'I was not armed when she offered me a truce,' Dora pointed out.

'I hope you're not plotting against me over there,' shouted Quil.

'Wouldn't dream of it,' Jana replied, sarcastically.

'You should come watch this.' Quil waved at the screens. 'Should be fun.'

Dora exchanged a glance with Jana, who shrugged. 'Why not,' she said.

Dora removed Sarah's apron, balled it up to use as a pillow and rested her mother's head upon it. Then she and Jana walked over to stand beside Quil at the wall of floating screens. More impacts rattled the house above.

'So,' said Quil, as if addressing a classroom. 'Before us we have four main screens. This one, top right, shows us an aerial view of the ridge to the east. As you can see, parliamentary forces have occupied the ridge and set up their cannons. I thought they might. It's the best vantage point. They got our range very quickly, which is impressive, but their fire won't be able to penetrate the forcefield I've erected around the house.'

'A forcefield is a kind of invisible wall,' said Jana. Dora swallowed her frustration and nodded thanks for the translation.

'I have a surprise in store for them,' said Quil. 'But let's allow them a little time to try and work out why their cannonballs are bouncing off thin air. First I think I'll deal with these gentlemen.' She indicated the screen below, which showed another aerial view, this time a column of men carrying pikes and muskets marching through the gate that marked the boundary of the Sweetclover estate.

'How are you seeing this?' Dora asked.

'Eyeskys. I have flying machines that send me pictures,' said Quil as if it were the most normal thing in the world.

Dora watched the screen, imagining what it would be like to see such a view for real, to be flying above the ground looking down on it like a god. What would that do, she wondered, to a person's sense of power, seeing people scurrying below like ants?

'My dear, should you not be closing your invisible door?' said Sweetclover, mildly.

'Patience,' replied Quil. 'I need to wait for the last man to pass through the gate. That'll take a couple of minutes yet. So let's see how the cavalry are getting on.' She indicated the top left screen on which a group of twenty mounted men were trotting, as casually as could be, across a large field, again seen from above but with a much steadier picture. 'That's the view from one of the cameras on the roof of the hall's central tower,' explained Quil.

'We are under attack on three fronts,' observed Sweetclover.

'Yes, we are,' agreed Quil. 'And none of them poses any threat to us.'

'Will you send your militia to fight them?' asked Dora.

'Militia?' asked Quil.

'The blue-faced guards.'

'Oh, you mean the Celts.'

Dora was not sure that she did, but did not argue.

'No need,' explained Quil. 'I've only got ten of them awake at the moment. They're good fighters, but they're not quite enough to win this battle. I've got them manning the tower guns. Oh look, they're through.' She pointed to the screen that showed the infantry, who had now all passed through the gate and were fanning out as they began to approach the outer edge of the hall's gardens. Quil turned to her husband and grabbed his arm, as if she were an overexcited girl. 'I'd forgotten how much I missed this,' she said. 'I love a good battle.'

Dora did not believe that anyone who enjoyed battle could be quite right in the head, but she kept the thought to herself.

'Can we please begin our defence,' replied Sweetclover, who looked far less enthusiastic than his wife about watching an army converge upon his home.

'Sure,' said Quil. 'Pick one. Who goes first?'

'Cannons, I think,' he said with a strained smile.

'Cannons it is,' said Quil, pushing one of keys on the board before her. 'Fire in the hole!'

The top right screen turned bright orange and a moment later they felt the ground beneath their feet rumble and ripple as if some great giant were stomping towards them. The screen filled with fire and smoke and then went dead.

'Damn, got the eyesky,' cursed Quil.

'What has happened?' asked Dora.

'I filled the ridge with high explosive, which I just detonated.

If I got my math right, the whole ridge is now gone. Just gone. No more ridge, no more cannons. I thank you,' she said, and bowed to imaginary applause.

Dora felt her mouth drop open at the scale of what Quil had done, the number of people she had dispatched with a single button-press; it made Dora feel ill.

'There was no need for that,' said Jana quietly.

'For my second trick, I will stop the cavalry,' said Quil, with a smile in her voice, ignoring Jana. She pressed another button and said, 'Open fire.'

There was a loud sound from somewhere above them, a repeated thud that sounded like nothing Dora had ever heard before. It had an almost musical tone to it. On the bottom right screen Dora watched as the horses and their riders were cut down by a devastating cannonade of what seemed to be explosive cannonballs. The bombardment lasted only two minutes, but when the guns fell silent and the smoke cleared, the field was littered with bodies, both human and animal.

'God,' muttered Jana.

Dora felt as if she were going to be sick.

Sweetclover was looking at the screen silently, but he had gone pale.

'And for my encore, the *pièce de résistance*,' said Quil. 'This requires a little more finesse.' Her fingers tapped away at the keyboard, which Dora noticed caused a grid of lines on the bottom left screen to move about. As she watched, she understood that Quil was causing the lines to move. She stared at the screen but could make no sense of what the lines represented, or what Quil was doing. Helpfully, Quil was happy to provide a commentary.

'First we erect the forcefield around the wall, to prevent our soldier-boys from running away.'

Dora saw a shimmering plane appear across the gate through which the infantry men had so recently marched.

'Then we erect a second field directly in front of them.'

Another shimmering plane appeared on the screen, this time between the soldiers and the house.

'Then we add two more, to make the sides of the box.'

Another tap of the keyboard, and two more shimmering planes winked into being at the far edges of the line of soldiers. The last remaining cadre of parliamentary forces were now enclosed in a rectangle made of invisible walls.

'Let's give them a moment to work it out, shall we,' said Quil, leaning back in her chair, folding her hands behind her head and putting her feet up on the table.

The aerial view showed a group of pikemen crash to a halt as they marched into one of the invisible barriers. Quil laughed, but Dora found the whole spectacle profoundly disturbing.

'This is sick,' said Jana.

'Now you have them trapped with your magic, there is no need to kill them,' said Dora. 'Why could you not have done this with the cannons and the cavalry? It appears to me that you had the means to end this battle before it even started, without a drop of blood being spilled.'

'Obviously,' said Quil. 'But where would the fun be in that?'

The calm, reasonable Quil who had agreed terms with Dora, and saved Mountfort's life with the silver wand, had been replaced by a monster. Dora watched the screen, her stomach twisting in fear and disgust. The soldiers now knew they were trapped, and they were running back and forth in blind panic, pushing up against the walls of their invisible prison.

'I thought I could witness nothing worse than the massacre

you effected upon the green, but this cruelty is horrible,' said Dora.

Quil turned her impassive mask to her. 'Shall I put a stop to this, then?'

'I wish you would,' replied Dora.

'Very well.'

The instant Quil said that, Dora knew something terrible was about to happen. 'Please, don't,' she began, but it was too late. Quil leaned forward and hit a single key.

On the screen, the walls of the unseen enclosure began to contract towards each other, reducing the size of the box rapidly. The soldiers were knocked off their feet, rolled along, pushed and thrown and tumbled together into an ever-decreasing area.

'Stop this,' cried Jana. 'Please!'

'Dear God,' breathed Sweetclover. 'They'll be crushed to death.'

'Too much?' asked Quil flippantly.

Dora turned her face away, unable to watch. She heard Jana gagging, as if to be sick.

After a moment Quil said, 'Pasted!'

Sweetclover broke the long, appalled silence. 'For all your talk of the battles you have fought, and the great war to which you must return, I had never . . . This is . . .'

'You thought I was making it all up?' replied Quil. 'That it was just stories?'

'No,' replied Sweetclover. 'But hearing a story of battle is a very different thing to witnessing one, especially one conducted in such a manner. Is this considered honourable in your future, killing from a distance, looking down upon the deaths of men who cannot defend themselves?'

'Says the man who just executed an unconscious man on a sickbed,' snarled Jana.

'He struck me down in my own house. Honour demanded recompense,' said Sweetclover, but Dora thought his protestation lacked conviction.

'Honour is overrated,' scoffed Quil. 'Victory is all that matters. Once you commit yourself to a fight, it's certain death to retreat from it. If the cause is just, any means at all are justifiable. We couldn't let them take this house. There are still things I must do here.'

'Like what?' asked Jana, her voice weak.

'Like get the data from your chip,' replied Quil. 'Oh, and fix Dora's mother, of course.' She turned to Dora with an expression of insincere regret. 'Sorry, sweetheart,' she said. 'Don't think your bro's going to be part of the package after all. He just got either blown up or squished. My bad.'

Dora could say nothing. Her words stuck in her throat. All she could see was blood. She felt as if she were not entirely present within her own body, as if the horrors of the day had shaken her soul loose from its cage.

She turned away and walked back to her mother, sat down beside her once more, lifted her head back into her lap, stroked her hair and began to sing a lullaby.

28

'I think I broke your pet,' said Quil.

'Screw you,' spat Jana. She could feel the none-too-gentle pull of shock herself, but was determined not to give in to despair, guilt, homesickness or any of the other options that her confusion and terror kept tempting her with.

Quil stepped forward until her mask was only inches from Jana's face. Through the slits in the stone Jana could see the fervour and excitement in Quil's eyes. 'We don't need to be enemies, Jana. In fact, we should be allies. If you knew my story, if you knew why I was fighting and whom, you'd support me. Together, there's nothing we couldn't achieve. This' – she swept a hand at the blood-soaked fields visible on the monitors – 'is nothing compared to what is coming. We could stop a far greater war from ever happening. All the bloodshed, the destruction, the hatred that I've seen – we could stop it all, Jana. You and me. Come with me to the future. Help me fix it.'

Jana stared into Quil's cold eyes, fruitlessly searching for a hint of compassion, kindness or sense. She saw no madness, not quite. Determination, certainty, passion, but no madness.

'What you just did . . . you want me to believe that you're the kind of person who wants to *stop* a war?' said Jana.

'This petty local conflict is a sideshow. My war's on a scale you can barely imagine. These parochial idiots, with their muskets and their horses and their cannons, they're not my enemies. They're merely an inconvenience. The real enemy's waiting for me back in the future. I'll do anything to get back there. So what if I have to dispatch a few unimportant soldiers in a minor war in a minor country in a minor century? It's no skin off my nose. And if you want to come with me when I leave, you'll need to get used to that.'

'Earlier today, some random guy tells me there's this woman called Quil who's hunting me, but won't tell me who she is, or why,' replied Jana. 'So I came to find you. Thought I'd ask you to your face. Sorry, sorry . . . mask. I have to stop doing that. And here I am, your prisoner. You want my chip, but you won't tell me what for. You say I can't go home, but won't explain why. You tell me you want us to be allies, but you won't say against whom. All I know about you is what I just witnessed – ruthless cruelty. And I can tell you here and now, we will never be allies. Somebody who can do what you just did is nobody I want to know. So if you want my chip and the information in it, you're going to have to take it. I know I can't stop you, but I'm not going to help you either.'

Jana held Quil's gaze for long moment, clenching her jaw and her fists, refusing to let her nerves betray her resolve.

'OK,' said Quil, nodding slowly with regret that Jana could not say for certain was faked. 'If that's how you want to play it. Hank, give me the knife.'

Quil held out her hand, all the while maintaining eye contact with Jana. Sweetclover, still staring at the screens, lost in thought, did not respond.

'Hank. *Knife.*'

Sweetclover twitched back to reality and handed his wife the blade without a word.

'I was going to get the data painlessly,' said Quil, holding the knife up before Jana's eyes. 'But if you're going to be such a pain in the ass about it, I'll cut the damn thing out and take that with me instead. At least I'll solve the biggest mystery of my life.'

'What's that?' asked Jana, conscious that she was starting to cry but unwilling to acknowledge it.

'How you died,' replied Quil. 'I spent years trying to figure it out and, wouldn't you know it, I was the one who killed you all along.'

She slid the blade cleanly in between Jana's ribs.

Jana remembered what it was like to feel a knife slicing through her flesh. It didn't hurt much, not if it was sharp and the blade didn't bounce off the bone. As she felt the strange, familiar pressure creep up into her chest she thought how ironic it was that her second death was so very similar to her first. If she had to die again, she would have liked to try something different. A fall, perhaps. But she'd attempted that and it hadn't worked. A gunshot, then. That'd be different.

Her vision went black at the edges; the sound of her heart beat loud in her ears. She felt dizzy. She knew what was happening and welcomed it. As she felt herself begin to die she realised that it had been inevitable all along. What her parents had done after her first death – bringing her back the way they had – was wrong, but it didn't matter. You can't cheat death. Fate doesn't forget you, and it can't be fooled. It had waited patiently for Jana, and now it had claimed her again.

She felt her knees buckle, and the ceiling spun around

above her as she began to fall. Her eyes were still sending signals to her brain, but the brain wasn't really paying much attention to them. Which is why it took a moment for Jana to realise that she had seen a bright rose-bloom of blood burst from Quil's left shoulder.

Jana hit the floor and the impact, which she had expected to be the last thing she ever felt, had the opposite effect. Her head cracked against the tiles and the pain in her skull lent her momentary clarity. She felt her chest spasm as she took a deep, ragged, excruciating breath that provided nowhere near as much air as she needed. The blackness retreated from her vision and her heartbeat began to fade out, replaced instead by shouts and screams, the clash of metal and the report of pistol fire.

Her chest spasmed again and she coughed, a terrible, racking convulsion that filled her mouth with blood. But still she managed to draw another breath. The pain was so intense she couldn't believe it. She knew what death by knife felt like, and this was not it. This was far worse, a pain so intense and immediate that death would come as a relief.

Then there were hands under her arms and she felt herself being dragged across the floor. She looked up and saw a blurred face looking down at her. She tried to focus and for a moment she was able to pick out the features. It took her a moment to recognise him, with his long hair and bum-fluff beard, but it was Kaz.

She liked Kaz . . .

. . . she coughed and screamed and frothed blood . . .

. . . he was nice.

And then her world went dark.

29

Kaz held the flintlock pistol awkwardly. It didn't sit as comfortably in his right hand as the gun from his own time had; something about the curved smoothness of the grip felt unnatural. It didn't help that the sword he held in his left hand was throwing his sense of balance off. You never saw cops on TV holding a gun in one hand and a sword in the other. They held the gun in both hands; it improved aim and response time. He uncocked the pistol and shoved it into his waistband, shifting the sword to his right hand. That was better; the sword felt good.

'This way,' he said, pointing through the trees. Thomas Predennick and the men of Pendarn, still wearing their white armbands and carrying their arsenal of makeshift weapons, followed him. Before they set out Thomas had shown Kaz how to walk silently in the woods. The secret, he said, was to place the whole foot down at once, not to roll your foot from heel to toe as you walked. Apparently it was the rolling that snapped twigs, and a snapping twig would startle the birds, which in turn would alert whoever was on the lookout for poachers. Kaz felt faintly ridiculous as he tried to walk flat-footed, like Frankenstein's monster or a Lego mini-figure, but stealth was important.

He glimpsed the door to the ice house through the trees and held up his hand to signal a halt. The men behind him stopped in a cacophony of rustling leaves and one particularly loud twig-snap. Kaz flinched. A partridge burst from cover, flapping clumsily and squawking an alarm, displaying the kind of survival instincts that made them the easiest birds in the world to shoot. Kaz glanced over his shoulder, and old man Squeer grimaced apologetically and mouthed 'sorry'.

Kaz surveyed his army. It was pathetic, frankly. How they'd ever thought they stood a chance against even a small force of soldiers, he would never know. He reckoned ten of them might be useful in a fight. The rest would probably either clutch their chests, wheeze and collapse, or wet themselves and run screaming for their mummies the first time someone with a weapon so much as looked at them askance. But they were here, supporting him and Thomas, bravely and without question walking into danger in support of a single lost girl from their community. Kaz felt a sudden, stupid rush of affection for them, and prayed that his actions wouldn't get any of them killed.

'There it is,' he told Thomas. 'That leads into the ice house. There's a door that leads to a corridor that will take us into the hall cellars. When we get inside, you follow my lead, yes?'

Thomas nodded. He still had this look of profound suspicion in his eyes, but he had at least stopped calling Kaz 'wizard'.

Kaz led the way towards the door, relieved and slightly surprised that they had made it this far without running into either Quil's guards or any outliers of the parliamentary force they had glimpsed earlier, progressing towards the hall down a narrow cart track. As long as this entrance remained a secret there was still a chance they would be able to get inside, rescue

Dora and Jana and escape again, even if the house came under attack while they were still inside.

No sooner had this thought crossed his mind than the distant boom of cannon fire came ricocheting through the trees. There was no need for stealth now.

'Come on,' shouted Kaz, and he ran for the ice-house door, the Clubmen of Pendarn hot on his heels. They reached the door and Kaz held it open as the men hurried inside. When the last one was through he glanced around the woods one last time, to check they were unobserved. But they weren't – a group of ten or so soldiers was running towards them through the trees, swords drawn.

He ducked inside and tried to pull the door closed behind him, but it didn't budge. Inside the spherical brick ice house, the men of Pendarn were milling around uncertainly.

'Soldiers,' said Kaz. 'Right behind us. We have to go forward, quickly.'

Before they could act upon his instruction, the sound of an unfathomably huge explosion penetrated the ice house and bounced around the curved walls as if in an echo chamber, making it impossible to tell which direction it had come from. The ground shook beneath their feet and dust showered from the ceiling, followed by clumps of dirt. At least two of the men screamed.

'What was that?' said Kaz, not expecting an answer. He felt someone grab his arm and turned to see Thomas, breathing hard but steadily, and in control.

'We have to go in,' he said.

'Right, yes,' said Kaz. 'OK, I'm going first.'

'Anybody with pistols, give them to me,' said Thomas. 'I'll go last. It's a narrow corridor, so the soldiers will have to advance in single file. Give me your pistols, I can keep them back.'

Three men handed Thomas weapons, but he refused to accept Kaz's.

'You know they have guns too,' said Kaz, but Thomas pushed him towards the internal door with a snarl.

Deciding that he really rather liked Dora's dad, Kaz shoved his way through the crowd of men into the dark tunnel. Without lamp or candle it was pitch black, but he remembered that it was straight and level so he forged ahead, one hand against the wall as he went. 'Follow me,' he called.

He reckoned he'd been walking into darkness for a minute or two when he heard a single pistol shot somewhere behind him. He increased his pace, not wanting to think about how Thomas was faring. A few moments later he caught a glimmer of light ahead of him, seeping around the edges of the still partially open internal door. He began to run, which wasn't easy crouched down in a tunnel this low, until he reached the door and pushed through into the undercroft. To his left, light flooded from the doorway of the hidden chamber; the hologram had been switched off and the door was plainly visible.

There was another pistol shot behind him, then another. Then there was a fourth, which meant the soldiers were firing back. But the shots were almost drowned out by the onset of a series of oddly harmonic crashes from somewhere above them, in the hall itself. It sounded like some kind of barrage, and it went on and on, shaking the floor and sprinkling the Clubmen with dust as they filed out of the tunnel into the undercroft chamber. Kaz was hugely relieved when Thomas burst out of the tunnel after them and gave him a look that told Kaz exactly how close his escape had been. Together he and Thomas put their shoulders to the door and forced it closed, even as a ball-shaped bullet sang through the narrowing gap, barely missing them. Unfortunately once the door was closed there was no way to lock it, so Thomas grabbed two of the youngest men and got them to sit with their backs to the door. Two others stood above them, pushing the door closed.

'That should hold them,' he said, a moment before the strange percussions from above ended. Both Kaz and Thomas immediately put their fingers to their lips and signalled for all the men to keep as quiet as they could. The men all stood silently, faces white, and waited to follow their lead. Kaz took point and crept down the corridor towards the door from which the light streamed. As he got closer he could hear voices inside, arguing. He made out Jana's voice, to his great relief, and Sweetclover's. There was a third person as well; a woman who he assumed must be Quil. There was also a soft voice singing; he thought it was Dora but couldn't be sure.

Kaz approached the door and lay down on the ground, poking his head around the edge so he could see what was happening. Jana was arguing heatedly with a woman in a strange white mask and a not very convincing wig; Quil. Sweetclover was standing behind Quil, holding a knife. Kaz craned farther and managed to see Dora cradling an older woman's head in her lap against the far wall. He felt a jolt of alarm at this, thinking the woman was dead, but after a moment he saw the soft rise and fall of her chest and realised she was asleep. This must be Dora's mother, he reasoned. He pushed himself back, rose to his knees and turned to Thomas.

'She's in there,' he said. 'Against the wall to the right as you enter, holding her mother, I think, who looks like she's asleep. We've got two hostiles I can see. Lord Sweetclover is inside on the left; he's got a knife. In front of him is his wife, who I don't think is armed. They're talking to Jana, who is arguing with them, like normal.' It was almost a relief to know that, even now, Jana was arguing with someone.

He could see, over Thomas' shoulder and through the throng of Pendarn men, the four boys pushing hard against the door. The soldiers must have reached it. He didn't know how long it would be until they managed to force their way inside, so time was of the essence.

'I'll take Dora and Sarah,' said Thomas. 'Can you handle Sweetclover?'

Kaz sheathed his sword, pulled out his pistol and cocked it. 'Oh yes,' he replied, smiling grimly. 'On three. One. Two. Three.'

Thomas and Kaz burst through the door side by side, the older man breaking right, Kaz running left, pistol raised. The men of Pendarn streamed in behind them, yelling and shouting and waving their sticks, clubs, swords and axes.

Things happened so fast that Kaz acted purely on instinct. As he crossed the threshold and ran towards where Sweetclover had been standing he saw Quil leaning in towards Jana with a knife in her hand. He spun in mid-run, trying a fast course correction, but he was too late. He saw the knife plunge into Jana's chest even as Quil's mask turned towards him to see what the commotion was. Crying out in alarm, Kaz raised his pistol and pulled the trigger. To his amazement, his aim was true. Quil staggered sideways, taking the knife with her, a splash of blood arcing from her shoulder even as Jana fell backwards, arms outstretched, collapsing to the floor.

Regaining his balance, Kaz ran to Jana, only vaguely conscious of what else was occurring in the room. She was lying on her back, blood bubbling up through her lips and nose, a red stain spreading across the tatty old baker's shirt she still wore. She looked up at him, but her eyes were blank, distant, as if she were looking straight through him. He dropped his sword and pistol, hooked his hands under her armpits, and began to drag her towards the room where he had touched, so disastrously, the bedridden patient. Jana screamed, her eyes rolled back in her head and she went limp. He felt a rush of fear at the thought that she was dead, but carried on dragging her, pursuing the half-formed thought that maybe there was some medical implement in there which could save her, something from the future that could make it all better.

The rest of the room was a blur to him. He'd gone through so much since he'd last been here, had been so determined to get back here and rescue the girls. And he'd done it. Despite the odds being so stacked against him, he'd actually fought his way back across time and space only to arrive literally a second too late.

30

Thomas broke right as he and Kaz pushed through the doorway into a chamber full of wonders.

Kaz had warned him about the strange things they would see when they fought their way into Sweetclover Hall – impossible illuminations, pictures that floated in the air, weapons that shot streams of fire. But although he registered the presence of these things, he barely acknowledged them. His focus was entirely upon his wife and daughter, upon whom he'd set eyes the moment he stepped through the door. Dora was sitting on the floor with her back to the wall; Sarah lay beside her, her head in her daughter's lap, asleep. Dora was stroking Sarah's hair and singing softly to her. Thomas knew something was terribly wrong, for even as he ran to them, Dora did not look up. Nor did she look up when a shot rang out behind him, or when the men of Pendarn streamed, yelling and shooting, into the room. Even as Thomas knelt beside her, took her face in his hands and raised it so he could look into her eyes, he already knew on some level that she would stare straight through him as if he were a ghost. There was an absence behind her eyes that made his heart ache. Could she have been taken from him so soon after her return? Could fate really be so cruel?

'Dora,' he said. 'Dora, it is I, your father.'

'Hello, Father,' said Dora in a dull voice.

'Is your mother ill?'

Dora nodded. 'Yes, but she's asleep now. Quil will fix her later.'

'Who is Quil, Dora?'

'Lady Sweetclover. Her.' She flicked her eyes over his shoulder and Thomas turned to see a woman in a white stone mask running towards a door on the opposite side of the chamber. Her right arm hung limp at her side, blood trickling down from a wound in her shoulder. Beyond her Thomas registered Kaz, dragging someone towards the same door. Lord Sweetclover was running after his wife, pursued by a group of three Pendarn men. The rest were standing, dumbstruck, staring at the strange floating pictures and the impossible globes of white fire that hung on the walls and illuminated the chamber.

Thomas saw no immediate danger and turned back to Dora. 'Has she bewitched your mother, is that your meaning?'

'She killed James, but she can lift the spell on Mother with a special thing called a machine.' Dora leaned forward and whispered conspiratorially in his ear, 'It's from the future.'

Thomas did not have time to respond, for there was a huge blast from the corridor outside followed by screams of agony, cries of attack, and the sound of running feet. He rose and turned to face the door as a group of soldiers burst into the room. Had it not been for the strangeness of the chamber, they would have fallen upon the Pendarn Clubmen and slaughtered them in an instant. But the lights and pictures caused them to falter for a moment and the Clubmen, who had already got over their initial surprise, charged into the fray without hesitation, swinging clubs, swords and axes with deadly effect.

Thomas ran to join them, but a soldier stood between him and the melee, sword drawn. He lunged forward but Thomas managed to swing his cudgel and bat the sword away so he could bend down and charge into the man, his shoulder catching him in the midriff. Thomas used his momentum to lift the man up and then slam him down to the floor on his back with all the force he could muster.

As the man fell he brought his leg up and kicked Thomas firmly in the crotch. The pain caused Thomas to lose his footing and the two men tumbled to the floor together, both momentarily winded by their separate injuries.

The chamber was filled with the sounds of battle. Crashes and thumps, cries, yells, screams; the occasional shot; the repetitive clang of swords as they parried and lunged.

Thomas felt the soldier heave him upwards and roll him off. Trying to ignore his pain, Thomas blindly reached around for any sort of weapon and, against all hope, his hand found the hilt of the sword the soldier had dropped. Rolling backwards, Thomas got to his feet and crouched down, holding the sword out in front of him. It was not much of a weapon in his hands – he had never fought with a sword in his life – but something about the heft and the length of cold steel made him feel safer. The soldier with whom he had tussled had also found his feet, and had grabbed a sword from the body of a fallen comrade. He once more lunged towards Thomas, who reacted without thinking, parrying the blow more by luck than judgement, knowing that he was now in a fight for his life – a fight he was almost certain to lose.

Another lunge, this time avoided by a quick step sideways. A swipe at his head, which he ducked away from. Thomas had no skill with which to attack; his defence consisted entirely of agility and luck, and the look of determination on the soldier's face told Thomas he should expect no mercy. He backed away another step, then another, always scarcely avoiding the razor-sharp blade, until his back was literally against the wall. The soldier smiled grimly, nodded once, as if mocking his imminently dead opponent, and raised his sword to deliver the killing blow.

At which moment Dora stepped in front of Thomas.

'No,' he said, reaching for Dora's shoulders so he could throw her to one side, away from the blade.

'Hello, James,' said Dora. 'I thought you were dead.'

'And I you, sister,' replied the soldier.

Thomas was frozen in place, surprise stealing the very breath from his lungs. He looked over Dora's shoulder at the face of the man with whom he had only moments ago been fighting to the death. Underneath the grime and the beard, through the changes that the years had wrought, he found the face of his only living son.

'James?' he whispered, feeling the same hollow ache of confusion and love that had overwhelmed him in the church earlier that day when he had held Dora for the first time in five years. This was his boy. His beautiful boy, grown to a man.

'I can't let you hurt Father, not like you tried to hurt me,' said Dora, her voice level and unemotional.

'He fights to protect a man who stands in opposition to Parliament,' spat James, his voice dripping with hatred. 'He worships at a church bedecked with idolatry. He consorts with the witch who created the magics you see all around us. It is my duty to God and man.'

'You do not understand what is happening here, James,' replied Dora. 'These events are not as you perceive them to be. You must put up your sword—'

Dora never got to finish her sentence, for James bellowed in fury, levelled his blade and ran forward, the tip raised above Dora's shoulder, aimed at Thomas' throat.

Thomas cried out, raised his own blade to try parrying the lunge, but he knew, even in the instant he lifted his arm, that he could not do it. He began to move sideways, trying to dodge the blow, but in this he knew he would be too slow. Then Thomas stopped dead; the blade came to rest on Dora's shoulder, the point steady and firm, an inch from Thomas' windpipe. Thomas stared over his daughter into the eyes of his beloved boy as they widened and changed from anger to puzzlement. James looked down, and Thomas followed his gaze to see that Dora was holding a sword of her own.

'Oh no . . .' he gasped.

'I won't let you hurt Father,' said Dora again.

James' sword slipped off Dora's shoulder and clattered to the floor. Thomas stepped forward and put his hands on Dora's waist, gently pulling her backwards, away from her brother. As he did so, he saw the sword that Dora held slipping from James' side, red with fresh blood. Once the blade came free, Dora's arm dropped to her side, but she still held the hilt tightly as the point hit the stone floor and the blood ran down the blade to collect in a small puddle by her feet.

Thomas stepped past her and reached out to take James' hands, grasping them tightly. James' legs went out from under him and he toppled forward into Thomas' arms. He took the weight but stumbled backwards and ended up sitting against the wall with James sprawled across him. He found himself cradling his son's head in his lap, much as Dora had cradled Sarah's only moments before. He could think of nothing to say. He opened his mouth three or four times, each time trying to find some words to express his love and forgiveness for his dying child, but nothing would come. There were no words adequate to the task. So he stroked James' hair as his son's breath came in shallower and shallower gasps. He cried over him, and soothed him, and took what solace he could in the calmness of his son's gaze, robbed of all hatred and anger by the certain knowledge of imminent death.

He was dimly aware of Dora sitting beside him, taking her mother's head back into her lap. And together they sat, father and daughter, holding the people they loved, singing lullabies to calm them, a tiny acre of peace in a world of war.

For the first time in seven years, the Predennick family was reunited.

31

Kaz dragged Jana through the door into the sickroom moments before Quil reached them. He could see that his shot had damaged her right shoulder, but she still held the knife tightly in her left hand and she brandished it menacingly as she advanced. Kaz put Jana's head down on the floor and stood, drawing his sword.

'Mine is bigger than yours,' he said as they stood facing each other, Jana lying unconscious between them.

'Oh, grow up,' said Quil.

'Is there anything in here that can save her?'

'Yes,' replied Quil. 'But only if I show you how to use it, and I'm not going to do that.'

Sweetclover ran up behind Quil, picked her up bodily and ran over the threshold of the room with her. Quil squealed in surprised protest and Kaz was forced to back away unless he wanted to run them both through. When he was inside the room Sweetclover dropped Quil, grabbing the knife from her as he did so. Then he dropped to one knee and held the knife to Jana's throat.

'Drop the sword and shut the door, or the girl dies,' he told Kaz.

Dismayed at how quickly he'd lost the initiative, Kaz had

no choice but to wave his approaching allies away from the door and close it in their faces.

'Think I'll keep the sword,' he said. 'Otherwise you'll kill me too.'

Taking advantage of the stand-off, Quil rummaged through the instruments on the medicine table. She found what she was looking for and began swabbing her wound with some liquid that she sloshed onto a piece of linen.

'Who's he?' asked Kaz, pointing to the man who lay on the bed. He was a mess; covered in blood, with a nasty red gash in his stomach and what looked like a bullet hole in his chest. Remarkably, he was still breathing, but his breaths were rasping and shallow, with a soft gurgle of blood; he didn't look like he was long for this world.

'Nobody,' replied Sweetclover.

There was a pistol shot outside, which told Kaz that the soldiers had broken through the door.

'Big fight outside,' said Kaz. 'My guys against Parliament soldiers. Fifty/fifty my side wins, but whoever wins, you lose.'

'Idiot,' laughed Quil. Kaz glanced over at her just in time to see her grasp the alarm cord and press the button. He cursed his own stupidity. After what had happened last time, he should have remembered the damn thing was there.

'Within a few minutes my guards will come down from the gun emplacements on the towers and kill everyone in that room.' She winced as she cleaned her wound. 'Hank, flip her over and cut the back of her neck open for me, would you? You'll find a small grey square thing attached to the spine where it meets the skull. Prise it off and toss it over.'

Kaz stepped forward quickly and levelled the point of his sword against Quil's left breast.

'Try it, Hank,' he said, 'and this monster dies.'

'Who are you anyway?' asked Quil, affecting nonchalance and continuing to staunch the bleeding from her wound. 'What is that accent? Russian?'

Kaz felt a familiar anger rise in his breast. 'Polish,' he said.

'Oh, right. Sorry,' she said, making it plain exactly how sorry she wasn't. 'But who are you, Kaz? I know Jana's story, I know how Dora got involved. But you're the wild card. Can't get a handle on you.'

'I am just a guy,' he said. 'Nothing special.'

'A guy who can travel in time. A guy who makes it his business to get in my way. What have I ever done to you, Kaz? What's your beef with me?'

Kaz shrugged. 'Where do I begin? You kidnapped me. Plugged me into a mind probe thing. Sent guards to shoot at me.'

'Haven't done that yet,' she replied. 'But I'll make a note so I can be sure not to forget.' She turned her attention to Sweetclover, who was still holding the knife to Jana's throat. 'Hey, Hank, she still breathing?'

'She is,' he confirmed.

'If she dies now, before I met her, there's a chance it could change history. Maybe it'd rewrite the timeline or something. I could vanish, you know. It could be like we never met.'

'That would be a shame,' replied Sweetclover dryly.

'You say the sweetest things.'

'If she dies, you die,' said Kaz, pushing the tip of the blade against Quil's chest for emphasis.

'Which would mean I couldn't go to the future and plug you into the mind probe thing,' said Quil, imitating his accent. Kaz really hated it when people did that. 'Another paradox.

Has anybody explained to you what happens if you change history, create a paradox, kill your own grandfather or whatever?'

Kaz shook his head.

Quil seemed disappointed. 'Shame, I was hoping you could tell me. Way I see it, there are three options. One: the universe explodes. Two: you create an alternate timeline that exists separate from the original, but with you in it. Three: time resets and you vanish in a puff of paradox. And I have no idea which is the right one. So if she croaks in the next minute or two, and you decide to kill me, thereby creating two paradoxes at once, and the universe doesn't go FOOM! you'll at least be able to discount one option.'

As she finished her little speech there was a cry from outside the door and Kaz realised that the sounds of fighting had faded away.

'Oh good, the boys have arrived,' said Quil. 'Open the door, Hank.'

Sweetclover rose and opened the door. Outside Kaz could see Quil's blue-faced guards standing over a line of men – both soldiers and Clubmen – kneeling with their hands behind their heads. The floor was littered with dead and wounded of both sides. Kaz could see both Thomas and Dora propped up against the wall comforting people, oblivious to everything that was happening around them.

Kaz cursed himself. The Clubmen of Pendarn, who had fought so bravely, had lost, and it was all his fault. He was the one who'd persuaded Thomas to help him storm this place to try and get Dora and Jana out. He'd tried to play the big hero, come running to the rescue, and look what had happened – half the men of Pendarn were dead or dying. Confronted with the consequences of his actions, the totality of his failure and the awful cost of his recklessness, he felt the fight go out of him.

Kaz dropped the sword.

'Screw it,' he said. 'You win.'

'I usually do,' said Quil.

32

32

Jana felt like she was swimming to the surface from the very darkest depths of the ocean. There was light ahead (or above, she couldn't be sure which) and she was clawing her way towards it through liquid agony. Even when sounds began to fade back in they were muffled and distant, as if she was sitting on the bottom of a swimming pool trying to listen to a conversation someone was having on a pool-chair by the water.

The first words that came through loud and clear were, 'Screw it, you win.'

That didn't sound good. She kept her eyes closed and tried to breathe calmly, as if she were still unconscious. Easier said than done; one side of her chest felt as if someone had cut it open and shoved a red-hot steam iron inside. She could taste blood in her mouth and throat. She could smell it too, and feel it caked around her nostrils and lips. She was lying down, had no feeling in her legs or right arm. She wanted to vomit, had the worst migraine she'd ever experienced, and generally felt as bad as she thought a human being can without actually being dead.

She heard footsteps around her head, and the voices moved

away. She lay still for another minute, somehow managing to prevent another bloody cough, and when she was sure there was no one directly beside her she risked opening one eye into the tightest of squints. Brick ceiling. So she was still in the undercroft. Even that small amount of light hurt and she winced as her brain found one more pain centre that it hadn't previously activated and gave it a punch, just to complete the set.

She risked turning her head, which was a very bad move indeed, because she almost passed out again from the pain of it. Once it had subsided to merely excruciating, she squinted again. She was looking into the undercroft, where Quil and Sweetclover were standing over a row of kneeling prisoners. They were an odd bunch – some soldiers, some civilians, and Kaz, who looked totally downcast. It didn't take a genius to work out what had happened. She closed her eyes and lay still for a moment, collecting her thoughts. She wasn't dead, which was a nice surprise, but she felt sure she soon would be unless she received urgent medical care. There were two options, as far as she could tell – persuade Quil to save her, or join hands with Dora and Kaz and jump to a year where they had hospitals.

Given how completely Quil seemed to have the upper hand, Jana quickly discounted getting her help. Which raised the question – how was she going to get to Kaz and Dora, when she couldn't walk, and there were guards looming over them?

She turned her head again, stifling a groan of agony, and looked around the room for inspiration. The first thing she saw, lying right by her hand, was a sword.

And that gave her an idea.

She moved her arm, which unleashed a fresh hell of pain

across her chest and nearly forced out a wet red cough, but she managed to grasp the blade, slick with fresh blood, and pull it to her, her fingers slipping again and again as she struggled for purchase. When the sword was close enough, she walked her fingers down the blade until she found the hilt and grabbed it. Then, trying not to think about how much it was going to hurt, she lifted her arm, put the point of the sword on the floor, and used it as a lever to sit up.

She wasn't even aware of having screamed until the sound had faded away, because her head was so light from lack of blood that she passed out for a moment as she was pulling herself upright. But when her hearing and vision returned she found, to her delight, that she was sitting up, sword in hand. And everyone was staring at her.

'Sorry,' she wheezed, and attempted a smile. 'That hurt.'

Gritting her teeth for another brush with darkness, she raised her other arm till she was holding the hilt of the sword with both hands. The wound in her chest felt like someone was trying to scoop out her heart with a blunt teaspoon, but she managed not to pass out again. Finally she rotated her hands and raised the tip of the sword until it was pointing at her throat.

'What are you doing, Jana?' asked Quil, her voice full of amusement.

'Going home,' she rasped.

'Really?' Quil laughed. 'Oh, this should be good.'

'Kaz and Dora. Where are they?'

'I'm here, Jana. So is Dora, but she's not so good.' That was Kaz, his face the picture of misery.

'Kaz and Dora are going to come and sit with me,' said

Jana. 'Or I'll drive this sword through my throat into my chip, and destroy it.'

The long silence that greeted her pronouncement was broken by a slow clapping.

'Oh, very good,' said Quil, ending her applause.

'I'll do it,' croaked Jana. 'Nothing to lose.'

'I can see that,' said Quil. 'So what's the plan – hold hands, jump to a time with a hospital, get yourself fixed up, live to fight another day?'

Jana tried to say 'something like that', but found she only had breath for, 'Yes.'

'The jump might kill you, you know.'

Jana managed a short laugh.

Quil made a show of considering her options. 'I do want that chip, and damn if I don't believe you would kill yourself just to spite me. If you stay alive, I can always catch up to you another day.' She shrugged. 'Why not? Kaz, Dora, go sit with your friend.'

Kaz rose to his feet and walked over to the wall. He had a mumbled conversation with Dora and then, holding her hand, he helped her get to her feet. Sparks shot from their joined fingers. Together they walked across to Jana.

'Hi,' said Kaz.

'Hello, Jana,' said Dora, in an odd, flat voice that told Jana she was deep in shock.

'Hi, guys,' breathed Jana.

'We leaving?' asked Kaz.

'Yes.'

'Sorry, I can't leave. My family's all here, I need to stay with them,' said Dora.

Kaz smiled at Dora patiently. 'That's OK, Dora,' he said.

331

'We can come back for them. But Jana and me need you to help us jump out of here to somewhere with a hospital. Or Jana will die. We cannot jump without you, Dora.'

Dora looked over at Jana and her face creased in puzzlement. 'Jana, why are you holding a sword to your throat?'

'Long story,' gasped Jana, wishing that Dora would shut up and hold hands already.

'You know what, Hank?' said Quil loudly, making a point of ignoring the three time travellers. 'I think it's time we got going too. Not much point hanging around here any more, not if Jana's leaving.'

'Go where?' asked Sweetclover.

'I thought Paris, the Grand Expo, my time. It'll be lovely. I can get a new face, you can try escargot, we can drink the city dry. What do you say?'

To Jana's eyes Sweetclover seemed relieved by Quil's suggestion, as if getting away from all this bloodshed was his fondest wish. He nodded and said, 'Yes.'

Quil turned to address them. 'OK, we'll be off then. It's been fun. Don't hang around too long, though, I'm going to set the self-destruct. Don't want to leave any evidence lying around to confuse the archaeologists. Just this room, though. Seal it up. For now.'

So saying, she typed a series of commands into the computer's keyboard. All the screens merged into one large image, showing a clock counting down from sixty seconds.

'I love a good countdown, don't you? Bye.'

She reached out and took her husband's hand, and they vanished in a blaze of red.

'Crap,' said Kaz.

Jana let her arms flop to her sides and the sword fell to

332

the floor. She was racked by a terrible coughing fit, and felt her mouth and throat fill with blood again.

Dora was staring at the clock curiously. 'What happens when the clock gets to nothing?' she asked.

Jana tried to warn Kaz not to tell her, but she was too busy coughing to get the words out, and the dumbass went and answered her question.

'This room will explode,' he said. 'We have to go.'

Jana gave Kaz the dirtiest of looks in which she tried to communicate as much of 'and what about her family, you moron?' as she could manage in a glare.

She saw Kaz realise his mistake but it was too late, Dora was already tugging at his hand.

'My parents, my brother, we have to get them out of here.'

Kaz held tight, refusing to let her pull away. 'Those guards aren't letting anyone out. We stay, we die. We are the only three who can escape, Dora. We have to go *now*.'

'Let go of me,' said Dora, pulling as hard as she could.

Jana, knowing that it was now or never, willing herself to ignore the pain, raised both arms, leant forward and grabbed Kaz and Dora's free hands with her own.

'LET GO!' screamed Dora even as the crimson sparks engulfed them and Jana felt the lightness in her stomach as she was pulled away from 1645. The undercroft began to fade away, and Jana felt her head go light and empty. She knew she was passing out again, but at least they were on their way. With luck, she'd wake up in a nice clean hospital bed.

Just as she lost consciousness, she heard a final despairing scream from Dora, and felt her hand slip from her grasp.

Jana's last conscious thought was of home . . .

* * *

333

Thomas did not know what was happening, but he did not much care.

He had seen his daughter disappear. Kaz had appeared before him earlier that day in much the same way, telling tales of pirate ships, enemies from years to come, and the peril in which Dora found herself. He had persuaded his friends and neighbours to come with him to the hall, to help save his wife and child. To a man they had agreed without question and it had made him proud. But now at least half the menfolk of his village were dead or wounded, and the rest knelt before him, threatened by the blue-faced militia and their strange fire-shooting guns. He, James and Sarah, prone on the floor, had been ignored by the militia. Clearly they were not considered a threat. The clock that floated in the room was counting down, and although he did not know his numbers that well, he knew enough to suppose that nothing good would happen when the counter reached zero.

But none of it mattered because his son was dying in his arms. Thomas had no idea how or why James had changed so. He had heard stories of young men consumed by religious fervour, driven half mad by Puritan zeal, turning upon their families and loved ones. He had shaken his head in wonder at such tales, unable to conceive of such a change. He could not comprehend it in the abstract, so what chance he could comprehend it in his own flesh and blood?

The clock ticked down to forty-one, and then . . .

Jana began the slow process of regaining consciousness almost immediately, although she could not have said how long she had been out. The first thing she became aware of was that Kaz was still holding her hand. The second thing was that Dora wasn't.

She opened her eyes and winced at the bright sunlight.

'Jana, wake up, please,' said Kaz, close by her ear. 'I think we have a big problem.'

The world swam into focus. Jana was looking across at Kaz, and she was ridiculously pleased to see him.

'Dora?' she asked weakly.

'She let go. She didn't come with us,' said Kaz. 'But that is not the real issue.'

'What is?' said Jana, laying her head on Kaz's shoulder and wishing herself asleep. 'We in the Stone Age or something?'

'No,' said Kaz, nervously. 'We are on a roof. And there are three men here who want to talk to you.'

Jana felt a deep knot of fear materialise in her stomach, as if it had jumped through time on its own and just caught up with her. She lifted her head and squinted to see three people she had hoped she'd never see again – ugly, sneery and short.

'You've got to be joking,' she said.

'I don't know what's going on here,' said the tall one, the ringleader with the mirthless smile and the chain. 'One second you're jumping off the roof, the next you appear in a cloud of fire with your boyfriend. What kind of freakshow is this?'

Jana began to laugh. There didn't seem to be any other response. It turned immediately into another bloody cough, and she sprawled forward onto reconstituted rubber, choking. She'd travelled all this way just to end up back where she started, about to be beheaded on a New York roof.

She closed her eyes and waited for death.

After all, she'd died once before and it hadn't been so bad.

* * *

The three men stood over Kaz, grinning the idiot grins of thugs about to dish out a beating. He was stranded on a rooftop in a time and place that were not his own, with his back literally to the wall. He and Jana had nowhere to run; without Dora they could not jump through time to escape.

Jana was sprawled on the floor before him, blood pooling around her, and although she was breathing he could not be sure that she was still conscious.

'We take the head as proof,' said the leader to the goon on his left. 'Cut low on the neck so you don't damage the chip. I'll take it back while you get rid of the body like I told you.'

'Don't you mean bodies, chief?' asked the goon on the right, pointing at Kaz.

The leader met and held Kaz's gaze and then nodded. 'Yeah,' he said. 'Sorry. Bodies.'

'Please, why are you . . .' Kaz started to say.

The leader kicked him in the face, a shattering impact that filled his mouth with jagged shards of broken tooth, smacked his head against the wall and left him stunned. His senses reeled.

Through his confusion he was aware of the leader of the three thugs kneeling beside Jana and raising his knife even as the other two brandished their weapons and moved towards him, ready to beat him to death, and then . . .

And then . . . ♦ ♦ ♦

. . . Simon snapped awake. There was deafening gunfire, smoke and a bright red flash of light through the haze which silhouetted three figures that were there one moment and gone the next.

Between him and the silhouettes was something far more shocking. His boss, Henry Sweetclover, was flying backwards through the air, blood spraying from a series of bullet wounds across his torso.

As Simon reached for his gun there was another bright red flash, this time directly behind Sweetclover. A woman in black popped into existence and caught him neatly as he fell. The momentum was such that they both toppled backwards and the new arrival was stuck underneath Sweetclover's bullet-riddled body.

There was a sharp clang of metal, as if someone were rolling a metal ball into the room, and Simon shouted in alarm as he realised it was a grenade. His cry attracted the attention of the new arrival, who reached out from underneath Sweetclover and said, 'Take my hand,' in a familiar voice.

He hesitated, momentarily distracted by Sweetclover's face, which had changed . . .

'NOW!' shouted the black-clad woman.

Simon reached out and grabbed her hand . . .

. . . and found himself somewhere else entirely.

. . . a sudden flash of crimson made Thomas wince. When his vision cleared he saw a young woman in black clothes standing before him, her face obscured by a woollen head garment the likes of which he had never before seen.

Without saying a word, and before the militia could react, the woman leant forward and placed her hands on Thomas and Sarah's heads. Thomas was opening his mouth to ask a question when the room around him went black and then reshaped itself into somewhere clean, white and dazzling.

Strong hands lifted James from his lap and a voice said, 'We'll take care of him.'

. . . the one on the left, with the scar on his cheek and the shock of bright red hair, stopped and looked down at his chest. The short one with the chain turned to stare at him, his mouth falling open in surprise.

Kaz saw the redhead tip sideways to reveal a young woman dressed in black, her legs apart, arms high, holding a sword with a glistening red blade. Her next movements were a blur to Kaz, possibly because of his concussion. Or maybe, he thought dreamily, she really was that fast. She pivoted and gestured with the sword and the short one was tumbling too, falling backwards off the building, arms outstretched as if reaching for salvation or comfort.

Another blur of movement and the leader, who was still kneeling over Jana but had not had time to so much as turn his head to see what was happening to his lieutenants, suddenly had no head to turn. His torso was frozen for a moment, kneeling, knife raised but with a fountain of blood where the head had been only a second before. Then the body collapsed in a heap. Kaz did not see where the head ended up.

The young woman crouched before him and removed her black balaclava.

'Sorry,' she said. 'Cut that a bit fine, didn't I.'

Kaz nodded, and spat out some teeth. He looked into the face of his rescuer, some years older than when he'd last seen her, her features harder, the softness of youth burnt away by time and experience.

'Yes, Dora,' he said. 'You did.'

The first thing Jana was aware of was the absence of pain. It wasn't the painlessness that steals through you in the moments before death, this was different. The absence was a thing in itself, a tangible fact that told her she was anaesthetised.

She floated there for a while, half conscious; awake enough to realise that she had been rescued, but drugged enough that she wasn't in any particular hurry to find out how or by whom. She just enjoyed the warm, soft feeling of painlessness until someone spoke to her.

'Your breathing has changed. I can tell you're awake,' said a voice. There was something familiar about it but she couldn't place the speaker.

'I am not awake,' said Jana, despite the numb heaviness of her tongue.

'The only alternative is that I am a dream,' said the voice.

'Do you feel like a dream?' asked Jana.

'You are Godless,' replied the voice. 'You don't dream. So I must be real. I feel solid, but I am floating.'

'Me too.'

'They have good drugs here. You were stabbed. I was shot.'

'Sucks to be us.'

'Sucks to be me.'

'And me.'

'That's what I said.'

Jana considered this for a moment, then opened her eyes. The light was low so she could not make out much detail about the room surrounding the bed in which she lay. She turned her head towards the voice and saw another bed beside hers. Sitting propped up on pillows was a woman, her face etched in shadow.

'Do I know you?' asked Jana.

'Kind of,' replied the woman.

Jana slowly raised herself up on her elbows, expecting a sudden shock of pain at any moment, pleasantly surprised when none arrived. She really had been given the good drugs. She peered into the half-light, trying to make out the features of her new acquaintance.

The woman leaned forward, her cheekbones catching the light. Jana gasped in wonder.

'Are you . . .'

'You? Kind of,' said the woman, who looked pretty much exactly how Jana thought she would look like in thirty years' time.

'What do you mean, kind of?' said Jana. 'Actually, forget it. You were right first time. You're a dream. Hallucination. All you are is very good drugs.' She closed her eyes and lay back on the pillow.

'Keep telling yourself that, kid,' replied the dream-who-was-not-a-dream.

Jana fell back into floating, anaesthetised sleep, but just

before she passed the threshold of consciousness she heard the dream say, 'Sleep now. But when you wake up, you and I have so much to talk about. So very, very much.'

And so Jana slept.

Dreamless.

Acknowledgements

The journey from a strange vision of an inverted cone made of shattered crystal that popped into my head just as I was on the threshold of sleep six years ago, to the book you're holding, has been a long one.

My Editor, Anne Perry, who sought me out, asked if there was anything I had in the drawer that she could look at, and then nurtured this book from a brief pitch to maturity, is wise, funny and almost certainly far cleverer than me.

My Agent, Oli Munson, who made the deal that allowed me to phone my father and tell him that yes, in actual fact, the patently absurd career plan I had outlined to him ten years previously had actually bloody worked, is the best ally a writer could have.

My friends Simon Guerrier and Jonathan Morris, who dissected large portions of this book and told me exactly what I was doing wrong, are both ridiculously talented and extremely generous with those talents.

My wife, who had my back as I worked myself to the point of madness and never wavered in her support for and faith in me, is awesome (and clearly deluded).

My kids are the most delightful people I have ever met and were super-patient as I locked myself away from them to write.

All my parents are supportive above and beyond the call of duty; the sound of my dad uncontrollably laughing with joy (and relief!) when I told him I'd signed with Hodder & Stoughton is one of the best sounds I have ever heard.

I also have to thank Jonathan Oliver at Abaddon Books, who took a huge gamble on me and launched my career – this book wouldn't have been written if he hadn't taken that initial leap of faith and commissioned *School's Out* off the slush pile.

Thank you all. Now brace yourselves – I'm going to do it all over again!

About the author

Scott K. Andrews is the author of three novels in Abaddon's Afterblight Chronicles series - *School's Out, Operation Motherland* and *Children's Crusade* - which follow the adventures of a group of schoolchildren trying to rebuild society after a viral apocalypse. He has also written audio dramas, comics, episode guide books and was the lead writer on Rebellion's Sniper Elite: V2 computer game.

Enjoyed this book?
Want more?

Head over to

CHAPteR 5

for extra author content,
exclusives, competitions – and lots
and lots of book talk!

Our motto is
'Proud to be bookish',

because, well, we are ☺

See you there . . .

 Chapter5Books 🐦 @Chapter5Books